Robert Holdstock w
educated at Gillingha
read Applied Zoolog
College of North Wa
take up research in M
writer in 1975. His ————— the award-winning
Mythago Wood, *Lavondys*, *Eye Among the Blind* and
Earthwind. Robert Holdstock lives in London.

ROBERT HOLDSTOCK

Necromancer

Futura

A Futura Book

First published in Great Britain by
Futura Publications Limited in 1978
Reprinted 1981, 1990 (twice)

*FOR NANCY, WHO WAS THERE WHEN THE
BEAST BEGAN TO ESCAPE*

ISBN 0 7088 1406 9

Printed and bound in Great Britain by
BPCC Hazell Books
Aylesbury, Bucks, England
Member of BPCC Ltd.

Futura Publications
A Division of
Macdonald & Co (Publishers) Ltd
Orbit House
1 New Fetter Lane
London EC4A 1AR
A member of Maxwell Macmillan Pergamon Publishing Corporation

ACKNOWLEDGEMENTS

I would like to acknowledge the work of Dr Anne Ross, Mr Arnall Bloxham, and the Institute of Psychical Research for invaluable inspiration during the writing of this novel; and I am especially grateful to the Pieria 'Psychic Vibration Group' who first demonstrated the 'talking rings' to me.

The Church does not deny that, with a special permission of God, the souls of the departed may appear to the living, and even manifest things unknown to the latter. But, understood as the art or science of evoking the dead, necromancy is held by theologians to be due to the agency of evil spirits.

The Catholic Encyclopaedia

This veneration of ancient stones and earthworks can . . . be seen as the last lingering acknowledgement of the power and importance of these sites for the welfare of the community, though the [modern] practices were surely far removed from the original manipulations of energy that occurred . . .

Tradition decreed that respect be paid to these ancient monoliths . . . and so, in their simple fashion, they peopled the stones with spirits and sought to placate them with offerings of food and animal sacrifices.

The Secret Country
Janet and Colin Bord.

PART ONE

OBSESSIONS

CHAPTER ONE

In the shadow of the ruined church of St Mary in the Fields, the man suddenly collapsed, face down, cracking his head very hard, very loud on the concrete pavement. He tried to get up, shaking his head from side to side as if to shake the pain away. Something forced him back to the pavement and he stretched out his arms, his fingers curled in agony. His head turned slowly to the right, and the tension in his neck and face, the closed tightness of his eyes, suggested that he fought desperately against the epileptic forces that were trying to dominate him.

His head hit the ground, hard, and for the first time he made a sound: he screamed. Blood stained his brown hair and ran, dirty and streaked, down his left cheek. He began to crawl towards the gutter, towards the slowing traffic. He reached out and cried a single word, incomprehensible, manic. No-one watching remembered that word.

At last someone ran to help.

Her name was June Hunter. She had appeared from behind the grey ragstone walls of the fire-gutted church, and when she saw the writhing man she scrambled across the fallen masonry and charred rubble and began to shout.

She was a tall woman, in her late thirties, and her fair hair was wild and uncombed, plastered to her face by sweat. She wore blue slacks and a thick blue car-coat against the October chill, and in each hand she clutched a plastic bag of shopping. As she ran across the short grass verge between the church and the street one of the bags split from its handle, and tins and jars spilled freely about the pavement. She took no notice, dropping the other bag as if in some way this balanced her. As cat food rolled, and polystyrene egg-packs spilled their yellow contents beneath her flying feet, she dropped to a crouch behind the now still man.

'For Christ sake somebody get help!' she screamed in anger, not-looking up at the people who stood, shocked and helpless, about the busy high street.

A bus, that had slowed and stopped nearby, suddenly surged away, the sound of its bell obtrusive and sickening in the autumn stillness. A grinning face watched the woman from the passenger stand, a youth, blonde hair parted in the middle, his ticket machine sparkling in the daylight. The bus weaved between cars that, prompted by the sudden motion, also began to move.

June Hunter, her hand resting on the sprawled man's bloody face, looked around her pleadingly. Then she looked down, saw the red smear on her fingers, the narrowed eyes of the man who lay so quiet. He was staring along the pavement, and his breathing was hardly noticeable; but after a moment he coughed, and shivered, and began to climb to his feet. June helped him, brushing her hair back from her face, staggering as his weight fell a little too heavily against her. Both hands supporting him she said, 'Are you alright now? Can I help you to a seat?'

He shook her off, shrugged her grip from his arm and rapidly brushed at the coat he wore, as if at the invisible marks of her fingers. He backed away from her, staring at her, and reached spasmodically to his forehead to wipe away the blood, to massage the bruised skin. He suddenly turned and ran down the High Street. The woman watched him go, puzzled and hurt, then bitterly angry as she turned from his grey-coated form, flying into obscurity, and surveyed the spilled remains of her weekend's shopping.

People around her, she realized, were walking and chattering as if nothing had happened; when she looked at them she could recognize none of the crowd that had watched the man collapse, and had stopped so frighteningly, so helplessly still.

There was not even a smear of blood on the pavement; orange juice, yellow and sweet, ran across the concrete and pooled between crisp autumn leaves, blown from the beech trees that lined the road a few yards away.

The sun broke through the clouds again. The shadow of the ruined church touched the far side of the street, brilliant streaks of white breaking the ragged outline of the tower and high-arched doorway which had crumbled and decayed in that intense conflagration of a few years before; an explosion and a fire and St Mary in the Fields had finally spilled her soul to the winds and downs of Berkshire.

Disturbed and dishevelled, June gathered her supplies together and abstractedly kicked glass from the broken orange-juice bottle into the gutter.

Gusting winds disturbed the fallen leaves and swept her hair back across her eyes. She turned, as she clutched her bag, and stared into the grey and now featureless faces of the church walls, and her gaze wandered beyond the proud walls and into the dark recess where Adrian was trapped, so helplessly, so cruelly.

'Bye, Adrian,' she said quietly. A car swept past, too close to the kerb, and she felt its wind, its heavy breath of contempt upon her legs.

She turned up the high street and began the sad walk home.

Where the main road from London swept beyond the town of Higham it made a sharp turn to the left, carrying the traffic of the metropolis away from the high street, and into the pinewood-bordered fields and downs of the west.

Beyond Higham were small towns and villages, modern and expensive, but still possessed of that certain rustic peacefulness that could be called English.

Higham itself was a place of double standards: where it reached towards London it was crowded and clustered, houses faced onto the street, and there was something almost shabby about the shops and gardens that formed the estates and side roads. But where Higham reached into the west, the first of the affluent residences rose majestically from behind its pallisade of alder and birch trees, and looked both across the town and into the setting sun, following the arrow-straight passage of the motorway to Oxford and the mountainous wastes of mid-Wales.

Here was where the Hunters lived, beyond their means, but in considerable comfort.

Exhausted after the half mile walk back from the town centre, June Hunter struggled up the steep drive to the front door of her house. She clutched her surviving carrier bag in both arms and was aware of the stickiness of juice that had coated her hands and jacket, but nobly ignored it, aware that there was nothing she could do for the moment to escape that awful discomfort.

Her ginger cat, affectionately called Treacle, scampered from the October shade of a stand of fern and rubbed ecstatically against her legs as she stood, for a moment, and stroked the animal with one white sneaker.

Hidden from the eyes of the town June placed her bag of supplies on the bonnet of her husband's Rover, parked irritatingly in front of the door instead of in the huge garage. Exhausted with the walk, shaken by her experience with that man having a fit in the town, she leaned against the black car and stared up at the front of her house, feeling relaxed and secure now that she was home.

They had painted the wooden facade during the long, baking summer. It gleamed bright, white, attractive, and the October sun cast the grey shadows of chestnut and silver birch in a jagged and artistic line between bedroom windows and the great lounge window that looked through to the rear garden. She peered through this, now, and saw the children at the far end, where the woodland encroached upon their land.

There was no sign of her husband, Edward. He'd probably left the kids to their own devices and was reading, his *Lancet*, perhaps, or a report from the World Health Organization; or if not that, then some of the comics that Adrian's friends brought over by the armful. It was unlikely that he would be working on his new medical textbook.

An emotion fled through her as she fumbled for her key and thought of Edward. She smiled, then frowned, pushing the heavy door open before turning back to clutch her sagging bag of food and pass through into the cool hallway. She could remember a time when it would have given her the greatest pleasure to surprise Edward indulging in their daughter's comics, reading each dialogue balloon minutely, and studying each frame to glean the greatest understanding from it; she would walk up behind him and read over his shoulder, and gradually he would become aware of her and he would cough very loudly and with an elegant flip of his wrist the comic would sail across the room. He would clasp his hands and stare solemnly ahead of him, his face red, whilst June went for the jugular, reading him adolescently torrid scenes from the badly drawn pages.

Have you finished, he would say, finally.

Science fiction I can understand, she would taunt, pointing to the bookcases crammed with Space fiction, a hangover from Edward's days of literary indulgence, before he had turned to physiology and more physiology. But girlie mags? Really!

Girlie mags! Indeed! The last time I looked at porn was . . .

She remembered how he had narrowed his eyes, half smiling.

Yesterday?

Day before, actually. Really quite incredible stuff. One of the students brought it in.

Disgusting.

Revealing. And all in the cause of sexual understanding. No, really! That's what it said. 'These pictures are not erotic, they are designed to be educational.' Bloody well were too, but not in the sense they meant.

June could remember conversations like this as if they had occurred yesterday. She felt a pang of sadness – they never joked together any more. She missed that. Idly she picked up one of the boys' comics and leafed through it. All of Karen's comics were still upstairs, filed away neatly in her cabinet. It was two years since she had left home for her boarding school (her *third* boarding school) but somehow it was improper to think of clearing out the childish junk that she – like all young girls – had accumulated, her heart-throb pictures, and flower dresses that no, she would never wear again, but no, don't throw them out, they have memories!

Perhaps now that Karen was coming home (again!) there could be some major sorting out of the crammed cupboard and trunks.

In the bright kitchen June scrubbed the sugary stickiness from her hands and the sleeves of her jacket. Edward had not been in the front room, so where was he? The kitchen smelled heavily of polish, and the veneer of their family dining table was bright, though streaked with wax around the edges. He had done his chores (he had even mended the faulty blind across the kitchen window. My God, and it's not even New Year!).

She put the food away, in cupboards, containers and baskets, and flicked the red switch of the automatic kettle. Instant coffee was called for, before the kids' party began proper.

She went to the sink and peered out through the large window at the long garden, its wild extremities carefully designed to contain highly productive stretches of well nurtured earth. A child's paradise, and a self-sufficiency programme, all neatly and cleverly contained in an acre and a half. Apple and pear trees supplied the summer shade, and helped cut down the appalling fruit bills that they had once suffered. A fruity family, Edward called them, and was the only one of the four who ate meat. June never touched the stuff, and Karen had followed her example for reasons more concerned with her adolescent yoga fetish; Adrian was actually allergic to red meat, but fortunately not to fish.

At the far end of the garden, where the late afternoon sun threw the shadows of the woodlands . . .

Late afternoon? Surely it wasn't much after two o'clock.

She put it from her mind and watched the kids, a small circle of seven and eight year olds, busy playing with their own, and Adrian's, toys. June smiled as she watched the two Pickersgill twins driving panzer tanks across the rough turf of the children's own piece of land, which Edward had solemnly sworn he would never cut. It was like a jungle, flattened grass and weeds, and only the absence of thistles and nettles told of her husband's secretive sorties with fork and trowel to keep the free range less temporarily uncomfortable to the kids they encouraged to come and visit.

Theirs was a popular garden; it was as well; Adrian was not a popular child.

Behind the war-making Pickersgill boys sat two solemn faced girls; one was dark and as pretty as her Spanish mother; the other had a tight mass of blonde curls that framed her cheeky face which watched Adrian, thoughtfully, from behind huge gold-rimmed glasses. They talked too seriously for seven year olds, but this was how it always was. June had often heard them talking of Adrian, and whether they should do more to help him. It was unnervingly adult talk for girls so young. The blonde girl was the daughter of their neighbours, Christine and Aiden Foss, and liked to be called Suzy, short for Susanna. The dark girl was called Davina and June could never remember her surname. Her father was dead, her mother a recluse who communicated with the world by phone and through her forthright and highly sociable daughter.

There was one other boy, who sat absorbed by the parts of a snap-together model plane. Tim Belsaint, Adrian's best friend, in as much as Adrian could have a best friend. The Belsaint boy was constantly round their house, talking to Adrian, helping him understand the simple toys that by seven most boys would have spurned. With Tim, Adrian occasionally laughed. The first time it had happened June had not believed that he *was* laughing. She had thought he must be making animal sounds, or perhaps sobbing, or hurt. But standing in the doorway of the playroom she had watched this mortal part of her son laughing loudly and unrepressedly at the antics of a lego-man that Tim had made. Each time Tim tore an arm or a leg from the model, laughter burst, like an explosion of sound, to be cut short, followed by heavy, expectant breathing, as Tim waltzed the gradually disintegrating brick man about the floor, ready to demolish another part of him.

Terrified, in retrospect, that Adrian's humour would be confined to death, demolition and such like, they had encouraged Tim to come round more and more, and asked him to play a variety of games. Sometimes Tim's elder brother, Don – who had romantic ideas towards Karen when she was home – helped in the design of games that did not depend so much on violence. Adrian had a real sense of humour beneath his impassive, mindless exterior – or so Edward believed. He laughed most easily at the breaking of an orderly pattern: a line of cars that Tim would plough a tank through tickled Adrian. A car that shot off the scalextric track sent him into a brief but genuine fit of laughter.

Edward lived in the constant hope that soon, very soon, Adrian would speak his first word. June knew, instinctively, that he would never utter organized sound. That part of him had been stripped from his head, along with his reason and his personality, many years ago. They lay trapped, in the darkness of a stone, in the shadow of a ruined wall, where even in summer it was cold, cold . . .

She shivered.

She stared at Adrian, seated quietly in the long grass, wrapped in his thick coat and scarf. He seemed uninterested in the war of noise and model that was occurring nearby, or in the fascinated scrutiny of his model Boeing. He stared at the kitchen, at the window, and through the glass into his mother's head. From this distance it was difficult for June to see what precise expression existed in his eyes, and she knew that he could not see her very clearly. And yet she felt the coldness, the coldness of stone, like the stone font in the church: but this stone was the stone of flesh, of bone, of a living being that could respond no better than a rock to her love, or to her words, or her song, or her laughter.

In the years since the accident, her love, and her laughter, had frozen as hard and as cold as quartz. This glance towards her, down the length of the garden, was merely the fascination of seeing movement, distantly, inside his symbol of security, the house, his home, his second skin.

The wind tousled his brown hair, cut long and parted nattily down the middle. When he was staring without expression he was such a pretty child, and yet he was so horribly angry looking when he cried, or frowned. His eyes were green, and when he had been born he had had a fine scalp-down of ginger hair that had lasted for a year before changing to a more auburn-tinged brown. He was tall for his physical age, but very thin, and sometimes he had to be actively prompted to move; it seemed to his parents that unless they took a hand in the matter he would sit in his room, or in the garden, and never move from one hour to the next.

Except for his eyes. He had the alivest, most active eyes of any of the children in the group.

This was Edward's hope.

No child with eyes that bright, that alive, is going to stay a cabbage all his life. Believe me, June, he'll grow out of it, you'll see. He's alive down there, really alive.

He's alive in the stone . . .

Stop saying that! That's bloody stupid, and you know it. The

17

boy is damaged, no question about it. He's badly damaged, but the damage is working out: He'll be alright! He's alive . . . his eyes give it away.

He's dead. His body's alive, but his mind is dead. We should have killed him.

For God's sake, June, don't say things like that. Please have hope, have something . . . anything . . . (just acknowledge the possibility. He's going to come out of it. Not this year, perhaps not even next . . . but soon. Soon. It's happened before.

Words! Just words! And these particular words had been spoken not yesterday, nor last year, nor even the year before.

June felt the sour taste of time and the passing of years in her mouth as she remembered the night they had lain in bed and argued like that until six in the morning, until dawn, until Karen had shouted at them for keeping her awake all night. That terrible exchange of defeat and hope had been more than four years ago, shortly after they had first come to realize that Adrian had been badly damaged by the accident at his christening.

They rarely argued about it these days. Edward's spirit, as the patronizing hope-bringer, had been drained away, drained like all waste materials into the deep earth of their enclosed garden; drained by June, by her obsession, and her own hope, that they could win the boy back from the place he was trapped.

Beyond the chattering, noisy kids, something moved in the woodlands. Puzzled, June leaned further forward and peered, her nose almost against the glass.

The movement was fleeting, almost invisible; it could have been a dove dropping from branch to branch, or a child running between the clustered, dark trees.

Quite suddenly the shape became clearer, moving forward from the darkness towards the long grass where Adrian watched the house, and the other children played quite unsuspectingly and innocently.

June caught a glimpse of the face of the moving figure and her heart missed a beat. The blood raced to her head and she felt a cold touch on her skin.

Oh no!

She raced into the lounge and pulled open two drawers, searching for something. She talked to herself as her fingers scrabbled among place mats and card packs and assorted objects and gadgets.

Where is it? Where is it?

Pausing to glance through the wide window, she saw the figure hovering at the very edge of the trees, watching the children.

In panic she ran to a cupboard and pulled out a small, black bag. She glanced at the electric clock and frowned in disbelief as she saw that it was after four thirty.

It can't be! I was only twenty minutes . . . it can't be!

She ran through the kitchen, and out through the back door. Adrian looked away as she appeared and the two girls looked up, waved at her, then frowned as they saw her running towards them.

She ripped open the bag and reached inside, her attention half on the children and half on the dark shape behind them.

Quite suddenly the figure moved out into the open. June stopped and slipped the tiny pocket camera she had found in the bag to her eye. She snapped and wound as the masked figure darted towards the children and sent them screaming and scattering.

It was horrible – blank-faced, and narrow-eyed, with a wide, grinning mouth, and candles poking from the pulpy flesh of its face; its dark robe swirled as it ran after the girls, who screeched and shrieked with laughter, then turned its attention to Adrian who stared at it in blank incomprehension as it picked him up and swung him high.

June snapped as many shots as she could, as fast as she could. When the reel of film ran out she put the camera back in her bag and walked resentfully towards the rough ground.

Why couldn't he have waited? He must have seen her . . . he could have signalled! He was such a bastard, such an angry, intolerant bastard. Those shots would show distant figures and a lot of grass, and they weren't the photographs that either of them wanted.

They were both snapshot fanatics and this party, to celebrate Hallowe'en and Adrian's birthday, was to have been an important source of entertainment for the following years, good shots in the album, and good things to look back on and laugh at.

God, how desperately she needed good things to look back upon.

Edward had removed the pumpkin mask and now Suzy had placed it over her tumbling curls and was chasing after one of the twins. Edward smoothed back his greying hair, and wiped juice from his face where it had seeped through the mask's paper lining. He smiled thinly at June, and leaned to kiss her as she came up to him. He was flushed from the running about, and the colour of his face looked unhealthy. A man in his early fifties, the age difference between he and June was becoming more noticeable all the time. He was a broad and strong looking man, but his face was becoming loose, lined around the eyes and mouth, and the world-weariness of his expression seemed just that – tiredness, not experience.

He was angry. It was written in every line of his face, every perfunctory gesture – the touch on her arm, the kiss on the cheek, the smile.

'Where were you?'

She said, 'I didn't know it was so late. I got held up.'

'You've been in that bloody church again.'

'I haven't, actually . . .'

Edward's glance at her was the most derisive expression she had seen on his face in long months. There was the hint of a smile on his face – not humour, but a sneering comment on the transparency of her lie. She had spoken too quickly, too obviously defensively.

She acknowledged the lie to herself, and then aloud, 'I've been in the church. Alright, what of it? I was only there for a few minutes; five minutes.'

'More like two hours.'

June bristled with anger. 'You still could have waited!'

Edward mocked her with his laughter. 'Why are you so upset? It was me that wanted the photographs.'

'I wanted them too. I like to see the kids enjoying themselves – I like to look back on them . . .'

'But not on Adrian. He's irrelevant, right?'

June shook her head, but said nothing. Around them the children played happily, Tim Belsaint now wearing the pumpkin mask while the girls played tag-and-run with him. Adrian sat quietly, his intense green eyes apparently unfocussed, but his gaze directed at his mother. She stared down at him and smiled. Edward laughed nastily.

'Well! That's the most affectionate gesture you've made to your son in a year.'

'Shut up,' said June, bitterly. She dropped to a crouch to kiss the boy. His skin was cold, his face colder. He stared at her as she drew back, and his breathing never changed. Then his gaze shifted towards the house and he placed his little finger in his mouth. June reached out and removed the hand from his face. 'Don't bite your nails,' she said softly, and stood again as the boy began to shake his head angrily. 'He's going to have a fit,' she said anxiously, and turned towards Edward. They had both witnessed Adrian's shaking fits before, his body racking from side to side, his hair flying free and wild, his eyes rolling; he made no sound during these spasms, but afterwards, sitting still, he howled like some bestial wind, his mouth open, his eyes almost white, his skin as pale as fresh snow.

'No . . . look . . . he's just angry with you.'

Adrian had calmed and replaced his little finger in his mouth, sucking contentedly.

'If you'll just show him love, and let him alone otherwise,' said Edward bitterly, 'You might actually help him.'

'Let's not argue,' said June, tired of these all too familiar words. The unusual warmth of the October day had gone and the evening was turning chill; it would soon be time to take the party inside, out of the pale autumn sun and into the secure central heating of the house.

'I helped a man having a fit in the street, outside the church.'

Edward looked momentarily interested. 'What sort of fit?'

June shrugged. 'Just an ordinary thrashing-about-on-the-ground fit. Nobody did anything to help him.'

'Nobody ever does.'

June laughed sourly. 'Even the man ran off from me when he'd recovered. I felt really angry for a moment. Aren't people awful?'

Edward said nothing. They stared at Adrian in silence.

'How has he been? Has he played with Tim?'

'Quite a lot,' said Edward. The cool breeze dropped and a sudden and pleasant wash of warmth swept across the garden; Edward squinted into the sun, suddenly freed from behind its veil of evening cloud. 'Let's sit down for a while. Adrian's hardly seen you . . .'

'I've been talking to him this afternoon,' said June, more for aggression than anything. Edward closed his eyes and controlled his annoyance, then he smiled.

'Sit down.'

They squatted on the grass beside their son and listened to the laughter and chatter of the children. Soon the pumpkin mask underwent the expected process of entropy, and the excitement changed to some vaguely-outlined war game. Adrian watched, his head turned to the right so that the sinews and veins in his neck stood out hard and strained. June, absently, reached out and eased him round, almost swinging him about by his extended legs. As she went to leave go of him his left hand came down upon her wrist, and his nails dug painfully into her skin without

21

breaking the skin and drawing blood. June made no sound, but felt angry enough to shout as she saw the flicker of a smile vanish from Edward's face.

'You never touch the boy except mechanically,' he said.

She looked at Adrian's brown hair and wondered whether some residual awareness in this human shell understood the words.

'What's to touch? Flesh and blood . . . God, Edward, he even feels like a corpse. His skin is cold and clammy. I can't bear to touch him, sometimes.'

'You know damn well that this is all part of your ridiculous obsession! June, I've tried to help you, to understand you, but you've gone over the edge, do you know that? Sometimes I believe you're actually mad. I've watched you kissing that sodding font, that stone . . . talking to it . . . sometimes I really believe you've cracked. This feeling of cold when you touch him, it isn't Adrian . . . it's *you* . . . the boy is as warm as I am.' As if to prove his point, or perhaps to reassure himself, he reached out and touched Adrian's face. He smiled, and the boy made a sound in his throat and shook his head.

Edward said, 'Warm. Like the ordinary child he is. It's getting chilly out here, but he's alright. If you'd only work with me, June, help me bring the boy to the surface again . . . but you can't, can you . . .'

Had he seen her inward shudder of revulsion? Had he spotted the cynicism in her eyes, the flicker of a frown, the slight tensing of her facial muscles? What had she thought at that precise moment, that exact second when for the billionth time he had asked her to help bring the lost Adrian up from his deep seated cage, a cage that Edward believed was in his own mind? She recaptured that moment, savoured it for all its empty dream, for its blind obsession with something every bit as reasonable and unreasonable as her knowledge that Adrian was trapped elsewhere.

I'll not waste my time on an empty vessel . . . believe what you like, Edward, but that's not my son . . . that's not Adrian . . .

They had never, she and Edward, communicated from heart to heart, or from soul to soul; at first, of course, they had questioned and learned about each other, but they had never been able to talk freely about those shadows that they feared the most. And yet . . . and yet Edward, for all his infatuation with work and the belief that his son would one day speak, become normal, could read her like a book, now spotting her every despair, now her every irritation. How could they converse when her answers to his

22

inane demands preceded her voice in the expression of her eyes, so that his defences went up instantly, and his next question, or statement, attacked not the common problem of their son, but she herself, her very fibre?

'I suppose creeping up on him in a demon mask is good for bringing him out of his shell.'

There was more bitterness in her voice than she intended. This made her statement somewhat hypocritical since she had approved that part of the party; what had she hoped for? A few photographs, some excitement, some smiles . . . yes, she had hoped for a few smiles, and maybe a smile on this golem who looked like her son. It had come to this, that to try and get a response, a happy response from the flesh of her flesh, she would approve the frightening of him with a slant-eyed mask leaping from the trees.

What are we doing, she wondered transiently . . . what are we doing, going to these extremes? Where must it end before Edward gives in? Must he mutilate himself, like Timmy mutilates those lego-men, pulling limbs, hacking off hands, in order that the golem will smile for our family album?

'There are a thousand things more frightening that Adrian will meet than a man in a pumpkin mask,' said Edward, predictably. 'I thought we'd had all this out.'

'We have. You needn't go into it again.'

'Sometimes I think you don't believe in *anything* I do,' persisted Edward, relentless, unstoppable, now that the flood-gates of his intellectual defensiveness had been opened.

Oh God, thought June. I can't stand a lecture.

Edward was saying, 'Fear is the most deep rooted response in the human species, in all animal species. It's defensive, and important . . . my God, it's important.' He stroked Adrian's hair as he spoke. 'Humour is something superficial, and humour occasionally sparks something in the boy. But fear . . . fear must strike deep to the core, to the primal root of him . . .'

Hack psychology, always hack psychology!

'If we can frighten the boy it might trigger the release of all his human emotion. Fear is the key . . .'

'I saw that. A good film, very good.'

'But is *is*, June. It *is*. Fear can corrode the barriers of disease, break through to the trapped persona in cases like this.'

'This isn't a *case*, you quack, this is your son.'

'*Our* son,' said Edward.

'*Your* son. *Your* zombie. You might as well try and frighten a tree.'

Unexpectedly, Edward smiled. June glanced at him and he reached out, a moment of warmth between them, touched her hand: she did not pull away. The breeze played havoc with his greying hair, and she found herself sympathizing with the sadness she could see in the tired, exhausted features of the man she had once loved.

He said, a shallow smile still playing on his tight lips, 'Sometimes I can't believe we're not just a couple of nuts.'

'I'd like to think that one of us was right,' said June stiffly. It grew cold very quickly. 'Shall we take the kids inside?'

'Yes,' he said, and climbed to his feet, lifting Adrian with practiced ease. The boy had been in a non-walking mood for three days, now, and Edward never questioned whether that mood might have passed. Adrian watched emotionlessly, staring back over his father's shoulder, but as Edward walked towards the house, so the boy's eyes moved to stare fixedly at his mother as she followed, the chattering children grouped about her, their arms full of Adrian's toys.

Inside, as Edward rang parents and asked if the children's party might go on a little longer, June set the table. Tim Belsaint poured huge glasses of lemonade for everybody (pinching a small cake while he was at it, June noticed). The girls pushed Adrian in his indoor racer.

This is the way life goes on, thought June, as she listened to the normality all around her. This is the way we hide our minds from what our eyes see. This is the way we age, remorselessly, inexorably, our whole lives dedicated to a dream, a hope, a selfish hope.

She stared at Edward, who was laughing, his charm oozing from his every pore as he chatted to one of the children's mothers . . . it was Davina's mother, the dark, attractive Spanish lady; she knew it was her because Edward's voice was a shade lower and softer than usual, and his speech was slightly more rounded, emphasizing vowels as if talking to a person whose natural language was not English.

June smiled wryly; Edward too was so readable, so predictable; she hated the way his charm came on, his pleasantness, his humanness, at all times except those when he was with her.

The party tea began, noisy, messy; Adrian helped himself to food and Edward watched him, glancing all the time at June who ate silently and slowly. Adrian was not incapable of any normal human function, such as walking, picking things up, even running and crying; it was just that he did these things so rarely. He never spoke, although he responded to such a wide variety of complex words that Edward was convinced he had the capacity for speech, but was again being lazy. Make the boy scream with fear, Edward had once said, and we'll reach down to the speech association centres. When he has to cry for help he will cry the word *help!* One word only, that's all it will take. You see, speech is there, it just needs the emotional release.

June had forbidden him to do many of the things he had wanted to do, but over the last two years she had gradually come to not care any more. Why should she worry what he did with the human shell?

Stop thinking about it!

The children sang a rousing chorus of Happy Birthday. Adrian watched impassively, unsmiling. The singing faded away, slightly embarrassed; extremely tuneless. The girls looked uncomfortable and Davina excused herself, but she had to be getting back home. June saw her to the door, turned to find Suzy wrestling with her anorak and smiling rather uncertainly.

'It was a nice party,' she said, and ran after her friend.

It *had* gone on too long, June knew, and she wasn't surprised that things had come to a rather strained end.

She went back inside to where the boys still greedily chewed on what was left. Tim, with all the easy unconcern of a boy who had spent many hours in this house, opened the fridge and helped himself to more lemonade. He filled Adrian's glass for him, and then made a frantic grab for the last salmon sandwich, which he missed and glumly watched being shovelled into Greg Pickersgill's mouth.

'I'll make some more, shall I?' said June, amused, but Tim shook his head.

'I'm stuffed,' he said. 'I'll have some cake, though.'

Edward said, 'How's school these days, Timmy? Have you got over that new maths yet?'

'No, sir,' said the boy, suddenly stiff, straight, awkward. Perhaps, even at his young age, he sensed politely trivial conversation. Edward said, 'Bring it round sometime and we'll have a look at it, if you like. How's your dad?'

'I don't see much of him. He's going to Scotland soon, with work. I'd like to go with him, but I don't think he'll let me. Don's going, though.'

Mention of Scotland made June think of Karen, coming home from her school in Yorkshire, and she glanced at the clock.

'Five o'clock,' she said, and Edward glanced over his shoulder.

'I'll have to get a move on,' he said. He rose from the table, wiping his napkin across his lips.

'Is Karen coming home?' asked Tim.

Edward nodded. 'Home for a couple of weeks,' he lied. 'Do you remember Karen very well?'

The boy nodded, but obviously knew her more from Don talking about her. It had been a long time since Karen had been at home for more than a few days, though Don, Tim's brother, spent a not inconsiderable number of weekends lodging close to the school where she boarded. Their romance had begun playfully, and yet seemed persistent, and Edward was not unhappy about it. When Karen came home for the vacations, the whole family moved away, to their country house in Wales, or camping in France, and Don always came with them. Both June and Edward saw, in Don, perhaps the only chance to settle Karen for once and for good.

'Adrian's looking forward to seeing Karen, isn't he?' said Edward, smiling and playfully ruffling the boy's hair.

That was when Adrian screamed.

June jumped to her feet, her face registering the awful shock she felt. Her chair flew backwards, and Tim stared at his friend, terrified.

Adrian, eyes wide, mouth opened, continued to utter the awful ululation of anger and fear until he exhausted his lungs.

He turned very slowly to stare at June and in his eyes was an expression she had never seen before . . . not anger, not fear, not excitement nor depression . . . something, perhaps, that was a mixture of all these things – and more.

The boy's lips moved, soundless at first, then the hiss of air began to form words, the first words he had ever spoken in his life:

'Don't let her come . . . hate Karen . . . hate Karen . . .'

'Oh my God!' said June, her face ashen. She looked at Edward. He seemed every bit as shocked at hearing words from Adrian, and slowly he met his wife's gaze. The blood had drained from his face and he looked nothing less than a corpse, lined and grey, slack and dead. And yet he should have been triumphant!

In the instant that their attention was away from the boy, Adrian put his right little finger into his mouth and began to suck. June noticed the way his eyes narrowed and how the signs of tension developed in the muscles of his face, but all this she saw in that strange wasteland of awareness that follows shock – she was aware of the kitchen, the wind blowing the long grass beyond the window, the breathing of her husband, heavy and noisy, the sound of the Pickersgill boys uncomfortably kicking the legs of their chairs as they watched this bizarre tableau of stunned surprise. She was aware of Adrian, doing more than just suck his finger – he was biting . . .

There was a sound like the dry cracking of a dead twig.

Adrian uttered a cry, like a man, hurt beyond control, yet manfully containing his agony. When June looked at him for a second she saw only the tears of pain and hurt in his eyes, the awful, angry gaze in them.

Then she saw the thick stream of blood that erupted from his mouth and flooded down his chin. Her legs went out from under her and as Edward began to shout his sudden horror, she hit the edge of the table with her head and passed into unconsciousness.

CHAPTER TWO

Something had called to him in the last few days, an intuitive cry that had at once excited him, and frightened him.

He had not been sleeping well; he never slept well during autumn, feeling too cold or too hot, or too restless with the thought of a miserable British winter just around the corner. And he dreamed, too, and his dreams were usually vivid, occasionally intensely violent. He remembered them, more often than not, and they could shake him for days, and for the last two weeks he had not slept a full night, nor passed a night without a dream. And somewhere, in those fourteen insomniac darknesses, was a call, a dream, perhaps, about something closer to reality than his frustration- or power-complexes.

The precise time of that feeling, that disturbance, escaped him now, and had probably escaped him the morning after it had occurred. But since then he had been restless and dissatisfied with the particular carvings on which he had been working, and his attention had come closer and closer to concentrating on that one small, lichen-covered fragment that had come into the museum a year ago, and had been pushed aside as uninteresting . . . the Higham fragment.

He smiled inwardly at the predictability of this, the familiar pattern of the uninteresting addition to a collection suddenly revealing itself as fascinating. It happened to him all the time, and to his colleagues as well. It was at once the bug-bear and delight of research.

With a bulging folio of papers beneath his arm, he hurried along Oxford Street, sensing rain in the grey November sky.

His name was Liam Kline, but he was always known as Lee. He particularly hated being called Doctor Kline. It made him feel old, and he was only just thirty – or was it thirty-one? He couldn't remember these days, and didn't care anyway. It wasn't the exact count of the rings in his body that mattered, but the pulsing beat of his heart, which beat like an adolescent's and often gave him an adolescent taste for fun. When some stiff and grey-suited Professor at the Institute addressed him ponderously as Doctor Kline it made him wince. When he called those same Professors by their Christian names in a seminar or student gathering it made them bristle, and he enjoyed that. It got him into trouble quite often, but it was impossible to maintain anger with Kline – he had a mischievous expression about him, a boyish grin, easy and relaxed, and sparkling blue eyes that always belied the mock solemness of his face as he listened to some accounting of his irreverent behaviour.

Kline was a Californian, born and bred in Berkeley, where he had also graduated. He had earned his doctorate in the same College and had then decided to make his move, to England, to London, to participate in a project on the population dynamics of pre-Roman Britain. Naturally, after eighteen months, he had broadened his horizons to include anything and everything that interested him, from Stonehenge to Celtic stone heads, from the ecology of prehistoric Britain to Alfred Watkins' ley-lines, a phenomenon in which he whole-heartedly believed. He had an informal, but highly disciplined approach to work, and was intolerant to the point of boorishness of people whose way of working differed from his own.

He could also be a bastard, and enjoyed the knowledge of this too. He used that same disarming smile to soften a victim to what could often be a devastating criticism of work and personality. He cared not that he damaged the confidence of a promising student. What the hell? They were at the Institute to work, weren't they? They should have as little time for personality problems as he. If they couldn't take a piece of strong criticism of their private lives when those private lives were obviously affecting their work style, then they'd not make much of their professional lives.

He enjoyed shaking people up. He couldn't stand maudlin, self-indulgence, not in his friends, not in anyone.

As he weaved his way through the crowds he felt rain on his face and pulled his woollen hat tightly down across his unkempt hair. Hunched inside his short leather wind-cheater, but still freezing cold, he broke into a run, hanging on tight to his precious package of newspapers. He made for shelter in the gaping maw of Tottenham Court Road underground.

The shower sleeted from the west for a few minutes and he watched the late season tourists clustered in every shop doorway, and the students, in faded jeans and denim jackets, moving unbothered and laughing in the suddenly easier streets. The traffic roared past, chaotic, impatient; everything looked so miserable in this weather.

The rain eased as abruptly as it had begun and Kline, anxious to begin his newspaper chase, turned his collar up and began to run towards the Institute building he could just see beyond the high, Victorian buildings of Tottenham Court Road itself. He hesitated only once, to smile broadly at a girl he recognized from the teaching hospital close to Russell Square, and she favoured him with a wave. Next time he saw her, in the sun, he'd see if she remembered November.

Moments later he was at his place of work, bounding up the concrete steps and pushing brightly through the swing doors. He acknowledged the security man on the reception desk and swore inwardly that if the little busybody should push back his horn-rimmed glasses and call him over he'd tell him what to do with his security.

Once inside his small, compact office he let his mind loose from its intense programme of thoughts concerned with his work project; walking was very therapeutic and very encouraging, helping him to sort out new angles, new approaches, even to write difficult letters. His acknowledgement to the streets of London would remain personal, but he was never in any doubt of their value.

Tossing the folio onto his wide desk, just in front of the small selection of stones and Celtic carved heads he was working on, he made himself a cup of strong black coffee, heaping in the dried granules and enjoying the moment of relaxation. He stood by his window, staring out across the small park, its golden-leaved trees shading and sheltering the activity within the narrow walks and small areas of green. Behind him the door was politely knocked,

29

and opened, and the departmental secretary walked in, placed his afternoon mail in his tray.

'Thanks,' he said absently, not turning.

When he had finished his coffee he sat down, put his feet on the desk and picked up the four letters. He chucked the two reprints into a big drawer without even seeing which ones they were. He kissed the small, beige envelope that contained his grant cheque, and then held the fourth letter before him, shaking his head.

'Well, well. Crazy Lady.'

He stared at the spidery writing, the awkward angle at which the French stamp had been stuck to the envelope, felt the thinness of the note-paper inside it. He sensed the woman's urgency and shook his head, smiling uncertainly as he tossed the letter into his in-tray for some quiet deciphering later on. It always took ages to work out what Crazy Lady was saying in her bizarre mixture of incomprehensible French and awkwardly structured English – all overlain with the most appalling handwriting (apart from his own) that he had ever seen.

The French woman had written, originally, just to the Institute. Kline had been put in charge of her. She had taken courage from his first courteous response to her and now regularly sent him some further listing of her bizarre and outrageous ideas about the standing stones of her home country, and Carnac in particular. Kline had absolutely no idea who she was, and it was only in her last letter – a disturbing letter indeed! – that she had given any hint as to what she was. Kline dismissed her outwardly as . . . crazy. Inwardly he was intrigued by her. She was uncannily accurate in some of her observations, which would testify to her being an expert in the Megalithic culture of Brittany (even Professor Thom had taken a serious and alarmed look at some of her ideas, writing frantic footnotes to his books as a result) . . . and yet no-one had ever heard of her.

Ultimately he had been moved to ask certain questions of her as to how she knew the things she knew. He had not liked the answer. This short letter, no doubt, was a polite request as to why he had been so silent since she had last written.

His colleagues had no hesitation in dismissing Crazy Lady as being part of the lunatic fringe. Kline agreed, but was nevertheless sympathetic towards that particular fringe; what he hated was its lack of discipline and research orderliness. He was well prepared to believe what some 'sensitive' people in England said, that there was a spiral flow of 'energy' up a standing stone; but before he accepted it he wanted machine and experimental proof: it wasn't enough to look at a solitary standing stone in a field, he wanted to see standing stones removed and replaced with other stones to see if the effect remained; he wanted to see different *types* of stone used. He wanted to see the whole thing done in the proper way, and he wanted to see the focus of this strange work, exploring the nature of the ancient stones, taken out of the hands of the Colin Wilsons – the journalists who were looking so hard that they would find something, even if it wasn't there – and placed in the hands of sceptical, irritable, mocking scientists.

Nothing is impossible, he always said, but if it's true it can be tested because there is no such thing as an unknown quantity.

He did not acknowledge that there might be some unknown forms of energy eluding detection, except in their tentative relationships with stones, leys and underground streams. He *did* accept that, under certain circumstances, known energy forms could be elusive. And it was people like dowsers, and sensitives, and, yes, even Crazy Lady who might be the 'machines' of a new technology, a technology for reading more from standing stones than that which the eye could see, and the mind could imagine.

All of which was nothing to do with the issues at hand . . .

He finished his coffee and pulled the artists' folder around, unzipping it to reveal its content of newspapers, ready for his first intensive search. He sensed he would find something in these papers of interest, but in the past, despite his certainty that newspaper reporting would always supply something of importance, he had more usually drawn a total blank.

He hesitated. The noise in the corridor outside – chattering, typing, walking – had faded away, and even outside his window an unusual stillness had descended. He felt alone, for just an instant, isolated in his room with his work, and his thoughts, and the heavy thump of his heart.

He felt hot.

His hands let go of the folder of newspapers and his gaze shifted to the filing cabinet across the room, and to the fragment of stone he had rested upon it.

The Higham fragment.

For a long while he stared at it, following its rain smoothed curves with his eyes, focussing hard upon the just-visible depressions in its surface that told of a design carved upon it. The stone seemed to whisper to him, to drive all thoughts from his head, and all sounds from the world. It demanded his touch, his caress, and after a while he rose and walked across the room, to pick the fragment from its shelf and turn it over in his fingers.

It weighed no more than ten pounds, not heavy, not the heaviest stone fragment he had come across with carvings upon it, but a comfortable weight – heavy, to indicate its nature, but light enough that he could carry it, to grow close to it. It was thin at one end, thick at the other, sheared from the block of stone it had been a part of by an enormous blow. His expert eyes could still see the marks of the tool that had severed this limb of the rock. He could imagine the religious fervour that had given strength to the blow, the superstitious fear that had angled the assault so accurately, so devastatingly.

What unholy properties had those medieval peoples assigned to this innocent relic of the past, he wondered? What had they feared in such stones as the Avebury megaliths, and even some of the memorial stones of the Celts, that they had felt it necessary to destroy them? What awful ignorance had fed upon their belief in magic and evil to set them so fervently to the task of obliterating those stones from their vision?

Kline had no doubt at all that the Higham fragment was the chipping of one such destructive orgy, perhaps four hundred years in the past, perhaps less. Since then the stone had lain in the earth, obviously half-exposed during the more recent years, for a thick layer of lichen, grey and dead, compacted to the rock as if it was a part of the rock itself, spread across most of the carved surface.

It had been found near Higham, in a copse of trees, and brought to the Institute's museum a year ago. Kline had seen it on its arrival but had not remarked upon it. And yet he must have seen the almost invisible markings upon it, the fragment of a spiral crossed by radiating lines, because at a later date that knowledge had surfaced and sent him racing to the specimen cupboards, searching for it.

Another example of his intuition, that famous Kline intuition as it had come to be known. Intuition perhaps, but nothing inexplicable. The unremarked information had merely surfaced from his subconscious and drawn his attention.

But that nightmare, that cry, resounding through his sleep . . .

He was still unnerved by that dream, yet that too could be explained as merely part of the mechanism of recall – the nightmare must have featured the Higham Fragment, and his mind had not been at rest until he had located that stone, and finally seen the surface markings for what they were – deliberate patterns, a small area of some larger design.

He held the stone to his nose, smelling its mustiness, its

earthiness, loving the ancient feel of it, and the call of the distant, dark past intrinsic in the shallow-etched markings.

His phone went, loud and irresponsible in his quiet mood. It jarred.

He placed the Higham Fragment back upon the cabinet and went back to his desk.

He finished with the phone-call then turned his attention to the newspaper chase. By now it was quite late afternoon, and he found it necessary to switch on his desk lamp since the rainy skies above London gave the city a veneer of dusk, and his room was quite dark.

He stared at the topmost of the local papers, with its broad, ugly logo, *The Higham Chronicle*. He had borrowed just one years' edition, fifty-two, or three, of the slender journals. It had not been easy convincing the middle-aged woman at the London-based offices of the conglomerate that owned the paper that he was to be trusted with their loan, but ultimately it had been easier than using the British Museum's collection. It's unheard of, the lady in charge had said, stiffly. He had gently cajoled her, eased her into his way of thinking, with promises and his urgent tone, so easy to turn on when necessity dictated it. He couldn't imagine settling to read fifty-two papers in the cluttered offices in Bond Street, surrounded by desks, noise and bulging files, for the place had been the location of what seemed to be hundreds of out-of-London weeklies.

He had won through. He could borrow *The Higham Chronicle* in units of one year, and heaven protect him if he lost even a single column, from a single page of a single issue.

He started to read, skimming the news pages that filled the first quarter of each issue. For a brief period he came to know much about Higham, despite trying to forget the enormous input of information as fast as it came in. He read about the shopping centre that had again been frustrated by the local council, the multi-storey car park that had gone ahead, despite the excavations for the foundation having turned up the remnants of a ninth-century house (a note on this one, just in case). He followed the exploits of a local fishmonger attempting to prevent the opening of a wine bar next door because of the lack of nearby car space, and the congestion that illegally parked cars would cause outside his shop. He discovered that a new Catholic Church had been officially opened, transferring the local priest from a temporary hall in a nearby town. What had happened to the previous church?

Then he found something that interested him more directly. In December of the year before a local man had killed a young couple, unrelated, unknown to him. There were exaggerated accounts of Black Mass rituals, and references to the man worshipping Satan, and claiming that he had killed the two people on instructions from the Dark Prince himself.

A note here. It was mundane, and familiar (there were over a thousand crimes a year that were claimed for Satan, or other blackly religious cults). But it was worth knowing.

He ploughed on, reading into the current year, wading through Winter in Higham, and the river flooding problem that had sent a million cockroaches into the kitchens of two local restaurants. Arrow heads (Stone Age, according to the paper) had been dug up in someone's garden. He made a second note here.

He read on, through council decisions concerned with the car park – which would finally be delayed so that the Historical Society might remove rotted timbers, and make a few more observations of the site. Road widening dominated the April issues or, more precisely, residential objection to what was seen as unnecessary measures to alleviate traffic congestion through the west end of the town. Two local business men were insisting that the old stone font should be moved to the new Catholic church from the ruins of St Mary's. The priest was fighting them for reasons that seemed very irrational. He read on, and in the first July issue found something that interested him more: an auction had taken place of the sketches and watercolours of a Victorian artist, by name of Bellamy, who had lived in the village of Higham, as it had been then. 'Sketches of the town and the surrounds, including portraits of several of the local dignitaries, were sold for four hundred pounds. Four watercolours, showing the downs, and the town as seen from the east, fetched sixty pounds.'

Across four columns, badly reproduced in this paper, was a sample of one of the pen and ink sketches, showing a wide dirt road and several wooden-fronted houses, as well as an ugly brick Victorian building that he guessed was the Town Hall, and a quite magnificent old church, standing back from the road, elevated as if it stood on the broad back of a low hillock.

He concluded his news search, turned the pile of papers over so that he was back at the bottom again, then settled back in his seat and looked at his notes. They were an average set of notes, a few points of interest, and one nice sketch (with the possibility of others, when he could track down the buyer) showing the sort of detailed view of the old town that he found so valuable to his work.

But there was nothing before him that sparked his imagination, or set his blood surging with intuitive excitement; he had hoped to feel something in connection with the Higham Fragment, but no such feeling had overwhelmed him, and though he was slightly disappointed, he was not overly surprised. It was always a long shot. And when the long shot missed, the whole point of his newspaper chase became shrouded in obscurity. Why *had* he spent three hours skimming fifty papers? What had he hoped to unearth?

The immediate answer was . . . just what he *had* unearthed. An impression of Higham, a sense of its place in the scheme of things; a sense of its past.

Which, though it created an atmosphere conducive to interest, was no help at all in understanding where the Higham stone had come from.

Nevertheless, a newspaper chase could prove fruitful. Stories, references to old buildings, local colour, local legends resurrected for fun . . . very early in his professional career Kline had been amazed at just what could be unearthed from a local paper. There was always space to fill when the news was limited. Old stories and tales were good space fillers and often had their roots in interesting historical facts.

Something . . . some inner feeling, urged him back to the papers. It occurred to him, as he opened the earliest again, this time at the centre pages, that there had been no reference to the discovery of the Higham fragment itself. If whoever had dug it up had thought it important enough to send to the Institute, then surely the local paper would have recorded *something* about it.

The obvious answer was that the fragment had been dug up years ago, had resided in someone's garage, or under the stairs, until a change of ownership, perhaps, had unearthed it again, and only then had it found its way to the archives of the museum. By going further back through the local papers, Kline might find more about its original discovery.

For the moment, however, he began to scan the articles, the small columns, the country life and write-ups of local activity.

In the very first of the year's papers he discovered a 'true' ghost story, and felt immediately encouraged. Ghost stories were amazing sources of information, he had not the slightest doubt about that. So many related, if not to prehistoric figures, mis-identified as 'white ladies' or some such, to a source of ancient strength, or magic. By following the more authentic ghost stories to their source he himself had discovered a few *leys* – and other workers many more – and sites of pagan ritual, including stones or the remains of sanctuaries, well hidden but not totally obscured, by more recent buildings.

So he read ghost stories with his scepticism riding high, but with the interest of a serious man. This story, however, did not bear re-reading. Told by an old woman who had lived on the outskirts of Higham all her life, it was an innocuous tale, and almost certainly untrue, concerning the impossible headless figure so favoured by ghost writers, and so blatantly phoney. Kline decided, dismissively, that the old woman was narrating a story she had read as a child, perhaps, and which had – over the years – become confused with her personal experience.

He turned to a second paper where the next in the series of stories about the ghosts of Higham was printed, and feeling less than enthusiastic began to run his eyes down the columns . . .

And then, with one of those sudden twists that can turn growing despair into almost uncontrollable excitement, he found something that sent him rocking backwards against the desk in delight.

The article concerned the ghost of a man who had committed suicide over a hundred years ago; the phantom was often to be seen (said the article) walking through the grounds of the house where he had lived before taking his life in the local church, St Mary's.

None of which was the full reason for Kline's excitement.

What had taken his attention was the reference to the font of St Mary's, an ancient stone font against which the man had died.

This was the second reference to that same piece of church furniture he had read today, but this new mention was all the reason he needed to go to Higham tomorrow – there was something about the font he had never experienced before in his life.

He *had* to see it.

The following morning Kline drove away from his small Hampstead flat, and joined the motorway leaving London for the West. He drove a small Austin – ten years old, much battered, much strained – and it amused him, momentarily, to note that try as he might he could not get the needle of the speedometer to touch fifty.

'Damn it, car, I can walk faster than this!'

At a sober, and safe, forty-eight mph he droned out of London, the map of the western suburbs opened on the seat beside him, his eyes keen for signs to Higham which would mean he need no longer bother with the map and just – what was that English expression? – *beetle* along, regardless, following signs to his destination.

At this very early hour, just after eight, the traffic was heavy coming into the metropolis, and almost non-existent leaving it. That made sense, he decided, grinning at the slow moving commuters as they shook their heads and bit their lips, leaning to the right to try and see what the hold-ups were.

They all looked as tired and dishevelled as Kline himself; but – fired by excitement – Kline was far from tired. His hair was unruly, sticking out at all angles, uncombed and unwashed for three days, and he hadn't bothered to shave; being naturally dark, this was noticeable. But he had felt there was no time to lose. After all, the stone he was going to see had waited two millennia. It must be getting fed up waiting.

He left the motorway and pulled into a petrol station, not for fuel but for breakfast – a bar of dark chocolate and a can of coca-cola.

Higham was on a fairly direct route out of London, and though a naturally bad navigator, he soon got onto the right road and was able to relax. Within minutes the town was signposted. A mile from its outskirts Kline pulled off the road into a convenient parking area. He climbed from the car, stretching his muscles, still stiff from the night.

He watched the traffic for a few minutes, then pulled his hat tightly down and began to walk. It was cold and he was wrapped in leather jacket and thick cotton shirt. The sky was overcast, but it didn't threaten rain.

This close to the downs of Berkshire, where vast forests had once concealed all manner of game, and community life, the roadway was thickly bordered by trees. It seemed that he walked in the middle of nowhere, joined to civilization only by the straight, tarmac road, and the whining lorries and cars that fled past him. He saw no houses, though when he looked hard through the woodlands on either side of the road, he could see open spaces, and distant clusters of buildings.

Soon the woodland thinned and houses sprang up, most of

37

them old, quite attractive, but the sort of place that Kline, a city-lover, hated.

The road dipped and curved, vanishing into the shade of a woody overhang, and when he emerged he found himself staring straight at Higham across its battered and dirty name-sign.

Once, he thought, an artist had sat around here and drawn the view along the road, into the wide square of the market town. He had seen grassy verges giving way to attractively fronted houses; a coach had clattered across the square, heading west, perhaps to Oxford; old buildings, works of art in themselves, had clustered beneath the gentle gaze of an old and remarkable-looking church.

He looked at Higham as it now presented itself, and felt no inkling of rapport with it: he saw red brick buildings towering high, ugly, one face of them lacking windows completely; he saw two vast estates of box-like houses, stretching across the land as far as his eye could see; white facades broke up the ugly monotony of the red brick, but the repetitiveness of the design was ugly in itself.

He walked along the roadside, ignoring the wind of passing traffic. Abruptly he was in the town itself, walking across the same square that the artist had drawn a hundred and thirty years before; it seemed smaller, now that a great clutter of taller buildings surrounded it, and it was black and hard compared to the muddy square of the Victorian era. The same ornate building watched him, as it had watched him from the sketch, and he saw that it was not a Town Hall, but a Salvation Army centre.

Out of interest he located the town's museum. It was a small building, old and dirty, the sort of museum that is run on sufferance by one or two local people in the employ of the council; or so it seemed to Kline as he peered through the tiny windows into the gloomy interior. The building did not open until eleven a.m., still over an hour away.

So he walked along the High Street itself, staggered by the mundanity of the town, increasingly depressed by its lack of character and the predictability of everything he saw. He knew this sort of town so well, and he had hoped for so many surprises.

It was as he stood in the street, vainly trying to sense something of the past, that he saw the church of St Mary in the Fields.

It lay back from the road, fronted by a wide grass bank, and a winding gravel-laden pathway. Its fire-blackened ruins were mostly hidden from his eyes, and from the old square, by the shops and offices that fronted the road more directly, and he moved quickly along the street until he stood directly opposite

38

the building and could drink in the atmosphere of its destruction more directly.

Now at last he felt excited. Its jagged profile, the buttresses of grey stone, and the perfect forms of its door and window arches, untouched by the holocaust of flame and smoke, appealed to the historian in him in a very special way. A church was more than just the building and the religious fervour that its confines had harboured. It was a reflection of a time at least two thousand years old, a survivor, in mood, of an age of innocence and of a more supernaturally oriented society. And if the church was as old as its design suggested, then it was undoubtedly sited upon something much older, an older place of worship, which itself was probably built upon a site of great power, pagan – certainly – but undeniably powerful.

Now he smiled, despite the stench of petrol, and the normality of life around him. He sensed that past, the rich harvest of memories locked in the earth upon which the church stood. And he sensed the stone that lay within it, the ancient stone whose mention in a ghost story had called him to the town.

He checked the traffic, planning his crossing of the busy road. As he started to run, however, he noticed a woman walking up the gravel pathway, and he hesitated.

He swore as he stepped back onto the pavement opposite, and watched the woman as she vanished into the ruined interior of the church. He willed her to re-appear, walking away from this place that he so urgently wanted to step within. He hated the thought of not being alone as he approached the stone. The woman was an intruder and he wanted her out.

But she didn't come out, and after five minutes he could bear to wait no longer. He ran across the road, weaving between the slow moving cars, and walked quickly up the pathway into the porch.

And saw her.

CHAPTER THREE

She was crouched in the darkness of a recess and he could hear the faint sound of her voice as she spoke to someone. All he could see in the morning shadow was the dull whiteness of rock, rising from the gleaming green-tiled flooring, and as he focussed his eyes he realized he was looking at the church's font, a font hewn from the rough surfaces of the ancient stone he had come to see.

He began to pick his way carefully across the fire-damaged floor. In places the decorated flooring was intact and wherever possible he walked on these surfaces, but the fire had had its major destructive influence on the roof and walls, which were badly and irretrievably cracked open in many places. Underfoot was mostly secure, accounting, probably, for the fact that the ruins were not closed to the public as dangerous.

He was half way across the church when the woman sensed his presence and looked round, the gentle drone of her voice cutting off abruptly, but not before Kline had heard her mention the name of Adrian.

She frowned as he approached, and rose to her feet, her right hand resting on the carved top of the font. Kline smiled narrowly, aware of her unease, and her suspicion, and of his own wild looks; when he was some ten feet from her he stopped, and nodded.

She never smiled, nor acknowledged him, merely stared at him, the slightest of frowns, of queries, upon her face. Kline longed to drop to his knees and embrace the stone, to study it, searching its every cranny for some sign of its true origins. But he lingered, a moment, on the woman, for he found himself drawn to her, attracted by her, even slightly puzzled by her.

He thought she might have been in her mid-thirties; her face was smooth and youthful, well cared for, and only around her eyes, and the corners of her mouth, were there the slightest of lines, fine lines, attractive. She had full lips, which turned slightly up and gave her that permanent smile that is so pleasing, and so inevitably comfortable. Her fair hair was cut quite short, and very neat, parted in the middle and turned up at the edges in an elaborate, contrived chaos of curls. She wore a blue blazer over a roll neck sweater, that hugged her figure, emphasising the fullness of it, a perfect match with flared and meticulously creased denim jeans.

She was Kline's sort of woman, casual but perfect, a perfect opposite to Kline himself, a complete complement.

He thrust his hands into his pockets and grinned. 'Hi.'

'Hi,' she repeated, and the frown deepened.

'I see we have the same idea.'

She cocked her head slightly. 'What idea?' Her voice was soft, her accent deeply English, with well rounded and well formed words; it seemed, to Kline, to be sensuous. It matched her appearance.

He pointed to the font. 'Visiting that lump of rock.'

'The font?' She glanced down at the stone. 'I come here most days; I've never seen you here before. What are you, a journalist?'

'A journalist?' He laughed, surprised, although there was nothing to be surprised about. 'No, I'm a historian. Does that seem unlikely to you?'

'Why should it? I've never met a historian before.' She looked him up and down, quite deliberately. 'You look more like a garage mechanic, I'll agree, but I'll take your word for it.' She turned away from him and stared down at the grey stone, running her fingers around the deeply chiselled bowl. Without looking at him she said, 'Why *are* you interested in the font?'

'Because of what it once was,' he said quietly, staring at her, and not at the stone. She was so obviously hiding something from him, and her anxiety at his interest was unexpected and almost improbable. He hoped her reasons for being so protective were trivial and sentimental and not because she was – herself – interested in the origins of the St Mary's font.

She glanced up at him, smiling thinly, but intrigued. 'Because of what it once was? What does that mean? It's always been a font . . . except when it was part of a mountain.'

Did she really believe that?

He walked across to her, now, and ran his hands across the cold, grainy surface of the stone. The sensation was thrilling to him, and he felt his heart speed up, sending a dizzying wash of blood to his head. He touched the shallow marks on the sides where inexpert hands had tried to carve Christian symbols and pictures, a dragon, and a serpent entwined about a cross. They were superficial and of no importance; they had hardly marked the original surface of the stone. Only at its base were there more intricate carvings, and these he soon discovered were in a plaster rim that hid the entrance of the stone into the ground. They were recent, and quite beautiful, and had been coloured to look as if they were a part of the font itself. But they were separate, and Kline was pleased.

He said, 'This rock was dug out of the mountain a long time before man used it as a holy well.'

'A *holy well*?' said the woman loudly, almost as if she didn't believe what he'd said. 'That sounds more pagan than Christian!'

'Damn right,' said Kline, boredly. He was fascinated by the font. He couldn't take his eyes from it, nor tear his mind completely away from the contemplation of it. 'I don't believe in your munificent, all-seeing One God. The old peoples had the best idea – nature as God, and many Gods.'

'Is that what you believe in?'

Kline glanced at her, smiling, then shrugged. 'Not really.'

'What *do* you believe in?' She seemed hostile, almost provocative.

Kline glanced around, at the ruins of the church. My God, he thought, grinning at the irrelevant invocation, what a fire this must have been to have cracked the stone walls like that! 'I believe,' he said aloud, 'In Fire as a symbol of progress . . .'

The woman laughed. 'This is progress?'

'You have a new, modern church in its place, don't you?'

She stayed silent. Kline went on, 'I believe in water as a symbol of life . . .'

'I don't. I believe in water as death.'

'Why?'

'You can drown in it, can't you?'

'You can burn in fire. You can suffocate in earth. The sky might fall on your head and crack your skull. I'm talking about a deeper meaning than the physical side of things.'

'So am I.'

Again she was staring at the font, and now her face was white. There was tenseness at the edge of her mouth.

'What's your name?' asked Kline, and the moment of unease passed.

'June Hunter. You?'

'Lee Kline. Are you a Catholic?'

She shook her head. 'There was a time, yes. I used to come to this very church. I used to go across into the back pews, over there, and sit with my friends, giggling and paying no more attention to the service than I paid to anything. I can remember being fourteen and using Sunday mass more as a chance to fix up a date than as a chance to commune with my God. I moved here with my parents when I was ten. I left when I was twenty, when I got married, and came back here a few years ago, just before my son was born. They say once you've lived in Higham, you'll never settle anywhere else.'

'I can't imagine why,' said Kline. 'It's the most depressingly awful, modern, characterless town I've ever seen.'

'Is it? Not all of us think so. There are families here whose ancestors were here during the Domesday census. We know some of one family like that very well – the Belsaints. I think it's the closeness to both country and London that makes it so popular.'

Kline looked thoughtful. 'It must be more than that. I can name a hundred towns that fit that bill.'

June smiled, shrugged. 'Yes, I suppose you're right. I don't know. Something attracts people to the place, keeps them here. It's a very secure town. It has a good feel about it, the longer you stay. It has a good community life.'

'Sure,' said Kline. 'I know just what you mean. You get ties with the earth, like there's always a part of you attached to the ground where you were born.'

June smiled. 'You mean like Roots?'

Kline laughed. 'Why not, by Christ? Why not?'

He turned back to the stone font and dropped to a crouch beside it. 'This stone is *fabulous*. Think of the history instilled into it –'

'What history?'

'Well, for a start it was almost certainly an ancient standing stone, thousands of years old. Then it was dragged here and used by the Britons, during the Roman occupation probably –'

'Used as what?'

Kline shrugged, pushed his woollen cap back across his head and scratched at his scalp, which was itching. 'Christ knows. Some ritual purpose, perhaps. When they'd finished with it they left it to gather the silence of time until the last few hundred years, when it was finally destroyed in such a subtle way.'

'Very poetic,' said June, but she was puzzled. She watched Kline as he walked around the font, dropping to his knees to touch gently the hidden side of the stone, searching for something, anything, that would indicate its original nature more thoroughly, more certainly, than his instinctive feel for it.

'Destroyed?' said the woman. 'It hasn't been destroyed. What are you talking about?'

'It's been carved into something that it wasn't,' said Kline, still running his index fingers across the coarse surface of the rock. 'It's been chipped and hollowed but that was nothing to the psychological destruction involved. A stone used to make acknowledgement to Man as God has been deliberately changed into a stone used to baptise man in the name of God as man.' He glanced up, grinning. 'You followed that, I hope.'

June laughed. 'Well, yes. But the stone is the same. If it has an historical meaning, the Christianizing of it hasn't changed that.'

43

'Not in actuality, no. In fact, it's fascinating. But all that mind power, all that religion, instilling itself into the structure of the rock, it must have gone a long way to wiping out the stone's memories.'

He looked at her, a half smile on his face, conscious that he was provoking the scorn of the woman, aware that he was saying things that he only half believed.

To his amazement the woman was staring at him, her mouth agape, her eyes wide.

He frowned. 'You must admit,' he said, 'That if stones had minds, then this stone has been pretty well screwed up.' To himself, more than to her, he added, 'I wonder how long this font has been a font . . . Any ideas? How long since the bowl was hollowed out?'

June Hunter ignored the question. She said, 'What do you mean, stones have memories? Do you believe that? Do you really believe stones can trap thoughts?'

She was either deeply frightened or deeply fascinated by the idea. The intensity of her interest was overwhelming and he rose to his feet, leaned heavily against the grey stone and stared at it. 'Well, yes. Or rather . . . no, I don't *believe* it. Because I've never seen it proved. I do not disbelieve it for the same reason. I believe that it is possible that a stone can act as a recorder . . . it's an enormously complex crystalline structure, after all; even sedimentary rock, like this, is made up of billions of tiny crystals of igneous rock. I mean; it makes sense to me that something that is crystalline, but dis-ordered like sandstone, or ragstone, or any of the stones that were used to build churches, or ancient buildings, or even chipped into what we call *dressed* stones, standing stones, stone circles, memorial stones, goddammed Stonehenge and all the rest . . . they all, surely, are potential recorders, of something more fundamental than noise and light.'

'The power of the crystal,' said June, and Kline laughed, thinking she was being slightly sarcastic. She was being anything but; she was staring at the stone, and her face was white.

When she looked up at him he started to speak, but her gaze went beyond him, towards the end of the church, and he heard her catch her breath, a gesture of anger.

Frowning he glanced round and saw a tall, angular man standing just inside the porchway, hands thrust into the pockets of his great coat, his head bare, his eyes almost hidden behind heavy, dark-rimmed glasses.

Kline shook his head and looked at June. 'Who is he? Do you know him?'

When he looked round again the man had gone.

June was shivering, shaking quite visibly, and now she seemed almost relieved, as if a moment of acute tension had passed. Slightly confused, she looked up at Kline and smiled. 'I'm sorry. I just can't stand that man.'

'Who was he?'

'A priest.'

'I noticed that much,' said Kline. 'Why'd he upset you?'

She shrugged and looked back at the font. 'He hates me as much as I hate him. He thinks I did something to hurt him once and now, whenever he can, he lets me know what he thinks of me. Sometimes he's almost obscenely abusive.'

Kline said, 'Report him. Why not?'

'I can't – don't ask me why. I just can't.'

She brightened, as if forcing herself to become more jovial, and brushed a hand nonchalantly across the stone font. Kline watched. She had something really big on her mind, and he wished he knew what it was and he hoped she would stay around long enough for him to find out.

Then again, she was stopping him sensing the stone in all its primeval majesty. He wished she would go away and leave him alone. And also . . . he wished she would stay, and open up, for he sensed something about her, something abnormal. And he wished she would take her problems elsewhere and leave him alone . . .

With the experience of long practice, he engaged gear and turned on his unfailingly successful overdrive: always assume that troubled people are people in trouble; people are interesting, and their particular personalities can give an insight into local affairs; troubled people give deeper insight.

He cleared his throat theatrically, gaining her attention again. 'I came here,' he said, 'To look at this font, which was originally a stone erected many hundreds of years before Christ was born, which was dragged east, to this place, to stand in an area of intensely religious but 'pagan' – you must understand there are quote marks around that word – 'pagan' practices. The people who used this stone in this part of the land probably sensed something about it, something primitive, and primal, something they wanted. They stole it from the western lands, probably around Avebury, and erected it here. I must say at once that not a word of this is necessarily true. A mixture of guesswork,

45

having seen the font, now, and of pieces of information received from an article in one of your local papers – most interesting of which was that this stone was once called the "suicide stone". So, assuming that something like this history *did* occur then I am fascinated, June, and I have come to Higham to extend that fascination into a brief period of study.' He smiled. 'Now, that's all very innocent and all very straightforward. So tell me exactly, and without embarrassment, why you are so resentful of my interest. Tell me what it is about this stone that bothers you so much. Please.'

She stared at him, and chewed the nail of her left index finger until it snapped, and Kline winced. 'I'm sorry,' she said, wiping her finger against her denims. 'What makes you think something is bothering me?'

Kline laughed. 'Nothing. Pure instinct.' His grin made it plain that he was being facetious and June recognized, immediately, that her behaviour had given her away. She shrugged. 'Stones as recorders, as memories . . . as prisons? Is a trapped memory a prison?'

Willing to say anything that would keep her talking, Kline said, 'I suppose. Does this font have good memories for you? Bad memories?'

'Good and bad,' she said. 'Like all things, all places, there are good and bad. Did you ever see that play about ghosts trapped in a church? Trapped in the stones of the wall?'

Kline hadn't, and admitted as much.

'It was silly,' said June Hunter. 'But then, it was a long time ago. Each stone remembered what it had seen, and could release its memories as ghost visions. Could it happen?'

'Yes,' said Kline, quickly. Too quickly, really, for his mouth spoke before his mind had managed to fully comprehend what she was saying. And besides, there was another thought nagging at him now, a recollection of his own, of a letter, of a woman who had confused and delighted him with her particular madness . . .

He tried not to think of that letter, instead looked down at the font, so quiet, so cold in the ruins.

If stones were crystal, and crystals were organized matter laid out in a disorganized, and therefore mutable, way, then of course stones could be recorders. That's what earth memory was all about, wasn't it?

He was amazed that, despite his feelings that standing stones, and old buildings could – as June had asked – trap the essence of the past, he had never before acknowledged that it might be totally physical, an electrical or magnetic property of the crystalline component of the stone, holding imagery, recollection, reflection, tightly in its impenetrable substance.

How many times he had watched the bizarre magneto–electric fields of stones demonstrated by students and other researchers; how many times he had argued that earth energy, the new energy being propounded by many thinking men, was merely an unexpected and difficult-to-define use of known energy forms.

And he had never linked – in his mind – the two things together.

June Hunter, he thought, may all your troubles stay with you!

But did she believe what she seemed to be implying, or was she merely teasing him, getting him to commit himself?

He asked, 'Do you believe that memory can be trapped in stone?'

'Of course,' she said sharply. 'And life too.'

'Life? Human life?'

As if the suddenness, and specificity, of his question had upset her, she looked angrily at him, then walked quickly to where her bag lay in the shadow. She picked it up and methodically opened it, searching for something, drew nothing from it and closed it again: it was the sort of meaningless gesture that denoted anger, that told of her unwillingness to let the conversation, or her acquaintance with Kline, go further.

'Have fun,' she said, but even as she spoke, walking away from him as she uttered the bitter words, he sensed her reluctance to leave. There had to be a final commitment on her part to this stranger who had caused her to confess so much of her obsession – her obvious obsession – with the font.

Kline read her this way, and was gratified that when he asked her to wait a moment, she stopped and turned.

'I didn't mean to upset you, prying like that . . .' Had he been prying? By her standards, obviously he had.

She shrugged. 'You didn't upset me. And I don't suppose you were being nosy. I'm sorry, I'm just very tense. You can't know what this font means to me.'

'I'd like to. Straight up! I'd like to know what it means to you.' The fish, on the hook, wriggled; uncertainty dragged it away from him as he smiled, playing the line tight, closing on her bodily as he tried to close on her mentally.

Suddenly he realized she needed help. He didn't know what,

nor how he might give that help to her, but he recognized her need, and her desperation to have that need acknowledged.

'Let me help,' he said, 'For God's sake, if I can do anything for you, let me.'

The fish was landed.

'You can't help me.' She was sad. 'No-one can.'

'How do you know? I don't even know what's bugging you. I can sense that something is, and that it goes deep, and painful. Maybe you're right. Maybe I can't help you. But have you asked anyone for help ever?' She shook her head, and he went on, 'So what have you got to lose? Even if I can't help, I'll promise you this: whatever is upsetting you, about this font, about anything, I'll respect your privacy . . .'

She was no longer looking at him, her eyes resting sadly on the font; but she was closer to him, now, than at any time in their minutes together, and he felt her closeness and tried to match it, to consolidate it, by staring at the font as well. As he walked to it, touching it again, so did she.

Their fingers touched, just briefly, the contact of smooth skin, warm skin, almost a shocking contrast to the cold, grainy touch of the stone.

'You'll think me mad,' she said. He reached for her hand and held it, not in a sexual way, but in a Kline way, firm, reassuring, a hint of deeper interest in the tentative way that he played his finger tips across the tense muscles of her palm.

'Okay,' he said softly. 'I think you're mad. You're crazy. You're the most insane person I ever met. You're full of crap, absolutely berserk, brainless, emotional, confused, idiotic. OK? Now that we understand each other . . . tell me about it, all about it. I promise you that if I can help you, that is, assuming you need help –'

'I do,' she said quickly, urgently, voicing something that had only been a suspicion in the American's mind, relieving him, for he now knew that he was not treading on ice as thin as the wisps of fair hair that curled, chaotic and untamed, from her scalp. Impulsively, unable to prevent the movement of his arm, he reached out and brushed the curls from her eyes. She let her grip slip from his and smiled, nervous, girlish, smoothed her hair back more firmly, pressing it into place.

'I do need a sort of help,' she said, confident now. 'And yes . . .' searching his eyes, aware of him, in one sense, for perhaps the first moment of their meeting. 'I think you probably *could* help me.'

'What does this stone mean to you? Why such an obsessive hold over you?'

She flushed bright red, every fibre of her body tightening – her eyes became wild, almost desperate, searching his own, for courage, perhaps, or for a sign that he would understand.

She said, 'Because the font is evil! Because my son is trapped in it, imprisoned. And I want him out, back where he belongs, in his body, the empty body that lives in my house.'

There was a moment's silence, and Kline felt the words sink like lead through his mind. Her gaze became hysterical as she sensed him searching for reason, and for words to continue their momentary understanding, words to reassure her, to let her know that he was still with her.

As quickly and as effortlessly as he allowed himself to laugh, not meaning to scorn her, meaning only to relax the tense moment of amazement, she grinned: it was a grin for all the world the most angry sign of pleasure he had ever seen. It said, 'you bastard, I knew you'd make fun of me.'

She said, 'I told you I was crazy,' and turning, she ran from the church.

Kline wanted to follow, but he remained, leaning against the font, watching her slim shape vanish from the ruins.

CHAPTER FOUR

To his surprise Kline discovered that he was quite shaken by the encounter. He had come to look at an unusual stone, and had discovered himself drawn into the uneasy world of a normal-looking woman with a very abnormal, very obsessive, belief in the impossible.

Or in the unlikely?

Kline found himself standing absolutely still and staring into the recess where the font was grey in the grey day, cold in the cold air. It looked so dead, that rock, and yet it lived for him because of the time it had seen, the steady journey through the ages that it had made, gathering memory, and lichen, dust and fractures.

Can a stone store memories, the woman had asked. And she had meant memories that were active and could be read and recorded, but when he had felt himself agreeing that it could, he had meant memories of a more passive, more metaphorical kind.

N.—3

And then he had argued emptily, and without knowledge, about the crystalline structure of stone and how, yes, it was not inconceivable that some form of information storage function could be inherent in a font, or a rock, or a squared brick of ragstone such as the stones that were used in the walls of the church.

He allowed himself the simple luxury of a self-deprecatory smile, then walked back to stand, leaning against the hollowed bowl of the font. It seemed very quiet around him, and the noise of traffic was distant, almost unnaturally distant. It was chilly, the mournful November day threatening rain, or at least the discomfort of uncertainty, brooding dark clouds, and a heavy, wet atmosphere. But as Kline stood above the font, so he felt warm, and the warmth extended around him until he felt his face hot, and flushed, save for the wind as it blew gently through the ruins, disturbing leaves and dust. His body began to sweat, boiling in his clothes, and he tightened the collar of his jacket, conscious that this was some sort of psychosomatic fever, brought on, perhaps, by his confusion over June Hunter, or by the delaying of his excitement over the discovery of the stone.

The heat would pass. He had experienced something similar before, and was not afraid of it.

The ruined church faded into darkness, and he leaned back heavily against the wall of the chapel where the font stood, and his eyes half closed, seeing the grey shape of the stone, and little else. Somewhere he heard a bird crying loudly, raucously, and sensed its wings as it fled through the jagged walls of the church. A crow, perhaps, or some large dark bird, and its shadow passed above him several times, its wings loud, relentless, as it circled. Then it was gone.

The heat passed, that strange fever that Kline found could take him so swiftly, so inexplicably when he was excited, or intensely uneasy. He stood and drew his notebook from his pocket and was suddenly aware of something.

The stone was no longer as well lit by the day as it had been. He checked his watch. It was late afternoon!

'It can't be! Three hours . . . ?'

He ran to the porchway and stared down into the high street, looking for the clock that he had earlier noticed hang outside the wood-doored corn-exchange. It read the same time as his watch, and now a different sort of sweat prickled his neck. He had never before experienced such a rapid passing of time, and his unawareness of it scared him deeply.

He felt cold, now, the cool air drying the moisture on his body and making his shirt stick icily to his back.

He walked to the font and knelt beside it, sketched it quickly, marking out the highlights, and chip marks that might not show clearly on a photograph. He carried a small Agfamatic with a twenty frame cartridge inside, and he photographed the font from all angles, to give him a clear idea of its shape, then he searched every inch of its surface for signs of earlier carvings than those which were obviously Christian. He found none.

At the base, where it was embedded in the tiled floor of the baptismal recess, layers of plaster had been stuck to the stone, and fashioned in ornate and elaborate patterns, to give the font a more Christian, and more romantic, appearance. He used a piece of broken tile to attack this plaster and found it came away quite easily, but not until it was well worked along its adhering edge. It was tiresome doing this and he gave up, but he tore up the tiles around the font's base and found dry, compacted earth below. Using a bigger piece of stone he smashed the tile flooring across an area of a square foot or more, then – using a stone and a technique such as Stone Age man must have used – he excavated down into that earth, following the rock base to see how deep it went.

And it went deep. He managed to dig down two feet, feeling the cold, earthy feel of a different sort of rock, before he gave up. He ascertained one thing, the sort of fact he was trained and expert in elucidating: below the church level the font was in its original shape, the surface rough and pitted and in no way 'dressed'. The stone had been erected in the church, and the font carved from it afterwards. Or perhaps the church had been built *around* the font? It was improbable, but it would explain the shallowness of the flooring around the stone, and the presence of natural earth so close to the surface.

He was, of course, being destructive to protected property, for the ruins of St Mary in the Fields were still standing – he imagined – simply because they were of deep historical interest. Soon, he had no doubt, the floor would be replaced where it was damaged by fire; he glanced about the church, at the cracked walls, and the long fissures that ran through the heavy slabs that made up the flooring. It was quite usual for roof and wall to suffer most from such a blaze, but . . . it occurred to him that the fire must have been of the order of a fire-storm to have done so much damage! And yet the font, and the plaster base, were unaffected.

He shook his head, surveyed his own vandalism and then quickly filled in his small excavation and replaced the broken tile slabs above it. He wanted that stone out of the ground, pulled up like a molar tooth so he might examine its roots before replacing it. And there were ways and means of achieving that end which would bring him into conflict with British bureaucracy, but not with the irritable arm of the law.

Someone walked through the church, using it as a short cut to the estate that sprawled nearby. The man never glanced at Kline and Kline waved silently to him as he himself walked to the porch, brushing the dirt from his hands and carefully buttoning his notebook and camera back in his pocket.

He wanted to see June Hunter again. The thought nagged him, surfaced to push down his interest in the stone font; the object of his visit would make an interesting account, and might fill in some gap in his accumulating knowledge of the behaviour and community life of that tribal kingdom of Britons – the Atrebates – who had lived in this area two thousand years ago.

But a woman, obsessed with the idea that the font was in some way evil and had trapped her son, that was interesting in a bizarre way, and Kline found himself excited by that bizarreness. He loved to link legend and folk-lore to the hard, grainy substance of his work. Wasn't this woman, in a sense, a contemporary source of legend?

He was used to tracing local legends to some sort of factual source, and he knew how many such stories, though manifestly medieval, usually related to a time much earlier. Each age updated a story, the children of different historical periods finding their greatest fascination in an age just gone. Thus to the Elizabethans it was the romantic age of Knightly Chivalry that overlaid their stories, but in the Eighteenth Century it was the flamboyance of the Tudor Age that made their imaginations race. And a folk tale, inherited for many generations, changed its clothes and its motivations, but still retained an almost invisible link with the darker past that had spawned it.

June Hunter represented an unusual, and very different, fantasy association. She believed something about the stone, almost certainly far more than she had said, for his laughter had sent her away, angry. How did she fit into a rational study of Celtic memorabilia?

Was she just crazy? Or was she aware of something non-legendary, some fact about the stone that had sparked her obsession, and which itself might be a valuable insight into the history of the font, in St Mary in the Fields?

He wanted to see June Hunter again.

There was a noise behind him and he glanced back towards the recess. A boy was sitting on the stone, grinning at him. Kline felt a guilty flush as it occurred to him that the boy may have been watching him digging around the font, and might not realize how embarrassing for the American such a revelation could well be.

Kline smiled. 'Hello. How long have you been there?'

The boy cocked his head to one side. He had curly brown hair, and wide, intelligent eyes. He ceased to grin, as he stared at Kline, and then said, 'I wish my sister hadn't come home.'

'Why?' said Kline. 'Does she fight with you?'

He figured the boy to be seven or eight years old, surely too young to be a nuisance to him.

'She'll be dead if she doesn't go away.'

Kline walked towards the boy, but hesitated as he sensed something like cold panic from the child. He frowned and studied the boy's face carefully.

'What's your name?'

The boy laughed loudly, and the laugh was more self-indulgent than humorous, as if he laughed at a private joke. 'Cru.'

'That's an unusual name.'

'Kline,' said the boy, suddenly solemn.

'How do you know my name?' Kline was uneasy. The boy grinned again, almost mocking him. His thin legs swung as he sat on the font, kicking the rock. He stared at the adult, fixing him with a penetrating, almost assessing gaze.

'Kline's fine, Kline's mine.' More laughter.

The American frowned. 'What are you into, kid? What's all this about? Who are you?'

'I'm glad you've come, Kline.'

And with that the boy jumped down from the font and ran around it, dropping out of sight. Kline frowned, staring into the grey shadow. 'Where are you?' he called. 'Come back a moment. Please. Where are you?'

He walked across the church and round the stone, and there was nothing there but shadow and mustiness. He looked around, and after a moment saw a small fracture in the wall, a heat fracture, where the bricks had split open and the wall sagged slightly. It was right in the corner, and a single piece of wooden beam had been used to ensure it moved no more. The space through the wall was just wide enough, Kline imagined, for an extremely agile child to slip through. It would have been a hell of a squeeze, but this was where the child must have gone, and must have been watching him from.

He was hungry, and in desperate need of a toilet. Hoping that any religious presences would not object, he went into a corner of the recess and relieved himself. Then he left the ruins and found a telephone box. He leafed quickly through the directory and found there were six Hunters listed.

He dialled the first. Asking to speak to June he was met with a query, and hung up instantly. He did not believe in redundant courtesy.

He tried again. A girl answered. 'May I speak to June?'

'June? Oh, you mean mummy. She's not in at the moment I'm afraid. Who's calling?'

'A rude American called Lee Kline. Tell her I rang, will you, and that I'm sorry.'

'What are you sorry for?' asked the girl, obviously intrigued, obviously slightly amused. He could 'hear' the smile, and the way her voice dropped conspiratorally low.

'Never you mind,' he said. 'Who are you?'

'I'm Karen. Does daddy know about you?'

'How old are you, Karen?'

'Old *enough*,' said the girl, irritation transparent in her voice. Kline found himself quite unable to decide whether this girl was early or late teens. He normally could.

'Well, no, daddy doesn't know about me, but only because I met your mother in town today and we had a chat about . . .' what had he heard June saying to the font? What name? He remembered. 'About Adrian.'

And to his astonishment the girl, Karen, put the phone down on him! He stared at the receiver for a moment. 'Freaky family.'

Then he went back to the directory and wrote out June Hunter's address.

He walked briskly back to where he had parked his car, and sat inside it, for a few minutes, listening to LBC, catching up on the news. Reception here was poor, and when he had recovered his breath, and was feeling more relaxed, he changed stations to find some rock music. Then he drove back into Higham, parking in the High Street near the church. He walked the hundred yards or so to a Wimpy bar and sat down at a table next to the window.

It was quite dark, now, and Kline watched the movement of traffic and the hasty departure of the working population from the town centre with an apparent fascination. He had eased his hunger with four cheeseburgers, and now lingered over a coffee, his eyes on the lamplit street, his mind on the attractive woman he had met in the old church, and on the font, and on what he could only call her bizarre obsession.

In one of those uncanny, yet commonplace moments of coincidence, he was just thinking of the tall man who had so unnerved June Hunter earlier, when that same man walked past the window of the cafe, hunched against the cold and pacing fast towards the new estates at the far end of the town. It occurred to Kline, for only the first time, that perhaps that priest had been the priest in the ruined St Mary's, before the fire. As such there were certain ways in which he might be able to help Kline fill in information on the origins of the stone font.

He drained his cup and quickly paid his bill. Pulling his hat down to his ears, and turning up the stiff collar of his jacket, he ran after the priest, who he could just see turning off the High Street some way ahead.

Kline raced after him and found himself out of breath and sweating as the road rose quite steeply to the start of the new estate. The priest was already vanishing into the shadows, and Kline could just see his angular frame passing through the light of a lamp. He ran faster and by the time he was walking, gasping for breath, among the red-brick, box-like houses that had so appalled him earlier, he could see the new church in the distance. It rose above the houses, clear and sharp yet in its own sort of darkness. On the bell tower was a huge white cross. The unlit windows were long, vertical gashes down the side of the main building. It looked alien and empty, uninviting.

Kline chased on, called out to the priest to stop, and was rewarded with the sight of the man pausing on the gravel outside the main entrance of the church, and turning to see who had shouted.

Kline came up to him, breathless, feeling slightly foolish. 'Can you spare a few moments to talk?' he gasped. The priest stared at him, slightly puzzled, then seemed to recognize him and his face hardened.

'I suppose I can,' he said in a clipped, very English tone.

'Excuse me – you walk very fast –' Kline leaned down and breathed deeply once or twice. When he straightened the priest was smiling slightly – the frostiness had gone. 'I'm Lee Kline. Father . . . ?'

'Alexander. Father John Alexander.'

'Nice to know you.'

And they completed the formalities of courtesy.

Alexander was a man in his fifties, Kline guessed, but being tall and extremely gaunt, with face and hands well cared for, he looked a lot younger. The eyes that watched Kline from behind the thick spectacles sparkled in stray light from the darkened estate. He was staring at Kline intently, and thoughtfully. 'What can I do for you?'

'Were you the priest in St Mary's when it burned?'

Instantly Alexander's pleasantry evaporated, and a shadow passed across his face. 'Yes. I was.' He was solemn, staring at Kline, frowning slightly. 'Is it about that you've come?'

Kline felt uneasy, sensing hostility about to break from the priest. He said, 'Not really. My interest is in the font. I was wondering why it hadn't been moved here.'

There was no change in Alexander's coolness. For a long time he was silent, looking away from Kline as several children ran noisily around the church and away among the houses. Their laughter was loud and hollow in the cold air.

At length the priest said, 'There were those who wanted to move the font to this new church, and there were those who did not. There were a few who wanted to destroy it. Those who wished the font to remain were very strong, very persuasive. I think that they would have gone to any lengths to prevent the stone being uprooted. I was not as fanatical about it, but I sided with them. Two reasons, really, the first quite simply that the font has always been there, in that church, and belongs there. Even now that the church is destroyed it should remain. Secondly, the stone from which the font is carved is a very unlucky stone for me, perhaps for those who took mass in the church before me, but mostly for the people of Higham.'

Kline said, 'I don't believe in lucky stones, or unlucky stones, or luck of any sort.'

Alexander shrugged, almost wearily. 'I use the expression figuratively. It was the stone that caused St Mary's to be gutted.'

Kline frowned. 'In what way?'

'A few years ago,' said Alexander, 'A child was baptized in the font. It's a very shallow font, as you've seen. It is very, very hard rock. There was an accident . . . the child was dropped, striking its head against the sharp edge of the stone. The child

56

never recovered. It was an accident. No-one was to blame. But the mother blamed me, and through me the church. She took her revenge on the church by putting St Mary's to the torch. That was her justice, her way of balancing the scale of fairness. An explosion and a fire, of such horrendous intensity that even the ancient stone walls cracked apart.' He shook his head, remembering, 'She is the most evil woman I have ever known, and she is still free, untouched by the law.'

Kline was confused, sceptical. 'I find it hard to believe that one person could have created such an intense fire . . .'

Alexander's voice was quiet, haunted, as he said, 'It burned like the fires of hell, Mister Kline. Never in my life have I seen such a fire, or heard such sounds of destruction. It was as if the flames fed upon the very stones themselves. It was frightening, truly frightening. We saved so little from it . . .'

Except the font, thought Kline, and the plaster around its base.

He said aloud, 'It would have taken an expert to have set that fire; no local woman would have the knowledge.'

Alexander's eyes were wide, almost fierce as he stared at Kline. 'She is friends with a family who have the knowledge. The Belsaints – I should not have referred to them, but somehow I no longer care.' He glanced away. 'One of them, the father, works with explosives all around the country. His eldest son makes working models of fire-arms. Between them they could have unwittingly supplied all the knowledge she would have needed, even the material, perhaps.' Again he looked back at Kline; the lights of the town were sparkling reflections in the lenses of his glasses. Kline looked beyond this to the tension in his face. 'As surely as I know God is within me, I know that woman put my church to flame as revenge for the accident. So you see, Mister Kline, the stone *is* unlucky. Had it been softer, perhaps more plaster than rock, the child would not have been so badly damaged.'

Kline was silent, watching the priest and noticing how old the man looked now, how suddenly the youthfulness had drained from his face; his features were white, drawn; it seemed that he looked at Kline from behind a wall of years, years of agony and bitterness, years that had eroded something within him, and had themselves been concealed and disguised by the healing passage of the seasons; now, bluntly confronted with the past, the true face of the man emerged from behind its mask.

A bitter man watched Kline, an angry man, a man who was

powerless because of his own beliefs to return that act of savagery to the one he believed had burned his church.

'I am a sinner,' said Alexander quietly. 'Every day that sin spreads. I hate the woman who burned that beautiful church, *my* church, I hate her with a vengeance. I am appalled at my hatred, and at my weakness, and thus I sin. I have never let the police know of my feelings. I don't think they would take them seriously. Many people know what I feel, and for whom. She herself knows. But knowing of her crime is not proof, when one knows purely instinctively.'

It was obvious to Kline who Alexander was talking about, and yet, without naming names Kline could not be absolutely sure he was grasping the point. He said, therefore, 'June Hunter. The child's name was . . Adrian?'

Alexander started with surprise, then relaxed and allowed a cold smile to touch his lips. 'She told you, then. I thought she would.'

Kline shrugged. 'She didn't tell me much. My real interest is in the old stone font. It's an enormously powerful focus, for people, for thoughts, for events. I felt it today, and I believe June Hunter feels it, and has felt it for years. Your feelings, your negative feelings towards the stone, probably indicate that you sense it too. The stone stands on a site of enormous power, an ancient site . . . of that I'm sure. This is why you find people reluctant to let it be moved. They sense the importance not just of the stone, but of the place on which it stands.'

'That is almost certainly true,' said Alexander, pushing his spectacles more comfortably onto the bridge of his nose. He stared thoughtfully at Kline, his tension gone for the moment. 'Is it possible that the church, perhaps the baptismal recess itself, stands along a ley-line?'

Kline shrugged. 'Ley-lines connect linear sources of power, if you believe the earth can mould power from the various energies that flow through it. But there are such things as isolated sources of power, not connected linearly with any others. I know of no ley that passes in this area, but then this part of the world has been torn down and rebuilt so many times I don't suppose there's much left at all.'

Abruptly Alexander turned away from Kline and walked up the steps to the church doors. He was fumbling with keys. 'It's cold out here, Mister Kline. Come inside for a moment.'

Kline followed the priest into the dark interior. Inside the wooden doors were glass doors, and once through these Kline felt warmer. The church was totally silent, still; it smelled strongly of candles and wood polish. In one far corner a few flickering yellow flames were enough to illuminate the red and white robes of a statue of Christ. Alexander's footsteps echoed in the gloom as he walked somewhere down towards the altar end of the church.

A moment later the back of the church was half lit by ceiling lamps. Alexander re-appeared and held out a picture to Kline.

'I understand the usefulness of having links with the past when one thinks of the past . . . that is what my parishioners do every Sunday, after all. You may borrow this.'

Kline smiled and accepted the picture, which was a pen and ink sketch made in 1827, of the inside of St Mary's, showing the font at the far end. It had been, on this evidence before him, a beautiful church, with a fabulous atmosphere. The artist had shown light, shafting in through the stained windows, and the baptismal font was high-lit in places.

Something about the picture disturbed Kline, but for the moment he was unable to say what it was. He puzzled for a second, and then gave up. 'Thank you. I shall take good care of it.'

'Please do. The pictures – there are two others showing the interior, but not the font – were in the church when I came, and they were among the few items that survived the fire.' He leaned against the back pew, staring at Kline as if trying to understand something about the stranger. 'It's very interesting what you say about people wanting something to stay on its original site: A hundred years ago a man tried to remove the font. I'm not at all sure why, though I expect you could find out. I was told by the retiring priest when I came here. The man, apparently, used dray horses and ropes. He managed to drag the font outside the church during the night, and some way into the country, but the next day was found dead – by his own hand – and the font was back in place. The law at that time were quite convinced it was murder made to look like suicide, but no-one was ever apprehended. So there you are, a mystery surrounding the font. The font takes revenge on the man who moves it. Say what you will, Mister Kline, that stone is an unlucky stone.'

Kline shook his head. 'No such thing, Father.'

Alexander shrugged. 'Have it your own way. The font was once called the suicide stone, or suicide well. That's something else you can probably trace in local records.'

'I know about that,' said Kline. 'I read an article on ghosts in the local paper; it was about the ghost of a man called Harker who committed suicide over the stone, and I picked up a few snippets of information about the suicide tendencies of Victorians inside the church.'

Alexander laughed emptily. 'I remember the article. There are lots of Harkers, by the way. They're one of our old families. The old families of Higham seem to have a predilection for suicide.'

Kline asked, 'So there is a basis of truth. People *did* commit suicide near the font, for no apparent reason?'

Alexander shrugged. 'Don't ask me about the basis of fact in any local story. We are a nation, and an age, of exaggerators. We can't palate anything that isn't outrageous or bizarre, and when mundanity comes along as news, we have to jazz it up to make it acceptable.' He hesitated for a second, staring at Kline. 'All I can say is that there have been a smattering of suicides that seem to conform to a ritual. The church was several times reconsecrated. I don't believe there have been nearly as many suicides as local legend would have you believe.'

'Who would know about those deaths, though?'

'I suppose the police might help. I really don't know, to be honest. The priest who was retiring so conveniently when I was up for a move from my previous parish told me a few tales of the stone, and from what he said I get the impression that the suicides came over the span of fifty years, followed by very little. There was a suicide in the church last year, did you know?'

Kline, his heart feeling like it might jump from his body, shook his head dumbly. 'Tell me.'

'Nothing to tell. A man who had been a little . . . you know,' tapped his head, 'for some years, slashed his wrists in the church.'

'Near the stone font?'

'There was blood *on* the font, but then there was blood over a large expanse of floor. He'd done a good job, with a piece of stained glass from one of the small side-windows. Only the main windows were rescued. They're both re-constructed in the museum. This piece, if I remember correctly, was St Peter's elbow.' He gave Kline a lopsided grin. 'I like details like that.'

'Was he a Harker?'

'No, I don't think so.'

'And that was the first suicide for, what, a hundred years?'

'I wouldn't think so,' said Alexander. 'I think there have been two or three, even in the last twenty years.' He suddenly laughed. 'The stone font was believed to be evil by one of the priests who practised here, a certain Father Albert MacAlistair. He had the font exorcised in the mid-eighteen hundreds. He was crazy of course. The exorcism apparently worked, the church was filled with maniacal laughter as he finished, and it is assumed that this was the evil presence fleeing back to the fires of hell. Unfortunately only Father MacAlistair actually witnessed these events.' Again Alexander smiled coldly. 'Such nonsense.'

Kline felt almost angry at the priest's cynicism. 'A man felt strongly enough about an ancient stone to exorcise it and you call it nonsense? Isn't that a rather narrow view?'

Alexander's gaze was openly contemptuous. 'You believe in Satan, do you?'

Kline could hardly believe his ears. Angry, but struggling to remain pleasant, he said, 'Not as such, no, of course not. In evil, yes, in an evil presence in the world . . . don't you?'

'Of course. As I said, I've already shown you how. I believe in evil as man. The most evil presence on this earth are all in the flesh ·and blood disguises of consciously destructive human beings. We are our own Satan; evil is inherent in the genetic make-up of man, and in some men it is stronger than in others, and in a few it is dominant and destructive, and truly frightening. It is, if you like, a part of the evolutionary process of our species. And the most evil person I know is here, in Higham, a woman who is so evil that when I see her in the street my whole blood freezes, and my stomach turns. The Hunter woman is Satan to me. And she has certainly condemned me to a death without my God, for I cannot help hating her.'

For the second time Kline sensed the ice in Alexander's heart, as if the mere mention of the fire, or the women, triggered some irresistible force of coldness within him. He stood up and walked away from Kline, down the side aisle to where the bank of light switches was located. 'I have evening Mass to prepare, Mister Kline. You must excuse me.'

Kline watched the man's gaunt frame disappear into the gloom. Moments later lights came on above the altar, and in the main hall of the silent church.

Kline called out, 'One other thing, Father. When was the stone made into the font? Have you any idea?'

'Hundreds of years ago,' came Alexander's reply. 'I'm sorry, I never thought to find out. But hundreds of years ago. Not as recently as Father MacAlistair.'

'Goodbye, Father,' called Kline, and walked to the double doors.

As Kline hastened away from the sombre shape of the church so the bell began to toll, adding to the atmosphere of desolation in this part of the town. He walked quickly through the dark estate, cold and uneasy. He was glad to get back into the brighter High Street.

Thoughts raced through his head. Should he go and see the Hunters tonight? Why, what would he gain? It was the woman's strange obsession that intrigued him, and its possible link with the history of the stone, but if truth were known she was probably neurotic, and of nothing but psychiatric interest to anyone.

Kline acknowledged the possibility, but was not convinced. Something about her – and not just her looks – attracted him, very strongly. He sensed something uncanny in her behaviour, and in her life, and that strangeness spoke to him, intuitively, as a stone, or an earthwork fort could speak to him, reaching beyond his conscious mind to the deeper levels of his awareness and provoking that Kline-sixth-sense that he found so useful.

There was more to June Hunter than just the second Crazy Lady in his life. And he wanted to know more about what it was.

And who had that kid been . . . what was his name? Cru? He'd known Kline's name, but that was understandable if the child had been eavesdropping on his chat with June Hunter. But again, there was something not right about the child. I'm glad you've come, he'd said, and he'd said it so certainly, so decisively. I'm glad you've come, as if Kline was going to help him in some way, or change something . . . as if he'd been waiting for him for some time, and now . . . he was glad the man had come.

He walked quickly towards his car, having finally decided that home, a couple of drinks, and bed were called for. As he passed the ruins of St Mary's he hesitated a second, and briefly recalled how furtively June Hunter had slipped into the building as he had watched. There was so much that he would have to clear up in his own mind, just for the simple sake of curiosity.

He started to walk on.

'Kline! Is that you?'

'Yes!' he called, stopping abruptly and swinging round to see who had called him. There was a man standing on the gravel pathway that led to the ruins; he was short, hunched up inside a trench coat; Kline couldn't see his face. He walked back along the road, staring at the man. 'Who are you?'

The man abruptly turned and walked out of sight, beneath the porchway and into the total darkness of the church. Kline, puzzled, lingered a while across the road, watching for the man again, but whoever he was he didn't reappear.

'How in hell do these people know my name?' said Kline, quietly, crossing the road at last and following the dark shape into the church. 'Where are you?' he called. 'What do you want? For Christ sake stop screwing about. I'm hungry. Where are you?'

There was no reply. Kline felt ice fingers run down his back as he stood in the darkness within the ruined walls. He was afraid. He looked to where the stone font was a vague shape in its recess, standing out from the darkness because of the lighter grey of its colouring. He walked carefully to that stone, now, feeling the blood throbbing in his temples, scared of the darkness, and the heavy silence, appalled at this fear, and perturbed by that same stifling sense of heat that he had experienced a few hours before.

Touching the stone he ran his fingers around its cold edges, and down into the shallow bowl. He whipped his hand away, crying out in surprised disgust at the touch of some warm, rather slimy liquid there.

'Oh God!' he said loudly, and ran from the ruins. He held his hand away from his body as he ran, appalled at the contact of that liquid, knowing what it was. In his car, with the dim light above the driver's seat on, he stared at the blood that caked his fingers and only after five minutes of silently staring at the awful sight did he wipe the stuff away, and use spit and his shirt tail to cleanse the stickiness from his skin.

'I don't believe it,' he said, repeating the words loudly and angrily, almost afraid to look at St Mary's.

He couldn't be sure, but as he reached for the ignition key, drowning all sound including the sound of his heart with the sudden roar of the engine, he thought he heard a child's laughter, very distant, very loud.

CHAPTER FIVE

Silently, drifting like some cloud shadow through the night, the figure passed from the woods at the end of the garden. It hesitated, and for a moment seemed to be watching the house. Then it moved swiftly across the lawns, and across the turned soil, and where its feet touched flower and vegetable alike, there was no movement of the plants; the soil was not disturbed.

Again it stopped in the darkness, then ran quickly into the invisibility of the small garden shed. Moments later it moved again, across the back of the house, towards the large windows that watched the woods from the kitchen.

From her bedroom window, from darkness, Karen Hunter watched the shape. There was cold sweat on her face, and her whole body was shaking violently. She lost sight of the figure, then saw it again, straining to keep it in view, knowing why it had come. Featureless in the overcast night, it seemed like a man, stooped slightly, massively built, almost huddled against the bitter cold of the early winter.

The shape ran to the back door and seemed to pass through it without moving the door at all, without sound. Karen gasped, suddenly petrified, even though she had known this would happen; for an instant, in that awful moment of fear, she lost control of her body and clapped a hand to her lap, pressing, trying not to lose herself to fright so completely.

She turned away from the bedroom window, and leaned one hand on the bedroom chair, her other hand still holding herself, her eyes wide. In the darkness only her white nightgown showed where she stood, petrified. Her breathing grew louder, the rhythmic thump of her heart so noisy, now, that she felt sure she could be heard all round the house. She listened, sensing the figure as it darted, animal like, up the stairs. She knew it had hesitated at the top of the stairs, on the landing, searching along the hallway, examining each door, seeking her.

It moved along the passage and pushed the door of her bedroom open. It stood there for a long while, watching her, and then it beckoned. Instantly Karen relaxed. 'Yes,' she whispered into the darkness, 'Oh yes . . . yes . . .'

And without hesitation, still damp and uncomfortable, she moved across the room towards it.

When she reached the door the figure crouched at the top of the stairs. She felt its eyes on her, smelled something leathery and sour, heard the rustling of leathery wings. Again it beckoned, and again she ran towards it.

When she turned to walk down the stairs it was waiting at the bottom, and she ran lightly down to the hallway, and followed it through the kitchen. When she opened the kitchen door, staring out into the freezing night, she saw it near the woods, darkness against darkness, but perfectly distinct. As she started to run towards it, smiling now, so the kitchen door slammed shut, loudly, shockingly . . .

The sound pierced the deadness of June Hunter's sleep. It was like a shot in the heavy silence of her dream, echoing and ricocheting, a warning cry disturbing her passive acceptance of slumber. She woke in an instant, sat up in bed and stared at the heavy curtained windows.

'What the hell was that?'

'What the hell was what?' mumbled Edward, beside her in the wide double bed. He shifted angrily, sleepily, dragging his pillow round to bury his head deeper in it.

'The kitchen door. Someone came in . . . or went out . . . oh God, Karen! Edward! *Wake up.*'

She jumped from the bed and ignored her robe, spread out on a chair. In just her thick, crumpled pyjamas she raced downstairs, and as she ran down the passageway she heard Edward running across the upper landing, himself suddenly jerked from sleep by the awareness of what was happening.

'Adrian!' she heard him cry, and she hesitated, just a moment. Edward was already in the boy's room. 'He's gone. Christ! Oh Christ!'

June tore through the kitchen, switching lights on, then realizing without consciously thinking that she'd be able to see nothing if she did that. In darkness again she pulled open the back door and stepped into the still, freezing night.

Above her head a bird, or some night creature, sped noisily towards the wood. She refused to say the word 'bat' to herself, hating bats with a vengeance, even though she knew they were tiny and harmless.

She saw Karen, running towards the wood, her gown flowing in the night as she darted this way, then that across the garden, getting closer all the time to the trees. As her eyes recovered from that brief moment of blazing light, June saw the girl was running with her arms outstretched; when she glanced round, searching for something, she seemed to be simultaneously smiling and crying . . .

Then she laughed, a gay sound, full of contentment and happiness. She stopped, turned towards the trees again and then began to run with greater purpose.

'Karen!' screamed June, and the girl stopped. Her mother raced towards her, and flung her arms around the girl's trembling body. June laughed, with relief, and then felt tears spring to her eyes. The girl was shaking badly, and slowly waking. A light came on in the big house next door, and two silhouettes appeared at the window.

'Go away,' said June softly, staring at the intruders with resentment. She was hugging Karen.

Edward ran past her, looking around the garden. He was like a wild man, panicstricken and ungroomed, hair on end, pyjamas twisted about his waist and crumpled. Since he wore no jacket in bed, his torso was naked, but he had grabbed a towel on his way through the kitchen and this lay about his shoulders. He held it across his breast as an old woman holds her shawl.

'Adrian! Come on Adrian, come back to bed. *Adrian*!'

Karen woke completely, realized where she was, and began to cry, loudly, frightened . . .

'Quiet,' soothed June, stroking the girl's sweat-saturated hair. 'It's all over. You're all right. Come on in, come inside.'

'I'm . . . cold . . . cold . . .'

'You'll soon be warm.'

'Adrian!' cried Edward again, running towards the wood and darting among the thin trees there, his grey form appearing and disappearing in the darkness.

As June reached the kitchen she heard something coming through the air and instinctively ducked, dragging Karen down with her. A split second later there was a terrific crash of glass, and the wide, plate-glass window above the sink shattered into thousands of fragments.

'My God!' June, horrified, stepped gingerly into the kitchen, reached for a tea-towel and stepped on it until she could reach the light. The kitchen was smothered with glass, and on the table, where a few days before a happy group of children had enjoyed a party, lay a red brick from the pile that Edward had placed up in the woods, out of sight, after work had finished on the outhouse.

Karen, still visibly shaken and very pale, stepped across the debris and went into the lounge, where she sat down in a deep armchair and stared at the cold, grey bars of the electric fire.

June fetched a pair of slippers from beneath the stairs and slipped them on, then took out a pair of Edward's gardening shoes and ran with them back into the night.

Edward was walking down the garden, Adrian cradled in his arms, the boy's bandaged hand trailing limply. June walked to meet them. Edward stopped in the spill of light from the kitchen and June brushed the boy's hair back from his face, marvelling at how saturated he was. Adrian watched her quite impassively, and she reached for his good hand and massaged some heat into it.

'There's glass all over the floor,' she said, dropping the shoes to the ground. Edward passed the boy to her and she staggered under his weight, but held him, not liking his sweaty closeness and the limp feel of his body. She knew he could walk if he wanted, and for a brief moment she thought of just simply dropping him to the ground, *making* him walk, but to her surprise he curled up against her bosom, moving his head so that his cheek made contact with, and gently massaged, her left breast. Edward had his shoes on and took the boy back, and they returned to the house. June found herself touching her breast almost tenderly. It had been a nice sensation.

'Who threw the brick?' Edward asked quietly, staring at the destruction.

'Didn't you?'

'Don't be so bloody stupid,' snapped Edward, angrily. 'Why the hell would I do a thing like that?'

June laughed sourly. 'I assumed you had. I assumed you were trying to prove something.'

Edward stared at her, uncomprehending. After a moment he repeated, angrily, 'Don't be so bloody stupid, June.'

June shrugged. She was confused now. She had never questioned for an instant that it had been her husband who had done this destructive thing on the spur of the moment — but now she wondered what part of her had so easily accepted that most unlikely explanation. She kicked at the glass and frowned, and looked up almost bewildered as Edward said 'Well? *What* was I trying to prove?'

She shook her head. 'I don't know,' she said quietly. 'If you didn't throw it, then who did? Adrian?'

Edward laughed, bitterly. 'A hundred and sixty feet from wood to kitchen? With enough force to shatter thick glass like that? Adrian? It would take a machine to do that.'

As if he had explained everything he went into the lounge. June heard him talk with Karen for a moment, and heard Karen's reassuring words. Then Edward's heavy step on the stairs, and his murmured conversation with the boy as he tucked him back in bed.

June stared at the glass, then picked up the brick and held it close to her face. 'Bastard,' she said, and her eyes lifted to the ceiling; her mind went beyond the wood and plaster to the room where Edward now sat, comforting his son. 'Bastard.'

But in her head images of Edward and Adrian were confused. The destructive act had been so senseless it almost defied a reasonable explanation – but she was disturbed to find herself suspecting Edward despite what her common sense told her. Was she beginning to believe, on a subconscious level, that Edward was crazy?

She flung the brick through the gaping hole in the window and turned off the kitchen light, walking stiffly to the lounge. Karen had turned on the fire, and now huddled on the floor in front of it, with the light out, her face lit just by the harsh glow of the filaments.

'How are you feeling? Are you still cold?'

Karen shook her head, huddled a little tighter inside her own arms. June watched her calmly, sensing the distance between them, wondering how much was natural adolescence and how much something deeper within the girl. Karen was just sixteen years old, although in some ways she seemed more mature; when she spoke of things she enjoyed she spoke with all the authority and knowing of someone ten years older; when in the company of girls her own age she could often sound the teenager she was, as silly, as flighty, as sulky as her peers.

'Are you wet?'

'Soaked,' said the girl. Her voice was quiet, filled with anger, and with embarrassment. For the first time June realized that the girl had wet herself in the childish sense, although she herself had been referring to the dampness of her hair. 'I hate it when it happens,' said Karen. 'I hate myself.'

'You shouldn't.'

'Why shouldn't I? It's so . . . so disgusting.'

'It's very normal. You *were* asleep. Lots of people have accidents when they're having nightmares.'

'Well, it's horrible, and filthy, and it makes me feel . . . *angry*!'

June winced as her daughter shouted the word at her, her eyes bright red with fire-light, with blood, and with the force of her

68

self-resentment. It made her so ugly when she was angry, distorting her normally very pretty face into a lined and twisted mask of adolescent fury. Her eyes, green and warm, were flaming ice; her mouth, wide, full-lipped and almost always smiling, was parted, tensed and mean, letting her teeth show through, the animal reaction of a wild beast at bay.'

Who are you at bay from, Karen? wondered her mother. Who is fencing you in, driving you into the cliff, your back to the wall? Who is making you scratch and fight for survival? Is it me?

She stared at the sulking girl, at the high points of flickering red light in her auburn hair.

Or is it yourself?

'What are you thinking, mother?'

The coldness of the question, the flatness of its delivery, sent a ripple of anxiety through the woman as she hugged her knees and stared at Karen. Karen was watching her, staring at her for all the world as if her mother was in some way responsible for the repetition of this horrible nightmare. June, for a second, said nothing, and Karen said, 'I know that way of staring. I know that steady gaze, full of self-pity and self-doubt. You're analyzing me, aren't you? You're wondering about your loving daughter, and why is she so broody, so hostile. Aren't you, *mother*?'

'Am I *daughter*?'

'Yes, you are. I know that look. You never talk about your feelings, you just sit and stare and think about things.'

She's right, I do!

'I *was* thinking about you, and wondering about you. Is that so wrong?'

Karen shrugged, staring back at the fire. The warm glow of the electric heat was at last driving the chill away from the two women, and June felt her mind relax as her body unwound, no longer tensed and protective against the internal cold.

She heard Edward busying himself with sweeping up the mess of glass on the kitchen floor. He grumbled as he worked, but he didn't stop working until he had tacked a sheet of thick polythene across the empty window. When he had finished he went straight back upstairs and climbed into bed.

Karen didn't appear to notice, or if she did, was less concerned about her father's behaviour than about her mother's. Edward had to be up very early, to go to London for a one-day conference on some Medical Aid programme to the Sudan.

Karen said, softer, more co-operatively, 'Why does Adrian always end up in the garden when I have my nightmare?'

To have the awful question voiced so simply made the blood drain from June's face. Her tongue felt thick, almost like cotton wool, as she said, 'I don't know. None of us know.'

Why did they always *forget* these things? Why did they always put them from their minds, as if by ignoring them they would go away, like the thing under the bed, the bogey man in the corner, the rippling shadow of a child's frightmare, sensed in the ceiling, disturbed by screaming, forgotten by hiding beneath the blankets!

'Why do I have so many nightmares, and always at home. Never anywhere else. Always at home.'

'Oh come on, you only have two . . '

'The same two, over and over again!' said Karen sharply, the edge of hysteria in her voice again. She relaxed, though. 'I was so frightened, for a while. Awfully frightened. Then . . .' she broke off, leaning forward so that her chin rested on her knees; her hair fell across her face and absently June reached out to brush it back behind her ears; her fingers touched the sensitive skin around Karen's temples, and June loved that touch, so warm, so responsive as the girl's eyes half-closed and she moved her head to increase the pressure of the contact.

Instantly June felt the warmth of mother love flood through her and she shifted closer to the girl, her arm gliding around her daughter's shoulder, their bodies coming close, touching; Karen relaxed against her, her hand reaching to the warmth between June's legs, gripping the flesh with an almost compulsive strength.

'I was so happy when it called me. So frightened at first, and then so happy.'

'Was it exactly the same beastie?'

'Yes. Horrible . . . man shaped, but dark, and huge, and without a face. But when it beckoned I just had to go, I felt it was right to go. So I just followed.'

'You didn't dream of being in the river?'

Karen shook her head. 'Not this time. I don't think so, anyway.'

June hugged her daugher tight. 'You have very realistic nightmares, little horror movies in your head . . . but that's all they are, Karen, just bad dreams. Something must be disturbing you, and when we find out what it is, the dreams will stop.'

'But it didn't feel like a dream. I can remember getting out of bed, and going to the window to watch it coming into the house. I could hear it on the stairs. I mean, it was just as if it was happening *now*. It didn't feel any different to this, to sitting here. It was so *real*. But when you came out into the garden I felt like I was waking up, suddenly, but you know what it's like when

70

you wake up. And it all went away, just like a dream does, except that I can still remember it clearly now, just like I remember shopping yesterday, and breakfast, and television. It was so real, and I just felt so happy following it.'

'It was just a dream, darling, a vivid, and real seeming nightmare because you are going through a difficult part of your life, and you have a sad little brother that makes you disturbed.'

Karen cried quietly for a minute, exorcising the last shadows of the nightmare with watery comfort. June, enjoying this closeness which was so rare, hugged her daughter quiet, leaning her face on the girl's still wet hair.

'Adrian frightens me.'

'That's just silliness.' Squeezing the girl in motherly reprimand. 'Adrian hasn't the . . . Adrian can't frighten anybody. He's just a gentle, empty little child, without malice, without love, without hate, without anything.'

'Daddy said he spoke.'

June clenched her eyes tight closed, quietening the sudden surge of intense anger she felt. In that instant she wanted to scream, to shout through the ceiling how much she despised Edward for his callousness. Why had he told her? Why did he go against everything they had agreed?

'Just words,' she said. 'Empty sounds. Adrian has something left, but nothing that should frighten you.'

'But Adrian *does* frighten me,' the girl repeated, obstinately. 'I can't help it, he does. And I know what he said, so you needn't try and hide it.'

Good old Edward, thought June bitterly. His fanaticism that Adrian would recover his wits was so great that those shocking words – words as shocking in what they implied as well as the fact of their utterance – would be the greatest news that Edward had ever had, and he would be totally unable to keep them from his daughter . . . it would never occur to Edward that telling Karen that her brother had implied he felt hostility towards her would possibly, ever so slightly, upset her.

What a fool. What a bastard. What a callous, thoughtless, self centred . . . man of science! The boy had broken his finger, nearly bitten it right off, but that was secondary to the words. The words were all that mattered.

'Words never hurt anyone,' she said emptily, hoping the platitude would cool the upset in her daughter's head.

Karen pulled away from her and sat up, smoothing back her hair. She seemed to be willing herself not to look at her mother.

71

'He watches me, sometimes. I can feel his eyes on me. Have you heard him laughing at night?'

'What, tonight?'

'No. Not since I've been home this time, but over summer, I kept waking up to hear him laughing, all on his own. And he watches me. I'm sure he comes into my room at night and watches me. I'm sure that's what gives me the nightmares.'

'I've never heard him laughing at night, Karen. I think you have particularly vivid dreams, and I think it's because you watch too much box.'

'Oh *mother*, that's such a stupid thing to say.'

Yes, damn you. It is.

'Karen, love, go to bed. Get some sleep. In the morning you'll feel better.'

'Cold light of dawn,' said Karen grimly. 'The new day will make all shadows pass away. OK. I'll go up.'

She leaned over and kissed her mother on the cheek.

June turned off the fire, then followed her daughter upstairs. She crept into bed quietly, and lay on her back, staring at the ceiling.

'I'll never get up in the damn morning,' murmured Edward, irritable, sleepy.

'I guess that means the end of the Sudan,' said June.

She hardly slept.

She lay awake, still and restful, but a million miles from slumber; she watched the brightening of the new day as it filtered through the bedroom curtains. Edward's breathing was gentle and drawn out, the breathing of an untroubled man. This, more than anything, irritated her almost to the point of reaching out and slapping his stubbly face.

As usual she controlled herself, even allowed herself the luxury of a bitter little smile. 'Sleep well, my beauty. Africa needs you more than we.'

It was always like this. No matter how troubled the family, or the wife, or the husband, or the world within or without this town west of London, it was June who lay awake and fretting and Edward who gently slept through the night, bridging the gap between one day's concern and the next with a brief period of total oblivion. No doubt that was how it should have been. His mind and body would be fresh the following day, and far abler to cope with stress. She would be a wreck, dark-lined beneath the eyes, numb in the finger tips, unsteady on her feet, perpetually reaching, like some human automaton, towards the coffee pot, fuelling the acid of her insides with the potent drug of the drink, trying to instil some coherence into her movements and thoughts. She hated Edward for so many things, and loved him for so many others. But she abhorred his ability to sleep!

'Do you think I should take up smoking, Edward?' she asked the prone form beside her. 'It might help me to become a zombie, like you. Perhaps I should drink. Would you mind if I drank a little? Just a little . . . two, maybe three bottles a day. Vodka, of course. All depressed women of the house drink Vodka. Whisky is so . . . so . . . passé, don't you find? And gin. Well. Anybody who drinks gin deserves a husband like you. Makes you depressed, did you know that Edward? Of course you did. You know everything. You're a man of science, a man of the *human* sciences. Gin makes you depressed no matter who you are, white or black, cockney or hunter of the Sudan. No. Vodka's the only drink for the Hunters of Higham. Did you get that? The Hunters of Higham . . . very funny joke . . .' she lay back on the pillow. 'You make me so angry Edward, so bloody angry. You really don't care, do you, that I'm failing to get back into my work. I'm a very good computer technician, did you know that Edward? Of course you do. You once listened to something I said, I remember it well. Whatever happened to those fervent plans to get me back into my career? What happened? Did I dream them? I distinctly recall that I was going to take no more than a year off after Adrian was born, but unfortunately I've let things slip a little. I agree with you, I'm apathetic. But if you'd do something more than just grunt and fart when I try and talk about my desires, my frustrated intellect, well, who knows . . . maybe I'd make it big in the Computer Dating industry.' She turned to look at him, sleeping peacefully. 'But that's about all you're good for, isn't it, the odd grunt, the occasional fart. And curing the Sudan. Yes, I'll grant you that, you're very good at curing the Sudan.' She leaned over towards him. 'I'd like to punch you right on the nose, you're so frustrating. God, Edward! Wake up you bastard. Talk about your daughter!'

He slept on, not even stirring as her raised voice thundered in his ear. He had woken earlier, when Karen had gone outside. But now, though the sound was louder, he remained motionless, and deeply asleep.

June smiled to herself, feeling a moment of despair overwhelm her, but chasing it away as she focussed on the strip of dawn-light peeping between the curtains.

This is how she had felt those days ago when Adrian had spoken. The shock of hearing coherent words in his mouth, and the sight of his blood, had knocked her out, although the bruise on her head was from a more physical blow. She had come round and there had been panic about the boy's finger, but though it had seemed appalling at the time, the damage was almost entirely restricted to the break, and it was a clean break and would heal quickly. Thereafter things seemed unchanged. Adrian went on being Adrian; Edward was thoughtful and easy with her, and she sensed this was partly a patronizing gesture in the wake of – he imagined – being proved right; Karen was down from school, facing the prospect of a wasted half a term as she decided whether to go on with her education in a new school or not, and inevitably, for the moment it was easier to ignore that issue than to worry about it.

But those words, those awful words . . . In her memory they became almost dreamlike, and as she thought back on them they had become incoherent and meaningless, and within a day she had rationalized them: they had been just parrot-talk, mimicry, words used by Edward, she imagined, that the boy had re-routed through his fragmentary brain.

Edward had not disagreed – nor had he agreed – but that night she had been unable to sleep, still disturbed, still upset by the turn of events. Edward, who should have been exultant, had fallen into peaceful sleep.

How little she knew of the workings of this man who had been her husband for seventeen years. How unsurprising *that* was. At eighteen she had fallen in love with the image of the brash young medical man, and the twelve years' difference in their ages had not seemed even worth consideration. He had been self-assured and popular, easy to laugh with, easy to be with; he had been romantic, and yet with a streak of anger that had frightened her a little; he had been strong in bed, gentle with her, but insistent. The speed with which she had gained experience had bonded her even tighter to the man who had become the centre of her world, unavoidable, inescapable.

Smiling to herself she understood something, now, that she had tried to understand earlier in the day. The American, Kline. What was his first name? She couldn't remember, but she remembered Kline because she always associated names with the sound they made, and she had made the association 'Klein bottle'.

She had been attracted to Kline-bottle. She had not understood it, nor liked it, and she had no intention of brooding about it. But

74

she understood – or thought she did – that in Kline-bottle she had seen the ghost – albeit with a foreign accent – of Edward at that age, the same self-assuredness, the same easy grin, the same unnerving knack for making her heart stammer just that little bit too fast for her not to notice . . . the same way of talking with his eyes.

The man had laughed at her, damn him. But thinking back she realized how hasty she had been. He hadn't been laughing scornfully at all! He had been taken by surprise. He'd called her back when she had run, swearing bitterly beneath her breath.

If he'd called her back, he was still interested. If he was still interested, then perhaps . . .

Perhaps what? Perhaps he could help her?

That would be nice. But help her how, and where? Break the stone open? Any muscular navvy could do that for her. What *did* she want? How could she be helped to get Adrian out of the stone?

'God, I don't know. I just don't know.'

In bitter frustration she lay back again, staring at the ceiling. But something was coming clear to her, clearer as each passing minute of the dawn brought the thin shaft of light deeper into the bedroom.

Until she had met Kline she had not really thought about releasing Adrian, she had been too wrapped up in her self pity and bitter depression at his entombment. But suddenly a man had come along who seemed to promise that almost unthinkable dream.

If anybody could get Adrian out, Kline could. She knew, she just *knew*.

'I haven't slept a wink,' she said as Edward climbed stiffly from the bed and moved quickly to the small bathroom attached to their bedroom.

'You should take up yoga,' he said, and June mentally strangled him. She listened to water running, and idly reached over to switch off the alarm moments before it was due to go off at seven. Then she climbed from bed and pulled on her robe. She opened the curtains, then went to attend to Adrian. She let Karen sleep on, but spent a long moment staring at the peacefully sleeping girl, and thinking about how frightened she had been.

Edward was out of the house by eight (promising to contact someone about the window) and she heard the high-revving, gravel-skidding departure of his Rover, and as the car was gone, so an immense veil of peace drifted down over her. She drank coffee, and cooked toasted cheese. At nine o'clock the domestic help arrived. This was a pretty woman in her late twenties called Stephanie; she was quiet, belying the blonde exuberance of her appearance. She vanished upstairs immediately, taking coffee with her, and set about the bedrooms.

When June went out she would take care of Adrian, and it was a relief to everyone concerned that Adrian, whilst not ecstatically demonstrative towards the woman, was quite content with her.

At ten she started to prepare for a shopping trip into town. Adrian would be going to the hospital later in the afternoon to have his finger checked. Karen needed shoes. The cupboards, well stocked, looked boring to June, so she wanted something more exciting to eat this evening. And she herself needed an Italian dictionary that was a little better than the pocket dictionary Edward had brought her from London when she had begun her Open University degree in the language.

As she gathered her thoughts, and made a quick list, the doorbell rang, loud and startling. As she stared towards the door of the lounge, where she sat, so she recalled – instants before – hearing a car gliding gently up the driveway.

She heard Stephanie running to open the front door, but she couldn't make out the sound of voices. Then the lounge door opened and the home-help peered round. 'Someone to see you, June.'

June rose, knowing instinctively who it was.

Kline, looking even more dishevelled and tired than the day before, stepped round the door and grinned at her.

CHAPTER SIX

Did she know yet?

Kline accepted June Hunter's proferred hand and gave it a friendly shake. 'Hi.'

Her smile told him what he wanted to know, that his vague doubts had been unfounded. She was glad to see him, almost relieved.

But did she know?

He had half suspected, the night before, what his drive through Higham this morning had confirmed. Waking, at a very early hour in his flat, he had wondered if the events of the night before had been dreamed – the bizarre talk with the very unorthodox priest, the blood on his hand, and the blood, warm and fresh, that had filled the bowl of the font.

He had laughed as he had walked around the heath for his dawn exercise. Blood in fonts, and hysterical men running from churches with the stickiness on their hands, was not the stuff of reality, it was the fare of Hollywood – or to put it into correct perspective, Pinewood . . . Hammer films might play with blood, and winternight hauntings. But come on, this sort of thing . . . what? This sort of thing what? Just didn't happen? Bullshit. There was his shirt, smeared with red . . . it was on his car seat, on the door of his car. It was on his jeans, and it was burned into his mind. It had happened.

And when he had driven through Higham this morning, he had seen the church cordoned off, and two blue lights flashing – police cars. There was an ambulance too, driven up onto the grass forecourt of the building. And the inevitable small crowd of the curious and the morbid.

He had not been allowed to stop in front of St Mary's, but a hundred yards further on he pulled into the curb and called to a leisurely looking man who was just breaking from the group of onlookers.

'What's happening?'

'Suicide,' said the man, grinning. 'Some bloke cut his own throat. Nice, eh?'

'Have you been inside?'

The man shook his head. 'But you can't hide things like that round here. Everybody knows what happened, and who it was.' He walked away. Kline lingered a moment, watching the activity – *oh God, what's going on?* – then turned and walked briskly back to his car.

He'd been very disturbed by the death, and instead of driving straight to the Hunter's house, using the instructions given to him by someone at the other end of town, he pulled right off the road into a small car park and sat staring through the windshield for an hour.

An indefinable thought was beginning to nag at him, and though sometimes he tried to pin it down, he found himself unable to identify the deeper cause of his uneasiness. The thought eluded him. And though he was shaken by the suicide, and uneasy because he had been in the church soon after the death had occurred, this was not the source of that elusive concern.

But what about the death? This was getting too close for

77

comfort to the realms of the ludicrous. A man calls to him in the dead of night, calls his name as if making sure of his identity. The man vanishes. Three minutes later – no more than that! – he's dead, his blood a great sticky pool in the baptismal font.

Three minutes, acted out in haste . . . that was one hell of a determined, and decisive, suicide. In Kline's limited experience, gleaned from reading and talking to people in social fields who had experienced such things, he knew that suicide was never so precise, so definite. This was the most unsuicide-like suicide he could imagine.

Try an alternative. The man called to him, and led him to the church, where a second man was already dead. But that blood had been *warm* and not gelloid. Did blood, spilled in such quantities, actually clot? Kline had a feeling that it didn't; but it had still been warm, and on a freezing night like that, it couldn't have been there more than seconds before cooling to the temperature of the stone.

Third possibility: the man who had attracted his attention had then raced into the church and killed the second man. Murder. And in the darkness he might not have seen the killer standing there; he had not seen the body, either.

It was – at the moment – the only thing that made sense. And it made him feel very bad, very guilty, for there was one thing he was in no doubt about: with blood traceable on the car, and in the fabric of his clothes, there was no way – without an alibi – that he was going to go to the police.

And still that nagging thought that he couldn't put his finger on . . .

He drove on up to the Hunter's place, and by the time he got there he was feeling less tense, and more in control of himself.

But did June know what had happened, and if she didn't, should he tell her?

'I'm sorry if I upset you yesterday. I wasn't mocking . . .'

June inclined her head. 'Mister Kline, *I* apologize for running off so dramatically. I was very tense, and very at the edge. I'm often like that, and I just blew a fuse.'

'Call me Lee.'

'Lee. Okay. Would you like some coffee, Lee? Or breakfast? You look a mess.'

'Like a garage mechanic?'

She laughed. 'I wouldn't have been so rude as to say it.'

'You were yesterday.'

'So I was. Well? Breakfast?'

Kline shook his head. 'Thanks, but no thanks. I'm feeling a little off-colour. Have you been to the town yet?'

'For my daily visit?' She emphasized the words slightly and Kline thought she might have been being cynical. 'No, not yet. I was about to go when you arrived.'

He smiled. 'Perhaps we'll both go down later. Going to the church as usual?'

'Why not?' Sensing something in his pleasantly light conversation she frowned. 'Why not?' she repeated, more meaningfully.

Perhaps his silence spoke more than silence usually does. She walked back to him, searching his eyes. 'Why *not*? Has something happened?'

'Somebody's been killed there. It's all cordoned off.'

'Christ, no! When? Yesterday?'

Guiltily, Kline shrugged. 'Sometime. Probably at night.'

June turned away, and slowly walked to the sofa, sitting down on its arm and staring out the window to the garden. 'Suicide, do they think?'

'Right. Apparently the place is famous for them.'

'It certainly is.' She shivered. 'I need some fresh air. Coming into the garden?'

Kline agreed, and they walked out into the long, wild and rather attractive back garden. Kline affected interest in June's brief account of its lay-out. Why, he wondered, do people always assume other people are interested in details of their vegetable plans for the following year?

They walked away from the house, and across the rough grass, now spikey and yellowing and beginning to show signs of its winter passage.

'You have your own wood; Christ!'

Kline was amazed that there was no fencing separating the house from the dense stand of trees. Some way off a second garden backed onto the same wood, but high fencing marked the border very carefully.

'We don't own it, but Edward is friends with the man who does and he lets us keep our garden open to it. Karen loved it as a girl . . .'

'Karen? Your daughter?'

'Yes. She's in bed at the moment . . . we had a nasty time last night, a nightmare. She's very adolescent and a little bit what you would probably call "uptight".'

'Know it well,' said Kline with a smile. 'How about Adrian? Does he play here?'

June glanced at him thoughtfully. 'You don't know all that much about Adrian, do you? I can't remember what I told you yesterday.'

They walked between trees, into the musty shade of them, their feet sinking into the rotting undergrowth; Kline brushed cobwebs away as they clung to his hair, and searched anxiously for spiders, but to his relief saw none. They would hardly have been giants, anyway.

'I know about the accident, when the priest let him slip and strike the font. I know you believe his mind became trapped in the stone. And I know the boy is still alive and semi-aware.'

'I'm not sure he's even that,' said June bitterly. 'My husband thinks I'm mad. He gets very angry when I spend hours with the font. But I think it would have passed if it had just been madness, don't you? I know he's there, trapped there, and I'm sure if it had just been an empty obsession it would have faded away years ago.' She snapped off a dead twig and tossed it into the gloom. Kline crunched his way through the wood, searching the bracken and leafy undergrowth for anything nasty such as snakes, or rats, but this late in the year no doubt they were all safely ensconced in their hibernacula below ground.

'Are you convinced the two parts of him can be brought together again?' asked Kline.

June laughed, empty, bitter laughter. 'I've clung to a belief that they could for years. And yet I've done nothing; all I've done is talked to Adrian. And grown apart from Edward, as I've grown to hate the shell of my son that lives and breathes and eats in that house. He's so . . . dead. Limp. He *can* walk, we even know, now, that he can mimic words, but he chooses to do nothing. That vital force is missing.'

'How do you imagine body and mind can be united?'

'Lee, I haven't a clue. You tell me.'

'Me?' Kline shook his head, aware, in any case, that she was not being fully serious. 'I have enough difficulty keeping my own body and soul together.'

She gave him a wry look. 'You're lying, Lee.'

'How so?'

'You wouldn't be back here unless you were intrigued. You wouldn't have given it a second thought unless you wanted to know more, and were half believing already that a human spirit *could* be trapped in stone. Confess it, Lee. You've taken an interest.'

He couldn't help himself laughing. 'Yes, I have,' he said. They'd stopped quite a way from the edge of the trees where it was heavy with a vegetable smell, and gloomier than the gloomy day above the foliage.

June took his hand, quite suddenly, quite unexpectedly. It was something he often did himself, with perfect strangers, enjoying the sensation of their momentary confusion. Now he was on the receiving end, and he was startled. 'Help me, then,' said June. 'Prove to Edward that I'm right, so that we can all help together to get Adrian out.' Her grip was tight, urgent. She was facing him straight on and he was overly aware of her body.

'Look, June . . . it has to be said that I don't really go one hundred percent with what you think.'

She said nothing for a moment, just stared at him, hard. Her grip on his hand relaxed slightly.

'How many percent, then?'

'I can accept that a stone could harbour images, perhaps memories, perhaps even some form of ghostly memory of a human. But you're talking about a real prison. You're suggesting that a living, thinking human is screaming around inside that stone, trying to get out. I don't go along with that.'

She let go of his hand and he looked away, sensing that she was angry. But a moment later he felt her arms about his neck; in the grey light he'd not been aware of this sudden shift, and he froze as she clasped her hands behind his neck, and stared up at him like some lost girl, clinging to the only safe thing around. She was faintly perfumed and he was aware of the heat in her face, the moistness of her lips, the shining intensity of her eyes.

She said, 'Lee, you'll think about it, won't you?'

He placed his hands on her hips, gently, unprovocatively. 'That's why I'm back.'

She frowned a moment, shook her head so that the tight curls of her hair didn't fall so much across her face. 'Because . . . because what? Because you like me? Because you think I'm mad? Because you're intrigued by my story?' With two fingers she nipped the back of his neck in mock aggression. 'Because what? Tell me . . .'

'Because I think there's something peculiar about that stone, and about its relationship with you, and vice versa, and because I think there's something going on, and I'd like to try and understand it.'

'Like a mysterious disease. Analyse, document, interpet, theo-rise, conclude . . . move on. But that's OK. You see, if there *is* something in the stone font that is Adrian, then whether or not you believe it's an echo, or whatever, you'll try and get it out. If it's an echo we get an echo. If it's his mind, we get him back. We get my son back. If we get him back, the Hunters are happy again. Edward eats humble pie. And we start over, fresh, as if from the moment of Adrian's birth. But I could cope with that. All I want is my *son back*! I've got to get him back. And he *is* in there, Lee. And you will help me.'

Disturbed by her, uneasy in this embrace whose meaning he could not fathom yet, Kline smiled and said, 'That's why I came back. I said that already. I just don't promise that I'll be able to do anything. Why should I? I'm just a crazy historian who wandered in by chance.'

'No you're not, Lee. A crazy historian, maybe, but you didn't come here by chance.'

Something tensed up inside the American. 'What do you mean by that?'

'I mean God brought you, Lee. God and all things good and kind. Lady luck. Fateful fate. A lucky star.'

Kline laughed. For a second, as she had said he'd not come here by chance, all the hair on his neck had stood on end, and the wood seemed to drift away with the passing of a moment of shock. There was something awfully uncanny about the words, but as she'd rambled on about luck and stars, the mood of unease had passed.

Suddenly she was kissing him, her lips hard against his, and quickly he kissed her back, parting her lips with his tongue. Though his hands reached towards her backside he kept them discreetly at her hips, then pulled away and laughed, almost self-consciously. She was looking at him slyly, half amused.

'What was that for?' he said.

She shrugged. 'Because I wanted to. No, don't worry mister American, that wasn't bribery.' She smiled sourly, then looked slightly abashed as he reddened. 'I'm sorry,' she said. 'I should be so lucky that my kisses could be used as bribes. I'm sorry.'

'Sorry for what. The insinuation or the actual kiss?'

'The insinuation. May I kiss you again?'

'Sure.' This time it was brief, almost embarrassing. Kline shook his head as June's hands slipped from his neck, away from him. 'It would be great fun reading a psychological profile into this. A quiet grope in the woods –'

'How dare you!' Her eyes had widened in mock indignation.

'Trouble with your sex life? Frustrated nymphomania? Tree trunk fetish? Mistaken identity?'

She reached up and squeezed his cheek, a gesture he expected to be quick, friendly, semi-concerned, and to his surprise she pinched him very hard, very painfully. Then she turned away to walk through the trees back towards the garden. 'None of those things,' she said in a tired tone of voice. 'I'm just an affectionate person who gets starved of affection; I want to love my son, but sometimes I can't bring myself to touch his body. I want to love my daughter but she's an adolescent and she's bloody cruel sometimes. I want to love Edward, that's my husband, but he's too bloody calm, he copes too well, he makes me despise him. When I'm feeling warm, and content, and hopeful, I like to kiss.'

He stared at the back of her head as they walked, at the curls that bobbed up and down as she picked her way through the bracken. 'That's my sort of thinking,' he said.

She glanced round, grinning. 'Keep making me feel warm and hopeful then.'

At the edge of the wood she stopped and he stood beside her, staring at the neighbouring gardens, and the grey, rain-filled sky.

'Can I ask you something, June; without you tearing a chunk out of me?'

'Go ahead.'

'Did you set fire to the church? St Mary's?'

Surprisingly she laughed. It had been bluntly stated, and he was tensed against her anger. Her laughter relaxed him and he stared at her, a half smile on his own lips.

She said, 'That bloody priest!'

'Alexander. I saw him last night. He's convinced you burned the old church. He's got a fixation about it.'

She was shaking her head, not looking at Kline. 'Do you believe him?'

'I'm inclined not to. Was it Alexander who dropped Adrian? At the Christening?'

'Yes,' she said, simply, and then she seemed to relax slightly, turned to look at Kline. 'Let's not talk about it. Here . . .' she suddenly stooped and picked up a brick, one of several that were scattered at the edge of the woods. She passed it to him.

'A brick,' he said. 'For me? As a present?'

'How far could you throw it?'

He weighed the object carefully. 'Not far. I'm no muscle man.'

'Could you hit the broken window in the kitchen?'

He peered at the window, noticing for the first time that there was no pane in it. 'You must be joking.'

'Could a muscle man?'

He shook his head. 'Shall I throw it?'

'Yes.'

He used a lob as if he was throwing a hand-grenade. The brick thudded into the dirt a quarter of the way to the kitchen window. 'No one could throw it that far,' he said.

'Someone did,' she replied with a meaningful glance towards him.

They walked back to the house. As they stepped into the kitchen Kline recognized the brown-haired boy who sat at the large table, absolutely motionless, staring at him. On the table was a pile of coloured bricks, and several cars, all in varying attitudes suggesting they had been roughly discarded. An electric fire burned close by, keeping the kitchen comfortably warm.

'Hello Cru,' said Kline, amazed to see the child here, even delighted – in the second before realization came – to have the boy who had so puzzled him actually inside a house where he might speak a bit more.

Then it dawned on him just who he was looking at. 'Adrian?' He turned to look at June. 'Adrian?'

June Hunter was looking confused. 'Yes, that's Adrian. What did you call him?'

'I thought his name was Cru. He was in the church yesterday, after you left, and he said his name . . . June? What's the matter?'

The woman had gone white; she stared at Kline, her eyes wide, filled with some stark terror. A moment later she spat out her anger.

'Bastard! What are you trying to do? How dare you make such filthy jokes in my house!'

'For Chrissake, I'm not joking. Calm down!'

'You couldn't have seen him, not in the church . . . you bastard, you're lying.'

Red anger replaced the white of shock, and though she was still furious, she was now confused. Kline realized his mistake, and how callous his statement must have been to June; conscious that the blonde and rather petite girl was watching him from the lounge, he tried to make amends. 'There must be a simple explanation.'

June looked at him, then back at Adrian. 'Oh God.'

The girl in the lounge discreetly closed the door. Was that Karen, Kline wondered. 'I was probably mistaken,' he said. 'The boy looked like Adrian, but it probably wasn't him.' He noticed Adrian's right hand, bandaged. The boy in the church had not had that dressing on his hand. 'I'm sorry, I wasn't thinking, and that was inexcusable.'

June said nothing. She turned and walked out of the kitchen and into the lounge. A moment later the girl came out and went upstairs. She was holding a duster, and a dustpan, and Kline realized this must be the cleaner. He found himself staring at Adrian, almost hypnotically held by the child's piercing stare. Blue eyes met green, and a flow of some energy, some force of awareness between them, made Kline's whole body go cold; his legs felt weak and shaky. The boy laughed, suddenly, softly, and the laughter was unnervingly hollow and unchildlike; it reminded Kline of that laughter he had heard last night, just before his panic-stricken retreat from Higham with the blood of a murdered man on his hands.

He walked to the table and sat down, closer to the boy, leaning forward. 'Why did you say your name was Cru? Who are you?'

The mask of false humour faded from Adrian's face and the blank expression of mindless incomprehension returned. Brown hair fell lank across his eyes. His breathing was shallow, but rapid. His fist was clenched, his whole body tense, such a thin body in its loose fitting clothes. A moment later June Hunter returned, stood in the doorway staring suspiciously at him. 'You *do* believe it was Adrian . . .'

'Yes,' said Kline. 'I'm sure of it.' He settled back on the hard wooden chair. He sensed he was not risking a renewal of her anger. June stared at her son, then swept back her hair and shook her head; she seemed tired, her face lined and tense; the girl-like prettiness of her features was subdued, for a while, beneath the middle-aged mask of anxiety that could make people look so old, so much older than they were.

'Adrian never leaves the house,' she said, simply.

Kline said, 'Can he walk?'

'Yes, but he never does. Except occasionally . . . sometimes he walks in the garden.' She hesitated, obviously wanting to say more. 'A lot of times he walks in the garden . . . at night as well. We have the back door rigged so it bangs shut if it's opened. His windows are locked tight, but he still goes out. If he wants to he can do anything a normal child can do.'

'The church is only a mile or so away. He could have sneaked out yesterday, and back, without you knowing.'

June shook her head. 'Look at him! He's dead. That's not

living, that's dead. He doesn't move from the place you put him, he's like a chicken with half its head cut off. It'll fly if you throw it, balance if you put it on a perch, but it has no will, no will of its own. You're not telling me that *that* actually chose to sneak from the house and made a round trip of two miles to St Mary's?'

Kline shrugged. 'He was there, June. And he spoke. He said he was glad I'd come.'

June leaned heavily against the doorframe and her eyes closed. 'I can't believe that.'

'Was someone with him all of yesterday?'

'He slept in the afternoon and early evening. Tim Belsaint, his friend, was round with Don, that's his brother; they played together until about eight o'clock. Don was visiting Karen. I put Adrian to bed soon after that. I can't believe it was him.'

The child suddenly laughed again. Kline jerked round to see June's reaction, but she was unmoved. 'He laughs with Tim quite a lot. He occasionally laughs on his own for no apparent reason. Edward thinks it's a reflex outlet after he's heard a lot of argument.'

'You have an answer for everything,' said Kline tiredly. He rose and reached out to ruffle Adrian's hair. As he went into the lounge with June, to fetch a drink, so the boy turned to watch him, and Kline's last sight of the child was of Adrian clenching his fist, holding out his bandaged hand, and beginning to shake from side to side.

CHAPTER SEVEN

After a while there was movement upstairs and someone ran across the landing and was noisy at a sink for a while. Kline drank scotch and talked with June, and settled into the house, which he found very comfortable. It was a very large house, short on rooms – he guessed about ten – but obviously each room was spacious, a house unto itself. The lounge was as big as his whole flat.

The home-help left and almost immediately a young lad in school uniform rang the bell. June let him in and introduced him as Tim Belsaint. He was on his way back to school after the lunch break and had a package for Karen. He said hello to Adrian and then left.

June told Kline about the relationship between the two boys,

86

and then the phone went. From her conversation Kline guessed she was speaking with Edward and he discreetly left the lounge and went back to the kitchen.

Adrian was seated exactly as he had been before, unmoved, unmoving. Kline was uncomfortable with the way June had just left him there, unattended, in a room whose insulation against the cold was hardly very good with the window gone.

Did she really not care that much?

'What are you up to with my mother?'

The girl's voice startled Kline. He turned sharply, then relaxed. 'You must be Karen.'

The girl looked older than sixteen. Her hair was cut short, very neatly styled. She had overdone the make-up around her eyes and lips, but that was probably fashion. She was wearing a thin dress, tucked at the waist, and her feet were bare. Kline allowed himself a glance at her legs. She saw that and liked it. She was very like her mother in looks, but there was something very hard about her eyes. Instinctively Kline sensed the girl's experience of life. Unable to help himself he communicated interest and the girl walked into the room, her cheeks slightly flushed, her body more relaxed as she – perhaps without realizing it – understood.

'You didn't answer my question,' she said.

'I'm not up to anything with your mother. I'm interested in Adrian.'

Karen turned to stare at her brother. There was no warmth in her eyes or face – the expression was more contempt.

'Why would anybody be interested in that little bastard?'

Kline laughed, unable to stop, at the unexpected language. Karen glanced angrily at him. 'Don't be shitty,' she said in her attractive English accent. 'I never was one for being ladylike.'

'Perish the thought,' said Kline.

The girl grinned. 'You like your women *gritty*, do you? Even a little *male*?' Her laugh was delightfully cruel.

Kline shook his head, half in amusement, half in puzzlement. One day, he thought, she'll be a fine player of games. The bitch.

He said, 'Why are you so hostile to your brother? He can't help what he is.'

'I don't believe it,' said Karen, coldly. 'Little Adrian is a master at getting sympathy. He not only acts out the role, he dedicates his whole life to the cause. Don't you, darling?' She leaned down and leered at the boy. 'Mummy's mad and Daddy's sad, but big sister knows the little bugger's secret.'

Straightening up she looked at Kline again, looked him quickly up and down. 'Where do you live? London?'

'Hampstead.'

'Really? I'd like to live there. Must be lovely.'

'Good pubs.'

'You'd appreciate that. As an American.'

Kline frowned. 'I appreciate it as me . . .'

The girl walked round the table and rested her hands on Adrian's shoulders, staring down at his head as she gently massaged his muscles. 'I can't go in pubs yet. I'm not old enough. But Don takes me in. I like to drink. I drink a lot of spirits, but Don's in CAMRA – that's the Campaign for Real Ale. So I get to drink a lot of good beers too.'

'Who's Don? Your boyfriend?'

'He's more than that.' She said it quickly, a touch of thrilled embarrassment in her voice, her look. Her eyes flickered up, meeting Kline's gaze briefly. She was bragging.

'Holds your hand, does he?' said Kline, thinking angrily at himself, are you jealous, you bastard? You *are*!

June came through into the kitchen, holding the parcel for her daughter. 'Edward will be home earlier than he thought.'

'Good,' said Karen. 'Is that from Don?'

June remembered the package. 'Oh, yes. Is it another gun?'

Karen opened the paper, and the shoe box inside. 'A birthday present,' she said. 'Belated,' she explained to Kline. She drew out a small flintlock pistol and held it up for him to see. She held it lovingly, smiling with genuine pleasure. 'Isn't that beautiful?' She cocked the hammer and triggered it. It made a loud 'clack'. Kline noticed that June was not happy, watching her daughter with a deep frown on her face.

'May I see?' he said to the girl.

Karen passed the gun across and Kline was surprised at the weight and good feel of it. He noticed it left grease marks on his fingers. The lock was tight to pull back and sprang satisfyingly when he pulled the trigger. There was no flint in the teeth, yet. He looked down the barrel and there was no bar. 'It works?'

'Of course it works,' said Karen proudly. 'Don's a real craftsman. We go pigeon shooting sometimes, always with his replicas.'

'Does he need a licence?'

'Probably. Hasn't got one, though. I've got two guns now. An English duelling pistol –'

'Ugly thing,' said June quietly.

'And this . . . It's an eighteenth century London pocket pistol. Doesn't it feel nice?'

Kline agreed and passed the replica back to the girl.

June said, 'You'll look after Adrian, will you Karen? I'm going into the town for a while.'

Karen smiled pleasantly, glanced at Kline, then sat down at the table next to her brother and started to explain the parts of the gun to him. Adrian watched blankly.

'See you later,' said Kline.

Karen didn't look up. 'I expect so.'

The girl disturbed him. As he left the kitchen and helped June into her coat, he found himself thinking of her and of her hostility. He couldn't fathom it.

As if reading his mind, June said, 'Don't take any notice of Karen – she's always like that, always cool, aggressive. To the church?'

'Why not?'

'Will they let us in?'

'There's only one way to find out.'

They left the house and climbed into Kline's battered car. He sensed June's amusement with this relic of better times, but she kept a straight face, looked vainly for a seat belt, and then settled – almost in resignation – back in her seat.

They drove into the town and pulled off the main road into a side street just a few yards from where the churchyard began. The ambulance had gone, and so had the police cars. Hunched against the cold they entered the ruined church through the front porch and stood inside, for a moment, watching the group of men who were almost boredly probing around the cracks in the walls, and turning over lumps of masonry. The font, Kline noticed, was smeared with blood, as was the floor. It hadn't been cleaned yet. There was a sour and unpleasant smell in the air.

June shivered, looking unhappy. 'Let's go,' she said. 'I don't like it.' She was staring at the font, and her face showed her unhappiness.

'You got a bad feeling?'

'Very,' she said.

'Hold on a while. Just a while.' Kline walked towards the font and when one of the plain-clothes men came across he said he was from the *Evening News*, not officially on duty, but he'd heard about the suicide and couldn't keep his journalist's nose out of it. If the policeman despised the press he didn't show it. He shrugged. 'Go ahead, look around. We're finished. The body was behind the font, and he'd smeared some mark with his own blood before dying.'

'A mark? What sort of mark?'

The policeman waved a hand towards the recess. 'There you are, go and look for yourself.' Then he turned away from Kline and called to the others. They left the church. Kline walked towards the font.

June Hunter held back, uneasy, walking a little way after Kline, but then standing by one of the walls, watching, hunched inside her thick coat. Kline ignored her. He peered into the basin of the font and grimaced at the blackening pool in there – not as deep as he had imagined it, but gruesome just the same.

He walked round the font, his sense of expectation rising, and almost immediately he saw it!

His cry was of surprise and delight, but he couldn't have known what emotion made him yell so loudly. He had eyes and mind only for the gory symbol that had been drawn out on the grey stone, out of sight of the main body of the church, where the recess was at its gloomiest.

'Come and see!' he called, but June, shivering, shook her head.

'I'm going home,' she said. 'I don't feel well. I feel frightened.'

'I'll see you later,' he called, and as an afterthought, 'Can I check up later this afternoon?'

'Of course.'

Speaking without warmth, without sincerity, June had turned and was running from the church. Kline watched her for a second, not understanding her sudden discomfort, and not particularly caring.

Then he stepped back from the font and stared at the bloody sign there, and all over again he marvelled.

Concentric circles, divided by rippling lines in the vague shape of a cross. Although the fragment of stone that had brought him there had only a part of a symbol upon it, that part matched this symbol perfectly . . .

Circles, and water signs, ancient marks used in a thousand ways in modern times . . . their ancient association forgotten consciously, but unconsciously? Their meaning was still there, it had to be. A thousand symbols, used without thought, accepted without question, but a thousand symbols that spoke in silent voices, reaching to some deeper vision in the modern human mind. And here was one of them, a symbol of the past, the dark past, drawn in living paint upon the stone that so intrigued him.

A thousand questions, a hundred feelings, filled him with a

dizzying sense of wonder as he crouched before that pattern and ran his fingers around the gory lines of the design. What did it mean, he wondered? What meaning to the dying man who had drawn it there; what meaning to the man who observed it, unaware of its ancient root?

He was aware that the curious, and the ghoulish, were wandering into the ruins and passing away, their intrigue satisfied. Kline remained, crouched on his haunches by the font, and later was only half aware that two overalled men came and washed out the basin of the stone. They scrubbed the blood from the floor and sides of the font, but when they came round to remove the design Kline stopped them. 'I'll do it,' he heard himself say, and the men shrugged, said words he didn't hear, and went away.

A heavy stillness descended about the place, and though the day was cold, bitterly cold, he felt hot. He heard a bird flying about somewhere, the sound of its wings loud and sharp in the still air.

He glanced up, seeking this avian intruder into his solitude, but he saw nothing. He imagined at times that a dark shadow wheeled above him, darting across the open sky, circling and flapping, touching down on the walls, then launching itself into space, flying above the recess and then vanishing again.

He could see no bird, and after a while he chose to ignore the persistent sound of its movements, and its occasional shrill cry.

He felt heat, as of some raging fire, close by; he sensed the crackling flame, the slow disintegration of wood and rock crumbling down into a heavy ash pile, while yellow flame licked heavenwards, and danced about him; the sweat rolled from him, dripped from his face, from the angles of his jaw, the prominences of cheek and nose; and all the while he sat and stared at the flickering blood symbol in front of him, and even when the symbol curled and dripped away, running down the stone in chaos leaving the face of the font clean and bare again, even then he still sat motionless . . .

Listening . . .

Wind, blowing the fire, fanning the flames; it whirled and cried about him, a wind across hills, raging through forestlands and across bare, storm-swept moors . . .

A bird, shrill of voice, loud of wing, darting about the skies above him, invisible to his eyes, its raucous anger sounding from some time that was not this time . . .

Laughter, then a cry as of someone dying, and the distant thudding of someone running across stone, nearer, nearer, the heaviness of the footfall echoing through some empty space, louder, more resonant, the running coming closer until it ceased, and there was a scream, and that scream was Kline's!

On his feet, holding his head, his ears, trying to block the loud and terrifying sounds that were flooding his mind.

Hands took him – he felt them and fought against them, but they were too powerful. In astonished horror he watched the flesh of his hands pinched and.twisted, white then red where invisible fingers tore at his skin, bent back his fingers against his will, bending them so far that he cried with the pain, but was helpless against it. He was thrown heavily across the recess, striking the font, grasping it for support only to feel unseen hands drag him from it, and take him about the neck, twisting his head while fingers plucked and pinched at his cheeks, pulling the flesh out and pushing it into the gap between his teeth. His hair was pulled, standing straight, then knotted, then yanked so hard backwards that he staggered with the wrenching suddenness of that agonizing grasp.

And as he sprawled onto the rough ground again he felt fingers on his genitals, tightening, tightening, until he screeched with agony and thrashed about in front of the font, beating at the thin air before his body, unable to strike at anything of substance, almost crippled by the cruel and merciless fingers that squeezed this most tender part of him, and finally reduced him to tears, of pain, and embarrassment, and confusion . . . and fear . . .

Somehow everything passed and he found himself lying on the rubble at the rear of the church, his eyes open, the stone font filling his field of view. He was shaking and saturated, and it took some minutes for him to come properly to his senses and remember where he had been, and what had brought him here. He was not in pain. Slowly he sat up, then stood up, and when he touched his body he found no bruises, little residual pain, no marks or scratches.

Rapidly, what had happened to him became unreal, insubstantial, fleeing his mind as a dream flees the mind of one who wakes suddenly, vividly recalling the events of slumber, only to lose them as quickly as water slips from clasped fingers.

He looked at his hands, and touched his throat, and walked unsteadily back to the stone font to see if the symbol was there. It was. It had not melted away, as he had observed . . . it was there as it had been, a gruesome reminder of what had occurred here the night before.

Badly shaken, and very confused, he walked from the ruins of

St Mary's and back to his car. After a while he calmed himself, and managed to stop the shaking of his hands, the weakness of his legs.

He smiled, staring through the side window of his car at the trees that obscured much of the rear wall of the church. Beyond that wall lay the stone.

The thought that had nagged him for so long – not even days, now that he thought of it, just hours! How long it seemed he had been here! – that thought had cleared in his mind, now, and he felt charged and excited by it. And even relieved.

When June, earlier that day, had said he had not come to Higham by chance, he had felt disturbed for a moment. But now he saw how she might have been right. Not chance, but not the goodness of fate, either. He had been brought here deliberately, and calculatedly. He didn't know by whom, or by what, but now that he was here, something was trying to keep him here.

Whoever it was had put on one hell of a good show to keep his curiosity at its peak. He hated to think of being used like this, it went against every grain in his body. But he conceded the round for he was intrigued, now – captured. He was as trapped by his own need to know who was using him, as was Adrian Hunter by the fabric of the stone font.

Before, until just minutes ago, he had been just a curious observer; but now he was a part of the tragedy, a player, a participant. Badly shaken, and inwardly quite frightened, he felt nonetheless an overwhelming sense of *involvement*. But involvement in what?

As he stared at the ruined church, and relived his memory of that endless agony of physical abuse, he began to wonder about June Hunter's obsession, and like it or not he found himself believing that perhaps there was something in what she claimed for the ancient stone font.

CHAPTER EIGHT

Again the hours had passed without Kline being aware of their rapid and impatient passage. He discovered it was dark, and that the hour of five had been and gone. He recalled inviting himself back to the Hunter's, and wondered whether or not to ring and confirm the date, or to ring and cancel; he was tired, and shaken, and felt an overwhelming desire to climb into bed and sleep.

On a sudden impulse he drove round the block and rejoined the High Street several hundred yards from the church. He drove slowly back through the crowded street, searching for an off-licence, and when he spotted one he parked briefly and bought two bottles of Hapsburg Liebfraumilch, his favourite white wine.

With this gift in hand he drove to the Hunter's. He curtains of the house were closed, but light shone from every down-stairs room, and after a moment's hesitation Kline locked his Austin and rang the bell.

June Hunter answered the door.

'I thought you'd be back ages ago,' she said; she was smiling in a rather forced way, and there was something strained and uneasy about her.

'I got held up,' said Kline. 'Can I eat with you tonight?'

'Yes. Of course. Edward's home.'

She stared at him hard as she told him this, and Kline guessed that her husband was the source of her concern. Not, he hoped, because of anything as ridiculously trite as jealousy. But he could never be sure.

Stepping into the house he presented June with the wine. 'One for me. One for the rest of you.'

'That's lovely, thank you. I love German wine. I'll cool them down for a while.'

She led the way through to the lounge and ushered Kline into its warm and cosy interior. Karen was sprawled in an armchair, reading, and she glanced at Kline as he came in, favouring him with a quick smile before returning pointedly to her book. Opposite her, reading a paper, was a severe looking man in his fifties, with slightly receding grey hair; he was dressed in white shirt and dark tie, as if he was incapable of dressing to relax even in the comfort of his own home. He wore half frames, and removed these like some officious professor as Kline entered. He rose to his feet, but remained where he was so that Kline was forced to cross the room and extend his hand.

'Mister Kline,' said Edward Hunter. 'Very pleased to meet you. My wife has told me something of you.'

'Call me Lee,' said Kline. 'And it's good to meet you too. And good of you to allow me to dinner.'

'I didn't know I had, but not at all, not at all. Sit down, Mister Kline, and I'll fetch you a drink.'

Kline grinned as he sat on the three-seater settee, winking at Karen who frowned at him, then returned to her book. 'Mister Kline?'

'Sorry? Oh . . . scotch, that'll do fine.'

'Ice?'

'Not needed, thanks.' There was enough ice in the room already, he thought with an inner smirk.

Kline raised the glass and toasted Edward's health. Then he sipped the drink and unwound a little. 'I really would like you to call me Lee.'

'I dislike familiarity with strangers,' said Edward Hunter curtly. He stared at Kline through half closed eyes, leaning back in his chair and watching the American's every movement. 'It may seem unsociable, but I assure you you are very welcome. I'm just a great believer in distance, and correctness, and attending to one's own affairs, not those of others.'

Kline shrugged. 'That's fine by me . . . Mister Hunter?'

'Doctor Hunter.'

Karen abruptly rose and stormed from the room. Kline had sensed her growing irritation, her long, angry looks at her father. She let the book fall to the ground and Kline reached down for it, placed it back on her chair. It was something called *Dead Babies*.

'She has appalling taste in reading,' said Edward, shaking his head.

'By whose standards?' teased Kline. He allowed no smile to touch his lips, and Edward Hunter was silenced. Kline found himself wishing desperately that June would come back into the room. He could hear the distant clatter of kitchen work. June's voice occasionally rose to an audible level, and she sounded harassed and unhappy.

Edward said, 'My wife is a very ill woman. I wonder whether or not you realize the full extent of that illness?' He sipped his own scotch, watching Kline through dark-rimmed eyes, his expression one of arrogance, of challenge. Kline met the gaze coldly, shook his head to indicate that he didn't know anything about any illness.

Edward frowned, then laughed in a pointedly cynical way. 'No? You've talked to her, haven't you? For heaven's sake, Mister Kline, in the twenty four hours since she met you she's talked about you as if nothing else in the world mattered. I feel like I've known you for years. You've had a quite remarkable affect upon her, and I'm not sure I altogether like it.'

'I offered my help, that's all.'

'I know that. But help at what? Instinctively she knows she can't be helped, but you've become – even in this short space of time – a symbol to her, a symbol of the help she needs, even a symbol of *hope*! She's pinned that neurotic hope upon you, Mister Kline. You have become her reason for living. And you don't know how ill she is?'

Again Kline feigned deep thought for a moment, shook his head and said sweetly. 'Can't say I've noticed.' He raised his glass before taking a mouthful of the warm drink.

'My wife is obsessed,' said Edward. 'Can't you see that?'

'I'm obsessed,' replied Kline, evenly. 'Most people are. For different reasons. I'm obsessed with the need to get regularly laid.'

Edward looked disgusted. 'That was cheap.'

Kline smiled bitterly, feeling irritated with himself. Edward was right: it *had* been a cheap crack. He said, 'All I'm interested in is the truth – in getting the truth.'

'Then why do you deny the truth of my wife's obsession?'

'Because you use the word to mean *neurotic*. You imply madness. You imply a bizarre and abnormal behaviour when in fact she is obsessed with something that for all *you* know may well be true. If a man, for a sound and acceptable reason, is obsessed with the idea that his missing son couldn't have been killed in the war, then he isn't as crazy as the man who just refuses to accept the death of his son.'

Edward Hunter adjusted his position in the deep armchair without taking his gaze from the American, without relaxing for an instant the growing superciliousness of his expression.

'I see,' he said quietly. 'Then you don't believe my wife's behaviour is on the borders of madness? Her obsession, to you, is a courageous and heroic belief in the unlikely, in the face of academic scepticism.'

'Something like that,' said Kline. 'The only obsession I can detect as being in the slightest neurotic, is your own obsession that your wife is wrong.'

Edward laughed bitterly. 'She's converted you, I see. Well, then: as far as you're concerned it is I who am on the borders of madness.'

Kline shrugged, angry, barely restraining himself from demonstrating that anger. In fact, he felt sour, and very uncomfortable. He had hoped this man would be able to enrich his understanding of the stone font and its alleged prisoner, but quite obviously Edward Hunter had no time even to question the astronomically small possibility that June was right.

Kline made a split-second decision to finish his drink and leave. He could visualize an unbearably uncomfortable evening, all defensiveness against contrived offence; small-talk laced with bitterness; probing questions not from the genuine heart and root-centre of concern, but from the cracked and struggling ego of this middle-aged man with his middle-aged intolerance of that which he could not comprehend.

'I do not necessarily believe that your son is trapped in the font in such a way that he might be sucked out, liquefied, and drained back into his body. I do not believe that because I cannot comprehend how such an imprisonment might occur, and in my research, and conversations with people who work in similar fields to myself . . .' some full time, some part time like me, he thought, thus avoiding the technicality of the lie . . . 'I have seen and learned of some very strange properties of stone, and of sites and locations on the earth's surface. To June, as a lay-woman, sensing as she probably does some intangible relic of your boy, Adrian, it must seem as if there is the possibility of his being alive. I do not *necessarily* believe in the life, but I do most certainly believe in the intangible presence. I agree that June's behaviour seems irrational, but only by your standards, and the common standard. By my standards she is a determined woman, and that determination is all I need to suspect there is something to what she says.'

And anyway, he thought, whilst simultaneously deciding not to tell Edward Hunter anything about it, I have myself experienced some force of aggresssion associated with that stone. If I ever needed proof, then that is it. But proof of what I'm not sure.

Aloud, he concluded, 'I am intrigued by the possibility that a "ghost" exists in that stone, and not just one, but many. And some of them very ancient.'

Edward laughed, loudly and insultingly. 'But that's so stupid! That's as stupid as some routine piece of TV occultism. That sort of belief is not worthy of a man as obviously intelligent as you.'

'Never mind the bullshit. I've learned long ago that minds like yours and minds like mine . . . and like June's . . . miss each other by whole numbers of miles. We're on – to use the charming phrase – different wavelengths. I'm an interfering asshole, and you're a dumbshit doctor.'

Edward frowned, slightly taken off-balance. 'I've never found American slang particularly provocative,' he said evenly, staring at Kline with that same blankness, the same edge of hostility. Yet he was quite white, and Kline sensed that he was inwardly seething with irritation. 'Tell me this, Mister Kline. Did you see anything or hear anything when you were up at St Mary's? Or have you only my wife's words to go on?'

'I sense *something*,' replied Kline, shivering as he thought of his encounter with the stone a few hours before. He stared down at his hands as he spoke, aware that Edward would be wildly misinterpreting that simple gesture. He stared at his white skin, which only hours before he had watched – or had dreamt? – rippling, twisting and being pinched. Had he imagined that? Did the church play upon his high expectations, the mood, the anticipation of the place causing a realistic vision, a very solid hallucination?

He couldn't believe that he had dreamt that encounter. He couldn't believe that there was not something there, something strange, something frightening in its effect, something with great power . . . but what? *What?* What could hurt him so much, and leave him undamaged? Surely not the ghost of a boy . . . surely not that!

He clung to his new belief that there was something associated with the stone, and he clung to it with all the obsessiveness that June clung to her own belief, and Edward Hunter clung to his despicable ignorance. There could not be anything *evil* in the stone, for there was no such thing as evil unless embodied in man. Alexander had said that, speaking familiar words, expressing very old, very routine feelings. Strange, how such routine ideas could – even thirty years into one's life – affect a man more strongly than ever before.

'You see,' said Edward, 'What my wife –'

'For Christ sake call her June! What's the matter with you, *Doctor* Hunter? My wife, my wife . . . you haven't used her name once whilst talking to me! Are you *that* afraid of her?'

'I'm not afraid of her,' said Edward simply.

Kline mocked him with his forced grin. 'I see . . . more of your distance and English properness. Never refer to Christian names in the presence of strangers.'

Edward shook his head. 'Not even that, Mister Kline. Pure and simple unease . . . with you, with her. You are quite correct to remind me that I am being bad-mannered, though why *you* have to be so bad-mannered I fail to comprehend. As I was saying, what June fails to understand is that Adrian is not a vegetable. He is not mindless. You've met the boy, you've seen him. He is unnervingly aware. I use that word in full appreciation of its provocativeness. He is unnervingly aware. At times he seems almost asleep, though open-eyed: suddenly his eyes, still open, become alive. What Adrian has lost is his ability to relate, to speak . . . to speak . . . My God, he has spoken once . . .' he

98

had trailed off, his eyes focussed somewhere between Kline and the fireplace. 'That frightened me, Mister Kline; he spoke coherent words, unexpectedly, suddenly, prompted by something. I had waited years for those words. When they came they scared me half to death. And since that day, several days ago, he has not spoken again, though I have tried to make him do so. But that was such a break-through Mister Kline. That was the sign I needed! I could turn to June and say, there, I was right! The boy *is* inside his head, his personality, his mind, it *is* there . . . but trapped. I've said all along that Adrian is repressed. Lack of speech, lack of outward emotion, or outward expression. Listlessness, followed by spontaneous and energetic bursts of high activity. The behaviour is peculiar, but I expect no less; a boy, nine years old, and highly intelligent, is confined inside the damaged cortex of his brain, emerging slowly. We must encourage that emergence. My wife – *June* – does not help. Even when Adrian spoke she would not believe me. Parrot words, she said, thrown out from his mouth like he throws out faeces and urine and spit and his arms and legs, mimicking, responding, in an instinctive, mindless way.' He paused, looked thoughtful, frowning as again his eyes slipped from contemplating the American to rest, unfocussed, on Karen's book. 'Perhaps I am afraid of June. Perhaps you are right. Perhaps I am afraid of her obsession because of what I see it doing to my son; or rather, what I see it stopping in my son, his spontaneous – the church would call it miraculous – recovery!'

Kline twirled his glass, watching the last drops of scotch fling themselves about the crystal walls of their prison. 'I hadn't been aware that Adrian had spoken for the first time in his life . . .'

'June didn't tell you that, eh?'

Edward was grinning as Kline glanced up. 'No. She didn't tell me. But then she didn't need to, because I spoke with Adrian in the church, yesterday.'

'Nonsense.' Edward Hunter, suddenly, was white again. The word was spoken so quickly, so nervously, that Kline was instantly able to detect the surge of apprehension that had invoked it. 'Nonsense,' Edward repeated when – after several seconds – Kline had remained unnervingly quiet and calm.

'June didn't tell you, eh?' said Kline with a smile.

'She did, in fact,' said Edward. 'I just don't believe you.'

Kline was instantly irritable. 'What the hell's the matter with you?' he said sharply, shaking his head. 'I don't understand. I would have thought this news would have delighted you. He spoke very coherently, this boy – Adrian. We had a talk about Karen, and me, and Cru.'

'Who?'

'I'd hoped you would know. That's what Adrian said he was called. Cru. Hi, he said, I'm Cru.'

'I still don't believe you. Adrian never leaves the house on his own. He goes to his special school and returns. We take him out some times. He visits Tim Belsaint. Otherwise he never leaves.'

'You just said he has occasional bursts of activity. The church is only a mile or so away.'

'I don't deny that. Adrian sometimes uses his hands and legs like a normal child. I've never seen him run, but he walks occasionally. It all helps to convince me that I'm right, that the blow on the head didn't drain him from his body, merely shuttered him up a little too much.'

'Never mind that. If he can walk in the garden, why can't he walk down the road to the church?'

'Why should he? What would he gain? The garden represents a different part of his secure home. I take him in the garden and he knows it's part of his environment. He would have no reason to walk down the road to a church which he doesn't know.'

'Not even to visit himself? His mind? To unite with his second part?'

Edward laughed sourly. 'Well I'd have to say no to that, wouldn't I! No, not even to meet his alter ego. He enjoys the garden, he likes it out there. He likes to listen to the wind, and watch the clouds. He often goes out at night, and we have to go and fetch him in. We've rigged the back-door so that it bangs loudly when it's opened . . .'

Kline frowned. 'Why don't you lock it, and hide the key?'

'Why do you think? I'm *glad* he does these things, Kline. I'm glad he goes outside and I want to know when he does it. But I don't want him to catch cold.'

Kline felt hot and aggressive towards this man with his stiff English mannerisms and barely concealed provocation. He shrugged as he said, 'Well, all I know is, I saw Adrian in that church. I suggest you accept the truth of that statement, or else give me one good reason why I should bother lying about it. He might have a double, of course. Do you think that's feasible?'

Edward grinned. 'Perhaps you saw the ghost of my son; perhaps you saw this ghost that June is always talking to. Perhaps he left the stone for a quick chat with you.'

'Perhaps indeed,' said Kline brightly. 'Yes, I'd never thought of that.'

The smile remained on Edward Hunter's face for a few seconds, then he fell suddenly solemn. He leaned forward, looking earnest and angry. 'Look Mister Kline, let me be frank with you.'

'Please do.'

'This is not a happy family. My wife, whatever you say, is a sick woman, a very sick woman. My son is fighting for his life in every sense of the word. Right? My daughter has been asked to leave the very good school at which she has been for two years: she is aggressive, bad-tempered, rough. She is a bad influence. They say. Also she has nightmares, bad dreams – she sees things, she forgets things. Her personality can change in the space of a single breath. It's strain, Mister Kline, the strain of the family situation that has done that to her. I find it quite unforgivable of you to come barging into this domestic scene of strained bliss and encourage my wife in the belief that is causing most of the trouble. If you want to help her, break her of this stupid belief. I've tried. And I've failed. She will not listen. I will be most upset if you encourage her in this nonsense. And I do not believe that an intelligent man like you believes in ghouls, and trapped persona, and voices in the night.'

Kline leaned forward. 'Oh but Doctor Hunter, I do, I do!'

As Edward frowned and sat back, barely restraining his anger, Kline rose from his chair and placed his glass carefully on the mantelpiece.

'You're a very evil man, Mister Kline.'

Kline laughed. 'And you're full of crap!'

And with that he left the lounge and walked through into the kitchen.

June looked up from setting the big table as he walked through the door. Karen was working at the sink, and Adrian sat quietly at the end of the table, watching everything, perhaps watching nothing. The kitchen window had been repaired, Kline noticed, and the new putty stood out stark against the rest of the painted frame.

'I think I'll be going,' he said quietly, picking a salad onion from the bowl in the middle of the table. 'I don't mean to be rude, but I'm very tired.'

June nodded slowly, irritation showing in her face. 'And Edward has upset you.'

'Not really. But he might, and I might, and I wouldn't want to ruin your evening.'

'That implies there is something to ruin.' She smiled, but there was something desperate about her. 'Please stay,' she said.

'I'm not running out on you,' said Kline softly. 'I need time to think about something, something that happened today. I've got to sort myself out a little, to distance myself again . . .'

'You'll be back then. You really will be back.'

'Don't pressure the man, mother,' said Karen irritably. 'If he says he'll be back, he'll be back.'

'And not alone,' said Kline. 'I'm going to try and get help, someone who can really help you. I promise.'

He turned away from her, but as he made to go, so he found himself staring at Adrian. The boy was slumped in his chair, hands dangling by his sides; his brown hair was untidy and falling across his face, and there were food stains on his cheeks. His mouth was open, and for a second there was an empty look in his eyes, a window into the void that was his mind.

Then the features tightened, the eyes focussed on Kline, and the boy smiled, just briefly, just fleetingly. When June turned to look at her son, the slack features returned in an instant. Kline felt icy cold, empty – and deeply disturbed. Again, as he made his way from the kitchen, he found himself unable to distinguish between imagination and reality, and that momentary smile was lost to him, becoming dreamlike and unreal as he thought about it.

He drove back to London hardly noticing the miles, or the darkness, or the traffic. He made straight for the Institute, and parked in Bloomsbury, then ran through the criss-cross of streets until he came to the front doors. They were locked, of course, but he called the night porter and identified himself. The porter admitted him, well used to Kline's lengthy working hours.

In his office he made himself coffee, and pulled the blinds across the window, obscuring the night and lights of London, immersing himself in the musty smell of stone, and the heavy stillness of the deserted building. He put his feet up on the desk and let his attention linger on the Higham fragment for long minutes.

Then he reached for the letter he had placed, unopened, in his correspondence tray, the letter from Crazy Lady. He opened it and read it quickly, and whereas a month ago he might have grinned and shaken his head, thinking on what she said with half seriousness, but not allowing himself to take her wholly seriously, this time he read her words in silence, thoughtful silence.

When he had finished, he reached into his desk drawer and pulled out an untidy sheaf of papers, mostly letters and the carbons of his replies. Out of the heap he drew Crazy Lady's last letter but one, the letter in which she had explained what she was, but not who she was; the letter that had plunged Kline into a confusion from which he had not extricated himself, not until today, at least.

When he had read this letter for the first time he had scorned it, then frowned over it, then shrugged it off. Now he read it and knew that Crazy Lady was his answer. It was his ,intuition working again, and he knew better than to quibble with his intuition.

So for a long while he sat in his bright, silent office and read her letter over, and stared at the spidery handwriting; again and again his eyes flicked down the page of scribble, re-assessing her words, letting them seep deeply into him.

And at last he reached for a pair of scissors and doctored that page of writing, snipping out the paragraph that concerned him, and which he knew would concern the Hunters:

'You ask me how I know the things I know,' she had written, 'things about the ancient cultures of my country, things about their behaviour and their looks which no-one could know. You suggest that I should be some brilliant researcher, but you have not heard of me. I think you have jealousy of me, and that makes me grin. You have no need to have this. My gift is very special, and very personal. You will think I am mad, but I shall tell it to you. I am psychic. You know what that is. When I touch an arrowhead I can feel what has been associated with that weapon. When I feel a watch from a man I can feel who gave it to him. When I sit in a house I can feel the people who were in there years ago. I can see the past so clearly, sometimes, that I am afraid for my own mind. Two hundred years ago I would have been called a witch. But there is a word that I think describes me better, and I like to think of myself as this thing.'

'Necromancer. I am a necromancer.'

PART TWO

CRAZY LADY

CHAPTER NINE

Less than twenty-four hours after leaving Higham for the second time, Lee Kline was in mid-air, searching the broken cloud for a glimpse of the French coastline below. The Boeing was an old 707, and the vibration was incredible. Kline was a bad traveller, and flying was the worst. The only relief to his constant sensation of nausea was that he could view the world from the heavenly realm of the Gods: he always remembered, when he flew, how an astronaut *en route* to the Moon, some years before, had extended his thumb and obliterated the moon-sized disc of the earth. It had been Buzz Aldrin, the second man to kick up silver dust on the dead world of earth's satellite. That simple act of blotting out the globe, and its people, and its past, and its future, and its potential *lack* of a future, had had a deep and disturbing effect upon the man.

Kline could well understand it. Seeing a town from ten thousand feet, its ugly regularity, its ink-blot shape, its insignificance, filled him with a sense of futility. I am one such unit of insignificance he found himself thinking . . . and there are so many of us, and we are so small.

The cloud broke just as the plane hummed its way across the north coast of Brittany. He had no idea what part of the coast they were crossing, but he could see cliffs and rocks, and the sluggish, magnificent whiteness of sea breaking against those rocks.

His stomach turned as the plane hit an air bank and tipped quite violently. Outside his small window the tip of the wing seemed to be melting as if in some unseen but intense heat – it was merely cloud condensing and spraying off the metal – an uncomfortable illusion. Then the clouds closed in below them again, obscuring the earth, and Kline settled back and ordered a second scotch from one of the prim, dark-haired stewardesses.

It was still light when the plane dipped below the stormy heavens and plunged from sunlight into dark, grey November France. Rain sleeted briefly across the window next to Kline's seat and the plane seemed to bump and creak far more than he would have thought safe. But they landed safely at the bleak and desolate airport of La Baule, and taxied towards the unimpressive and uninviting passenger terminal. He ran from the plane to the tunnel, and passed through customs quite quickly.

Tired, and rather apprehensive at the thought of driving in the dark, Kline checked into a small hotel over-night. He sent a telegram to Crazy Lady telling of the alteration in his plans. Early the next morning he hired a car, a beaten up, rather decrepit Citröen that was not what he had been promised when he had phoned from London to arrange the hire. It was also very expensive. He said nothing, beyond swearing, and as grey daylight spread across the land he put his foot down and raced along the straight road towards St Nazars. If the Citröen gave him difficulty for the first ten minutes, he was soon driving it smoothly and effectively.

Somewhere along the tree-lined road, after less than an hour of driving, he saw the sea, and sheer looking cliffs; he pulled off the road into a convenient lay-by. An occasional car roared past him, but swiftly the sound was lost. The slopes above the road were wooded with tall pines and thick brambly undergrowth; but towards the sea was an expanse of open field, newly turned earth much covered with tiny plant life, and very stony. He walked across this field and swung over an iron gate. A second field, and he could hear the sea.

He was on the edge of the land before he knew it, climbing through thin gorse and bracken until he discovered a winding trackway down to the wind-swept shore. Dark rock, soaked by rain and spray, rose from the sand and grew out of the cliff, like some enormous, gnarled life-forms. Gulls flew above the beach, and as Kline ran between the pinnacles of rock, sinking inches into the dull brown sand, the sea-birds scattered from the shore, shrieking in their shrill and raucous fashion, swirling above his head, crying in anger.

He sat on the sand for a while, using his jacket as a seat, and watched the wild sea surging towards him, only to seep into the sand and recede backwards into the heaving, white-flecked ocean. He loved the feeling of desolation, and the sense of being in a place of primeval nature – though children's plimsoles had swarmed about these sands for generations, the beach was essentially as it had been before a 'day by the sea' had been quite so commonplace.

It was a question of perspective. To look through the right eyes, and from the right angle, the sea and the cliffs – with not a house in sight – might have been features of any age. And yet – in the interests of accuracy – Kline knew that this coastline had changed radically in just the few thousand years that man had lived here, and built structures here, whether wood and brick and modern, or earth-covered tombs dating back to some four thousand years before Christ.

At the tip of a small island, called Er-Lannic, which lay close to the land in the Gulf of Morbihan, was a ring of stones, a Megalithic structure every bit as enigmatic as those at Avebury, in Wiltshire, or Stanton Drew in Somerset. The ring was submerged beneath the sea which had risen over the centuries, and half of a second circle, attached to it, was also submerged, its nearer stones rising from the waves when the tide was low, as so many dark fingers. It was into that Gulf that he now peered, though that particular small island lay hidden behind a headland to the north. Sea level changed, and this coast and this gulf had changed, and so there was no real understanding of what the sands had been like when they had first witnessed ancient man beaching upon them in his black skinned craft, reaching for this new land, leaving the old lands far behind.

The signs of those ancient arrivals were everywhere to be seen. They had built massive tombs, of stone and earth, and cleared land for their farms and houses. They had erected stones in lines and circles, to mark their existence in mortal fashion. They had had no need of forts, not in those early days, not in those times of struggle against an enemy that fought not with sword and spear, but with nature herself. They had left their mark, as proud and prominent as might any man of money. They had worked in stone, and stone – unlike wood or metal – sees down a million years of time, is as strong and permanent as the earth itself, for it *is* the earth itself, crystallized and shaped, and forged into symbols of mankind's strength and determination by the forces of the earth that man, at this time, was learning to tame.

Here on the shore, drenched by icy spray and deafened by the thunder of crashing waves, Kline thought of all these things, and recognized, too, stone shaped by those same forces, but in a more natural way: crags and pinnacles of rain-scoured rock that seemed to speak their earthly origin as if to remind him that it was the earth that initiated, and man that mimicked. Here we are, cried the grey rock on the storm shore, here we are, a memorial to a darker past than that of your stone-age workers in our fabric.

And for long minutes, loving the isolation and the presence of older times, Kline was content to listen to those voices.

After a while, feeling refreshed and excited, he weaved his way through the tangle of bracken on the steep slopes, back to the Citröen. Across the wild sea he could make out the faint outline of land, much obscured by distance and sea-mist; he couldn't be sure what he was looking at, because he had no real idea where along the road to Vannes he was. But he sensed instinctively that he was looking at the peninsular of Quiberan, where there were so many ancient monuments, and where Crazy Lady lived.

He drove on. In Auray he asked at the gendarmerie for precise directions to the farmhouse where Crazy Lady lived. They knew of her there, and while one man gave instructions in near-perfect English, two others laughed quietly, made jokes about her and annoyed Kline intensely, even though he had done much the same a few months ago.

He almost missed the trackway to her house, flying past it far too fast, and only realizing his mistake when he caught a glimpse of the sprawling white-walled house through a cleared area of the tall pines that lined the road here.

He backed up and drove along the bumpy track, and found himself in a wide, chicken-filled yard facing an attractive, well-thatched building, with low doorways and shuttered windows. Open barns and sheds blocked his view of the wooded land beyond the yard. Buckets and sacks were stacked in no particular order, and a long, ancient-looking saloon car was parked close to the house, its boot open, its passenger door open and its radio playing loudly.

Kline sat in the car for a few minutes and watched for movement. He saw none. Finally he climbed from the Citröen and walked to the open door of the farmhouse; he knocked loudly and peered into the well-lit interior. He was staring into a wide, low-ceilinged kitchen, its bare floor-boards scattered with sawdust and substantially covered by an enormous unpolished wood table on which plates and cutlery were piled. An open fire burned pine-wood, and the smell was exquisite. He also smelled coffee, and chickens. The wall above the fire was hidden behind a single, enormous black and white photograph of a standing stone, taken in the correct conditions for emphasizing its mystery: against a dark sky, with stormy clouds in evidence, and its features highly emphasized by light and shadow. Kline felt the mystery of that stone. For over a hundred years artists and photographers had attempted to capture just such an atmospheric quality around the stone circles that were their subject matter, reasoning that lumps of rock photographed on sunny days didn't impart the same 'druidic' mystery as bleak and desolate stones photographed on bleak and desolate landscapes. And this stone, he could tell, was no more than three feet high, though in the picture it seemed enormous. Everyone wanted to make the stones seem to tower above man's head; at Stonehenge those bronze-age memorial stones *did* tower above the human spectators; even so, early artists, Stukeley and his like, had increased the height of the stones in their pictures to give that extra meaning to the word 'megalith'.

A woman entered the kitchen; she was well wrapped against the outside cold, and carried a basket in both arms. She was about sixty and her grey hair was tied in a tight bun on top of her head. Red faced, she immediately smiled as she saw Kline, not startled, nor wary.

'Madame Jeury?' asked Kline politely. She was a lot older than he had hoped, and expected, but really that didn't matter now.

But the woman was shaking her head. She spoke quickly, too quickly for Kline to make any sense of her words, apart from the negative reply to his question.

He smiled and looked politely dazed. 'Jecompronpas. Pardon,' he said, pleased with the effective run of words, and the Frenchness of his French.

'Ah, Americain!' said the woman. 'M'sieu Kline. Forgive me. I forget you come.'

How did she know I was American? Kline grumbled quietly. Was his accent that bad?

She was saying, 'Madame Jeury is at Le Menec. She asks that you meet her up there. You know where that is, Le Menec?'

'I have a map,' said Kline, producing a holiday brochure and then frowning. The stylized map showed tents and fishing sites, but no tourist attractions. 'I didn't have time to get a proper map,' he explained, stuffing the brochure – the man had assured him it possessed an excellent map of the area – into his jacket pocket.

The woman led the way outside the house and loaded her basket into the car. 'I go to Carnac, so I must lock the house. Otherwise you could stay inside.'

'That's OK,' said Kline. The old woman pointed out directions to him and he followed her to the road before waving briefly and travelling north again. He felt slightly annoyed that Madame Jeury had not been at home to meet him, after he had so specifically mentioned his arrival time in the telegram. But perhaps it was too much to expect people to change their working plans at such short notice. And he *was* an hour later than he had said. That stop on the beach, and the drive being longer than he had anticipated, had thrown his timings considerably.

Despite the instructions having been complicated, he reached the hamlet of Le Menec in ten minutes, parked the car and stood up to survey the land before him. His attention was rivetted upon the stones, line after line of them, stretching away to the East as far as he could see. Some were tall, most were short, and the further away the lines of monoliths stretched, the smaller the size of the stones.

But they made a breathtaking spectacle, and as he walked among them, touching their cold surfaces, treading down the bracken and gorse and scrubby grass, he forgot about the nearby houses and the closed tourist-information shop, and the Volkswagen that roared noisily along a road nearby. He had eyes only for the standing stones; he had ears only for the wind, and the rustle of bracken; he smelled only the heaviness of the air, the mist, the sweet smell of late autumn vegetation.

He had walked two hundred yards, intellectually immersed in this enigmatic roadway of standing rock, when he saw the woman ahead of him. She was seated on a stone, her legs dangling from it, not quite touching the ground. She was looking away from Kline, to the north, and the wind was blowing her short, brown hair away from her face so that Kline could see her eyes were closed, her whole expression one of exultance.

As he approached her she heard him and straightened, turning slightly to watch him walking towards her. She didn't move from the stone, but her face hardened. Her skin was very tanned, and there were attractive lines at the corners of her mouth and eyes. She was dressed youthfully, in a short fawn coloured raincoat, with a red scarf tied tightly around her throat and long brown boots. Her fingers were covered with rings, gold and silver rings, with green stones – just green – flashing in the daylight. Kline thought she might have been in her late thirties. She was no older than that, he was sure, but she didn't look as young as June Hunter.

Why was he so obsessed with age, he wondered? Was it because he was obsessed with his own age, with growing older? It was certainly not that he had hoped in any way that she might be young and impressionable. The opposite, in fact. He knew, instinctively, that he would not have been able to fully trust and relate to a young woman claiming what Francoise Jeury was claiming. An old Crazy Lady was far more acceptable; but a Crazy Lady in her thirties was a challenge.

She jumped down from the stone and smoothed back her wind-blown hair. When she extended her hand Kline grasped it warmly, and she pressed his fingers tightly, firmly, as if reading things about him in the strength and easiness of his grip.

'M'sieu Kline,' she said, her accent not pronounced, but attractive. 'I'm glad to meet you.'

'And you. I'm sorry if I've interrupted your quiet mood.'

'Not at all.'

Kline was surprised at how well she spoke, and sounded, in English. Was this the woman whose letters in English took an hour to decipher?

He asked her if she had ever been to England, or America. She shrugged. 'To England a few times, on holiday. Why?'

'You speak the language very well.'

She laughed, a very pleasant sound, a very easy laugh. 'So do you.' She thrust her hands deep into her pockets and hunched a little against the cold. 'Shall we walk? Have you seen Le Menec before?'

'First time,' said Kline, glancing along the seemingly endless rows of stones. Francoise Jeury turned and began to walk slowly through the damp undergrowth.

'I love this place,' she said quietly. 'Sometimes by September the ground here is trampled absolutely flat by people. Other times, other years, it always seems wild among the stones. But by this time of year the fern grows up again, and the stones seem to settle a little bit more. They seem more relaxed, like your Horseguards outside Buckingham Palace. They know they aren't going to be pestered . . .' She chuckled, and Kline smiled politely.

'They're not *my* Horseguards,' he reminded her. 'And they're not outside Buckingham Palace. How many stones are here? Thousands I should think.' I ought to know, he thought to himself.

'Just over a thousand,' said Francoise more precisely. 'I don't know why anybody would want to count them. There must have been hundreds more once. The figure means nothing.'

'What do the stones mean, I wonder?'

She glanced back at him, her breath frosting slightly in the crisp air. 'You'd be surprised.'

'What do they mean to you?'

She stopped and considered his question, her face showing certain signs of suspicion. She was polite, but politely wary.

'Peacefulness,' she said. 'At this time of year, anyway. This area is full of peace, and silence, and the voices of other times.'

'I know just what you mean,' said Kline. 'I stopped on a beach on my way here and the atmosphere was just great; so natural, so undisturbed.

'I'm glad,' she said with a quick smile. Her eyes searched him for a moment, and she seemed pleased with what she saw. 'I guessed from your letters that you were a romantic. I knew you would like this place.'

They were out of sight of humanity, now, at least, if they didn't strain too hard to see. The grey stones, slick with moisture and coated with that grainy surface of dark lichen that so characterizes ancient stones, rose from their beds of bracken and browning grass, silent yet loud with the sounds of their enigmatic natures. Kline touched them, leaned against them, found himself searching for signs and carvings although he knew there to be none. He kept seeing a single carving from another stone, three hundred miles away. He kept seeing a stone of lighter grey, carved and pummelled into a different shape, a newer shape, but which would always be a relation to these aligned and fascinating Menec monoliths.

There was mischief in her eyes as she looked at him and said, 'So. You've come to Brittany to see me. Have you come to laugh at me?'

'To laugh?' Kline, taken aback, stopped and frowned, staring at her as she looked at him half amused, half challenging. 'To laugh at you,' he repeated. 'Why do you say that?'

'You laugh at me at home, don't you?'

'No. No, I don't. What makes you think I do?'

She shrugged, walked on, and after a second he followed, watching the way the wind tangled her hair. He was puzzled by her, finding himself slightly on the defensive, which was a place he hated to be.

'There is laughter in your letters,' she said. 'Always. I can tell. You write seriously, but there is always a smile on your face.'

'At first, perhaps . . .'

'Perhaps always!' She looked back at him, grinning, then biting her lip as she saw his discomfort. 'But I don't mind. As long as you don't laugh to anyone else.'

Kline said, quickly, 'Okay, dammit! So I laughed at you all the time. If it makes you happy to know that, then it makes me happy. But I'm not laughing now. I need your help.'

She seemed slightly disappointed, just for a moment, a fleeting second as she looked back at Kline and he saw the shadow on her face. 'Oh,' she said. 'Not a social call.' It was not a question, it was a statement, and Kline felt a twinge of unease, as if he had spoiled some developing dream of Madame Jeury's, or had trodden upon forbidden or difficult ground.

'I rarely make social calls,' he said. 'But I like to mix fun with business whenever I can.'

He had not intended the tone of his voice to be in any way suggestive, but being Lee Kline he had not been able to help it coming out that way.

Francoise's eyes shone, again, with that girlish mischief she had demonstrated before. 'Ah, I see. You want to have some fun with me as well as business, eh? Well, I don't know about that. You seem very young to me.'

'I'm thirty-two,' said Kline, going along with her.

'That's young,' she said, definitely. 'Too young.'

Trying to sound light-hearted, though he was burning to ask her about her work and her strange power, Kline said, 'You can't be much older than that.'

She turned on him sharply. 'Liar!' she said, then shook her head, vaguely amused, perhaps slightly irritated by him. 'My God, what an awful liar you are. I am much older than you and you know it too well.'

'Thirty-eight?' he said, suddenly lost, unable to determine whether this was mischief or anger that Madame Jeury was using against him.

'Forty-two, m'sieu. Ten years more than you. So be careful. I am *much* more experienced.'

She turned away again, walked on, crossing from one alignment of stones to another. Kline laughed quietly, uneasy, half amused; he followed her, kicking at the gorse and watching the way her body moved with such gentle ease. 'Don't bet on it,' he said, more to say something than to play her game.

Without turning she made a noise of scorn. 'Listen to him! He tries to become the man.'

'Madame Jeury, this isn't really . . .'

'Madame Jeury! My God, he even thinks I am his mother! So you see, you are much too young to have any fun with business.'

'You win,' said Kline, tired of the game. 'What do I call you?'

She laughed. 'How about "hey you". Or "you there".'

'I take it I can call you Francoise.'

'Why? Why should you call me that? It's only my name. People don't call people by their names, do they?' As if suddenly tired of this meaningless, and childish, banter, she said, 'Of course you can call me Francoise. You are Liam.'

'Lee.'

'Well, Lee. I am very glad you have come to see me, because not many people do that. In fact, I was thinking of perhaps coming to see you in London, but I never knew quite how to ask.'

'You'd be very welcome.' He refrained from mentioning that it was to get her to England with him that had brought him here. He sensed she would need subtle persuasion.

Always assuming she was what she claimed to be, and of that, for a while, he was not totally convinced.

The rain that had been threatening for some minutes began to fall, lightly, and freezing, causing the two of them to stop and turn back towards the distant cluster of buildings where both their cars were parked. They still walked slowly, hunched inside their coats, staring at the ground in thoughtful silence.

Then Kline, deciding it was time to break the ice on the subject of Francoise Jeury's alleged mysterious powers, said, 'I'm here because of your . . . ability. You know that.'

'Of course. I don't understand your embarrassment.'

He glanced at her, irritated, but she kept staring into the distance, walking carefully between the stones. Kline said, 'When you touch objects you can really . . . *see* things to do with the person who owns it?'

She smiled. 'Sometimes. Not always. Enough times that I know it is a real ability.' Now she looked at him, slightly puzzled. 'There are many people like me, Lee. You know that, surely. In London alone there are many people with abilities similar to mine. Some years ago I wrote to a few of them, to talk about what we were, what we represented. They are all interested only in . . . fairgrounds.' She smiled, shrugged. 'It's sad. Such a terrible way to abuse such a wonderful gift. But when no-one takes you seriously . . .'

Kline recalled, now that she mentioned it, having seen a bespectacled old lady on Irish TV a year back, when he had been on holiday; she had been telling a man in the studio audience facts about himself that were frightening him; she was holding his watch. He recalled how a second man had asked for the same treatment, sending his watch down to her and awaiting her revelations. There were none. She had said the watch must have been new to him, or not very personal. He said it was ten years old, and had been on his wrist all that time; it had been a present to him from his father whom he loved, and who had died a few days later. He had laughed. The old woman had not been embarrassed. Sometimes I get the feeling and sometimes I don't, she had said. Of *course*, the man in the audience had sneered, as if her failure with his watch had in any way negated her startling success with objects earlier in the show.

There had been someone else with her on that programme. An artist. A woman who sensed the spirits of the dead and drew them, like lightning, confident stroke upon confident stroke until features emerged, and always someone in the audience recognized the person. Kline remembered how the picture of a boy had brought associations of a *duck* into the psychic artist's mind. The woman in the audience who recognized the boy (she was in tears) explained how he had died of a fall from his window, holding his toy Donald Duck in his arms. Kline had been much impressed. The picture of an old man that emerged next sent one of the *camera crew* scampering home by taxi to fetch a photograph of her grandfather from her flat. The likeness was quite remarkable.

And of course, there was one sad, middle-aged lady in the audience who recognized *every* picture that emerged, bursting into tears (to the joy and delight of the audience) every time the face took shape.

It was a question of susceptibility to suggestion – of gullibility, to put if bluntly. There were always those who were too willing to believe and who could affect the serious assessment of the psychic in as damaging and negative a way as those who were totally unprepared to give the possibility of mental power the time of day. Fake psychics cashed in upon this readyness to believe, and though there were far fewer fakes than had been thought even recently, they were the only rationale for the shaky egos of those who doggedly, and with admirably persistent ignorance, refused to accept the evidence of their own eyes, and ears, and reasoning powers.

For Lee Kline it was not a question of belief or not in the alleged power of Francoise Jeury, but a question of whether or not she truly possessed the power she claimed. Kline was well prepared to acknowledge such power existed, but he was also well aware that what she claimed to be able to do could be accounted for by cryptamnesia, plus a superbly refined imagination. It would be very easy to *imagine* the events of the distant past, making them feasible and realistic even though they came, not from the unexplored depths of her association with a genuine 'recorded' atmosphere from the past, but from her highly inventive mind. She might not have been able to tell the difference.

But the power she claimed to possess could be tested, and could be tested easily and effectively, for it could be tested upon Kline himself.

His problem – which he was well aware was a major stumbling block – was in presenting his need for proof without totally alienating the woman from him, and from his cause. He knew, from the bitter experience of many students of the subject, how fragile, and sensitive were the egos of psychics, and how destructive to them was any scepticism and voiced doubt.

Whatever force was involved with the various uncanny powers, it was tenuous and insecure, and could often not operate under apparently perfectly relaxed conditions, conditions which in fact contained a strong measure of healthy doubt.

They reached the cars. Kline said, 'Back to the farm?'

'Of course. I need coffee. And it's a warmer place to talk in.' She smiled and climbed into her own Citröen; only two years old, it was as battered as Kline's. She roared in a wide circle and bumped across the grass verge at the side of the road before vanishing swiftly out of sight. Kline followed as best he could, but his own car would not give him the same peak of speed. When he came to a stop outside her farmhouse she was already inside, messing at the kitchen bench, preparing ground coffee.

Kline closed the kitchen door and stripped off his coat, stretching his arms and walking to the wood fire that burned at the dining end of the large room.

'You don't mind sitting in here, I hope,' said Francoise. 'The other rooms are freezing. I spend most of my time in here.'

'It's very cosy.' Kline sat down on a wooden chair, adjusted his back so that the ribs didn't jar with his shoulder blades. He watched Francoise as she set the coffee percolator into action, then came and sat down across the wide, pinewood table.

After a long moment's silence, she said, 'Are you wondering if I'm just a little bit mad?'

Kline laughed, not as taken by surprise by the question as he might have been earlier in the morning. He was more relaxed, now, aware that Francoise Jeury was exactly the sort of woman who could make a fool of him if she tried, and that was something he not only hated (it left him very bitter when he was shown up, in private or in public) but *required* should not occur with this particular relationship.

'Well, yes,' he said. 'You make way-out claims. You suggest you can do outrageous things. It so happens I believe those outrageous things exist – I think the balance of evidence is in their favour. I also believe many people think they have powers they don't in fact have. But the powers you claim are pretty bizarre. I mean, they beat all, Francoise. Hands down. They stand apart from the rest because of their pure zaniness.'

'Excuse me?'

'Bizarreness.'

She smiled, shook her hair back and thought hard for a second. 'I see. Well, yes, I agree. Ten years ago I would not have agreed. Ten years ago I thought myself no different to anyone else . . . I just didn't know that most people couldn't feel about things the way I do. Think about that, Liam –'

'Lee.'

'Sorry. Lee. But think about that. I was just about your age, thirty-two. Pretty old, no? Pretty experienced. I had been married for five years. I had had . . . three lovers? Maybe. I can't remember. I was well adjusted, a very alive person. Thirty-two years of age. And I didn't know I was unusual.'

'But by thirty-three?'

'By thirty-three I knew. In one short year, just one summer and one winter, I knew what I was, and then . . . well, I became more of what I am. The power, or the ability, or the gift . . . whatever you choose to call it, increased; or perhaps I just became more aware of it.' She stared at Kline through eyes that were narrowed and filled with the sadness of remembered hurt. The deep tan of her face could not hide the pallor of her skin, a sickly pallor, the colouring of one who is reliving something most awful.

'Was it when your husband died?' said Kline, deciding, without really consciously coming to the decision, that callousness was the best way to break what he saw as an imminent wave of self pity.

She frowned, looked angry for a moment, then looked down. The coffee percolator was bubbling away, making strange abdominal noises. 'Yes,' she said quietly. 'He died. And when he died my nightmare began.'

Kline couldn't – wouldn't? – help himself. 'Oh Christ,' he said with barely concealed derision. 'How about that coffee?'

But Francoise leaned forward on the table and clasped her hands in front of her. She studied Kline for a long moment, and he felt her gaze on his lips and eyes and hands. Finally she smiled, in a patronizing, almost angry way. 'Some people would have been sympathetic. But not you . . .'

'Not me,' agreed Kline. 'I'm sorry, but that's the way I am.'

'Did you think I was going to become boringly sentimental?'

'I didn't think. Period. As I say, it's the way I am. The past is dead, and I have no time for being sorry about it. It fascinates me, excites me, but I don't expect it wants my tears.'

'It doesn't . . . and nor do I.' She stared at him, her face deep coloured with her angry flush. 'But you asked me a question and I was trying to answer it. I'm not like you. I find the past painful to talk about, to re-live.'

'Then don't talk about it.'

She smiled thinly and finally shook her head, almost in resignation. 'No. I don't think I will. You seem almost proud of your coldness. I should hate to be inside your head.'

Kline mimicked her hand-clasping posture, leaned towards her. 'Francoise, I really don't want you to think badly of me. I really hope you can accept me as I am. But I haven't the time to worry about what people think of me. I haven't the time to drum my fingers on the table and listen to sad stories. Ten years is another age.'

'Not for me.'

'But why? You seem to have centuries at your command. You have a thousand lives you can share. You have a rare gift, and a great talent. Why squander time on empty memory. He's dead; you're alive. Why regret the status quo?'

She exhaled slowly, angrily, but after a moment Kline noticed the flare of hostility fade a little; her features softened. She said, 'I loved Antoin very much. I think you know that, and I don't believe you are not sensitive to my feelings. Your rudeness is not honest, it's a game. You are trying to deny my problems so that we can talk only about yours.'

'Bullshit.'

'Excuse me?'

'Merde du taureau,' he said with difficulty.

She hesitated, puzzled for just a second, then grasped what he had said. Unexpectedly she laughed. 'You don't think I have problems?'

'Of course you have. Everybody has problems. Problems are passé. Problems are irrelevant.'

'Irrelevant,' she repeated, allowing herself to smile. 'Ah, m'sieu Kline, how young you are. How naive.'

'Jesus!' said Kline, before he realized she was teasing him. Then he grinned as Francoise laughed and rose from the table. She fetched the percolator and dismantled it on the side, then located two large, earthenware mugs. 'Black? Sugar?'

'Black. No sugar.'

She poured, and for a few seconds their attentions were rivetted on the gushing black liquid, as if in that ebony stream of taste and perfection they could observe some common ground between them.

When his mug was full Kline reached for it. 'Smells good,' he said.

'Smells good? I wonder . . . is that an insult, or a compliment? I don't understand you enough to know. It must be an insult. You obviously don't know how to be kind.'

'Oh yes I do, Madame. I know how to be kind.'

'Kind to young women.'

'Kind to *everybody*.'

'That's what I said. Every young woman's body.'

Kline settled back in his chair, staring at the older woman, finding himself torn between sharing her narrow, teasing grin, and leaping to the defensive.

How hard it was to read this lady. Was it mischief or malice? Did she really think of him as some child, too young for any interest apart from a patronizing interest? He couldn't believe that. So she was playing games, challenging him to some sort of a verbal and emotional duel. He'd started it, though more by accident – he couldn't keep his instinctive feelings bottled – than by design. He'd known he was being crass when he dismissed her grief so easily, so insensitively. It happened to be the sort of crassness he approved of in others, and in himself, so from his viewpoint it was not a crime. It was honesty, and a pragmatic approach to their new relationship calculated to establish a working basis without an emotional one.

But then, why didn't he want an emotional relationship?

As he watched Francoise sipping her coffee he sensed her repressed sex, and found himself stirred by her looks, and by her strength. She threatened him. He knew that. He wasn't that unaware of his ugly maleness that he couldn't spot his own ego bristling with irritation when confronted with a woman who was stronger, and quicker, and sharper than he was.

He decided that perhaps he should rectify any damage that might have been done, and try and be less aggressive. 'I apologize,' he said.

Her eyebrows rose and she looked momentarily astonished. Then she said, 'Knight to Queen's Bishop four.'

'Excuse me?' he mimicked.

'You play your relationships like I play chess. Each move calculated, each concession part of a greater plan to enable you to win.'

There was no denying it. He conceded the point without embarrassment, saying, 'Okay. I'll go along with that. I *still* apologize. I *still* need your help. I still have nagging, I hope not destructive, doubts about your talent.'

'Now we get to the point! You want proof.'

'I want proof.'

'And if I said, go to hell? Accept me as I am, or not at all?'

He hesitated only moments before he said, 'Then maybe I'd . . . beg?'

She scorned him with her laughter. 'You wouldn't. You've never begged in your life. No, Lee. If I said to hell with your proof, you would shrug and accept me as I am. If you have come to Carnac because you need my help, it is because you are more prepared to believe I can supply that help than that I might be a *long shot*. Am I right?'

'I guess you are,' said Kline, raising his mug to her, which she acknowledged by raising her own. They drank coffee and sat in silence. The fire crackled in the grate, and Kline turned to watch the logs of pine slowly darkening and crumbling beneath the flames.

Francoise Jeury said, 'Give me your ring.'

'Which ring? This ring?' Kline held up his left hand and toyed with the ebony signet ring he wore on his little finger. It was onyx, set in twenty two carat gold, and it had hardly been off his finger in twelve years. He twisted the jewel so that its gleaming face watched him, and as he most frequently did he brought it to his mouth and licked the cold surface of the stone. 'This ring?' he repeated.

'That ring,' said Francoise. 'I obviously know it is important to you. Maybe I can learn a little more about you than you would like. It's up to you. If the ring is close to you, I will certainly be able to sense why, and from whom, and for what, and when, and why you are sad about it.'

'Who said I'm sad about it?'

'You did.'

'I said nothing. I uttered not a word. Who says I'm sad about it?'

'You did.'

'But I didn't.'

'Not in words. Words are only the newest and crudest of the means of communication at our disposal. You understand?'

'You read my sadness in other ways. In my eyes perhaps, or my mood. Yes, I understand.'

'Good. Give me the ring.'

Reluctantly he obliged her. She detected his reluctance and grinned, perhaps sensing something she was well acquainted with – the hesitation of the sceptic when faced with the possibility of incontrovertible evidence to prove him wrong. But this was not why Kline hesitated. The ring was almost a part of his finger; he took it for granted. It had been there so long, and witnessed so many hours of his life, and his emotional fluctuations, that he was almost reluctant to let that store of personal memory be released.

Realizing this, understanding, his first impulse was to refuse her the courtesy of demonstrating her talent; he no longer needed the proof. He was convinced – the inner man that haunted him, that ruled him, was convinced, or he would not have been so afraid of allowing another human being access to his privacy.

But he placed the ring in Francoise's palm, and watched as she closed her fingers over it. He met her green-eyed gaze, and nodded, and for a second she sought his soul in that gaze, an intermingling of silent comment and a brief glimpse beyond the mask he wore so aggressively – it was a moment during which she entered his body and his mind, and allowed him, too, a glimpse into her own head.

In an instant, that instant of submission, he was sexually aroused, and flushed deeply; he was awkward and embarrassed, and yet, whereas an hour before she might have commented on the fact, she allowed his momentary release to pass unobserved by voice; but she had noticed, and by all the signs she gave him, she was pleased. Kline felt warm, the warmth of disconcertment, and the warmth of comfort, of relaxation. He wanted to reach out and clasp this woman's hands in his, to hold her, to feed upon her life force and grow closer to her.

He recalled June Hunter saying something similar to him, and in that momentary loss of concentration, with the images of another place, and another woman flooding through his mind, he withdrew from this intimacy with Francoise Jeury, and sat back in his wooden chair, staring at her hands.

As was she, her gaze centred and concentrated on the fingers that closed about the onyx.

And she seemed disturbed.

Abruptly, startling in the heavy stillness of the kitchen, the door was flung open and the housekeeper entered, shivering and making sounds of chill, slamming the door behind her as she tried to prevent the cold air swirling into the warm kitchen. Francoise smiled, and said something in French that Kline missed, but which made both women laugh. The old woman left the kitchen, shrugging off her coat and making a vague acknowledgement to the American. In stillness again Francoise reached out and placed the onyx ring back in Kline's hand.

'I am very sorry,' she said. 'Your watch might have been less personal, and less embarrassing.'

'You saw, then . . .'

'Stevie?'

The blood drained from Kline's face. Even ten years after they had split, mention of her name sent his pulse racing, and a cold chill fleeing through his deeper regions. He hated to hear her name, *that* name. It explained his reluctance to be seen with straight-haired brunettes. He liked women with fair hair, or blonde hair, or red hair, or anything that wasn't deep brown, like wood, like dark, smouldering wood, because it always reminded him, and he was, after all, a weak and drifting human soul.

'How can a man as insensitive, and unemotional as you, manage to be so strong in his feelings for a single woman?'

'Perhaps she drained me,' said Kline, and that, he knew, was probably true, because when he had found her in *his* bed, with someone he had very much respected, he had sworn that he would never again make a fool of himself with a woman. He loved women, and he respected women, in the same way that he could love and respect humans of either sex, people who were friends; he was not a cold man. But there could never be *that* sort of love again, not when love could be so easily, and so disgustingly, shattered in the space of a few days.

Francoise had obviously seen everything. Gently, speaking carefully as if she searched for the right words, not because of her different natural language but because of the temperament of the man who sat opposite her, she told Kline what he already knew far too well; she recounted images that were tightly locked away in his mind, but which he too frequently found surfacing without his bidding. She let him know that *she* knew, and that she had found it through the ring that Stevie had given to him, when they had decided . . . so long ago now! . . . that the stately, and ordinary, and clichéd institution of marriage was definitely for them.

That had been two years before she had proudly boasted that she had been to bed with every one of his friends (and Francoise reminded him, with horrifying precision, that he had countered with the fact that he had been to bed with every one of *hers*).

Why did he continue to wear the ring? He didn't know. When he had stormed out of Stevie's life, the angry hypocrite, he had been sorely tempted to destroy the ring, but then . . . something . . . something had changed his mind.

So Francoise Jeury told him that too, explained it to him as if he was a child learning basic human attitudes from an older, wiser, more experienced psychologist. She told him only that which he knew to be true, but which he had repressed. In the ring was a symbol of success, for he had succeeded . . . he had won Stevie's love, and gone on to establish what in most other times, and in most other places, would have been a lasting and successful relationship. It was *his* time and *his* place that had defeated that initial success – Berkeley, the age of flowers and grasses, and peace and ignorance, and opposition to war, and opposition to progress . . . it was that age that had destroyed the dream, and in the ring was a symbol of the moral attitude he despised. And it symbolized his single moment of weakness, of defeat, for thereafter he had resolved never to be defeated again; the ring, while he wore it, reminded him of the fact that his moment of weakness was past; he could never be weak again, he could never fail again. The ring was his failure. He wore it as a shield against the future.

It was something else, too, Francoise went on. It was Stevie. She had given the ring to him with love, and while he wore it he possessed the ghost of that love. Without that ghost, he sensed that Stevie could not love again. To wear her ring he wore her love, as a trophy, a severed head, an enemy head: it made him think that she would not be happy, wherever she was, because she had given him something and he would never give it back.

'Damn right,' he said quietly, as Francoise ceased speaking. He slipped the ring back onto his finger. As the woman had been talking to him he had felt his anger rising, anger not with her, but with Stevie . . . that same anger, all over again. He felt cold, now, as cold as he had felt when she had publicly bragged her conquests. It was not the deed that had broken them, he didn't acknowledge the relevence of the word 'faithfulness' or 'betrayal', not in that way, not so superficially. But she had used it as a weapon against him, and his love had turned to bitter hatred in less than the passing of a single breath.

'Damn right,' he said again, and kissed the ring, and grinned.

It grew hot in the kitchen, uncomfortably hot, and Kline sensed it was not the gathering warmth of the log fire, but some strain between them. Francoise seemed ill at ease, now, almost worried. She watched the table, and her clasped hands, and Kline could almost see the frown that her face doggedly refused to display. After a while he began to look lingeringly about the kitchen, finding no comfort in the shadowy movements on the walls, put there by the fire as the skies, outside, darkened enough to make the light filtering through the tiny windows almost dusk-like and inadequate.

When Francoise abruptly suggested a tour of the farmhouse, Kline readily agreed. He hated such conventional niceties with a vengeance, but this time was glad of the distraction. Francoise called for her house-help and gave concise instructions for lunch. She had ordered steak for him, and chicken for herself; she was partially vegetarian, hating red meat. At times, she told him as they walked through the creaking farmhouse and looked at plaster walls and bitumen-painted wooden beams, she existed totally on fruit. But only during the summer. During the winter she made vague acknowledgement of the carnivorous part of her soul.

Still, however, she was tense and almost upset. Her hands shook a little as she pointed things out to Kline, and the lines, etched around mouth and eyes, now evidenced as lines of tension, the wrinkles of skin drawn taut with anxiety.

'You haven't upset me,' he said, fishing, 'by exposing my sordid and clichéd little love hassle.'

'I have upset myself, though,' she replied quietly; she looked at him, frowning and harrowed. 'My God, Lee, can't you even tell that? You say you're not upset yourself, well, maybe you're not. You have your proof, and ten years . . . well, that's ten ages as you said.' Her smile was token, a reminder that she referred to his own words. 'To you, though it still hurts, it is the dead past. To me . . . oh, I don't know.'

'But if I'm not upset . . . I don't understand why you feel it necessary to be.' He took her arm, stopped her slow amble through a low-ceilinged room with no furniture in it but a wooden chair and locker. A single picture, of a man in the uniform of the French air force, hung on the otherwise bare, white-washed wall opposite the door. Francoise closed her own hand over his, pressing his fingers into the flesh of her arm. She stared at the picture, then released Kline and walked towards the ornate, chipped, gold frame. 'My husband,' she said. Kline had guessed.

'He's a handsome man.'

Francoise laughed, bitterly, scornfully.

'I'm sorry,' said Kline, recognizing that he had responded in a childish, male way.

But Francoise herself apologized. 'He *was* handsome, yes. Inside and out. He was such a very strong man, Lee. Peacefully strong. He knew what he wanted, so well, so precisely. He could sense alternatives for our future as I could sense the past. He was so precise, so ordered – he planned for his death. He died in one of the ways he had worked out, a crash . . . and I just sat back and an immense machinery took care of everything. There was nothing for me to do except to cry. Even now I do nothing. I clean, I run this small farm, I sell things, I write, I walk, I teach languages sometimes, and sometimes I allow tourists to stay in my farmhouse for high prices. I don't need the money. Antoin had taken care of everything.'

They walked away from the picture, back the way they had come, towards the kitchen. 'At first,' she went on, 'I was glad. Then I was so angry! He must have thought I had no ability whatsoever. He must have mistrusted me so much that he couldn't bear to think of me fending on my own for the rest of my life. I hated him for some years, then. I am a strong woman, and he had smothered me with orderliness, and I could have coped. I have coped. Soon I was glad of what he had done, because I needed to hide here, without concern and without worry.'

'Because this strange ability came on very strong, right?'

'I suppose,' said Francoise reflectively, 'I suppose that I always had some sixth sense. It was always there. I always could play games of guessing things so very well, especially as a child. At school I was either hated or loved because I knew so much, could see so much. I thought it was luck. You know, if you are a really good card player, things like poker, always winning, people say "lucky streak". They can win all their lives and never wonder about how bizarre that is. You know? I was the same. I never wondered that I knew so much about my girl-friends at school, finding out about them before they even spoke about their home lives. I frightened them, sometimes, but gradually the sixth sense seemed to go away. This happens a lot, Lee. Children are enormously powerful psychics; most children are psychic to some degree. I think it's because they need to be constantly aware of their parents, of where they are, like wild animals, always aware of what the adult animal is doing, always ready to follow. I'm sure this happens, and of course, not just in man, in animals too, as I say. We have it very refined, but as children become mature, as they are expected to defend themselves and not depend on their father and mother for protection, the ability wanes. With me, when Antoin died, it came back very, very strongly.'

'Why? Did you ever wonder why that happened?'

'Oh yes. I'm sure it is the security, the need for security. Antoin, so organized, so dependable, so smothering, was a very secure symbol to me. When he was gone I needed my animal power, to be aware; I was like a child again, loose in the herd. I needed all my wits. But I was settled, secure in myself. When my grief was gone, the ability remained. I had friends, and they came to hate me. I understood them too well. It was frightening for me also. I would find myself bending to people or away from them according to how I sensed they needed me. I would sympathize, or criticize, or respond on levels that they were unaware of, deep levels, that to me were very obvious levels. Can you imagine how disturbing that was for people? They became very uneasy with me. It was as if they knew I could see; their own powers, unrefined, were enough to make it clear to them that I was a sort of spy. I would touch their hands, all the time, holding hands with friends. I love to touch people. I was reading from their rings, their bracelets; I sensed it from objects in their houses, and perhaps a little from their bodies themselves.'

They were back in the kitchen, now, cool from the walk through the unfurnished, unwarmed parts of the house, and they stood for a minute in front of the fire. The housekeeper was busy at the stove, and Kline could smell steak, and it was a pleasant smell; he felt as if he had not eaten in hours.

'All my life, Lee, I have been haunted by this terrible inability not to see people deeper than they want me to. I came here soon after Antoin died . . . this was our country house . . . I came here to escape them, to hide. For a long time, Lee, I have hidden here, away from people as friends. I see people all the time, in a market, where the emotions are like a fog, a haze. I can be normal here, on my own. Lotte . . . ? Well, we never speak very much; we are not great friends. We are comfortable with each other, and she is gone by evening, and usually I am out during the day. So it works.'

Kline stared at her for a moment. She was more relaxed now, and the tense lines in her face had softened. She looked very attractive, and the yellow glow from the fire in the grey room gave her face an almost unreal appearance, a mask. Her hair had fallen across her cheeks, and she brushed it back almost irritably. Kline suddenly realized she was smiling. Her glance, when she looked at him, was mischievous. 'What are you thinking?'

'I was wondering why you chose to let me know about your power. In one of your recent letters.'

'I don't know.' Her smile vanished, but she did not grow cold. Suddenly she turned from the fire and leaned against the wall that surrounded the open place. She reached out and took Kline's hand, and pressed the fingers warmly. Cocking her head she searched him, and for the life of him he didn't know what she was looking for. 'Perhaps,' she said, 'I felt close to you in your letters. You write very warmly. I saw laughter, but I also saw a compassion that for a while today I thought I must have mistakenly seen. But you *are* a compassionate man, with a terrible fear of letting it be seen. But it was there, in your writing. Your first letter was formal; but by your second I felt that we were friends. Do you understand what I mean?'

'Very much so,' said Kline softly. 'Thank you.'

'For what?'

'For what you said. Now I think of it, yes, there was a feeling of being relaxed with you as well. Your letters scared me, puzzled me, but I felt very close to you very quickly, even though you told me nothing personal – nothing that was not about the past.'

'Words can be very powerful,' she said.

'When you can read them,' he added, and with a gasp of amused resentment she pinched the flesh of his wrist and let go his hand.

Kline's steak was ready. They sat down at the table and he ate quietly. It was tough, and cooked medium rare. He didn't object to either state of nature, for his income was so low that he could rarely afford steak at all, and when he did it was just such cheaper cuts, cooked just as indifferently. What did bother him was the lack of any vegetable, but he said nothing. He had finished when Lotte brought Francoise's chicken, two breasts, sliced thin and gently fried. She ate these on their own too, and Lee felt slightly glad that he didn't have to depend on eating here too often.

When they had finished Francoise went to a small cupboard and fetched out a bottle of red wine, unlabelled. She drew the cork and sniffed the rim of the bottle, smiling appreciatively. 'This is a good one. You like red wine? This is local wine, and it varies enormously in quality. But this bottle, it's good.' She fetched two glasses, then sat down again, filled the tumblers until Kline felt uneasy with the quantity of alcohol he would have to consume, then raised her glass to him. She drank several mouthfuls and made a childish lip-smacking sound of enjoyment. 'Good wine,' she repeated, and prompted Kline to drink.

It was sharp wine, with a lingering aftertaste, what he referred to as a *fur*. It was the most appalling red wine he had ever tasted, and after one mouthful he doubted he could finish the glass.

'Good?' she asked. He smiled. 'Yes. Thanks.'

Now she laughed, her eyes shining as she regarded him. 'Lee. Don't do things like this!'

He forced a pleasant expression, though right then he felt more like throwing the glass of drink all over her. *Dammit!* One moment warmth, the next moment a stupid game. What was she trying to prove?

'Don't do things like what? Like being polite?'

She nodded. Her eyes were on his lips, disconcerting him. 'Yes,' she said. 'No need. It's awful wine. I don't mind if you say so. Unfortunately it's the last bottle until tomorrow.'

'It's awful wine. I can't finish it.'

'But Lotte will. Lotte! Du vin!'

Lotte laughed as she took Kline's glass away and practically drained it. She thanked them both, and seemed well content. She had obviously enjoyed it. It occurred to Kline that she'd probably made it.

'Now, Lee, we must come to the point of your visit. You said you wanted my help. Well, I'm prepared to offer it. What is it you want?'

'I want you to come back to London with me.'

Her face shadowed, and she stared at her glass. 'Well, I don't know about that.'

'It's important, to me, and to a woman there, and to a boy . . . a nine-year old boy, who needs help very desperately.'

She looked up, her lips pursed thoughtfully. She said, 'A boy needs my help? What boy?'

'That comes later,' said Kline. 'First . . . there's something else I want to know about you.'

'Stones,' said Francoise, and Kline frowned, feeling the blood race in his body, and a rapid wave of irritation fly through him. 'I'm sorry,' she went on quickly, leaning back and sipping at her glass again. 'I'm afraid you rather telegraphed that. I don't think I was spying, you just let me know too well.'

'Yes. Okay, it doesn't really matter, does it? Stones. You and standing stones. Your ability and stones.'

'What has stones . . . *have* stones, excuse me . . . to do with a nine-year old boy?'

'Later,' insisted Kline. 'You read about me from my ring. You understand people from objects in their houses. Can you read the past in a standing stone? Can you?'

She hesitated just a moment, an uncertain moment, before saying, 'No.'

Kline collapsed backwards against the uncomfortable wooden back of his chair. He exhaled loudly, shaking his head with all the despair he suddenly felt.

Francoise finished what she had begun. 'Not always.'

'Not always! Then sometimes you can . . . sometimes . . .'

'Not always, therefore sometimes. Yes. That follows.'

'Don't play games with me, Francoise. You *can* read standing stones. What do you see? Tell me! Tell me what you see in them!'

'*Tell* you, *tell* you what I see in them!' She mimicked angrily. 'Why? Why should I *tell* you, *tell* you what I see in them? What business is it of yours?'

'Come on, lady, stop fucking around. I need to know.'

'Well that's so nice for you, but I suggest you learn some manners before you go demanding that I do just what you want.'

'For Christ's sake, Francoise . . . what is it with you? I'm not attacking you. I'm not trying to bully you. I'm excited by what you tell me. You can't say that standing stones are emotional. You can't tell me that what you see in them upsets you like a ring, or a watch or your friends upset you. Now can you?'

She shrugged; she looked bitter, but just a little repentant.

'How do you know? Did you ask me? No. I have explained . . . badly, I know . . . just what I am, and why I am hiding, and why my feelings are disturbed. But all you care about is how you can use me, how you can manipulate my talent to your own end. Deep concern I would not expect from you, not now, not having met you. But a gentle approach to your grasping demands I *do* expect.'

Kline stared at Francoise, his eyes narrowed, his breathing slow and considered as he tried to calm his suddenly tensed body. Why did she have such sudden, and bad, effects upon him? He was perplexed by her anger, by the unexpected outburst. There was no mischief now, no game playing, no gentle teasing. She was angry with him, angry because he had been excited. Damn the woman, he thought bitterly, what is *eating* her?

Francoise had drawn back her brown hair and squeezed it tight behind her head, trying to get it to stay put. There were tears in her eyes, in the corners, and her eyes glistened, shining with some intense brightness. Her lips were moist and looked fuller, almost pouting, at once both an attractive and angry feature. Her hands, clasped before her on the table, shook slightly, and her thumbs played criss-cross with each other.

After a moment she took a deep breath. 'I will not apologize for that,' she said quietly. 'I shall accept your nature, your insistence on *utility*, your lack of feeling. I accept that, but I shall not for the moment tell you what I see in a standing stone. I shall show you. Is that fair enough?'

Kline smiled in a friendly way. 'Yes. That's fair enough. But will you come to England with me?'

'Perhaps. I shall decide later.'

'I didn't mean to upset you.'

'What you mean is, you don't know *why* you upset me, but since you did, and since it stands to ruin your plans for me, you'd better put a humble mask on. Am I right?'

He shrugged non-committally. 'If you *keep* reading me, I'll clam up completely.'

She grasped his meaning after a second and laughed very pointedly. 'That won't stop me reading you, Lee. Oh no. You read like a book, like a child's book, with big print and explanatory pictures.'

'I get the message,' said Kline, unable to stop himself smiling at the image, hurtful though it was. 'Okay. Listen . . . you show me your stones, and tell me as much as you think you want to tell me. Then I'll tell you about a family in West London, and I think you'll want to come back with me to England more than anything else in the world. Is it a deal?'

'It's a deal,' she said, rising from the table and reaching for her coat.

He had expected to go by car, but she shook her head as they stepped into the cold, overcast day. She led the way through the yard, and behind a decaying wooden barn, through whose imperfect side-walls red, fat and inquisitive hens strutted and pecked.

A low wire fence bordered the edge of her land, and she walked, with Kline following, to a ramshackle gate that she pulled open, then re-latched behind them with a piece of wire. They were now on gently rising land, which was overgrown with weed and the remnants of some vegetable crop of a few years before; they walked steadily up towards a dark copse of pinewood that breasted and covered the top of the rise.

Kline scanned the woodlands, looking for the tell-tale breast-like hump of a tumulus, or the probing grey fingers of a stone circle, drowned in nettle and bracken, but just reaching a tip or two above the undergrowth. He saw none of these things, and when he walked into the shade, and warmth, of the trees, he asked where they were going.

'You'll see,' said Francoise, her breath frosting as she spoke, her progress loud and hindered as she weaved between trees, crunching and kicking at the dead and dying plant-life beneath her feet.

The ground sloped down again and they emerged from the trees onto a darkly grassed bank. A hundred yards away the silvery thread of a stream ran, winding and overgrown, through high earth banks and dense stands of dead-looking reeds. There were sheep here, and they scattered, adding their own dun colour to the land as they went.

Silently, Francoise led the way at an angle across the slope, gradually approaching the stream.

Where the soil was deeper a small stand of birchwood hugged the bank, their branches covering over the water; autumn leaved, the stream appeared to vanish into a dark tunnel, and Francoise entered this unhesitatingly. 'It's slippery,' she said. 'Watch your feet.'

Emerging from these trees they came out onto an unusually shaped bank of earth. Piled high and steep where the stream

133

curved tightly, but widely, to the left, the bank was covered with thorn bushes and small, almost shrublike trees which grew from the surface at a variety of angles. In summer, Kline recognized, this place would be totally hidden by blossom and growth of many forms. In winter, at the height of winter, it was probably reasonably accessible.

He followed Francoise almost to the stream itself, and managed to slip into the water and soak his feet. He cursed volubly and she laughed quite unsympathetically. 'There,' she said suddenly, and Kline ceased to shake his feet and murmur his irritation. He lifted his gaze to where she was pointing.

Half hidden by earth and brambles, three thin stones rose from the very edge of the stream. The tallest was perhaps five feet high, the other two, one on each side, were only just visible, perhaps three, three and a half feet in height. They had been erected in deep earth, and in summer – again – Kline realized they would be totally buried by plant growth. Even in winter, because of the high earth banks, and inaccessible route alongside the stream, they would probably remain concealed.

'Not many people know about these three stones,' she said. 'And I am glad about that. I found them by chance. Perhaps farmers here have known about them for many years, many centuries, but they have never reported them as far as I can find out. And they will never talk about them. They call this place the *la digue criant*, the *screaming dyke*. They don't know why it's called that, and they probably never heard a scream from here in their lives. Perhaps the legend began because someone, like me, saw what the stones were, and talked about it. If they were like me then they would hear screams all the time. Legends can begin like that.'

'I know,' said Kline, watching her.

As she had spoken so she had kicked through the tough bracken, easing the twisting, thorny stems away from her before applying the soles of her leather boots to the brambles, to hasten winter's killing task. Kline cleared a way to the stones before her. He was surprised to find them warm to the touch. They were lighter grey than the stones at Le Menec, and very different indeed to the irregular, towering stones in Avebury; in fact they reminded him of no standing stone, ancient or very very ancient, that he had ever experienced. He found he could not consciously define why.

As Francoise reached out to place her hands gently upon the tallest stone so she closed her eyes. After a moment Kline saw that beneath her healthy tan she had blanched considerably; her skin became pallid, awful.

After a while she shivered and drew her hands away, rubbing them together, perhaps to remove the dry and mossy dust from them, perhaps to brush away something more cloying, despite its intangible nature.

'Only that stone?' prompted Kline, watching her closely. As if he might share in what she had seen he too touched the stone again, running his hands across it as if he caressed some warmer, smoother surface.

'All three,' she said quietly. 'These are the strongest. A few of the stones in the alignments allow me access to the time of the builders, and just one in all those hundreds at Le Menec means something. But at Le Menec there is an atmosphere, a complete sense of the past. I don't always receive it, not today, for example. But once, in the snow, I walked through the stones and My God, Lee, there was such power there, such strength of vision. I could hear the language of those people, such a flowing language, unlike anything we know, not like Brythonic, or Welsh, or French or German. It runs smooth, like Chinese, very flat, and when the syllables are hard, they almost bite them out. When they cry out in surprise they cry *Cathug brin!* When they meet among the stones, in their great swathes of fur and skin, they exchange a fragment of carved bone and say *famus ranot reld.* It means may the power of rock and earth be in your bones and your sleep. I can hear the words so clearly, I can smell them . . . sometimes I can almost touch them . . .'

'You understand the meaning of language? Languages you've never experienced?'

'Not always. Sometimes my focus seems sharp, my senses acute. Other times everything is blurred, unreal. Almost dreamlike. I always see the same thing at Le Menec, a vague vision of some of the stones being drenched in animal blood, then painted in elaborate patterns with what I believe is human urine. I don't understand the meaning of it, or why only certain stones in the alignments were treated in this way. Some stones have animal carcasses tied to them. I have seen stones with human hair bound by cords of vine to the upper parts of them. Most stones stand then as they stand now, and I sometimes see meaningless rituals being carried out with sticks and cords, and blue-robed men who are constantly making respectful gestures towards a torch, carried and fuelled by a boy of no more than ten. I don't understand the rituals. The men of the communities here wear furs and skins stained a very bright blue, not a dark blue like the men of worship. They have green and red stripes on their skins, especially on their arms. The women have close-cropped hair, but there are younger girls with long tresses plaited a hundred times, and some have the thin plaits intricately twisted about to form bizarre patterns. The men are bearded, the beards cut square; their hair is tied back with leather, and many of them wear a circlet of leather, with a loose crown-piece of bramble, two twigs, crossing, fixed to the circlet at front, back and sides. It looks very peculiar. They all carry long spears, a whole bundle of them, but they seem very light-weight; they carry shorter tools with notches and designs carved on the hafts.' She broke off suddenly, glanced at Kline and frowned slightly. 'Did I already write all this to you? I did, I remember . . .'

'Sure. But it's good to hear it again. When you wrote first I found myself laughing. You were right, I did laugh at you. I wondered how the hell you could have known. I figured you were making educated – but wild – guesses. It was only after something happened – very recently – that I reconsidered what you had said, and wondered if you might be using the power you'd mentioned on the stones themselves. You mentioned arrow-heads, but never the stones.'

'Well now you know. I was. Stone axes tell me much, but the atmosphere of the stones tells me much more. If I said nothing in my letters it was because I felt it was my business only. Since I was a child I have had a love affair with stone, and earth. A real love affair . . . can you understand that?'

Kline understood that very well indeed, and said so. He added, 'What were these stones? Screaming dyke . . . screaming stones? Death stones?'

She glanced at him sharply, an expression he didn't understand; then her features softened and she smiled almost wryly. 'Well guessed. They were sacrificial stones. When I touch them I feel very close to death, and blood. It is truly a horrifying feeling, and yet . . . so much power from these stones, so much fear, so much pleasure, so much . . . sexuality. You understand? As the people were killed here, sacrificed to the gods of this water, and the earth around the water, they were often loving the earth and the stone across which they were being killed. I feel the intensity of that sexuality. It is often overwhelming. When I first touched this stone, this largest stone, I reached a strange sort of . . .' hesitating, she glanced towards Kline but did not quite meet his gaze; she seemed slightly embarrassed, something that passed and she looked almost challengingly at the American. 'A strange sort of orgasm. It was beautiful, in a cruel sort of way.' Touching the large stone again. 'They placed the severed heads upon the stones, and then baptized them with water from the river. Each man and woman and child sprinkled water across those horrible slack-jawed offerings, while the blood seeped down the stone, fertilizing and nourishing the earth.' She folded her arms about her, but this time not for relaxation but for some form of warmth, trying to drive away the chill of what she had glimpsed in this brief communication with the past.

'Let's go away from here. Do you mind?' She spoke not so much in earnest as with finality, moving back along the route they had come before Kline could answer. Kline glanced ruefully at the stones, his mind filled with thoughts, and ideas: there was a thought that he might make something of the reporting of these stones, but this he tried to overwhelm, for he recognized – within that selfishness – an enormous potential for dishonesty towards this bizarre French-woman, who was so willing to give of herself, and so insecure in the giving. There was also something approaching ecstasy as he realized that if the stone font in Higham contained any form of violent secret, which might help his understanding of the Hunter obsession, then Francoise Jeury – surely! – would be the woman to discern it.

He followed her, catching up with her as she scrambled quickly, almost breathlessly, up the scrubby slope towards the trees on the hill-top. Sweating hard, coldly damp inside his clothes, he tugged her to a halt and leaned heavily against the sticky bark of a young pine.

'You're unhealthy, M'sieu Kline,' she said, smiling. 'You should live in France, and walk three kilometres every morning and evening. And you eat red meat like you will die unless you get blood. That's very bad.'

'I know,' said Kline, 'but I like it.'

She made a sound that seemed to dismiss his words as not being worth the saying. 'Do you always give in to your desires? If you like something can you not rest until you get it, and enjoy it?'

'No games, Francoise. I'm too bloody tired. Jesus, you walk fast . . . and I don't understand why.'

'Why I walk fast?' she said quickly, annoyingly, deliberately mistaking his meaning. 'I do everything fast . . . except make love . . . oh ho, M'sieu Kline flushes. He *has* been to bed with me already in his mind.'

'No *games* Francoise, please! Why did you get upset down there, by the stones?'

She turned from him, solemn and suddenly serious. Her hands were thrust deep into the pockets of her beige gaberdine, and she looked like someone who has nowhere to go, nothing to live for. She ambled slowly away from Kline, hugging the edge of the wood, her head lowered, then lifted so she could gaze out towards the gulf. After a while Kline recovered his breath (how right she was about his fitness . . . she didn't need psychic powers to spot that) and walked after her. When she heard him coming she acknowledged his presence by a quick, searching glance across her shoulder. Then she said, 'It's the power of what I see, Lee. Not the power of memory, or the power of the men who kill those young people for their gods . . . it's just the power of everybody at that time.'

Kline shook his head, not understanding the precise nature of her allusion to 'power'. Did she mean power of personality, of wealth, of muscle? What *did* she mean?

'No, none of those. Not power like we understand power. But power like a psychic understands it. What you might call magical power, or supernatural power. The power to commune with nature . . . we can do that, you know. There are men who can talk to plants, and affect the way those plants grow. There are men who can relate to animals, even though those animals are ferocious, and wild.' Her voice lowered dramatically. 'Power such as I possess. I am . . . *espion* . . . spy, I am a spy, a necromancer. That's how I like to think of myself, Lee, watching and using the dead from my position of life.'

'I know. You said that in your last letter.'

'Did I? Oh yes. I did. I remember. Well, now you've seen me *necromancing*. I sense them so strongly, so powerfully, and I am sure they sense me . . .'

Kline gasped his surprise. 'You're joking . . . are you saying they can, what, sense the future, and see you watching them?' He shook his head. 'No, that's not possible.'

'Anything is possible. My God, Lee, their powers. They do things and take them for granted that we would write books about. They know their futures, their destinies. They consult strange oracles, strange augurs . . . they read the flights of birds, the ripples of water, the shape of sticks cast at random, the cracks in heat fractured stone. And there are other ages, more recent, a warrior age with iron swords, and the same sort of powers are there, but limited by then, restricted to a few. But I can still see them. They are aware of everything, and aware that they are a small part of something vast, and yet complete. Understanding their place in the nature of things they can use the whole of nature. It's wonderful. They read so many omens, and speak so many strange, magical words, but I believe that they work from their own deep powers, using these symbols only as a focus. Does that make sense?'

'It makes a lot of sense,' said Kline, thinking of the way an *ouija board* could be made to work. By focussing on the moving glass, and the letters and the board, and the atmosphere of the room, in fact by taking the concentration into the trivial, any local spiritual force, or energy, or whatever people liked to call it, could communicate its meaningless message through the *psyches* of those present. It was not, always, evil. There was so much raw energy in the so called spiritual atmosphere, or plane, that even a man alone in a room, contemplating nothing in particular, could tune himself into it. With the more organized focus of the seance it was like receiving the screaming energy of many of the dead; they were just echoes, ghosts. They gave their names, and their places of death, and if they had been in the army they might even have given their serial numbers. What they communicated was trivial information, because it was merely a recorded energy form that was communicating, and not a living, pulsating, evil creature, waiting to possess the unwary.

Or so Kline believed, having experienced evenings with a ouija board, and heard the fear of those who believed the board opened the way into a dark, frightening Universe of restless souls, and the beliefs of those who saw it as a way to communicate with those who had 'passed over'. He was convinced that the ouija board worked, and was more convinced of its essential meaninglessness.

In fewer words he told this to Francoise Jeury, and the woman looked thoughtful, and impressed. 'You believe in what the ouija does? You believe in living spirits?'

Kline sighed in irritable despair. 'No! I said I believe in spirits. I also believe in tape-recordings, in electromagnetically transmitted life and death on a television screen. I believe in the permanence, what J. A. Lawrence calls the "persistence of memory", not just in the human guise, but in many guises. The astral plane represents one. Your rocks, the things you see, represent another.' Still irritably: 'Comprenez?'

She flared, angered by his momentary facetiousness. 'Ah oui, I onnerstan meester Kline. Sankyew forr bee inga zo 'elpfool.' And without the silly voice. 'Bastard.'

'Oh Christ,' said Kline, quickly, ashamed of himself. 'Look, I apologize. And this time I mean it. Really.'

She inclined her head, smiling thinly, enjoying his discomfort. Then she reached out and took his hand. 'And this time I accept it. But I believe you are wrong not to believe in living spirits. There is more than "memory" involved.'

'But I have no proof of that.'

In mock frustration she bit his hand. 'You and your proof! If I told you we were at war again I suppose you would not believe me until you were shot.' She had stopped, leaving go of his hand. She turned and looked through narrowed eyes towards a place on the horizon where a low hummock, topped by stone, suggested the weathered presence of a tumulus. 'I see the past, and in a sense it lives for me, speaks to me. What I see there, apart from the way of life, and of death, is frightening. They play with magic, and with the soul of man. We always think of them as primitive, dressed in furs and chipping stone, but Lee . . . My God, they play with the forces of nature like we play with . . . with . . .' mischieviously, as she failed to find an apt metaphor, 'With each other. There was such awesome power in those days, such terrifying abilities to summon the dark spirits of a world which, when you think coldly about it, is *this* world, *this* earth on which we stand. The earth has not changed, man has! What was in the earth then is in the earth now. And what was in man then . . .' her eyes, when she turned to stare at Kline, were filled with something that was not fear, nor excitement, nor mystification, but something that was a mixture of all these things, and deeply disturbing to the American.

Francoise said, 'If the power was in man five thousand years ago, then it is still in man, enormous power, shrouded, hidden beneath what we call reason and common sense; we are like a pulsating, living critical mass, just waiting to explode from behind the protective barriers that were erected during our change to a civilized race. And that appals me, Lee. That frightens me . . .'

Nothing more was said, then, until they reached the farmhouse and had stepped in from the November cold. Without removing her coat Francoise turned and fixed Kline with a lingering and thoughtful stare, and the American frowned, wondering if she looked at him, or at what he had come to represent. After a moment she said, quite simply, 'Perhaps I shall come to England with you. I don't know. You must convince me that you need me.'

Kline felt greatly relieved. At least there was a chance! He said, 'I promise you – if you come to England you won't regret it.'

She shook her head. 'I'm not so sure about that.'

PART THREE

DEEPER THAN THE DARKNESS

CHAPTER TEN

Damn you, Mister Kline-bottle; damn you!

Rain sleeted against the kitchen window, so hard at times that June Hunter, sitting at the wide table, drinking coffee, was worried that the newly appointed plaster would melt and run in the storm, freeing the pane of glass, and exposing her kitchen to the fierce elements. She heard Adrian laugh shrilly, and Tim Belsaint's more reserved chuckle. From where they played, in the corner of the lounge, came the sound of cars impacting with other cars, tinny clashes appropriate to the tiny scale of the crashing machines.

It was such a bloody miserable day. She watched the rain as it ran in a solid, mournful sheet down the window, not even painting natural pictures for her on the crystal clean glass.

Tim Belsaint came running into the kitchen, clutching his glass.

'Lemonade time again?' asked June, smiling.

The boy nodded, seeming breathless. They'd probably been running about the room, or rather, Tim had probably been running about the room; perhaps he had discovered some new way to amuse Adrian, his friend by appointment and profession.

'He seems happy,' said Tim.

'You think so, do you?'

The boy tugged the fridge door open and removed the lemonade bottle. 'Where's Karen?'

'Out with your brother, I expect.'

Tim frowned, then looked thoughtful. 'They spend a lot of time together, don't they.'

'They're in love,' said June, sensing that her adult cynicism would be lost on the boy.

Tim said nothing, replaced the bottle and walked out of the kitchen. Outside the rain eased and he hesitated in the doorway, peering at the garden. 'I wish it would stop. I want to climb that tree again.'

'I wish you wouldn't,' said June, 'not after it's rained.'

'No, okay.'

Tim vanished, back into the lounge. June finished her coffee and went to the sink, rinsed the cup and set it to drain.

The phone started ringing.

She hesitated, staring into the hallway, unable to stifle her surging hope that this would be Kline. Damn the man, it was days since he had left saying he would be back. Over a week! A week of waiting, and wondering, and hoping.

Rationally, June knew he wouldn't be back. He had been upset by Edward, and exposed to her own craziness, and no doubt enough was enough, and he had politely and painlessly taken his leave for more rational corners of the world.

But for a second, as she went towards the phone, she felt her heart beat fast in anticipation of hearing the American's voice at the other end.

The ringing stopped; Tim had answered it. He came running into the kitchen. 'It's Karen.'

June smiled, unable to stop her self-mockery. 'Thank you, Tim.'

Karen would be late. Don Belsaint was driving her up to London to a film. That was alright. Don was a nice lad, from a nice family, and anyway, this was the seventies and people trusted people with their daughters these days, didn't they? Or perhaps they didn't care any more. Karen was going to see *Star Wars*. It had been showing on and off in London for ages. June had seen it, and loved it, but Edward's early fascination for space fiction had descended to his daughter who lapped up the imaginary trips to the stars in whatever form. Her reading was more fundamentally novelistic, but her visual tastes were all fantasy.

In a week Karen would be starting school near Staines, much to her own chagrin. The girl had had enough of education. She wanted work, but Edward would not hear of it. June was of the opinion that they had been lucky the new school had even considered Karen, let alone taken her on. She was at A-level standard, and should take her exams at the end of the coming school year, but no doubt the headmaster would insist that she wait two years. Two years at one school was going to be quite a task; Karen's behaviour so quickly became perverse, destructive, that she would probably not last the year. Only her cleverness and learning ability helped her pass crucial exams with a minimum of work and a maximum of disorientation during the preceding months. She would probably get her exams, and maybe even secure a place at University, and that would mature her, and simultaneously remove the responsibility from her parents. It was a day that June looked forward to. It wasn't that she didn't love Karen, it was just that she was . . . tired of her. Yes, tired, anxious to relax with the ghost of her son, and the hope, however frustrated, which Kline had brought to her for those few brief hours.

To hell with you, Lee Kline! To hell with you for walking out on me!

She hesitated at the door of the lounge, turned back to watch Adrian. He sat in the corner, watching as Tim stacked up the model cars into a pillar. Red on green, on blue, Rover covered Austin, covered the bright yellow Simca that Tim called Glowworm. The column of cars rocked a little when there were – June strained to count – ten cars in the heap. Adrian leaned forward, his green eyes aglow with anticipation and the slackness of his mouth suddenly gone. For a second he looked up at his mother; he did not smile, but a tautness of his lips suggesting some internal emotion that was about to release itself. She found herself impaled on that gaze, and missed the swift motion of his left hand that cut through the pile of cars and sent them scattering beneath the wine cabinet and small, colour TV.

Adrian's laugh was shrill, bouncing around the room like some darting animal, dark and scary, at once away from her, then flapping around her head so that she felt her skin crawling and her neck prickling in that customary, and uncomfortable, response to the unpleasant.

At once Adrian's lips were slack and a glistening bead of saliva appeared at the corner of his mouth. His gaze went down to the scattered cars and he sat back heavily, watching Tim's hands as they gathered the machines together. 'Again?' said the boy, but Adrian was unresponsive. 'You do it,' said Tim, handing the Glowworm to his friend. Adrian stared at the car, then began to twist. His upper torso writhed from side to side and his hands slapped at his legs. Tim reached out and pressed down on Adrian's hands, careful to avoid the thick plaster around his finger. 'Calm down,' he said, glancing round at June. 'I'll do it again, alright?'

Adrian leaned his head against the wall, his eyes narrowed, as if tired; he looked at June, almost blankly. His legs were splayed out in front of him, his hands resting beside him. His hair had fallen across his face a little, and Tim, the eternal nurse (bless his heart), took a moment to reach and brush the brown locks back across his head. 'Look at this,' said the boy, and began to arrange the cars into a V-shaped pattern. As the pattern was completed, and he reached for the green, heavy metal tank, so Adrian lurched into a more upright position and began to watch intently.

Tim ran the tank, zig-zag fashion, towards the column of cars. He swivelled the turret to right and left, making shooting noises, and each time his childish cry, mimicking an explosion, sounded loud in the room, so Adrian jumped, and smiled, soon echoing the sound with a sound of his own.

The tank ploughed through the cars, turning them over, exploding them with voice-sound, reducing them to imaginary smoking rubble. Adrian loved it. He laughed at it. He exploded cars with his foot before the tank could reach them, and then suddenly reached forward and rested his hand on the turret of the war machine, twisting it so that the long barrel pointed at June. She frowned as she watched, imagining that he would greet her with that frighteningly aware gaze of his and calmly, almost arrogantly, make the sound of a shot – got you! But he didn't; he turned the turret full circle and banged his fist against it, upturning the tank and giggling as its caterpillar track turned lazily on its clockwork control, released from the frictional hold of the carpet.

June felt cold. It was not the cold of winter, or the chill of her clothes, still damp from her brief visit to the shopping centre this morning. It was not even the cold she normally felt when watching what she believed to be the mindless shell of the child of her love with Edward. It was a new cold, a chill that came from her rational mind, that surfaced from beneath the self-pity and dedication to her belief in Adrian's spiritual existence elsewhere. It was a cold brought about by watching a perfectly 'normal' retarded boy, playing and enjoying himself; it was being aware, though she found it hard to acknowledge this, that Adrian – this Adrian, this solid, fleshy Adrian – was in fact her son, and that his spontaneous expressions of total awareness were indisputable, and indisputably evidence for Edward being right. There was a soul in the boy, somewhere, buried. Edward didn't believe in souls, but a soul is a mind, an awareness of self, and the relation of self to the needs and flow of the environment. Adrian had such a soul, and more of it was in the body than she had at first believed. She no longer denied this. But she still believed that much of Adrian's awareness was locked in the stone font. It was now a question of balance, of understanding the balance, and of reaching it.

Damn Kline, she thought. For running out on me may you rot in hell. But for making me aware of Edward's side of things, I thank you, Mister Kline-bottle, wherever you are.

She smiled at Adrian, who was not aware of her any more, being too engrossed in Tim's latest game.

'Perhaps you *are* in there,' she said softly, but audibly. 'The ultimate split personality.' She laughed.

Tim looked up at the murmured sound of her voice. 'Were you talking to me?'

'No, Tim. To nobody.'

Tim was suddenly aware that the rain had stopped. He jumped up and peered through the window at the driveway. 'Blue sky!' he yelled delighted. 'Can I take Adrian in the garden? Please?'

'It's saturated out there. Why don't you wait a little while?'

Tim looked disappointed. He stared back at the outside, and June could read his despair at the thought of being cooped up with Adrian much longer. This was no way to pass a day off school! If she wasn't careful the lad would make polite excuses and go home. 'Tim?'

'Mrs Hunter, would you mind . . .' He was obviously thinking exactly what she had feared.

She said, 'Tim, come here.'

The boy walked over, tall, reserved, his eyes filled with childish apprehension at what this much older woman was going to say. June leaned down and kissed his forehead. He was, of course, horribly embarrassed. He smiled unsurely. She said, 'I don't know what I'd do without you, Tim. You're so good to Adrian.'

'Okay. But I think I've got to go now.'

'Will you stay a while longer? I was just thinking of your clothes. That tree is wet and dirty, and your father will throw a custard pie at me if you go back filthy.'

Tim laughed. 'That's okay. I mean, about getting dirty, not the pie. These really *are* my old clothes.' His eyes, big and brown, kind, childish, were filled with such an earnest desire to go outside that June almost laughed.

'Take him out. Get wet. I don't care. Build mud pies. Have fun. I'll take the custard pies in my stride.'

'Great! Come on Adrian.'

He reached down for Adrian's hand and pulled the boy to his feet. Adrian stood there staring at the cars, then – propelled by Tim Belsaint – walked stiffly, then more fluidly, towards the door. June thrust waterproofs at Tim as they passed, and Tim shrugged on his red sailing jacket and helped Adrian into his army style anorak. June listened to Tim's laughter as the two of them burst out into the unexpected, and probably short-lived, sunlight; then she went back into the lounge and picked up the phone.

She hesitated for a moment, then dialled the London code, and the number of Kline's Institute. After what seemed an age the ringing stopped and a gruff, male voice answered. She asked to be put through to Kline's extension and after a brief moment his phone was answered. A stiff, formal sounding woman informed her that Doctor Kline was not available. When would he be available? She didn't know. Doctor Kline was on unofficial vacation.

Good on you, Kline-bottle, thought June Hunter grimly as she hung up without a further word, carefully, and satisfyingly, avoiding the nicety of a thankyou.

And in your own language, *screw you!*

She had missed her Open University programme, and glanced guiltily at the TV for a second, and at her books on top of the set, waiting for her interest. She was not interested. She had lost any keenness that had been there at the beginning of the term, and now the Open University was just one more amusement that had served its time and faded into oblivion.

Almost distractedly she picked up a brush from the sideboard and combed lazily through her hair, staring at the pale reflection in the oval mirror that hung above the teak-wood furniture. A few days ago the face that had stared back at her had seemed younger, brighter. There had been sparkle to the eyes, and a healthy flush to the cheeks. This was the shadow face that she had become so familiar with, back again, haunting her as a shadow haunts its owner, inseparable, unreal.

And as she stood there, indulging in her wash of self pity, she grew aware of the scream. Turning to face the window the unreal sound became horrifyingly real. It cut off short and sharp and, in a sense, painful.

'Oh God, what's happened now . . . ?'

She ran through the kitchen to the back garden, and took a few paces across the slick, muddy pathway that led between the vegetable patches. She stared at the woods and clearly saw Adrian, wrapped in his anorak, almost lost in its bulkiness. He was staring at his mother, something of a smile on his face. Above him, clinging on for dear life to the low-hanging forked-branch of the children's favourite tree, was Tim. He had obviously slipped whilst climbing, and now dangled precariously above the six foot drop to the ground. His arms were crooked, his fists gripping each branch desperately. June couldn't help laughing.

She walked towards Adrian, shaking her head. She ignored the bright cold, though she wrapped her arms about herself to try and keep in what warmth she possessed.

'I told you not to climb that tree, you silly boy,' she called.

But she felt a certain sympathy, for as a girl on her father's farm in Kent she had often (frighteningly often) got caught in a tree that had seemed so easy going up, and so desperately hard coming down.

That six-foot drop must have seemed like six yards to Tim, dangling there, blind and cold.

'Okay Tim, don't panic. It's a short drop and I'll catch you. Are you alright?'

She approached the boy, smiling at Adrian who backed away from her. Perhaps it was that unexpected, and poignant motion that made the blood drain from her face and made her stare up at Tim again, this time less amused. 'Tim? Are you alright?'

The boy didn't answer. Frowning she took a step closer, and in sympathy with that erratic motion Tim's hands fell away from the branches and dangled limply by his side.

The boy's head was twisted to the right, his neck stuck firmly and awkwardly in the tight Vee between the branches. His body, limp and unmoving, dangled from the tree, and from the slackness of his mouth, and the dullness of his open eyes, June knew instantly that he was dead.

The easiest thing was to scream. The sound of her voice was as a storm-wind, shrieking through the sky and across the earth, bringing people to their windows, and setting a new, more emotional cold on the autumn chill that froze the boy's body faster with each heartbeat that passed, each stationary moment that watched the frozen group in the garden.

June cried, bitter tears, of fear, of sadness, of sickness. Through her watery gaze she watched Adrian watching her.

'I didn't do it,' he said in his halting, husky voice. And smiled, shocking June to the deepest part of her. 'I really didn't do it.'

The worst day she had ever lived through.

Worse than the day when Adrian had bitten through the bone of his little finger, after speaking words every bit as meaningful as those he spoke now; worse than that terrible day when she had first come to realize that Adrian's wits were not united with his body. The worst day of her life, and she sat through it without a word, except to answer the questions that the thin-faced, youthful policeman asked her; and to nod appropriately; and shake her head instinctively; and watch as Simon Belsaint, Tim's father, wept as he had wept here, in this room, when his wife had died years before, and clasped his hands, staring at the carpet and ignoring the double whisky that sat on the arm of the chair beside him.

Of course it would go to the coroner's court, but that would be a formality. No-one would even have contemplated thoughts of foul play. Why should they? The boy had slipped on the water-slick trunk of the tree, and the death – tragic – was accidental.

I told them not to climb there, June said, surprised at the sound of the words she spoke without thinking. It was as if her body was taking over for a while, speaking the platitudes and phrases of comfort, and reassurance, necessary both to the deeply shocked parent of the dead boy, and the deeply susceptible conscience of the woman in whose garden the accident had occurred.

Somewhere among the shadows an Edward-shadow appeared. He was calm, cool; he was collected. He talked and comforted, drank and reassured. He wept, he laughed, then spoke quietly and patronizingly and gave forth what the ears and eyes, of those too numbed by shock to understand, required. He was the man for all occasions and he coped magnificently, and his shadow passed away into the dusk of evening while June sat quietly and thought of the stone in the church and the brash American who had deserted her.

She was not aware that she passed out, and even less aware when she came to; at eight o'clock, smiling all the time, Edward slipped her two sleeping pills and a glass of warm milk, and like an automaton she swallowed them. So sleep came, and dreams, and the terrible day passed into yesterday, and out of her immediate concern.

When Karen slipped in through the front door, sometime after ten, she almost smelled the terror in the house, and stopped, instantly afraid. There was a dim light on in the lounge and she walked towards it, smoothing her hair down, touching the parts of her neck that were sore, and which she knew were red. She knew she looked dishevelled, and she knew that her father would instantly know what had been happening this evening whilst she had pretended to be at the cinema. But she felt that any accusations should be faced, and any truths that were required to be voiced, should be voiced.

She pushed open the door of the lounge.

Her father sat in a deep armchair, close to the cold fire. The lamp that normally stood on the side-board was balanced precariously upon the arm of his chair, and he sat, bathed in light, staring at nothing.

Karen pushed the door wide open, staring at him. 'Daddy?'

He started, looked up in surprise, then smiled almost tiredly. 'Hello Karen.'

'What is it?' she asked. He looked away from her, his hands meeting before him, the fingers entwining nervously. Suddenly he smiled again. 'Good film?'

'I didn't go to a film,' she said, too quickly for the coolness she had intended to portray. Her father frowned, staring at her from his pool of light. She walked forward until he could see her more clearly, then knelt close to the chair and leaned against its arm. The lamp shook, the light throwing their shadows chaotically across the walls of the lounge. Karen wondered if she was advertising her evening's experiences with each breath, each pulse of her heart.

'I thought you were going to see *Star Wars*?'

'So did I,' she said. 'But I didn't. Please don't be angry . . . but we really must talk, now. I hate being deceptive, and I don't want to be deceptive any longer. I want you to know things about me, and then I'll be a lot happier.'

To her surprise, even to her annoyance, the words that had taken so much courage to speak seemed to fall on deaf ears. Edward was gazing at nothing, his eyes filled with a blank unconcern. But he said, 'It's been sad here today, Karen. Very sad.'

'Why? What's happened?' She was still angry, but realized that the time was not right, not from her point of view, but from her father's.

Edward shook his head, turned to her and kissed her. The lamp tumbled from the chair and they both frantically reached to catch it. They laughed as the lamp was saved, then Edward frowned. 'Have you been running?'

She shook her head, looking straight at him. 'Loving,' she said quietly, her heart feeling like it would burst from her chest. What would he say? What would he do? She felt herself tense and uncomfortable as she waited for his reaction.

He smiled, shook his head in a more fatherly way. To her immense frustration she realized he was thinking in terms of innocent kissing and the only slightly less innocent passage of hands. He just didn't have the capacity to imagine she meant something else, something . . . complete.

'Go to bed,' he said. 'You looked tired.'

'Goodnight daddy,' she leaned over to kiss his cheek. 'See you in the morning.'

Disturbed by the unfamiliar pattern of behaviour in her father, Karen walked quietly upstairs, staring thoughtfully at the slightly opened door of the lounge. Something had upset him, deeply and lingeringly; it was evinced in his eyes, his quiescence, the weariness that had shadowed his speech and movement.

Tired herself, confused by the uncertainties that seemed to plague her maturing awareness, confused more by Don Belsaint whom she loved so much, but who seemed so immature by contrast with other men she knew, she walked to her room and pushed the door to. In the darkness of the small place she felt peaceful, isolated from the haunting questions she continually asked herself. Leaning against the wall she stared at the night's unnatural brightness (a light from a house nearby) and how it made the patterns of the curtains and windows so stark, so clear.

She had been going out with Don for two years, on and off, on her brief returns from school, and often on the long holidays her family took, with Don as their very welcome guest. He was intelligent, and pleasant, with a grand sense of humour, and all the signs of being a strong and dependable adult . . . like his father, like all the mature male Belsaints. They were a good family. Hers was a tragic family. Perhaps uniting the two through a more tangible bond than Tim's dubious friendship with her brother would do wonders for the flow of energy in the Hunter clan.

Perhaps.

But while thoughts of marriage appealed to Karen romantically, this, she recognized, was her staid and English upbringing, the indoctrination by parent and school that certain things were joyous and to be made life's goals – marriage, children, security, and an active role in the community in which she settled. They seemed romantic because she had nothing with which to gauge them. The older she got the more she recognized the fallacy of her adolescent ideals, and the more she doubted Don, as a prospective mate (in the traditional sense) and even as a prospective companion, despite her undeniable love for him. And she was doubting herself.

And she still had the dreams.

And she still had the temper that could consume her like some awful disease and send her raving mad for long minutes, long destructive minutes that had marked her education as an erratic journey between schools, testing the patience and coolness of the teachers she met wherever she met them.

She sat on the bed and undressed. Naked she combed through her short hair in the darkness, not wanting to see the signs of Don's overwhelming vampirism. She smiled, though, because she had felt truly wicked in his car, and had found the sensation itself extremely erotic, even without the clumsy, rather unsatis-factory consummation.

Slipping into her nightgown she jumped into bed and pulled the sheets up to her chin, lying flat and stiff, staring at the ceiling, waiting for sleep to take her.

By degrees the room grew warmer, the alertness of her mind faded, the darkness of the room became greyer, more distinct, and yet her focus drifted, unable to stick at one point on ceiling or wall. She felt drowsy, and warm, and the heat of her body increased. She shifted, sensing that she was damp with sweat again. The warmth was uncomfortable. She needed cool. She could hear the river, shallow where it bubbled over stones in the broad curve as it passed through the woods, before running on through the village, deeper, more dangerous.

She ran towards it, cool in the dawn, isolated and glad to be so in the thin mist that hovered above the dank grass. On her bare feet the grass was icy and thrilling. Distantly the trees rose beside the river, shrouding it, protecting it, their reaching branches almost covering the water in a natural archway. Sleek, grey-furred rabbits scattered as she ran among them, shedding the short, woollen gown she wore so the wind was fresh and exciting on the naked smoothness of her body. She felt moisture condense on her flesh, rubbed it into the pores of her skin, delighting in the cool and sensuous touch of the dawn.

She could hear dogs barking, distant, so distant, away across the rise of land here that marked the edge of the community.

She ran lightly between the trees, unbothered by the cracking, sharp undergrowth that seemed to part beneath her feet. She came to the water and splashed in, up to her knees, then crouched. The water was icy against her legs and loins, and she splashed it across her stomach and breasts, getting used to the coldness, and when she felt brave enough she lay out in the current, turned upon her back and luxuriated in it. Her arms outstretched, she floated with the river, turning slowly as she drifted downstream, kicking against the slick stones beneath her as she sank too deep.

She dived and darted, then, swimming strongly on her belly and her back, sweeping her saturated hair back across her head and wiping the streaming water from her eyes; she laughed as the birds cried on the wing, panicking among the foliage, screeching and wheeling through the dawn above the river, at once angry with and intrigued by the slender-bodied intruder below them.

She spread-eagled on her back, watching the dark-feathered

birds as they spiralled above her, in turn watching her as she loved the cold waters, feeling them penetrate cool and deep into her openings of her. Her smile was the smile of a woman loved by a powerful and gentle man, and her fingers gripped the water with each tender thrust of the current, until soon she was gasping with the hot pleasure of a climax, and twisting in the river, drawing her legs up to her belly so the river could find her differently and enjoy her again.

As she basked here, eyes closed, she heard the panicking flight of birds, and the swift and cautious movement of some animal through the dark woods. She stood up in the water, brushing her hair back, sweeping water from the flesh of her breasts and hips, staring at the trees.

There was movement there, and something came out into the light and beckoned to her. Instantly she recognized it, and backed away, screaming with terror. It jumped into the river and though she turned and ran the thing was too fast for her, and its massive fingers, horny and jagged with the deadness of its skin, closed about her neck and leg, upturning her into the water, then dragging her, thrashing but helpless, to the bank . . .

Her eyes opened.

Icy sweat ran from her, soaking the sheets and her nightgown. The darkness was greyness, and in the greyness something stood watching her. As the dream fled, leaving the weakness of leg and the tightness of stomach to mark its passing, Karen eased herself up onto her elbows and stared at the dark figure that leaned across the foot of the bed and stared at her.

It might have been dressed in a black, leathery suit, with a black mask across its face for all the detail she could see, but she sensed its eyes upon her, and the heavy breathing that emitted from a wide and hideous mouth. It nearly reached the ceiling, massive, man shaped, and as she watched, knowing that at any minute she would give way to the terrible surge of fear she could feel rising from deep within her, so the creature beckoned, and instantly she felt relaxed.

Quick, for all its massive size, the figure darted to the bedroom door, hesitated and called to her with a gentle wave of its hand. She climbed from her bed and laughed and ran from the bedroom to follow it, down the stairs and out through the kitchen door. And as she opened the door she stopped, and closed it gently so that it clicked shut with hardly a sound.

Leaning against the door she watched the dark garden until she saw movement at the other end, and she ran towards this, hoisting her thin nightgown to her knees so that it did not hinder her running.

She was smiling as she ran among the tiny barbed thistles in the rough grass near the trees. She hardly noticed the pain, but turned her head to try and see where the figure had gone.

A hand touched her arm and she turned quickly, ready to reach for it, ready to do anything it bade her do. A man's voice said, 'What on earth are you doing, Karen?'

Her scream was short, sharp, as sharp as the nails she raked across the man's face, beating him instantly afterwards so that he staggered. Then she reached to the ground for a brick and fell upon the startled body of Don Belsaint, driving the brick hard and viciously against his nose. He grunted in agony, and threw her off, but as she began to run, away from the garden, climbing the fence into a neighbour's house with all the ease and agility of a cat, so Don collapsed forward, stunned and shocked, and momentarily too weak to rise.

Someone laughed as she raced past him, running through the dark, wet streets of the town, her nightgown billowing, her hair saturated with sweat, her breath loud and painful as she made her body run in a way it was not accustomed to. Someone else called to her. Others watched, silently, and perhaps among them someone thought that perhaps the girl was in trouble.

No-one did anything.

She ran into the silent tomb of the church, stopping just inside the archway to catch her breath. Where street light spilled into the ruins she could see the cracked flooring, the marks where the wooden pews had once rested. Flapping things disturbed the heavy silence, but were soon silent themselves.

Turning towards the dark recess at the end of the aisle, Karen saw the vaguely outlined shape of the stone font. A boy stood beside it. It was difficult to see, but . . . Adrian. It was Adrian. She recognized him, and if her face frowned, her mind accepted the fact without blinking. She walked, stumbling twice, into the darkness.

A voice – perhaps Adrian's – said, 'You're too dangerous, Karen.'

In her hand she felt something cold, something sharp, not a knife, perhaps a knife shaped fragment of glass. She heard something laughing, not aloud but in her mind. She grew hot.

Without consciously doing anything she felt the sharp and painful edge of the glass cutting into the skin of her left wrist.

Harder, prompted the voice, and obeying instantly she tried to drive the cutting edge deeper into her vulnerable flesh. 'Quickly!'

'KAREN!'

The voice, loud, terrified, was Don's. He scrambled through the rubble, reached her and bathed her in the full light of the torch he carried. 'What the hell . . . ? Karen, *don't*!'

Even as she tried for a last desperate time to cut open her arteries, he had kicked out and knocked her right hand away. The glass sliced through her palm, but skittered away into the recess. Karen screamed, and the scream grew, turning eventually to sobs. Don placed the torch on the font and reached for the girl. She jerked away, but he stopped her, swung her sharply round and slapped her hard across the face; she kept crying. She felt her hands held away from her body, and then his fingers exploring the cut.

'Don't move,' he said, and, 'Christ, why is it so hot?'

He had dropped to a crouch and was tearing at the hem of Karen's nightgown. He tore a strip, clumsy and inefficient in the deed so that he ended up with a piece of cloth that was triangular and not bandage-like. He started to wrap the cloth around her hand, binding it tight.

He was troubled by something other than Karen's wound; everything about his thin, pale features showed the fact. He kept shaking his head and running his now-bloody fingers through his dark hair. He kept glancing about him, and at the font. 'It's so hot,' he said, his face lined with anxiety, wet with discomfort. 'Why is it so bloody hot?' He wiped a hand across his face, streaking blood across his cheeks.

He suddenly backed away from Karen, shaking his head, then rubbing his hands together, then rubbing his arms and legs. 'Karen . . . Karen, what's happening to me?'

He was gasping. His eyes, one moment wide with fear, the next had narrowed as if he were in pain. 'Oh GOD! What's happening to me? What's happening to me?'

She ran to him. In the light from the torch she saw how white he was, sensed and saw the growing agony he felt as some fit overtook him.

'It happened to me before, outside here . . . before . . . twice before . . . Karen, get me out of here . . .'

The torch suddenly flew across the church and cracked and was broken against the stone walls of the building. Karen struggled with Don Belsaint, helping him towards the archway that led from the ruins.

Unbothered by the pain in her hands she got the youth outside, and in the cold, crisp night they stood together, shaking uncontrollably and recovering their wits.

'My car,' said Don, and pointed to where his Vauxhall stood against the opposite kerb. 'I didn't know where you'd gone, but you were running through the street like a mad-woman. Christ, Karen, I was scared just then.'

She was staring at her bandaged hand, at the great spread of blood. 'It hurts,' she said, dully.

'You were trying to kill yourself,' he said. She looked up at him, blank, uncomprehending.

'Trying to kill myself,' she repeated, not a question, but a dull statement of something she could not dispute, and yet could not understand. 'I wonder why?' Then she remembered something. 'Adrian! Adrian's in there!'

She made as if to go back into the ruins, but Don stopped her. 'I'd have seen him if he was. He isn't. You must have imagined him.'

'But I didn't, Don. I saw him in there.'

'Well he must have slipped away bloody quickly, then. He's not in there now.' He reached for Karen and entwined her in his arms, kissing her damp hair and hugging her tight. 'I'll take you home.'

They walked across the road and climbed into the car.

Almost as soon as they were in the relative darkness, and security, of the Vauxhall, Don began to cry. He cried for several minutes, quietly, and Karen watched him, not understanding. Then he dried his eyes and started talking about his brother. When Karen obviously behaved as if she knew nothing about the death, he told her what had occurred. Karen listened in silence, then closed her eyes.

'I just came into your garden to look at the tree,' Don whispered. 'I don't know why . . . it just seemed right . . . I just had to see where he died . . .'

'Oh God, how awful. That's why daddy was so upset. I knew there was something.'

Don's hand on hers was reassuring, strong, and she leaned towards him; he put his arm about her and they sat there, quietly, staring at the almost deserted High Street for over an hour.

When June Hunter abruptly awoke from the deep sleep induced by her intake of sleeping tablets, she sat bolt upright in bed and stared at the diffuse grey light that told her dawn was breaking beyond the net curtaining. She drew up her knees, hugging them, and though she wanted to think of Kline, she could only think, for the moment, about how fresh she felt, how alert and awake.

She wanted to get up; she wanted to ring London again, to chase the bastard all around the city until she found him and told him, flatly, to get back here and help, like he'd promised.

She wanted to hit him in the face! She had flown so high on the wave of his enthusiasm, his manifest interest; she had plummetted so painfully as each day wore on and the young American failed to make contact with her. He had gone on holiday, and would come back, refreshed, amused by what had occurred, but ready for something else, something new, something as strange – perhaps stranger – than the Hunters and their obsessions.

Quite suddenly she was aware that Edward was awake. She turned and stared at him, and saw that his eyes, wide in the dimness, were fixed on her.

'How long have you been awake?' she asked.

'I haven't slept.'

'That makes a change. I thought you could sleep through anything, any horror, any tragedy. You always have.'

He said nothing for a second, and June felt his gaze move from her. 'Not this,' he said. 'It's too upsetting. I really liked little Tim. I can't get his father's face out of my mind.'

June turned away, hugging her legs tighter through the bedclothes. 'I know. That smile, as if he was trying to put *us* at our ease, when we should have been allowing him the sort of tears he needed. He was most worried about telling Don. He must be going through all kinds of hell. Poor bastard.'

Edward sat up. 'Did he hear what you said to the police? About Adrian?'

'What about Adrian?'

'That he'd said loudly, "I didn't do it". The sort of thing a child says when he *has* done something and knows its wrong.'

'I didn't really eat that worm,' said June quietly, remembering how Karen had horrified them, when she was three, with that particular statement of innocent fact. She smiled at the remembered thought, then shrugged as she remembered Edward's question. 'I don't know, Edward. I just don't know.'

'What don't you know?' prompted Edward, confused for the moment by the delay in June's answer. 'That Tim's father didn't hear?'

'I don't know that either. I don't think he did.'

'And do you think Adrian . . . do you think he *did* tug Tim's leg and make him slip? Could he have reached the boy's legs and pulled him that hard?'

'He could have reached, but not comfortably.' She looked round at Edward, staring hard at him, at his stubbly cheeks and the heavy lines across his forehead. 'Are you doubting your chrysalis, Edward?'

'My what? My chrysalis? Is that how you see Adrian?'

'It's how you see him. The beautiful boy emerging from the ugly shell. Do you doubt that the emerging boy is as beautiful as you were expecting?'

'I thought you meant an insect,' said Edward, distracted, thoughtful. 'And I don't believe Adrian would kill. I don't believe he *could* kill.'

'The ultimate destruction. The ultimate amusement. He loves to see things destroyed. He laughs at them. Perhaps his latest amusement was destroying his friend. You should have seen the look on his face when I walked down the garden to them. It was repressed mirth, Edward. He was fighting to hide his grin.'

'Isn't that rather too much of a human reaction for that piece of "dead meat" as you call him?'

June looked away, towards the window. 'Until he talked at the party, yes, I might have thought so. I was wrong, Edward. There *is* something there . . .'

'Thank Christ for that. Sense at last.'

'Something,' she repeated pointedly, emphasizing the word. 'Not everything. He speaks, and he moves around far more than we knew –'

'I don't believe that.'

June laughed, cynicism not humour. 'I don't know whether to or not. I'm inclined to think that he probably does. It's interesting, isn't it, that the only place he seems to go is to the church, to the stone, to neurotic June Hunter's stone font . . . interesting?' When Edward said nothing June laughed briefly, a pointed gesture to let him know what she felt of his dogmatic insistence in his own beliefs. 'The font holds the key,' she said. 'I know it. That American knew it. Adrian knows it, your Adrian, your half.'

It was Edward's turn to laugh, sneering at his wife's persistence in the duality of their son. 'You don't really know what to believe, do you?' he said.

'No. I don't. I thought I did, I thought I was getting closer to it. But . . . but I don't any more.'

Damn you, Kline!

Edward reached up and ran his hand down her back. She

enjoyed the touch and turned towards him. He said, 'It's been a long time since we made love.'

She smiled. 'I know. I'd like to, but . . . I don't want to.'

'Why not?'

'I'm too . . . tight. Tense. I'm sorry, Edward. I just can't.'

'I shan't force you.'

She looked away, saying quietly, bitterly, 'Did you ever?'

She pushed off the covers and swung out of bed, walking to the window to lean against the ledge, staring out at this earliest part of the day. Edward rose too, pulling on his robe. He walked to the bedroom door, treading quietly, but when he opened it he caught his breath, and June turned, puzzled by what had made him react so.

'Karen?' said Edward, vanishing through the door. June followed and saw Karen standing outside Adrian's room. She looked from father to mother, then held up her roughly bandaged hand.

'Oh darling, what have you done?' June ran to her, took the wounded limb and cradled it. 'How did you do this?'

Karen said nothing. She was shivering, and saturated. Edward was staring at Adrian's door, pointing to the thin cellotape seals across it.

Karen frowned. 'What are you saying, daddy? What are you trying to say?' Angrily she reached out and tore one of the three strips away. 'Are you trying to say that little bastard has been in his room all night? Are you?' Her voice, rising, approached an hysterical tone. June quietened her, looked perplexedly at Edward who was quite amazed at his daughter's sudden fury.

'I didn't think I would hear if Adrian went out,' he said. 'So I just stuck these on so I'd know if he had.'

'Well, he has.'

Edward looked back at the door, peeled the other strips from the painted wood. 'Then he got out of the window . . .'

He entered the room. Adrian was asleep, his breathing peaceful; his body was hunched in a tight ball, just a few wisps of hair showing above the blankets. Quietly Edward walked across the room and peered through the glass, at identical strips of tape on the outside. In a rare moment of melodrama he had put them there earlier. He shook his head. 'I don't think Adrian has left this room. Why do you say he has?'

Karen, angry, turned away and ran to her own room. June went after her, but her daughter slammed and locked the door before she could enter. 'That cut needs attention,' she called, and Karen screamed, 'I'll do it! Leave me alone!'

Edward went downstairs, confused and dishevelled, and June followed him, cold in just her flimsy nightdress. She walked into the kitchen and flicked the switch on the kettle while Edward sat at the table, staring at his fingers.

Nothing was said.

After a while June made coffee and took her own cup to the window so she could stare out across the garden. A sudden feeling of pleasure overwhelmed her, had been creeping up on her for some minutes; it was more than pleasure – something indefinable. She sipped coffee watching the day brighten, feeling her own spirits rise.

She knew what it was. She knew without knowing, she sensed without seeing, or hearing, or touching . . . she *knew*.

Kline was back. He was coming back.

CHAPTER ELEVEN

Shouting a French expletive, her face suddenly ashen, Francoise Jeury let the Higham fragment slip from her fingers and crash onto the floor of Kline's small office.

He jumped towards the suddenly trembling woman, but reached down for the stone before he extended his hand and tried to lead her to a chair.

She shook him off, looked transiently apologetic, but then focussed hard upon the piece of weathered rock. She was pale to the roots of her brown hair; her eyes were wide, and Kline could see the rapid pulse of an artery across her temple. Finally, after an abortive attempt to touch the stone again with a trembling forefinger, the woman shook her head and sat down. She leaned heavily on the desk, staring beyond the window at the overcast London day. Kline, behind her, gazed thoughtfully at the fragment before walking with it around his desk, sitting down with the object between them.

'I guess you saw something.'

'Shut up,' said Francoise, more sharply than she had intended. 'For a few minutes. Just let me sit quietly.'

'Of course.'

He stared at her, frustrated by her silence, desperate to know what the stone had meant to her. What information had she gleaned from this small, cracked fragment? What information about its origins . . . perhaps as part of a larger stone, a stone shaped like a font?

Colour returned to Francoise's cheeks and she smiled, almost apologetically. 'I hate blood,' she said. 'It's what disturbs me about the stones near my farm, that and the death. But this . . . this stone. My God, Lee. I felt like I was drowning in it. Drowning. Such evil, such . . . I don't know how to describe it!' She was angry with herself for losing the words, her hand waving, her brow furrowed with the effort of trying to voice the shockingness of the experience she had just undergone.

'Evil?' he said. 'You mean like . . . religious evil?'

She shook her head. 'Power,' she said. 'Enormous power, but repressed, contained. I could feel its frustration, and the way it was trying to seep into me. I felt . . . yes, that's it . . .' she brightened, livened up as she saw the key to her emotional contact. 'I felt like something was trying to move through my fingers and hands, into my mind. Some fragmentary power, perhaps just an echo of that power – but awesome power, Lee. Dark, evil . . . My God, listen to me. I sound like some satanist.' She laughed, emptily, rather nervously. 'You must understand that it is difficult to put words to power like this. Dark power, perhaps, or misdirected power. There was nothing good about it, nothing that could be called useful. I sensed only death and agony, and the screaming sound of something . . . something trapped.'

Kline said nothing, watching Francoise as the colour drained from her cheeks again. She had approached the stone, leaning towards it, and now she ran her fingers lightly across the grainy surface. She frowned all the time, and finally removed the touch and shuddered.

Looking up at Kline her smile was wan, almost desperate. 'I think that this is not the stone you have brought me to touch. Is it?'

'No. But right now I'm wondering if . . . well, if I should take you to it.'

'Why not? The sense of horror from this was perhaps marginally more strong than from the screaming dyke. It always surprises me, that's all. This other stone, is it a bigger part of this fragment?'

Kline shrugged. 'I don't know. It's the same *type* of stone, but it doesn't obviously fit like two pieces of a jigsaw, so there's no way of telling.'

But he would have put money on there *being* a connection. It was an irrational idea, not at all the sort of logical conclusion that he favoured among his colleagues, and tried to practice himself.

Instinct again, the Kline intuition. The Higham fragment he knew, he just *knew* was a broken-off fragment fron the stone font in St Mary's. And it might not have been broken off so long ago, either. The picture that Alexander had loaned him had disturbed him in some way, and only recently had he realized why that was. The font in the etching, depicted as it had been over a hundred years ago, was standing higher by nearly a foot and a half (as best he could measure). It occurred to Kline that when the font had been dragged out by the roots, someone might have smashed the base, where signs and symbols appeared that had been concealed for several hundreds of years in the foundations of the recess. It would have taken much strength, but the base of the stone might well have been savaged, and the whole thing shortened. Alexander had merely said that the man had tried to destroy the font, he had not known the details of how.

Francoise Jeury, looking grim but resigned, shrugged her shoulders and sat back, staring beyond Kline into the daylight. 'I think we should go,' she said. 'And get it over with. If the response I get is strong – if I get a response at all – it may take some days to adjust to it, and to read it properly.'

After lunch in the Institute's canteen, and a double whisky in the crowded bar nearby, Kline spent a while on the phone breaking those engagements he had lined up for himself during the coming week. There were not that many, but courtesy demanded a certain time spent in apologizing and re-arranging.

That done he packed the stone fragment into his brief-case and the two of them drove out of London. Within an hour they were passing along Higham High Street. Kline had said nothing to Francoise about where the other stone was to be found, but as they paused in the fairly heavy traffic, close to the ruins of the church, so the woman turned her head sharply, straining to see more of the church than the shop fronts allowed at that moment. As the traffic moved Kline drove on, but Francoise asked him to slow. They idled past the church, to the annoyance of a Jaguar impatiently close behind, and Francoise studied the lawn and the dark walls of the building.

'It's in there,' she said. 'I can feel it. I'm right, aren't I?'

'You certainly are,' said Kline, excitement making his heart race. 'You can sense it this far? My God, Madame Jeury, I think we're going to have to chain you down when we get close.'

They had passed beyond the church, and now she stared ahead of her, slumped slightly in the seat, her face a mask of worry. 'Lee, I'm frightened.'

'Me too. But if we approach it gradually, perhaps you'll get enough warning if it's going to freak you out.'

'If it's going to . . . what?'

'Upset you.'

'Oh. Well, yes. Maybe. But I feel very nervous. I felt that probing again, the same as with your fragment of stone, but this time more active, more . . . alive. I've never felt that before. I don't like it, because it isn't possible. So what am I feeling?'

Kline said nothing. He was tense, impatient to go back to the stone font; he could hardly bear to drive on to the Hunter's house, but he knew this was the right thing to do.

Karen Hunter admitted them. She looked pale, almost tearful; she looked tired too, dark lines etching her eyes, and she gazed at Kline sulkily, affording only the slightest smile when Francoise was introduced. Her hand was bandaged, Kline noticed, but thought no more of it.

'Mother's in the garden,' she said, and as Kline led the way through the house, Karen vanished upstairs.

June came in through the kitchen door as Kline reached it. She smiled, placed a muddy trowel in the sink, then looked at both of them. 'I'm glad you came back,' she said quietly. 'I'd almost given you up.'

'I always keep my word,' said Kline.

'And you've brought . . . help.' June was staring at the French woman, and Francoise extended her hand for the functional handshake. '*Are* you Mister Kline's help?'

Francoise said, 'We'll have to find out. I want to do anything I can, but so far I know very little of what's going on.'

With a sideways glance at the American, June said, 'You're not the only one.'

They went through to the lounge and talked, though Kline kept fairly quiet, disturbed by something about June Hunter, something distant, something confused that had not been there when he had left, a few days before.

She told Francoise everything that Kline had already told her, yet the woman listened fascinated, occasionally puzzled, sometimes sceptical, then fascinated again. They drank scotch and Francoise began to question, laughing continually, and probing in ways that Kline admired her for. But at the end of it he knew only what he had known already, although Francoise had obviously obtained much more information, and perhaps some different, or extra, insight.

Then June told them of Tim's death, and that set Kline's heart racing again. And she went on to tell how Karen had tried to cut her wrists open in the church, whilst sleepwalking, and at that point Francoise turned to stare hard at the American, frowning slightly, thinking hard. 'That girl who let us in . . . yes. There was something strange about her. Not just that she had obviously been crying, and was upset . . . something deeper.'

'Are you a psychologist, Madame Jeury?' asked June Hunter, stiffly.

'No, I'm not, and I want you to call me Francoise. I *hate* "Madame".'

June said nothing, continued to stare fixedly at the other woman. Kline wondered what was going through her mind, whether disbelief in the possibility of Francoise being at all useful, or annoyance that Kline had brought her into the scene at all. Naturally, as he contemplated the sour look on June Hunter's face, Kline thought of a sexual reason for the coolness. Perhaps she could sense Francoise' lack of inhibitions, the freedom of choice in which she basked without being aware of the luxury of that freedom. Perhaps June was tense because she began to understand, or continued to realize, how chained she herself was.

Perhaps nothing of the sort, he finally came to agree with himself. This was the reaction of a woman, tense within herself because of her isolated stance in her beliefs, faced with the second possibility in the space of a few days of being laughed at. And perhaps, if she believed that Francoise was genuine in her agreement to help, perhaps she was already worried at the possibility of failure.

She had lived with the knowledge of Adrian's entombment for several years; so close to confirmation, and the possibility of his release, the days must have seemed like eternities.

As soon as he got the opportunity he asked June as much. She had gone to the kitchen to brew some decent coffee, and Kline excused himself and followed her.

'Partly,' she said, as he asked whether she was nervous of a total failure. 'Which is silly, because I don't even know how she's supposed to be able to help. And it's partly that woman herself. Oh, Lee, I'm sorry.' She smiled apologetically at Kline. 'I feel tense with her, with Francoise. She unnerves me. I feel like she is reading me, and I really hate that. Didn't you notice as we talked how she kept jumping to conclusions, and bloody . . .' she glanced guiltily around, then back, 'bloody *right* conclusions, like how the priest hates me – I'd never have told her that – she just guessed! That really does unnerve me, Lee.' She shivered, fussed again with the percolator that she was obviously not used to.

'I feel the same,' said Kline. 'Live with it, if you can. That's all part of her talent.'

June looked up sharply. 'Her talent? Then she *is* a psychologist.'

'Not exactly. She's a psychic.'

June stared at him in substantial disbelief for a moment, then smiled uncertainly. 'A psychic? You're joking.'

'No jokes,' said Kline. 'She can really see, June, see things that to everybody else are hidden. She can touch a ring and know about it . . .'

'And she can touch stones . . . standing stones, like the font . . . she can *see* . . .' Sudden excitement, childish, genuine, billowed from the woman, swamping Kline so that he too felt a second surge of anticipation. 'How did you find her?'

'She'd been writing to me; I'd guessed what she might be into, but a few weeks back she actually laid it on the line. We call her Crazy Lady at the Institute, but not any more. That lady is just one thing that you and I are not: she's rare.'

'And frightened,' said Francoise Jeury from the doorway. Kline felt himself slightly embarrassed, but she was smiling as she stepped towards him, giving him an amused look. 'Crazy Lady, eh? Well, that's nice after everything I've told you.'

Kline gave her a wry glance, but before he could retort, June said, 'Why are you frightened, Francoise? Why?'

'Because I felt something as we drove past the church. I felt it very strong, like you can feel when a needle is probing in your skin for the vein. I felt I was being watched, probed. An enormous power resides in the church, and I can only suppose that it is in the stone font. I am frightened because my flesh is only mortal, and from what you tell me, the power that lives there can reach out and touch, softly or violently, according to its whim.'

June was shaking her head, looking angry, perhaps a little shocked. 'What *power*? What are you talking about? It's Adrian that's in there, my son . . . you talk like there was some raging force of evil trapped there, but it's just the spirit of a boy. How can he be so powerful?'

Francoise reached out and quietened the woman with a reassuring touch on the arm. 'June, if I am to help, I must say everything I feel. I am sorry but there is more than just a boy trapped in the stone, more than just a child's spirit. I know that already . . .'

'There can't be!' June Hunter was close to tears, Kline could tell. And he couldn't really blame her; he himself was still shocked by Francoise's simple statement.

The French woman said, 'Unless something strange has happened to him, then there *is*. I sense only memories, echoes, but they are very powerful echoes; and what worries me is that perhaps they will drown the cry of the child.'

Kline said, quickly, 'We're already confusing memory and actual existence.' He stopped for a second as Francoise glanced at him, and he realized that she had been deliberately so doing, perhaps to put June at her ease. Nevertheless, he went on, 'Don't you think we should wait until you can explore the font closely before we start getting ideas about powers that may or may not be there.'

'Yes,' said June quickly . . . too quickly. 'Let's wait.'

'I don't want to wait,' said Francoise, almost angry. 'What good is that? I know my talents, and I know what I can feel.' She looked from one to the other of them, hostility in her eyes making her face seem to burn like flame. 'There is a truth in the stone, June; the truth may be that you have been wrong; it may be that you have been right; it may be that you have been partially right. Whatever that truth, it is the *only* truth you will get, and you must start to prepare yourself for it; you must put from your mind all ideas, all hopes, until I tell you which you may live with. Otherwise I fear you will not survive my contact with the stone. And I tell you,' her eyes rested on Kline for a moment; she was frightened. 'I tell you, already I fear for my own sanity. I must make that plain, Lee: that if the feeling I get is too strong, too frightening, I cannot and shall not go through with it.' She looked at June, almost sympathetically. 'I'm sorry to say that, but *my* life before anyone's. Self survival, you understand?'

June's voice was almost inaudible. 'Yes,' she said. 'It seems only right.'

Francoise pulled out a kitchen chair and sat down, brushing her hair back from her face and staring out at the garden. The day, still cold, was now quite bright, and Kline felt he would have liked to walk down in those woods with June again; he felt she had slipped from sympathy with him, just slightly, just enough to bring back an unwelcome edge of suspicion, or tightness.

Francoise said, 'I would have liked to see the boy first, before we go to see the stone. But I think I want to get it over with.'

June poured coffee into three glass cups. 'Edward insisted on taking him well away from the town. When he woke up this morning – Adrian – he seemed very irritable, very upset.

Yesterday he was totally unconcerned.' Kline saw her shiver, guessed she was thinking of Adrian's smile – triumphant, she had called it – when she had come into the garden and seen the dead boy.

Kline accepted his coffee and leaned against the work top, watching the two women both light cigarettes. Francoise allowed herself five filter-tips a day. He had never seen June Hunter smoking, and when he watched the woman puffing the French brand he wondered whether this was some suddenly courteous gesture to put Francoise at her ease. Or perhaps it was for the hell of it, for the hell of doing something that she didn't normally do.

Kline felt that way sometimes. It was an enjoyable feeling. Impulsively he called for a cigarette and Francoise, frowning, smiled quickly and threw him one. He lit it from the stove, and chuckled as he puffed.

Francoise laughed too, and after a while so did June. 'Revolting,' she said suddenly, and stubbed the thing out.

Sensing a more relaxed atmosphere, Kline asked her if she now thought there was more to the mortal side of Adrian than she had acknowledged before.

June shrugged. 'I don't know; I suppose so. Edward asked me that last night. He didn't wave my sudden uncertainty like some triumph, which I was grateful for. I still don't believe I'm wrong about the stone, though. Christ, Lee, you know that. I've heard him talking there, I've seen him, I'm sure I have, but always so far away. But I've heard him. And he sounds so helpless.'

Francoise was quite pale, watching the other woman. 'Don't say any more,' she said. 'I know that feeling too well. Despair. Despair is one of the most powerful of emotions, stronger than hate, stronger than love. So few people realize that, so few.'

And though she said nothing, June Hunter silently agreed.

Less than a minute later Francoise rose from the table and glanced at Kline. He nodded and placed his cup down, and the three of them left the house and stood quietly, shivering in the chill, outside the front door.

'It may take a while for me to get the courage, if the stone has such strong associations,' repeated Francoise, as if trying to talk herself into this act. 'So perhaps we should go there now, and come back in a few minutes. And then go again tomorrow . . . Shall we drive or walk?'

'I'm damned if I'm walking,' said Kline, and unlocked his car.

June watched them go. Impulsively, and perhaps unnecessarily, Kline lifted a hand in a wave as the Austin revved high and vanished down the sloping driveway. He drove slowly into the town, reassured and comfortable with the crowds. People were everywhere, teeming, and it helped to stifle the apprehension that was clawing at his stomach. Francoise looked at the shop windows, saying nothing. Perhaps she too was trying to normalize her behaviour prior to entering the ruins. But in a few minutes Kline pulled off the High Street and parked in the nearest side road to the church.

He turned off the engine and stared at Francoise. She was white, her lips, normally full and attractive, were thin, pinched. She was enormously tense, and yet – conscious of Kline's scrutiny – she smiled thinly and said, 'Anticipation, Lee. Nothing more.'

'You can't feel it strong yet?'

'I feel nothing,' she said. 'Perhaps I was imagining things before. I don't usually experience such power like that. It takes much closer contact, a touching contact.'

There was little point in sitting there quietly, putting off the inevitable. 'Are you going inside the ruins alone?' asked Kline. 'Or shall I come?'

Her hand reached out and pressed his wrist. 'You come,' she said. 'I need your strength. But be careful how you react. I sometimes cry, and that's alright. I can cope with the depression I usually feel. OK?'

'If you say so.'

They walked across the well-kept grass on the street-side of the church. Francoise shivered twice, sensing – she told Kline – that this had been part of the cemetery in the very early days of the building's existence. Most of the graves were at the back, away from the street, but around the side of the church, near to the sacristy, were piles of very old stones, relocated when the road had been widened, and the front lawn turfed over.

As they stepped into the shadows of the church, Kline heard the flapping wing-beat of some bird and looked up. Francoise was staring into the sky as well, and when neither of them saw anything they exchanged a nervous glance, and then smiled. '*Was* that a bird?' she asked.

Kline shrugged. 'I've heard it quite a few times. There's the stone.'

Francoise turned away from him, then nodded as she saw the font. She walked warily towards it while Kline watched, but after a moment she walked more swiftly until she was standing right beside it. She seemed thin and frail in her short gaberdine. She had tied her hair back inside a red scarf and Kline could see the loose material blowing in a draught he could not feel.

He watched as Francoise extended her hands very gingerly and then rested them upon the surface of the font. She didn't move for a moment, and then slipped her hands about the stone, in that sensuous motion that Kline recognized from his own touch of such monuments.

He wanted to ask her what her strange sixth sense was telling her, but the words did not emerge; he was dumb, with anticipation, and fear. He felt hot. That damn bird was still flapping loudly above him, its noisy wingbeat almost echoing in the space of the ruins. He refused to look up. He was *afraid* to look up.

Instead he dropped to a crouch, wrapping his jacket tightly about him, and folding his arms. He felt the uncomfortable prickle of sweat on his face and neck, but made no move to ease the sensation. He could see, quite clearly, that moisture was pouring from Francoise' skin. She seemed to glisten, to shine, and Kline was most apprehensive of what she was going through . . .

Much too late she realized her mistake.

The quietness, after that initial, transient but shocking contact, was due entirely to the source of the power withdrawing its reach, waiting for her . . .

It *was* waiting for her.

She saw that it had sensed her fear, her apprehension. It had made itself approachable so that her natural human courage had made her enter the realm of its influence, and slowly, almost insidiously, it reached out and touched her.

Fear, like sparkling drops of water, dripped from her. She couldn't remove her hands from the stone, though she tried, desperately, almost hysterically . . . she tugged and twisted, trying to move her fingers from the hot stone, but all she could do was slip along the surface, feeling its contours, hard ridges of rock beneath her fingers, as excited by *her* touch as she was by *its* . . .

Like Antoin, like his body, so hard and ungiving, except when she touched him here, and here, and then he twisted, laughing, and the seemingly granite-hard muscles gave, rippling beneath her fingers which thrilled at the feeling of his soft skin, so well kept, so supple.

She ran her hands across his body, from chest to groin, holding him, remembering him, and the sweat of sex poured from her, and she basked in it, bathed in it, loved every tickling rivulet that coursed down her back and her belly, to be lost in the greater heat of her desire . . .

'Antoin,' she breathed, 'Oh, Antoin . . .' and bending, pressed her lips to the warm/cold flesh/stone: abruptly drew back, the grainy taste of stone dust on her lips and tongue. Frowned as she stared at the font, then gave way to the surge of disappointment as Antoin slipped from her – an agonizing amputation – and she realized where she was.

Games . . . a trick . . .

Still touching the carved stone font, she sensed, now, the crying agony of a child. It was a more powerful image than she was used to; it was stronger, more vital. There was something about it that was unfamiliar, and after a moment she realized that it did not have the static feel of the sort of emotional image that might have been a memory in the rock, as memories could be trapped and stored in a watch, or a ring, or a precious object of any sort. This image was dynamic, almost pulsating, and as it shifted and twisted in the dark void of her mind, so she sensed its depair, its unwilling entombment, its agony, its terror at the crystalline world that had become its universe.

This was the terror of the unfamiliar, for all human life is adapted to a world of air and water, fire and sun; instinctively, though it had never seen these ingredients of a normal environment, the dynamic energy, the psychic presence in the stone, knew it was in the wrong place, and it was bitterly, almost unbearably afraid.

For a second – just a brief moment – she drew away from the stone; her hands came away from it and she straightened, feeling the way her clothes eased from the stickiness of her body; she shivered, wet and uncomfortable. Kline was crouched some way from her, and as she saw her breaking contact he rose.

'Stay there,' she said. 'I'm alright.'

The American hesitated, then crouched again, and from his earnest gaze she knew that he was burning with curiosity. And she herself was burning with an almost addictive desire to return her hands to the stone, to probe with her strange mind more of the secrets of the stone font.

She said, 'The boy is here. Adrian. I can feel him.'

'Alive?'

Kline's voice was hollow, as if coming across a valley from one slope to the other; distant, almost unearthly. She heard the words, but ignored them, and soon – unable to resist the gently calling voice of the stone – she returned her palms, flat and wet, to the dry surface. For a second she relived that momentary ecstacy, the sensation of pressing and stroking the body of her husband; whoever, or whatever, was watching her, it knew just how to appeal to her, just how to trap her into physical action with the promise of imaginary sensuality. She stroked the stone, and the gentle, watching force moved and shifted restlessly . . .

It was not the boy, not the stone-memory of the child whose head had been struck so hard against the rim of the bowl. That spirit form now faded, sinking away from her, out of her reach. There was something else . . .

As with the stones from near her home, as with any stone, or object of great emotional value, she felt something of the past, an atmosphere, a dark vision of a dead time, an unreachable moment from the lost years of the world.

Most pungent, most noticeable, the heady smell of clean air, of grass, pollen, of tree and water, an atmosphere so pure that she felt dizzy with it; bitterness on her skin, the crisp touch of a winter's fingers, and a panorama of unspoiled countryside, glimpsed, almost, through a half-opened shutter. There was a snatch of hillside, heavily forested, and the tiny, almost unreal sight of a settlement in a clearing, the miniature houses clinging to the world with all the apparent strength of limpets on a sea-shore rock. Thatch, and the muddy walls that had not yet been replaced by stone, and a scene of such animal mayhem in the dark earth compounds around the houses that at first it was hard to believe that this strange, strangely sharp, vision was also showing her people: dark-haired people, with loose clothes and thick cloaks, highly coloured, heavily painted. They moved almost dreamily through the settlement as she peered from her future age into a valley that was being seen, and enjoyed, not by the stone, but by . . . by someone who stood against, or atop the stone, and in deep communion with the rock so that his sensory impressions were drained into the rock, and stored there . . .

She sensed him, sensed his ecstacy at this peacefulness and tranquillity. He was cold in the winter chill, but wrapped heavily in woollen garments. He was old, too, and like Francoise herself he possessed talents beyond and above the normal human talents. He was watching the settlement, but there was a darkness in his mind where he reached beyond the tenuous veil of reality, into the realm of what would become known as the supernatural.

There were more, then, more of his kind, images and time flitting through her mind's eye with startling rapidity. She saw them, and sensed them, she could hear their voices, a strange tongue, gutteral, clipped, but she sensed meaning in their noises. They grouped together, about the stone, beneath leather canopies in rain and snow, and basking in sun during summer sessions. They were questing, delving, exploring, and she felt the probing nature of the enquiry into the nature of the world they saw, and of the world they could not see. She sensed their power, awesome, sometimes simple, but so much more than she possessed, and so taken for granted!

As she grew familiar with the strange memories of the stone, as she herself probed deeper, more confidently, she sensed darkness, then the cries of those who were sacrificed. She recoiled, upset and alarmed, as blood spilled across her mind; she felt it, warm and sticky, alive . . . she felt the fingers of those who had died here, holding onto the fabric of the rough-shapen stone with all the desperation that they clung to the last moments of their lives.

She grew confused; there were deaths and sacrifices from many times. She sensed a recent death, powerful, explosive, the spirit draining into the rock to be swamped by something greater. She sensed humour, laughter, the transient, almost pitiful emotional record of something Holy, something good – words, the Latin words of an exorcism, desperate, drowned by laughter that was not laughter, but a wind sound, a storm sound, issuing from the deep thing that still eluded her.

A woman, naked, cruelly opened so that her body spilled its life across the stone, then a boy, a child, his head taken from his living body and the juices smeared in spirals and circles, and squares and lines, the stone decorated with blood, and one symbol over and over again, drawn by different hands, from the lives of different victims, while in the background, submerged beneath the screaming power of the deaths that had occurred here, she could sense the strange words of the dark men, the old men, the druids, the priests, the magicians . . . and she could see the awe and respect in which they were held, and the abuse to which they were putting that position of privilege.

They were . . . creating something . . . *it was so difficult to see!* The blood and the words, the smearing of faeces and mud, the positioning of limbs from nature, from trees and plants, from animals, and humans themselves . . . all was part of some spell they weaved, to bring something forth that they had sensed existed.

It was so difficult to see . . .

But they were trying to . . . to capture something, to bring it

175

into reality . . . something that would help them, some power greater than all the human power in the world, something . . .

Like a God, or a demon, or a force of darkness that could be used by them, to fight the enemy from the East . . .

Then there was a moment of terror, a long drawn out moment, terror from the past, trapped and stored in this stone that had been so central to the spell; the old men found themselves overwhelmed; she couldn't see what it was that took them, and almost halved their numbers in a split second, but she felt the jumble of fear and hatred, and the desperate measures used thereafter to reduce the power of that which they had released . . .

There were other spells, garbled too fast for her to hear or understand; there were terrible sacrifices, awful scenes of butchery and mayhem; there was a cloud of red across the settlement, an awesome symbol of what was occurring in the valley.

Watching, she probed deeper, trying to see, trying to understand through the confused, darkening images of a world more than two thousand years dead . . .

And that was the moment it came out and tried to take her.

Suddenly –

Swiftly –

Flooding into her so that she saw everything about it, and knew everything about it, and was momentarily powerless to fight it . . .

Kline, from several yards away, knew she was going to scream seconds before the sound erupted from her: harsh, hysterical, heartfelt. Her mouth had opened and her face had contorted; she still clutched the stone font, but her eyes, always closed, were now squeezed tight shut. Her mouth moved as if she suffered some unbearable pain, but had not the breath to emit the sound to illustrate the measure of her agony.

Then she was bodily flung away from the font, striking the wall of the recess with a loud crack (of her head) and thump (of her body). The scream came, and she reached up her hands to hide her face, but she was lifted from the ground and hurled at Kline, so that they fell in a heap, sprawled and ungainly. He struggled beneath her, eased from under her and tried to quieten her as she continued to scream. People were running into the ruins, and someone helped them both to their feet, but still Francoise Jeury seemed at the mercy of some unseen abuser who tore her this way, then that, flinging her from wall to wall, tripping her and twisting her. Kline watched in stark fear as the woman's clothes were torn and shredded, ripped from her body until she was almost naked; her hair was yanked and twisted, huge locks of it falling free, bloody and fleshy at the base. And he saw her skin, pinched and twisted, white where unseen fingers tried to pain her.

And yet he himself felt nothing, and nor did those who watched, a small group of people, five of them. They backed away slowly, and even Kline, sensing his helplessness, just stood and stared at the quivering, thrashing body of the woman, her skin now red and angry, the last vestiges of her clothing stretched on her body so that the thin fabric almost cut her open.

Abruptly she stopped screaming, and in that same instant Kline had run to her and fallen upon her, trying to protect her body with his own. Tears welled up in her eyes, and Kline cried too, sympathetic with the pain and abuse, though by the look of the woman she was beyond any awareness, now, and it was merely her body that cried.

Soon she was quite still, but as she stiffened, then relaxed, her eyes half closed, glazed, almost dead, so a touch of a smile appeared on her face.

Just a touch, a hint. Blood streamed from her scalp, and soon formed a thin, evil mask across her skin; but as Kline picked her up, and someone placed a jacket across her body and said words that Kline didn't hear, so she grew aware for a second and looked at him. She passed out, then, but not before Kline had seen that look of triumph in her eyes, a look that in any language said, 'I won!'

CHAPTER TWELVE

'You can sleep downstairs, on the couch.'

'Won't Edward mind?'

'He won't have to mind.' June smiled pointedly, moved around the bed in the dim-lit room. Francoise's breathing was soft, now, less laboured than before. She seemed peaceful and the rising anxiety that Kline had felt about her condition rapidly evaporated.

June Hunter said, 'Mind you, the deal's off if your socks smell.'

'I changed them last week,' said Kline, but June ignored him. She was bending close to the French woman, and reaching out to touch the nasty wounds on her scalp. Kline walked round the other side and crouched, staring at the sleeping woman's face. In the half-light Francoise looked very young, very pretty, all tension, all adult knowingness, gone from skin and muscles. She was a girl, peacefully sleeping off the terror of a nightmare, the awful experience of a few hours before.

June had bathed the wounds, and patched them, and now only the scratches and bruises on her skin were apparent evidence of her battle with . . . something.

Kline shivered to think that whatever had attacked this woman had also attacked him, but had allowed him to escape with both skin and modesty intact. He doubted that Francoise would have been too bothered by being stripped. She had stripped easily enough in her farmhouse, in front of him, unabashed, unbothered by the way he had watched her, and overtly wanted her.

Her whole life, she had explained, was lived for the living, for the enjoyment of moments without restrictive fears that owed allegiance only to a group of ancient celibates. The allusion escaped him, but he had gathered that she was morally her own master.

It appalled Kline that morally he, himself, was not; the urgency to return to England, to Higham, had become second consideration as he had spent several days with Francoise, talking and growing closer, finding himself involved emotionally with her in a way that she was not with him. What a fool he had felt when he had used those awful, naive words, the words that told of the liar he was, the liar to her and the liar to himself. She had laughed, he had been embarrassed. The conflict, for three days appeased, had begun again. They were good friends, but they were like cats at each other's beliefs and principles.

He liked Francoise, but she was a teasing bitch. Francoise liked him, but he was a self-centred bastard.

He watched her now, sleeping away the fear, the pain, and he liked her even more. He wanted to reach out and touch her skin, smooth her face, the fine down of wispy blonde hair that dotted her cheeks, so feminine, so attractive, so sensitive. But his hands wouldn't move, and he was unable to remove June Hunter from his mind – he was aware of her pointed stare.

When he looked at her she was watching the sleeping woman, but he knew her eyes had been on him, frowning, wondering what he was thinking, and whether her own wishes – to understand what Adrian was – were now threatened.

He rose to his feet again and inclined his head questioningly towards the door. June shook her head. 'You go. I'll just be a moment. I'll tuck the bed-clothes in a bit tighter.'

He passed Adrian's room as he went towards the stairs, and

glancing through the door saw the boy sitting in a circle of toys. Karen was crouched against the opposite wall, her knees drawn up almost to her chin, her arms wrapped about her legs, her eyes thoughtful as they stared at her brother. She had not combed her hair today, and the spiky appearance, and dishevelled look, made Kline grin.

'What are you up to?' he asked quietly, and the girl jumped as she realized he was there.

'Waiting for him to say something,' she said. 'But he plays a good game. Don't you Adrian?'

The boy's hand swept out and scattered toys, but his face never changed; he was staring blankly at his sister. Kline noticed that the bandage was no longer on the girl's hand. He asked how the wound was getting on, and she held up her hand, palm flat, so he could see the plasters. 'It hurts,' she said.

Kline moved on and went to the lounge, where Edward was at his work on the dining table, spreading a whole selection of photographs out for possible use in his book. The study, though large, was not large enough apparently.

Kline helped himself to a large whisky and walked over to the doctor.

'How is she?' asked Edward without taking his eyes from the photographs.

'Restful,' said Kline. 'The raw patches on her scalp should heal over fairly fast.'

'Got nice hair, that woman,' said Edward. 'Should be able to hide the scars easy enough.'

'Everything's okay then,' said Kline. 'As long as the scars can be hidden.'

Edward straightened, his face showing weary annoyance. 'Not again, Mister Kline. For God's sake don't be so aggressive all the bloody time.'

'Francoise Jeury was damn near killed trying to help you and yours. You don't seem to realize that, somehow. The importance of what she did hasn't somehow entered your thinking framework.'

Edward said, 'Mister Kline, you are the only one here who believes she did anything important.' He leaned back over the table, sorting through the photographs; he turned one over, marking its back with a cross. He picked it up again and looked at it. It showed a group of children, skinny and happy, standing in front of a sparkling, shining white building, low-roofed and cool-looking. 'A new bush hospital,' said Edward, as if that explained everything there was to know about the building. He laughed. 'Those little monkeys regard it as their second home. They come miles, from their villages, just to get inside the place. I wish I knew where the little buggers got their energy from.'

He placed the photograph back on the table and picked up another. It showed a negro male, eaten and emaciated by disease, and the expression on his face was pure desperation. He was propped up, staring at the camera . . . touching his lips was a smile. Kline took the picture, held it close, frowning. Yes, the man was *smiling*. He probably weighed no more than six stone, and his upper body was ulcerated and vile. He was dying. He was smiling.

'What's he got to grin about?' said Kline, then with calculated sarcasm, 'I suppose you asked him to say cheese.'

'Cheese?' said Edward. 'He doesn't know what cheese is.'

Kline tossed the photograph onto the table. 'Someone asked him to look happy. I find that quite disgusting.'

Edward said, 'The man is smiling because he thinks that when the camera takes his picture it will take part of his life and keep it. Normally, being of a superstitious tribe, that would scare him. But he knows he's dying, and he is glad we are immortalizing him. Do you see that, Mister Kline? He wanted to be immortalized in a happy mood. There is no pain where he is going – he's gone, actually. He wanted that no-pain life with a smile on his face, not agony.' Triumphant, Edward Hunter moved away from the table and poured himself a drink. 'Can you understand that? Or is that to "silly" for such a socially pragmatic man as yourself.'

'Keep them happy,' said Kline with an angry smile. 'It makes sense. Coming from you. Keep the buggers happy because they won't know any better when they're dead.'

'Not really. But is there any harm in that?' Edward turned, sipping his scotch. Fleetingly, the look in his eyes was one of panic, replaced instantly by aggression. Kline liked that; he liked people who gave themselves away by their eyes, or faces, or words. Hunter was desperately afraid of the American, afraid of what he would find out, what he would do to June, to Karen, even to himself, not bodily, not even psychologically in a destructive sense, but in terms of their beliefs, and the necessity of changing that which they had spent years building together – a life style, a balance of pleasure and tragedy with which they could now cope.

Edward Hunter did not want that balance upset. He was secure in grief, in tragedy, he was secure in his work, in the relationship he enjoyed with his wife, and his daughter, and his mindless son. He was secure in house, and cash, and booze and boots. He had adapted. He sensed that his family had adapted. Everyone fights evolution, for evolution means change, and change means losses and shifts in priority, and a concomitant loss of security. Edward, in order to pursue his career as doctor, consultant and writer, needed security and Kline threatened that.

And Kline knew it.

And Kline was not going to let this day go by without Edward knowing that he knew, and finally beginning the rot, or revolution, that would change the blinkered lifestyle of this irritating man.

'The harm, Doctor Hunter, is that you have no right keeping June happy by trying to discredit me, or send me away. I know the way your mind works. You want things perfect, but you can't have them perfect because your son's retarded. Okay, so you want them secure and as perfect as they can be with that fault in mind. You've established a status quo, and you're damned if you're going to change that. It's fine that June is obsessed with the font, just so long as nothing happens to increase or decrease that obsession. You resent me because I threaten that security. I think you resent me too because I stand to make you revise your thinking, and that hurts doesn't it!'

Unexpectedly Edward said, 'Yes. It bloody well does. Look, Kline . . . I'm not going to deny that I think you're five forms of bastard. You interfere, you challenge, you upset, you're rude . . . Christ, I hate people who are rude! You're right when you say I don't want to alter the way things are in this family. Why should I? Adrian is retarded, yes. But I am convinced he can be rescued, from himself. I don't know how to do it, obviously, or I would have done it years ago. But I know it's possible. I know that as much as June knows he lives on, alive and vital in that bloody font. I know he's capable of returning to normal because of his speech, because of his laughter, because of those aware expressions of his that you seem to think are expressions of triumph, or evil, but which could well be the manifestations of an expression of *anything* . . . pleasure, fear, love, despair . . . his mind, Mister Kline, has had no training; he doesn't know *how* to register the different emotions, so he registers anything. You think he looks calculated and evil. I just think that My God, he's *emerging!*' Edward smiled. He had enjoyed the lecture, and felt he had scored a point. All this was obvious as he returned to the table and idly touched the photographs, looking at them, but not thinking of them.

When Kline said nothing, the man went on, 'And you see, a long time ago, just after you came on the scene, I decided that at any cost I should protect June from useless hope. Don't you see, Mister Kline, that it does her no good anyway to know that some sort of image of Adrian is locked by some fantastic means in the font? I mean, *does* it? He can't be got out. He can't be reached. You can't transplant a two-ton stone into his two-pound brain. So what's my wife going to do if you confirm that some echo of her son really *is* there? What's she going to do, Kline? How's she going to feel? Desperate, that's how. She's going to become obsessed with something even crazier than just talking to the stone. She's going to want his mind released by fire, or explosion, or breaking it up with sledgehammers. She's going to be actively obsessed, instead of passively obsessed as she is now. I can cope with her talking to the damn thing. I can cope with the arguments we have, because there is an underlying co-operation between us. Once your French so-called psychic starts declaring the boy *is* there, all co-operation is gone, Mister Kline. The family is split. I don't want that.'

Kline said, 'You underestimate your wife to such a degree I'm surprised you've lived together so long.'

'Our business. Not yours.'

'My business, Doctor, is any business I choose to make mine.' Angry, Kline felt the heat rise to his face. 'I don't give a fuck about privacy, or *business*. If I'm invited into a situation, then I take all the liberties I want.'

Edward, bristling yet calm, said, 'I'll allow you the luxury of not telling you what that comment makes me think of you. You can stay here, Mister Kline, until your French companion is better. Then you go. No questions asked, no argument. You go, and you don't come back. June invited you to stay – I know because I heard her – and I shall not interfere with that invitation. But I am making it plain to you that I don't want you here a minute longer than you have to be here . . .'

Cutting into what he sensed would be a speech of rising passion, Kline said, 'Let me tell you something, good Doctor; let me tell you something about my "French companion". Firstly, she is not a fraud. I resent the implication in your tone that she is. I have been satisfied to that point. Secondly, I am not a liar. Call me what you like, but if I tell you I believe something: fact, Doctor Hunter, *fact*. Right? Third. My "French companion" has already indicated to me that there is a very strong psychic presence in that stone font. And part of that presence . . .'

He grinned. Edward's face paled, his eyes narrowed and he said, 'Adrian?' He spoke quietly, almost afraid.

'Adrian!'

'I don't . . .'

'You don't believe it? What a shame. You'd *better* believe it, Doctor, because it's the truth. You cannot escape it. You can avoid it, you can hide your eyes from it, you can go to South America and change your name, but you cannot escape it. Something of Adrian is in there, in the font, just as June believes.'

Triumphantly, Edward smiled. 'But not his soul! An echo, perhaps, but not the human entity. You see, that is what I'm saying. What good does it do June to know this?' He shrugged. 'So he's there as a memory. He's in photographs as a memory. So what? We can't *do* anything about it, can we. Can we!' A moment's doubt, a shadow.

'I don't know. I'll have to wait until I can talk to Francoise.'

Edward finished his drink, then leaned down to the table to touch the black and white face of the dying man in that picture. After a moment's reflection he said, 'Come on, Kline, what really happened in the church? What really happened to Francoise whatshername?'

'Jeury. What happened? She got beaten up. You've seen her. I didn't do it, unless I had a momentary black-out. No-one watching did it.'

'What did, then?'

'I wish I knew.'

'No ideas at all? Not even the shadow of a notion?'

Kline, after a brief moment's thought as to whether discussion with this man was worth the effort, said, 'She talked of often sensing desperation. At times, as she did her crazy thing with the stone, I sensed desperation coming from her, or coming through her.'

'A psychic yourself, Mister Kline? Since when did *this* miracle occur?'

'Sensitive, Doctor, sensitive. Sensitive to the way people feel. Not cold and callous, Doctor Hunter. Not that, not me. Are you interested in what I think or not?'

Edward raised a hand, shrugged as if to say, of course, of course, go right ahead.

Kline said, 'Desperation is an emotion most common in

adolescents and the aged. The desperation of *age* is passive, insular. But that of adolescence is dynamic, out-going.'

'Poltergeists,' said Edward quickly. 'Do you believe in such things?'

'Absolutely. Virtually everything sensible I've read on the subject of poltergeists centres around an adolescent – usually female – who is going through something more than the usual adolescent hassles.'

'Karen, then. You blame Karen.'

Exasperated Kline threw up his hands and laughed. 'Jesus Christ, why do you insist on jumping to stupid conclusions? Did I say Karen? Did I? Where was Karen when Francoise was thrown all around the houses? She was here. Don't you think that if Karen was manifesting a poltergeist phenomenon it would occur here, in this house? No, Doctor. Not Karen. But yes, a Karen character in some way associated with the stone font. Perhaps someone who died there, and whose ghost lingers, perhaps . . . and listen to this, and listen carefully . . . perhaps the innate poltergeist in us all, stimulated and magnified by something in that church, or the stone.'

Edward's face brightened as he discovered a formula he could relate to.

'The residual adolescence in us all? The link with childhood, the ever-present force of the immature and irrational . . . yes, that makes sense. Theoretically. So you think that when you were attacked –'

'June told you that?'

'Yes. Shouldn't she have? We have no secrets. Not yet. You think you were attacked by a tangible force emanting from your own mind. The same with Francóise . . . and the people who died there? Genuinely suicide?'

'It makes sense. Theoretically.'

'Monsters from the id,' said Edward and laughed, but the obvious allusion was lost on Kline. 'But . . . but who could be the source? I mean, what could be the source . . . in the stone? What could it rationally be that can so affect our own hidden faces?' Edward's eyes were wide, now. Searching. He stared at Kline, and Kline sensed himself drawn into the man's awesomely powerful web of uncertainty, and fear of the unknown. Hunter was so overtly a man who liked to understand the world about him. He could cope with disease because there were books that made diseases not a matter of agony and emaciation and ultimate demise, but a set of statistics and graphs of immune response, and immune competence, and failure of the body's defence mechanisms, and protein fluctuation, and muscular change, and elastic tissue deterioration, and so on, and so on . . . if it could be seen beneath a microscope Edward Hunter could accept it.

If it was in the realms of the unknown, it frightened this man who was frightened of so much . . . the unseen, unknowable world of the supernatural, the way a mind might think that was so different to his own . . .

Poltergeists, those real, witnessed and indisputable manifestations of adolescent psychic frenzy, they were the only aspect of the supernatural that came within his focus and he could accept that without blinking.

Kline pitied him for his staid and dogged adherence to the understandable. But Kline had met too many people like him to devote much time to feeling patronizingly sympathetic; he felt a little pity for Edward, perhaps, but sympathy? There was no time for that.

'Are you asking me,' said Kline, 'If the echo of Adrian could be the source?'

Edward frowned. 'I suppose I am. Could it?'

'What makes you think I know? It occurs to me that Adrian, in his retarded – your word, Doctor – in his retarded way, in his prepubescent way, he must be quite a little atom-bomb of fears and frustrations . . .'

'Wait a minute, Kline. You're talking about the Adrian that's upstairs. I'm talking about this echo, this memory in the stone. Different thing.'

'Is it?'

'It has to be, doesn't it! There's no link between stone and boy. Come on, we're talking about two different things, like Adrian and a photograph of Adrian. Space and Time separates them. The echo in the stone, if it exists . . . okay, the echo in the stone that exists for certain, is no longer a part of my son. Right? I mean, come on, I'm coming a long way across to your side, to June's side. Can't you hear me? I'm actually saying that there was something in June's stupid obsession. I'm *giving*. But don't tell me that the photograph and the living boy are connected in any but an unimportant way, an *image* way.'

'I repeat,' said Kline. 'I just don't know. Until this evening I didn't know that poltergeists actually harmed people. It attacked me and hurt me, but there wasn't a mark upon me. The same thing happened to Francoise Jeury and she was badly damaged.

It's as if two different forces were at work, except that I don't think there *are*.'

The door to the lounge opened and Karen stepped in. The conversation between the two men ended, and they both looked at the girl.

'Still arguing, daddy?' she said, with a bitter smile, and walked to one of the deep chairs. She plumped herself down, legs spread out, the tight denim of her jeans striking Kline as uncomfortable, and rather disturbing. The girl watched him, and slowly her features softened. Edward went back to his task of picture sorting, and Kline walked over to sit with Karen.

'How are you? Over the shock?'

The girl shrugged. 'I don't know. Does one ever?'

'One doesn't know,' mimicked Kline deliberately. Karen laughed.

'One may be able to say in a few days,' she said, then fell solemn again. 'I'm leaving. I'm moving up to London.' As she said this her eyes focussed beyond Kline – she was glancing at her father, who worked on at the table, apparently unaware of what Karen had said.

'Why?'

'Get away from here. Try living on my own for a while, really on my own.'

'I thought you were in love with Don.'

She smiled in a catty sort of way. 'Maybe I am, maybe I'm not. I'm sure I don't know. Anyway, Don's a typical Belsaint. He'll never move away from Higham, onto better things. His roots are here, his ancestry. Nothing will drag him away.'

Kline thought about that for a while, then turned his attention back to Karen. 'Bedsit land, then. A tiny room at the top of a house, in Shepherds Bush, or Highgate.'

'That's it. I can't wait . . .'

Again her attention was more on Edward than on Kline. Edward had heard alright, because he was quieter than before, feigning his involvement with the process of picture selection. Kline watched the girl, half amused, half puzzled. There was colour in her cheeks, emerging from behind the awful layers of pale make-up. Her eyes were bright with that intensity that is at once intelligence and increased determination. Kline knew that much of her loud cry about London was a cry for help, and not for his help but for her father's help. Resentful of Edward's fixation with Adrian, bitter because of the artificial relationship with June it enforced upon her, Karen was making a vocal bid for Edward's attention.

She was manifestly failing.

Kline said, 'London's a desperate place, Karen. Desperately lonely. Awful.'

'Don't try and discourage me,' she said, grimly. Her hands clasped before her, and perhaps unconsciously she was emphasizing her breasts. Kline couldn't help but glance down, and when he caught himself staring he realized Karen was staring at him, and smirking. 'I don't mind,' she said.

'Don't flatter yourself,' he said quickly, angrily. She shrugged.

'What's wrong with London? Anonymity never did anyone any harm. And there are so many places to go at night, and all the fun of the young pubs and discos.'

Kline laughed. 'I guess there are things like that. People do have fun, the right sort of personality, anyway. If you're a bit shy, London's a hell-hole. You talk about meeting people like there's a big signpost pointing the way. But there isn't. It takes a long time to make friends in London, a damn long time. Through friends you meet others and so on, but people . . .' he broke off, thinking hard, looking at the girl through narrowed eyes. 'I don't know . . . people aren't ordinary. They're cold, they're slick. They seem to be in competition with each other all the time, socially, everything. There's no warmth.'

Karen pulled a face. She shook her head for a reason that Kline could not fathom. 'How many friends have you got, Lee? You could introduce me to a few people . . . you could help . . ,'

The American sat back, the smile he wore a forced, hollow gesture. 'Karen, I haven't got a damn friend in the world.'

'You must have. Girl friends . . .'

'Well, yeah . . .' Aware that Edward Hunter was listening more intently than ever, he shrugged. He felt a moment's anger with the man's manifest complacence. His interest seemed fixed at the level of the voyeur -- why hadn't he come over and said something, something angry, something cynical -- anything? Perhaps he was afraid, or unsure of his daughter and of his relationship with her. Perhaps he didn't really give a damn. Perhaps he thought she was playing games and saw no reason to stop her. Loudly, Kline said, 'Sure. I have a lot of woman friends. Christ, I'm thirty two. I need a lot of women.' Karen giggled, self consciously, slightly embarrassed by his frankness. Kline sensed nothing from Edward Hunter; either the man wasn't listening, or he didn't care. Kline decided to speak louder. 'By the

187

time I'm forty I'm going to need a lot of re-loading. I have to take my opportunities. I have to take advantage of my *youth*.'

Karen said, 'There you are, then. You can introduce me to a few people . . .'

'But they're not my friends, Karen. I use them. They use me. Honest to God, girl, there's not a sonovabitch in London that I'd call a friend.'

'Then it's by your own choice,' she said quietly, almost with hostility.

Damn right, thought Kline. Aloud he said, 'I suppose it is. I don't have time for such things. I don't need such things. I'm very content with my work, and my pleasures. It really bugs me when people start depending on people, like at work . . . the students are always going off boozing with each other. Well, Christ, how the hell do they expect to make it when half their time is spent like that? So much time wasted and so much to do!'

'You sound like daddy,' she said with a grin.

'God forbid.'

Abruptly Karen rose, and smoothed down her red blouse. She did it in an obvious way, and Kline watched her, half amused, half annoyed that she was provoking him so. And part of him was puzzled as to why she was doing it.

'I'm going outside, onto the porch. Come and stargaze.'

'Cloudgaze, you mean,' he said, but rose and walked stiffly after her, conscious of Edward watching him. As he left the room he glanced at the older man and smiled, waved his hand.

Outside, in the light from the lounge and the street lamps, they leaned against Kline's battered car and shivered in the cold. The girl seemed relaxed, though, perhaps because of being out of earshot and eyeshot of her father. 'I meant what I said,' she murmured. 'Honest, this isn't a come on. It's perfectly innocent. I want to go up to London with you, just so there's someone there while I settle. I'll even buy you dinner every Wednesday.'

'Wednesday's my fast day.'

'Liar. Friday is, you already told Mother.'

Kline laughed. So he had, so he had. The girl had folded her arms about her shoulders, hugging the warmth to her. She stared at the open front door, and the spill of light from the hallway. She said nothing more, and after a while Kline couldn't understand why he was so hostile to the idea.

'Okay,' he said. 'I'll introduce you to the City. When I go back, if your folks are agreeable.'

'Tonight. Now.'

Earnest, anxious, she turned on him and reached out a hand to touch his. 'Let's go tonight, Lee. Right now. You can come back and pick up Francoise when she's recovered. Let's get out of here.'

Kline was puzzled, but perhaps he could understand her anxiety to get away. She'd been through a rough time, not just with her nightmare, and the sleep-walking suicide attempt, but at school and in life for the whole of her adolescence. He squeezed her hand affectionately, and was taken aback when she grabbed him harder, closing both palms around his fingers and trying to draw him closer than just in body.

'Lee . . .'

'Karen, there are things I need to do here. Things to do, questions to ask, lives to understand.'

'You've done what you said you'd do. You came back and brought help. Francoise can help Mum, not you. You're not needed here any more.'

'I am though. June – your mother, well, she'd be uptight if I just left in the middle of things.'

'No she wouldn't,' said the girl quickly; her voice sounded angry. 'She doesn't care about you any more. She said so. She said she didn't care if you dropped dead right now, because you've served your purpose . . . she *did*, she *said* that . . .'

For a second Kline felt the heat rise to his cheeks and his heart race with some rapidly surfacing anger. He glanced up to where Francoise lay in her darkened room, then slowly frowned. 'When did she say that, Karen?'

'Upstairs, after you left her looking after Francoise. That's why she stayed up there. She clings to what she needs, and now she needs Francoise. She clung to you only when she needed you. It's true, Lee. Believe me.'

'Well, I don't believe you . . .'

'It's *true*!' she shouted, pushing herself away from the bonnet of the car and standing in front of him. He could hear and see the fine edge of hysteria approaching in her; her eyes were wide, anxious, and her lips were slick with moisture, parted as her breathing became heavy. Every pore of her body exuded the stale smell of fear. For some reason she desperately wanted Kline to leave, to go with her to London. She wanted to escape, to get away, and that was rational enough – but it was this uneasy, aggressive anxiousness that concerned him. It was unnatural, and he could not believe it was true.

'Karen . . .'

'I'm a grown woman,' she said. 'I'm not a virgin. I'm good,

very good. I wouldn't worry if you wanted me; that would be alright. I wouldn't want to live with you, Lee. Just help me. You can have what you want . . . anything . . .'

'You're making me sick,' he said quietly, pointedly, only half aware that she couldn't possibly be speaking these words from the heart.

'Bastard!' her hand slapped across his face, and quickly, without thinking, he struck her on the jaw. He had meant to slap, but the blow was harder than he could control. Karen reeled backwards and stumbled.

Kline leaned back against his car. 'Hurts, doesn't it.'

'What a cowardly thing to do,' she said, standing up, bristling with anger and brushing herself down before she tenderly cradled her jaw. In the half light he could see the tears in her eyes.

'Bullshit,' he said. 'You slapped me, I slapped you. Fair's fair. Chivalry costs, these days.'

'I know,' she said, looking down. 'I was silly to slap you. I'm sorry. But you were a bastard to hit me. Now we're square.' She looked at him, still hurt, but now perhaps worried that she had overplayed what was obviously an important hand to her. 'Leave here, Lee,' she said. 'And take me with you. Honestly, they don't want you around any more. You'd be better off gone.'

He reached out and gently touched her face; she didn't wince. She was a tough little lady and though she'd have a bruise, it would be small. Psychologically she had already adjusted to the blow, and had forgotten it. That, to Kline's way of thinking, *was* tough.

'Maybe,' he said, in reply to her last earnest plea. 'But I'm not going. Not yet. Not until June herself dismisses me, and not even then. Not until I *want* to leave.'

'Big, tough Lee Kline. Screw the world as long as Lee Kline is OK.'

'That's right.'

'That's also why you have no friends. Now I begin to understand.'

Kline shrugged and went past her into the house. He stopped just briefly and looked back at Karen at the sound of her loud and uncouth expectoration. Looking at him as he frowned his distaste she deliberately spat again, letting the long stream of saliva dribble from her lip and hang down her chin. Then she smiled and turned away from him, almost fleetingly passing a hand across her face to dry herself.

CHAPTER THIRTEEN

Restless, and uncomfortable on the couch, Kline wasn't sure whether he had been asleep or merely dozing when the furtive sound of movement outside the lounge woke him and roused him to a full state of alertness.

He lay on the couch, smelling the mustiness of the thick blanket that covered him, and watching the thin shaft of moonlight that was sneaking along the top of the join in the heavy, dark curtains. It was a fine autumn-winter night outside, cold and now cloudless. It would be a good day tomorrow.

He listened again and heard a gentle creaking, as of someone's weight coming down upon a bed. Too awake, and too nosy to leave things be, he stood up, pulled on his jeans and walked out into the hallway.

His heart leapt into his mouth as he saw someone vanishing into the kitchen, a shadow in the darkness.

'Who's that?' he called, and followed. The kitchen was dark, the light from outside shining from the stainless steel of the sink, the white paint of the freezer, the polish of the kitchen table. Through the window Kline could see the man running away into the garden. He hadn't heard the door open or close, and when he walked to check it he discovered the door to be locked.

His heart was thundering as he stared after that dark shape and wondered whether he had really seen it, or whether the night played tricks with him.

Then he turned and crept back along the hall, easing his steps onto the stairs and climbing them with elaborate discretion.

The door to Karen's room was open and as he stood in it he saw a shape crouched above the girl, leaning down close to her face, almost touching her, almost . . . kissing.

'Francoise?'

The shape jerked up, then raised a finger to indicate quiet. Francoise was standing there in a voluminous night coat. Her hair was down, and the white strips of plaster on her scalp almost shone in the night-glow in the room.

Again Francoise bent close to the sleeping girl, and Kline thought she looked as if she were listening. Her breathing was almost inaudible, and at times she actually *held* her breath.

At last she straightened again and shook her head. She walked round the bed and took Kline's hands in hers.

'I feel lousy,' she whispered, the accent strong, almost comical.

'I'm not surprised,' said Kline quietly. They walked to the room where Francoise had been put to bed. The woman jumped into the sheets and flattened them around her.

'How many people saw what happened?'

'Not many,' said Kline. 'Four or five. I don't think they really understood what they were seeing – one man put his jacket over you and helped me get you quickly to the car, and he obviously thought you'd had a fit.'

Francoise laughed quietly. 'So they'll talk, but only like people talk about one car bumping another. You don't think it will get to the local paper?'

Kline shrugged. 'I can't see how. But if this sort of thing goes on, well, yes, it's going to break eventually.'

'We must be discreet in our investigations, then,' said Francoise, dramatically.

In the darkness Kline thought she might have been grinning at him, but he couldn't tell. Her eyes shone, high spots of light as she stared at him.

'I was terrified, Lee. I was absolutely and completely and utterly terrified.'

'So was I. I thought you were going to die.'

'Not die. I was too strong.'

'Who were you fighting?'

'*What* was I fighting, you mean. I don't know. Something. I don't want to talk about it yet. Tomorrow perhaps. Or the day after. I just need to think, to clear my thoughts.'

'But . . . you saw something of the boy, Adrian.'

'Oh yes. Very strong, very alive. June was right.'

'Christ!'

'Exactly. Knowing makes it so bizarre, so frightening.'

Kline looked away from her, thinking of how a woman had known this strange, almost ridiculous state of affairs for six years, and had fought against those who scorned her because of the sincerity of her beliefs. And he thought of how he had laughed, and doubted her, then come to believe that perhaps she had sensed something about the font, but how he had not really believed it, not deep down. And when Francoise had said the boy was there, during her time at the stone, even then he had believed she meant as a lingering echo, like the echoes of Stevie in his ring, and in his mind.

But now she said he was there and he was alive. A boy. A human being, somehow held in place, in prison, in the matrix of sedimentary rock that made up the font.

'So what do we do now?' he said quietly. Francoise said nothing, questioning him with her silence. 'About Adrian,' he said. 'Maybe Edward was right. What good *does* it do us? Can we somehow . . . remove him?'

Francoise laughed, not scornfully, nor with amusement, but as a symptom of her own uncertainty. 'Time will perhaps tell. Who knows.'

'Perhaps.' Kline stared at the woman in the semi-darkness; she was staring ahead of her, not at anything in particular, thoughtful, and slightly confused.

He said, 'Why were you in Karen's room?'

She shrugged. 'Something. Some reason.'

'What reason?'

She hesitated, then said, 'I don't know what it means, so I shouldn't tell you.'

'You should tell me everything. What reason?'

'I wanted to get close to her, to touch her . . .'

'Oh Jesus, what does that mean?' Kline could not hide the transient irritation he felt as he came to the obvious conclusion. 'You're not getting emotional feelings for her, are you?'

'Bastard,' she said quietly, unprovocatively. 'Not, not emotional feelings. That's the trouble I think. I ought to get some. Then I'd understand better.'

'Understand what better?'

Pause. Eyes, brightly reflective in the half light, turned on him, huge, thoughtful. 'I saw her in the stone too. I saw her face.' She stopped as she sensed Kline's surprise, then went on, 'It wasn't the same feeling as with Adrian, or the other thing. It wasn't even like the stone's memories, the record, the psychic echo that you call it. It was like . . . like an image, perhaps in someone's mind. Oh Lee, I'm confused. I don't understand it and I'm too weary.'

'But you definitely saw Karen's face? No question that it was her?'

Francoise shrugged, shook her head. 'Maybe it wasn't. It just looked like her, very strongly. It disturbed me in a certain way, and I was just listening to Karen in her room, wondering if I could sense something. But I couldn't.'

Kline frowned. 'Your powers are not restricted to objects, then. You can sort of . . . see into people's minds?'

'Thank God no!' she said loudly, with feeling. 'But sometimes when I was making love with Antoin, I would feel him very strong, very powerful in my mind. I could see myself as he saw me. So I think that sometimes I might get some feeling for a person when I'm very emotional . . . you understand?'

'I understand. But what –'

She cut him off. 'Lee, I'm tired.' She reached out and touched his hand. 'I'm tired. I'll see you in the morning. We'll talk about what happened. OK?'

Kline nodded and rose, stooping above her to kiss her forehead. 'Sweet dreams,' he said.

'Don't be callous,' she replied, slipping down into the bed clothes and turning over.

Francoise slept undisturbed until midday; Kline was almost ready to wake her by force at ten in the morning, but June restrained him. He knew it was right that the woman should sleep off her shock, and fear, but he paced restlessly about the garden and the lounge, and when he finally saw the curtains at the back of the house open, and Francoise waved down to him, he raced back inside like a child called in to receive a present.

Over a light lunch, which Kline found indigestible – a vegetable concoction that June had prepared mainly for the French woman – Francoise told them what she had experienced, what she had seen.

She told them of Adrian, little more than she had told Kline. It had been an awareness of him, struggling somewhere in the stone's fabric, as if he were being held by great hands and not able to escape. June cried, not bitterly, more with relief than anything, and she made Francoise say it all over again.

'Mrs Hunter,' she said, 'please . . . don't take what I say as the absolute truth. It is very difficult to understand something that is not normal.'

'You saw him, though. I was right . . .'

'Perhaps . . .'

'There's just one truth in the font,' said Kline sharply, irritated, 'that's what you told us, Francoise. Just one truth, and we would have to accept it. Are you changing your mind now?'

Francoise shook her head, herself a little annoyed with Kline's impatience. 'No, I'm not changing my mind. It's merely that what I saw . . . perhaps it was what . . .' she trailed off, uncertainly. June prompted her to continue. 'Well then, let it be said. Something is playing games with you, and with me, and with Lee and Edward, and Karen, and Adrian, and everything and everyone. Something in there, in the font, something very very old, and very very evil. And it has played games with us, and perhaps this seeing Adrian was just another game. I can't get it out of my mind that perhaps it showed me Adrian so I would tell you, so that we kept interested in that stone font, so that we kept busying ourselves there. Whatever it is, it knows what we all need. It plays on our emotions, on our curiosity . . .' she glanced at Kline, 'On our feelings. It watches us.'

'My God,' said June quietly. 'Are you sure?'

'I'm not sure of anything. I only know what I instinctively feel.' Francoise sipped tea from a blue mug, while Kline watched her intently, frowning.

Something in the stone, something evil. But that wasn't rational, nor even sensible. She was talking about a demon, or a devil, something from the religious doctrines of the middle ages. So what *had* she sensed?

'Why is it watching us?' June was saying. 'Why? Why us?'

Francoise turned to look at Kline. 'Well?' she said. 'Don't you know?'

'If there's something there . . . *if* . . . then I suppose because of Adrian.'

June frowned. 'It has Adrian in the stone, and out here . . . are you saying that it's using Adrian? It watches us because we're his family. But why is it even *doing* that? What can we have that is of interest?'

Kline said, 'Freedom. A means to freedom.'

'Exactly!' said Francoise. 'It is trapped, this dark being. And it wants to be released. And I'll tell you something else . . . it is close to escape even now. Every contact it makes with us, it helps to get it free some more. And when I touched the stone I'm sure I weakened the hold of its prison upon it very greatly. Whatever it is, it will not be held much longer.'

'Don't interrupt me – you scorn me for using the words demon or devil, Lee, but these are just names, given by one group of people to strange things they did not understand. Lee, something – it is easiest to say, a *demon* – lives in that stone font. It lives there because it is trapped there, it was imprisoned there in some dark time, many hundreds, even thousands of years ago. The men who trapped it I sensed were powerful; they were men with powers like my powers, only more so. Never have I sensed it so strong, so overwhelming; never have I met anyone with powers like that. You remember, Lee, that I told you of my fears and my beliefs that such power did not leave man, but had become shrouded, and hidden, and it was people like myself who showed some signs of what each and every one of us can do . . . well, these men, these priests of the earth, they were . . . how to explain? . . . they were in *harmony* with the Universe, and with their world. They could speak with the wind, understanding the way it gusted and formed. They could commune with plants, encouraging them to grow, sensing the way plants observed their own environment; they knew about space and stars, the murmurs of time and the void; they knew about the depths of the earth, and the reality that existed beyond the matter of their own lands. They knew of Gods, and demons, of spirits and all the strange things that we call supernatural. No, Lee, don't interrupt! I sensed this, and they sensed it; they had never *seen*, not as with eyes, nor had they heard, or smelled, or touched; they just *knew* that there existed a powerful, but hidden and unbothersome world of beings, perhaps we should say *spirits* that owned the world in their own way, in the same way we own the world, and owned it then. They needed something different, if you like, some part of the Universe that co-existed with man, but did not interfere. And hardly ever overlapped. That slight overlapping gave rise to brief, much-feared visions of these powerful forces. With man's need for Gods, for forces of good and evil at war in the skies, fighting for possession of his soul, naturally the *need* and the occasional *visions* became the same.

'What these priests were trying to do was capture such a spirit, manipulating it into their own world, confining it in the stone from which it could be sent out on . . . errands . . . missions . . . It is hard to see exactly what they wished for, but I sensed briefly some tremendously avaricious souls at work; there was power to be had, and control over a world that seemed so dark in the valley but which they knew was bigger and brighter and richer beyond the shores of this land. They had come a long way from their own lands, these priests, looking for the right place . . . this valley was it, and now they needed the power of the Gods to assist them. They used their knowledge of their own power to drag it forth from the earth it inhabited. We would say they used magic, or spells, but this was science to them, this was technology, and they used this mind technology, and they used it very well.

'But the creature they captured was hostile and violent, it was infuriated and loathsome, and in the instant that they attracted it from the deep earth, it turned on them and killed many of them. Perhaps they had misunderstood the nature of the beast, perhaps it had been deformed during the passage to the stone, perhaps its violence was only violence in the eyes of man. Whatever the reason, it was useless to them, and dangerous to them. It was bound in the stone, however, and its power was weakened. And as far as I can see, those priests who survived used further magic to trap the demon more firmly, more bindingly. It has lain there ever since, but the hold of the stone, as I said, is weakening. Destruction, fire, the influence of the Christians and the contact of human beings, in violent and usually suicidal fashion, all have helped to slowly turn the key that will unlock the beast.

'I sensed, but very briefly, and very poorly, the way to lock it back, but I am afraid, now, afraid to touch that stone again. Because I might bring about the total release of the thing, and that would be terrible.'

As Francoise finished speaking, so June Hunter rose and walked to the kitchen door, stepping out into the garden and allowing the door to swing gently shut behind her. Kline said nothing, watching the woman as she leaned briefly against the wall, then began to walk slowly through the garden, immersed in her thoughts, perhaps trying to conquer her fears.

Francoise remained placid, staring at her clasped hands, studying the features of fingers and nails as if they were something of prime importance.

At length, Kline said, 'I find it very hard to believe.'

'I thought you did.'

He laughed, not with humour but with uncertainty, sublimating his confusion with a cheaper emotion. He felt very hot, and while Francoise had spoken the kitchen had seemed to recede, to become almost unreal. Her words, each syllable punctuating the stifling quietness of the room, had seemed unreal; her breath, slightly sour as she had looked towards him, seeming to be some wind that carried from a distant tunnel, high pitched and keening . . . he had lost all touch with the real senses of his world, caught in the sounds and pitches of her words, and the images, and the strange meanings they conveyed.

'A demon; earth Gods; priests – probably druids, or whatever were the magic-working equals; stone prisons; awesome mental powers.' He looked at her, shook his head. 'Not easy to cope with all that. A two hundred yard football pass from the quarter line, that's easy to accept. But demon Gods struggling to escape rocky tombs.' Again he looked overwhelmed. 'That's what I call a real bummer!'

'You must believe it, or I am useless and have been useless.'

'It goes against reason. It goes against modern religious thinking . . . it's just . . . it just doesn't ring true.'

'It *is* true. Man has summoned demons through all history. Obviously he learned how to control them better . . .'

'Jesus, Francoise! That's exactly what I mean. That's all crap. Satan is a psychological factor, not a real, live manifestation. Good and evil are symbols with which different societies establish their different rules. Some societies humanize the symbols, others don't.'

She said, 'I don't see the problem. We believe in ghosts, why not in dark powers, dark forces . . . Satan, demons, devils. Yes, your religious societies of the middle ages labelled things like that in Hebrew terms, related perhaps perfectly normal supernatural existences to the Christian belief in Angels, bright and dark. Don't confuse evil as symbol-humanized, with evil as symbol-associated-with-the-supernatural. One is fiction, one is fictionalized fact.'

Kline sat back his eyes popping. 'What language was that?'

Francoise laughed and pinched the back of his hand. 'You know what I mean!'

'I guess I do. It's interesting, in Western Europe one of the strongest God images is the Horned God. There is Cernunnos, who wears antlers and is identified as a Stag, but there are Ram gods, and Goat gods . . . all animals were god-like spirits to the ancient peoples, and if the Horned God, in particular this Cernunnos, was not the most important, he's certainly the one recalled the most. The horns were the ultimate animal symbol. The one thing that exists in the animal world, but not in the human world . . .'

'And tails,' said Francoise. 'Don't forget tails.'

'That's true. Horns and tails set a creature clearly as animal, not human. Man with horns and tail is thus a cross between man and animal, and therefore a God. So it really isn't hard to see how such powerful images arose in the ancients.'

'And were finally discredited by making them into Satan, the Ram of Mendes, or the Goat, whichever it is, I can never remember . . .'

Kline laughed. 'Cavendish would disagree with you, but he's almost certainly wrong.'

'Don't be clever. Who *is* this Cavendish?'

'Richard Cavendish. He wrote a book called *The Black Arts*, and dismissed the link between Faustus's Satan and the celtic

Horned God in about three lines. That will probably go down as the great oversight of the century.'

There was a moment's silence, then Francoise said, 'This thing had no horns, not like that.' Her face darkened as she re-lived her experience, and Kline could see the pain of recollected agony in her eyes. 'I caught only a glimpse . . . it was quite repugnant . . . a sort of man-shaped thing, leathery, horny skin, twisted but immensely strong, and horrible, staring eyes . . . insect eyes, dead, deadpan . . .' she shivered and fell silent.

Kline was thoughtfully quiet, watching as Francoise's skin paled, then flushed again, visual symptoms of the emotions she relived. At length he spoke, quietly so as not to arouse her hostility.

'Francoise, you said you felt that something was playing games.'

'Yes. Tricks and games, using us to its own end.'

'Could it be . . . I don't know . . . Adrian; could it in some way be Adrian? Perhaps he has access to the stone's records, and can manipulate them to *his* own ends. What do you think?'

Francoise stared at him, at first puzzled, then slightly angry. 'I told you what I felt, what I experienced. It is this powerful presence, this demon . . .'

'I don't believe in demons,' said Kline quickly. 'I'm not knocking you, Francoise, I'm not questioning your feelings. I'm just saying –'

'That you don't believe in demons.'

'So could it be Adrian, putting up this image to frighten us and confuse us?'

'I know what I saw. Can you see the nose on my face? You don't question that, do you? Don't question what I say I saw, then. It is this thing that is playing tricks. It is the demon that wants very desperately to escape. Adrian is his link with the outside world, a poor link, and a tenuous link, but a very real link. But Adrian's mind is not strong enough for it to grip, to haul itself from the stone. Nor was yours, it realized with some anger – that was why it punished you, but it wanted to keep you interested, because it sensed you could bring more help to it, better help. But when I came, I fought it. It was so angry, so violent, it nearly killed me. Frustration had made it ready to do just that. Now war is declared; it knows that you and I are strong. It must be on its guard. It is back to square one: Adrian.'

Kline considered her words for a long time, trying to swallow the feelings of bitter resentment that obsessed him as he came some way to accepting that he had been used.

'We were both thrown about; that is indisputable. June says she saw a man thrown about in the street, shortly before I arrived in Higham. What was he being punished for?'

She said, 'I don't know. Perhaps he wasn't. How do you even know it was anything to do with the font? Anyway, even if it was, perhaps this demon was beginning to flex its muscles, to try its strength. I'll tell you something: after it beat me, it was exhausted. I sensed that very strongly. Its power is limited while it is trapped.'

Kline accepted that as reasonable, but was still uneasy about the factual basis that Francoise insisted upon. He said, 'How about the suicides? A man committed suicide over the font just a week ago. Other people have done an identical thing over the years. I don't deny those suicides, Francoise, but they have to fit with your demon, and that's hard to do. I don't question that there is something very strange going on, all I question is the nature of the force that is behind that "something strange". I find it hard to believe in Gods and demons. I don't find it hard to believe in tortured human minds playing vicious tricks –'

'Poltergeists?'

Wearily, having only the evening before been over this same ground with Edward, Kline nodded. 'I'm fairly convinced that we are up against some form of poltergeist activity. Different, I grant you, stronger, more obsessive, more horrific. It *must* come from the boy, from the boy's mind in the stone.'

'That mind is infantile!' said Francoise loudly, angrily. 'Lee, the baby was not even a year old when it was dropped. The mind is not the mind of a grown boy, like Adrian is now. It's Adrian as a baby . . .'

She stopped. Kline frowned as he saw the sudden doubt in her eyes, a moments inner questioning of what she had said.

Kline leapt. 'It wasn't! It wasn't infantile, it was grown!'

'Yes.' She spoke distantly, emptily. 'How is that possible?'

'The mind has grown in the stone; perhaps it fed upon June as she poured out her soul into the font, not just occasionally, but for hours, every day. The mind has grown, become tortured, become frighteningly aware. It *has* to be that . . .'

Francoise sneered. 'And that's more feasible than the demon?'

'It makes more rational sense.'

She laughed. '*Rational* sense?'

'You know what I mean. It fits in with modern thinking on the matter.'

Francoise threw up her hands and laughed. 'Listen to this

200

mindless man. Four hundred years ago, talk of demons would have fitted with modern thinking. Our thinking will soon be as outdated as that. I said to June, and I say it to you. There is truth, and there is belief. Truth is more potent. Truth is undeniable. Truth is its own proof. The presence of an evil, powerful, demonic entity in the stone font is a *truth*, not a belief. You must accept that, or you are useless.'

'Useless! What the fuck does that mean?' He'd had enough of being called useless, of being told to bug out because his job was finished. Last night, and again this morning, he would dearly have loved to tackle June on the question of Karen's accusations, but it suited his ego better to believe that Karen had been trying to entice him with empty threats, rather than speaking the truth.

'It means you are not needed,' Francoise was saying. 'Not if you talk so negatively. Not if you won't believe in the real danger that threatens not just . . . not just this family, but everybody!'

'Demon doomsday?' mocked Kline. 'If it gets out the whole world is threatened?'

'You enjoy your sarcasm. But that makes me think very little of you. I am frightened, Lee, and not for my life, but for what that stone threatens to release into our world. You play with fire, as those priests did, and you burn not just your fingers, but your house and your lands. We have to stop that thing getting out, but if you refuse to accept it, to believe it is there, then you must leave. You must go now, right now, because evil preys on conflict, Lee, and your disbelief is causing conflict because it is causing confusion among the people around you. This whole family is in conflict, with each other, and within themselves; they are food and drink to this creature, draining them through the boy, and the more they argue, the more their relationships decay, the more it feeds and grows strong. It laughs at us, it encourages us, it frightens us, it puzzles us, it does everything it can to drive us in circles of confusion and conflict, and it grows stronger and stronger . . . and it will soon break free!'

Kline raised his hands to try and quieten the woman; he smiled, trying to explain with his eyes and gestures that he didn't want an argument. 'I'm not denying anything you say,' he said. 'I'm just saying that we should think of everything –'

'Merde!' cried Francoise, jumping to her feet. 'My God, Lee, you are so infuriating! You are so stupid!' And she ran from the kitchen still muttering loudly. Kline heard her pause at the bottom of the stairs, then walk up them quickly, not particularly quietly. After a moment he guessed she had gone into Adrian's room.

Stretching out, trying to ease the cramp in his body, a cramp induced, he could only suppose, by the unrealized tension during listening to Francoise, he rose and walked just outside the house, watching June. 'You OK?' he called.

She shrugged, then turned and nodded. 'I suppose so.' She looked up into the sky and Kline could see the sparkle of tears on her cheeks. Unashamedly she wept again, quite quietly, undramatically, her eyes tight closed, her lips pressed together to choke back the sound. Kline felt helpless and made no move, nor any attempt to speak.

After a minute or two June said, 'I just . . . I just can't help thinking of him . . . I can't get him out of my mind, that poor little boy . . . my poor little boy . . . I can't stop thinking . . . what she said about confusion, and terror . . . I can't . . . I can't bear to think of what he must be going through.'

Kline reached out and took her arm. June glanced up, then smiled. 'Let's walk, June.'

'Okay.'

They strolled slowly down the garden, their breath frosting in the chill. Kline felt cold, but somehow from a distance – he was unbothered by it.

They came into the trees and beneath them the ground crunched where they walked. Finally June stopped and hunched slightly, but she turned and looked at Kline, then brushed the chaotic curls of her hair away from her face.

'Francoise may have been wrong,' said Kline gently. June said nothing for a moment, just stared at him. Then she said,

'But she's never wrong, is she? She knows what she sees, and she doesn't believe in deception.'

Kline agreed with that. He reached out and took June's hand, warming the cold fingers. Unexpectedly June stepped up to him and put her arms around him, resting her head against his chest. She squeezed and Kline laughed. 'Ouch.'

Then he tilted her head so she was looking at him and said, 'What's this? More security?'

She nodded. Kline kissed her forehead and then relaxed his hold on her. She pulled away, solemn again, hunched again, with her hands folded across her chest.

Kline said, 'Maybe Francoise is never wrong about what she *thinks* she sees, that's all I meant. The world of that font, if Adrian's spirit there is aware, is the only world he has known. Terror and confusion may just be how Francoise reads the emotional charge . . . it may not mean the same thing to Adrian himself.'

June thought about that for a moment, then looked resigned. Tears again glistened in her eyes. 'I hope you're right,' she said, brushing at her cheeks, then rubbing her eyes more pointedly. 'Poor little boy,' she whispered. 'My God, Lee — I can't even *contemplate* what he must be going through.' She looked down towards the house, shivering. 'Do you think they sense each other?'

'Who?'

'Adrian,' she looked up at Kline and in her eyes was confusion, and something Kline thought might have been desperation. 'Both parts of him . . .'

'I don't know. I didn't think you felt there was anything in Adrian — the flesh and blood Adrian — that *could* sense anything.'

June shrugged, then smiled almost grimly. 'I don't know, Lee. I'm confused. I'm just confused.' And she walked out of the trees and back down towards the house.

Kline watched her for a moment. He felt disturbed by something but couldn't say what. After a while he followed her into the house, and when he couldn't see where she had gone he went upstairs to Adrian's room.

Francoise was sitting by the bed, on a hard wooden chair, her legs stretched out before her, her arms crossed. She was staring at the boy, who was sprawled out on the bed, fully clothed. His head was turned and he was staring at the woman. The room was full of light from the fine day outside, and heavy with the smell of sleep and childish aroma; no-one had opened the window.

As Kline entered, Adrian's eyes moved, though his head remained still. He gazed at the American quite blankly, quite unfrighteningly, then looked back at Francoise.

Francoise had sat up abruptly as Kline had entered, and he had heard the sound of her surprise.

Now she relaxed, sitting back again and folding her arms.

'How long has he been awake?' asked Kline. 'I thought Edward had sedated him.'

'He was awake when I came in,' said Francoise, distractedly. She looked round at Kline and then called him over. Adrian stared up at him, expressionless, his white hands resting easily on the covers by his side.

'I'm sorry about the row,' said Kline.

'I'm sorry I took such exception,' said Francoise. 'I am afraid that to convince you I am right might cost you your life.'

'A cheering prospect,' said Kline. He couldn't tear his eyes away from the placid, almost pathetic boy who lay on the bed. It amazed him that he could ever have believed this tiny body to be capable of acts of mayhem. 'Do you get any instinctive feelings from him?'

Francoise shook her head. 'Not much. Not until you came in.'

'Me?'

She nodded, thoughtful and almost reluctant to voice what she meant. 'It was quiet for a while. I sat and looked at him, and he sat and looked at me, and there was quietness and a sense of him watching me, not understanding me. It was very peaceful. But the moment you walked in I felt something much stronger . . . a sense of being watched that was much more than just his own eyes. It was as if something, just briefly as you opened the door, were glancing *through* his eyes.'

'I've often felt that Adrian was watching me when I've been on my own, in the lounge, or the kitchen. Just moments when the hair on the neck prickles and you turn, expecting to see him, and he isn't there.'

Francoise shrugged, and stood, turned to face Kline and smiled at him. 'We must reduce conflict,' she said. 'Not just for the sake of demons and spirits, but . . . for our sake. It is bad to argue.'

Kline agreed. Francoise looked back at Adrian, then said, 'Lee, he's not possessed, I'm sure of that. He's used, but he's not possessed . . . but he's very close to being so, very close. I know, I just *know*, that he is being used. You must accept what I say, or I'm afraid the boy's fate will be much worse than just being a shell with less than half its wits.'

CHAPTER FOURTEEN

On an impulse Kline left the house and drove out into the country, stopping for a drink at the first public house he saw that promised an English atmosphere, and quietness. He stared through the small windows of the lounge bar at the November fields, and slowly the tension that had been building within him drained fast, and pleasantly, and he closed his eyes, listening to normal dialogue, and laughter, and the normal life of people unaware of the obsessive fears that were shrouding a community just a few miles east of them.

After a while he grew restless with deliberately leaving his mind blank, and turned his thoughts to what had caused the argument this morning; he thought of the difference between truth and belief, and wondered if he could find it within himself to accept something that had not been proved, only witnessed, and then by just a single woman.

In his office, in London, Francoise had dropped the fragment of stone, upset by the images she had gleaned from it. Those same impressions, though stronger, more frightening still, had leapt out at her from the stone font itself. As far as she was concerned this was irrefutable evidence for the two stones having once been a part of the same. Kline couldn't help the nagging mistrust he felt for such tenuous evidence, but he was in no doubt of her ability, and her power! He just hated not being able to *see* with his own eyes the evidence she was asking him to accept.

There was little point in self-admonishment. It was the way he was made, doubting until the evidence was concrete . . .

But if, in fact, the fragment *had* been broken off from the font, then it should be possible to see the place where it had been. The font was lower in the ground than it had been a hundred years ago; he had seen this from Alexander's picture, and another thought was nagging him: had the man who had tried to destroy the font in fact been trying to destroy the *symbol*?

What *did* that symbol mean?

His thoughts drifted, around and around, like the narrowing circle of a spiral, until at last – quite abruptly – he found himself thinking of something else entirely.

Devil worship.

Perhaps his doubt about the stone fragment was merely a sublimation of his doubt in Francoise's frightening vision of something ancient, and dark, and 'evil'. Perhaps his cynical subconscious needed to throw as much shadow on the woman's talent as possible so that Kline could more easily believe in the boy, Adrian, as being the confined force of 'evil', and not just one prisoner among several. He did not like to admit that something non-human, and ugly, was entering the framework of the Hunter's obsessions. He did not like to think of himself pitched, body and soul, against something that was effectively a religious menace.

He did not like to admit that he was narrow minded; and in this case . . . wrong?

But *demons*! Wasn't it far more likely that she was misunderstanding the impressions the stone was giving her? Or that

Adrian, the malicious persona of Adrian, was playing tricks with her, and with her inner senses?

The frustrating thing was that there was no way he could know, not unless something – or the boy – was released from the stone, and although in the one case that was highly desirable . . ..

Confusion!

Kline shook his head, finished his drink and drove back to Higham. It was mid-afternoon, and he remembered there was something he had wanted to do for several days.

Visit the museum.

It was a fairly typical small-town museum, mainly Victorian and Edwardian exhibits, the emphasis on dress, and agricultural machinery and tools. There was a small Roman case, with coins, pottery and two miniatures of the God Mithras, one of them incorrectly labelled Kline noticed as he paused and admired them There were stone axes, arrow-heads and neolithic pottery, several cultures jumbled together in the same display. Nothing bronze, except that which was Roman.

The whole place was uncomfortable; it was shadowy and musty, and Kline disliked such relics of an age when anything that was itself a relic was somehow hidden away in dark, silent corridors.

He walked around the displays for a few minutes, alternately bored, amused or intrigued. He was on the point of seeking out the curator when he saw a new display, quite intelligently arranged – a series of panels, covered with photographs and drawings of a church . . .

And when he drew near, excited, expectant, he was delighted to discover that this was a display of St Mary's.

The story of the fire was there, and dramatic shots of the church burning, the dark walls framed by flame as it poured above them and through the windows in them. It had been a massive fire, almost unbelievable! Kline had never known it was possible for a building of such solid, cold stone to burn with such fury.

The recent history of the church was there, and Kline read it, fascinated. There was a long item on the history of the site which he decided to come back to because his attention had been caught by photographs of the church interior prior to the destruction. The font was there, of course, looking ordinary and uninteresting; the altar; the windows, the richly coloured stained glass, obviously the work of a real craftsman. Above the altar there had been a double figure of Christ, each over twenty feet high, Kline guessed.

One figure was Christ crucified, the other his white-robed figure, hands extended demonstrating the stigmata; the face of each was that strong, compassionate face that graced so many Catholic idols.

Below the picture were water colour paintings of the same interior, donated by a local resident. They were the work of a local man some hundred and fifty years before, and when Kline searched his memory for the name of the artist whose black and white sketches had recently been auctioned, he realized that this colour work was by the same man. The colour was beginning to fade with constant exposure to the light.

Fascinated, Kline bent close to scrutinize them. What had caught his attention, for the first few seconds, was that the windows shown above the altar were different to those that had been destroyed by the fire – they were more abstract, the contrast of light and dark glass more pronounced . . .

For a second his eyes had been confused by the undefined shapes, and hinted scenes; he had seen colour, depth, and experienced a sense of peacefulness in the abstract scene. It emerged through this sensory confusion as if it had been moving towards him all the time and had only now come into focus. The symbol from the Higham Fragment! The symbol that had been painted in blood on the font!

He was still leaning close, and staring at those enigmatic circles of bright glass when a hand touched his arm, startling him.

A middle-aged man stood there, smiling. 'Are you alright?'

Kline straightened, wiped a hand across his mouth, frowning. 'What do you mean?'

'You were shouting . . . I thought perhaps . . .'

'Was I shouting?' Kline looked back at the picture, feeling slightly embarrassed now. 'No, I'm fine. I saw something that surprised me, that was all.' He glanced back at the older man. 'Where do I find the curator, can you tell me?'

'I'm the curator. Kevin Lester. I've looked after this museum since I left Oxford, twenty years ago. I make models . . .'

He had extended his hand and Kline gave it a perfunctory shake. 'Lee Kline. Models? Historical models?'

Lester shrugged. 'All sorts, but yes, forts, houses, ships, anything that brings the dead past alive in the imagination.' He glanced at the display of St Mary's. 'There'll be a lot more displays like this going up. I've just about got the money together to start brightening this place up. Are you interested in the church?'

'Very much so.'

207

'So am I. I'm building a model of the site, to show the various structures that were on it before the church. All models will be cut away, a sort of religious progression from stone age to ruined modern age.' Both men looked at the closely typed information sheet on the early history of the church. Lester said, 'It was a tragedy when the church burned. A church has stood on that spot for centuries. The earliest remains were late sixth century. Before that there was a tumulus. There were some excavations in the thirties beneath the foundations of the church when they were digging out the medieval crypt. It had been filled in two hundred years ago, no-one knows why. They went deeper and found traces of cyst burials, bronze age, but the cyst burials themselves had been placed over cremations very much like western-coast neolithic burials. Perhaps once there was a fairly large stone-age mausoleum here, and the Bronze Age chieftains, the priest culture, dug into it for their own burials. But that site was of importance for thousands of years pre-Christ. And the fire finished it. The ruins are protected, and they will stand, but as a curiosity, now. And that makes me sad. The place has a vitality, a living vitality all of its own.'

'I know,' said Kline evenly. 'I felt it.'

'Have you?' Lester nodded thoughtfully, sweeping back his long, straight black hair. Kline smiled inwardly at the man, at the way he spoke like one of his information sheets.

Lester went on, 'I think everybody probably feels it. You stand there, in the rubble, and it still has something remote, something ancient about it. You can feel the power of time. Have you encountered Ley lines?'

'Occasionally,' said Kline with a polite smile. 'The church doesn't lie on one.'

'Places of enormous importance often don't.'

'Isolated foci of energy,' said Kline, and Lester smiled broadly and said, 'Yes, that's right.'

They looked at the display in silence. Christ regarded them passionately and sorrowful from the large photograph. He seemed to stare at Kline, holding open his palms to let the American see the mark of the beast, the mark of man, of the devil in man.

Noticing the way Kline was watching the face of Christ, Lester reached out and gently touched the colour photograph. 'It's beautiful, isn't it? Every day, no matter how sunny or dull, a shaft of light reached from the face of the Christ, here, right the way to the end of the church, to the baptismal recess and its promise of life. From the face of death to the dark corner of the womb. They designed the window to do that . . . the priest who ordered the glass to be changed. Dark glass around the bright face so the face would give a solid shaft of light.'

'Which priest ordered the glass changed? Not my old friend Albert MacAlistair . . .'

'Indeed, indeed!' said Lester, and smiled. 'By all the signs he was a real bible thumper. He thought that abstract design of the window was pagan, unholy, and he smashed them himself, with stones thrown in anger.'

And quite suddenly Kline became aware of something that had been obvious all along; his mind, still excited, still distracted, by the fact of the ancient symbol in that old stained glass window, only now added the fact of the symbol to the fact of the shaft of light, playing its Holy Energies across the source of Holy Life . . . the font. As he looked again at the symbol . . . dark glass emphasizing the light glass of the design itself . . . as he thought, now, of the shaft of brilliant sunlight that had carried that incomprehensible image to the stone font, so he laughed out loud and cursed his slowness.

And in answer to Lester's spoken query he said, 'Our friend MacAlistair might not have been as crazy as we think. I don't suppose for an instant that he knew what he was doing, but he was almost certainly obliterating something thoroughly and utterly non-Christian, there can be no doubt of that.'

Lester had grasped the source of Kline's amazement. 'Of course,' he said, himself much pleased. 'The priest copied the sunlight effect . . . you're saying that whoever designed the early windows consciously built in a pagan symbol that would unify the mixed religious beliefs . . .'

Kline shrugged. 'I don't know the motive, and would not like to guess at it. But I'll stake a great deal on that symbol having once been carved on the font. And I'll stake even more on that symbol being the *key* to the font.'

Lester smiled as he stared at the pictures of the church. 'Well there you are. How very strange. The old peoples who built those fantastic rock tombs used to do a similar trick. They'd leave a small gap in the tumulus, held open by stone, and on certain key days of the year the first light of day would send a shaft of brightness through the passage in the tomb right to the burial recess at the end. Egyptians did it too. Perhaps it's something that man finds inescapably fascinating – directing the energy of sun in a controllable form to touch that which he reveres . . .'

Kline nodded soberly, liking the words, liking the idea, worried by an inadequacy in them. 'Or something he . . . fears, perhaps?'

Lester smiled and shook his head, not in disagreement, perhaps in surprise. He removed his glasses and cleaned them elaborately with a red handkerchief. 'The key to the font,' he said quietly, watching Kline through dark-lined eyes, narrowed to a penetrating squint. 'That suggests some sort of mystery.'

Kline agreed but refrained from commenting further. He walked away from the panels on St Mary's and Lester followed, walking ahead of him to turn on several more of the museum's lights.

'Are you aware that the font in St Mary's was carved from one of the Avebury stones?'

'How do you know?' said Kline sharply, frowning.

Lester laughed and shook his head. 'It's just a story, but one believed by an enormous number of people round here. It's just a convenience of course. Some of the Avebury stone circle is missing –'

'A lot is missing.'

'Indeed. And the font is the same stone type. It's a romantic story, but of course where it originally stood can't be known. Some say they instinctively know it was carved and erected exactly where it now stands as a font.'

'That makes more sense to me,' said Kline. 'It would have been dragged into position first, then used for whatever purpose. It would have been no difficult task at all for even stone age man to have dragged that lump of rock across country.'

'And less problem again for the iron-using Britons. They could easily have dragged the stone for several hundred miles, not just a few tens . . .'

Intrigued, Kline glanced at the man. 'Now that's very interesting you should say that. But why *do* you say that?'

Almost anxiously Lester said, 'Because of the Ogam prayer stone.'

Kline, stunned, then sceptical, finally laughed. 'You're not saying there's Ogam script here as well.'

'You're standing next to it,' said Lester, and Kline turned to peer in the glass exhibit case.

There were fragments of flat carved stone, with deeply incised lines in rows, and the small horizontal and angle-groups of lines that each represented a roman letter. Kline stared in amazement, then frowned. Then shook his head.

'It's Ogam, but it's not genuine.'

'That's what the British Museum said, years ago when the slabs were unearthed beneath the church. They would have nothing to do with them.'

'I'm not surprised. Ogam was a very late Celtic written form, the only written form before they adopted the more usual script. And you only find it in Wales and Scotland, and of course Ireland.'

'And Higham.'

'But it just never arose in the Roman province. Everybody here would have written in Latin, using Arabic script. Ogam was a Celtic backwaters script, developed by Irish scholars and priests and imported into Wales and Scotland years later.'

Lester shrugged. 'You don't have to tell me. And it was always written down the edge of a memorial stone, and spelled out the Latin form of a name or a place.'

'Right. And this . . . well, it's like a book.'

'It's a prayer,' said Lester, unlocking the case. 'The slabs were found below the church foundations, close to the font, when the underlying burials were being excavated. I think they relate to the same period of time as the erection of the stone. It's a prayer, perhaps of a Celtic revival group trying to keep alive the old ways as the Romans set up parallel cultures around them, and the two cultures slowly mingled and became confused. Perhaps the elders of the community here sent to the far west for men who were closer to the old ways; and they used the hidden script, which few Romans, or Romanized Britons, would have known. Isn't that possible?'

'Anything's possible,' said Kline, romantically taken by the idea, deeply sceptical. He accepted one of the slabs. 'I just never saw it written like this before, that's all.'

'Well, that's the influence of the East for you. The old script, the new way of writing it.'

Kline held the first fragment and touched the faint (and obviously newly cleaned) marks. He felt thrill after thrill run through him, and he stared at what was written and slowly, piece by piece, he worked it out: IN ÆTERNU . . . *until the end of time*; AD TERRAM MASTABIMUS . . . *we sacrifice (will sacrifice?) to the earth*; VIGOR SAXI . . . *strength of stone*; LUNAE CORNUA . . . *horns of the moon (horned moon?)* CATENIS DARE CRUACHOSEM . . .

Imprison Cruachos! Cru . . . the name the boy had used . . . a shortened version of Cruachos. But who or what was *that*?

Had the boy known the name because he had seen these marks

translated? Or had he known through some other way, through a deeper, more spiritual source of information?

Cruachos.

Even saying the name through the silence of his mind, it filled him with apprehension, sent a nasty shiver through him.

Cruachos.

The name of the beast.

PART FOUR

EARTHFIRE

CHAPTER FIFTEEN

It was shortly after eight. June and Edward Hunter were sitting quietly in the lounge, relaxing. Edward was flipping through the pages of manuscript of his latest chapter, his mind only half on the words and content. He seemed distracted, and Francoise Jeury, relaxing with them, felt that she herself was the distraction. June's eyes were closed. It had been an emotionally draining day for her and she looked exhausted. Francoise herself felt bright, but dizzy; her scalp was sore, and when she moved there was an aching pain in her ribs that she knew was an enormous and discoloured bruise; but apart from that she felt unbothered by the damage to her body. She sat in the deep armchair, glad of the stillness of the warm lounge, and allowed her mind to reel chaotically about the events of the previous day – images and excitement, memories and the fluctuations of her emotions, all whirled through her head, intriguing her, fascinating her, exciting her more with each minute that passed.

The stillness had lasted for an hour.

At ten past eight June opened her eyes and stood up. 'I'm going to make some coffee.'

And at that precise moment there was a deafening explosion and the front window erupted inwards, showering glass across them, and plaster, and fragments of wood.

June screamed and dropped to the floor, and Francoise ran into a corner and dropped onto her haunches, wide-eyed and terrified, feeling warm blood run from several small scratches on her face and arms. Miraculously her eyes were undamaged. Edward Hunter, bleeding from a single cut on his cheek, remained stiffly seated for a moment before shouting loudly and angrily for his wife to shut up.

The curtains that had blocked out the night were in tatters, ripped and holed, and it was these that had reduced the killing impact of the explosion.

Nevertheless the shot-gun blast had been powerful enough to have killed them if it hadn't been directed upwards, where it had buried itself in plaster and wooden flooring.

As Edward rose to his feet, and walked shakily towards the window, so Karen raced down the stairs, and Adrian's high-pitched wailing announced that he was terrified by the sudden noise, and the way the floor must have shaken.

Edward, acting with almost unbelievable foolhardiness, wrenched back the curtains and stepped up to the shattered window. Only small fragments of glass remained in the frame, and he stepped onto the low sill and jumped outside.

Francoise followed, more cautiously, and soon saw that there was no further danger.

Tim Belsaint's father was kneeling on the driveway, his head hanging, the tears flooding from him uncontrollably. He was shaking like a leaf, and sobbing loudly. Don, pale and frightened, was holding the now broken shotgun and crouching by his father. There was blood on Don's face, his lips, as if he had been punched.

He looked up at Edward, then across at Francoise as she jumped through the window and ran towards Simon Belsaint. She put her arms around him and whispered to him, while Don rose to his feet and confronted Edward.

'What in the name of *God* is going on?' stormed Edward.

'It was my father. He went berserk . . .'

Edward stared angrily down at the older man. 'You bloody fool!' he screamed. 'You could've . . .'

'Shut up!' screamed Don, and then, 'Shut up for Christ's sake!'

June ran to him. 'It's alright Don. We're just shaken. Calm down.' She turned on her husband. 'Why don't you go inside the house and blow your brains out? Do something constructive . . .'

'But this man . . . !'

'Oh *do* be quiet Edward. Can't you understand anything?'

Edward, white with fury, reached up and wiped the blood from his cheek, stared at the smear on his hand, then turned with fresh fury upon her. 'I understand that my wife and myself have come close to being blasted to blasted Kingdom Come. What else am I supposed to understand? What the *hell's* going on?'

Don said, 'My father, Doctor Hunter. He went out of his mind. He got the gun and threatened to kill Adrian . . .'

'Too many bloody guns in your house!'

'I only just managed to stop him. He knocked me down twice; he had a maniac's strength. I only just stopped him shooting in a straight line, but the blast still went into the house. I'm truly, truly sorry for this, but since Timmy's death . . .'

'It's alright Don,' said June. 'Bring your father inside. Oh God . . .' Don caught her as she stumbled, and in the event it was he who helped June inside, and Francoise who lent support to

Simon Belsaint. Edward had preceded them into the house and was busy at the phone when June entered the lounge.

'If you're ringing the police,' she said evenly, 'I'll empty the other barrel into your brains. And that's the truth.'

Edward stared at her, white faced. After a moment he returned the phone to its stand and looked away.

They sat in the lounge, brushing glass from seats and kicking it out of sight, and June replaced the single bulb that had been knocked out by a fragment of shot. The plaster was still flaking from the ceiling and Francoise took the opportunity of the moment's quietness to run upstairs and calm Adrian.

Karen was already with him, herself in a state of shock. Francoise was surprised that the girl's first concern was for the brother with whom she was so ill at ease, and not for the boyfriend whose presence in the confusion outside the house she must have known about.

'How is he?' she asked.

Karen glanced up, the frown on her face making her seem old. 'He's shaking.'

Adrian lay in bed, staring upwards at nothing, and his whole body racked and shook.

'He's not been hurt . . . ?'

'No, not at all. I think he's just frightened.'

The boy's lips moved, as if he was trying to speak. Puzzled, Francoise went nearer to him, and as she stooped so she momentarily jerked up. His breath was foul, fetid. 'He stinks.'

'Yes I know,' said Karen. 'He doesn't usually.'

'He's trying to say something.'

'No. He often does this.'

But Francoise bent closer, trying to ignore the boy's strongly unpleasant breath. 'Adrian, what are you trying to say? Say it louder.'

Still the boy's lips moved, and his eyes rolled. His hands grasped the sheets as if he were in some intense pain. Then, quite suddenly, he said with his hoarse whisper of a voice, 'Kill Kline. Kill me. Kill all who danger. Danger. Danger kill Kline danger all kill Karen french, Kline danger Cru Cru danger kill . . .'

Francoise's eyes were wide and she was white and shocked. She watched the moving lips and listened to the repetitive words, meaningless except for the continual use of the word kill, and the steady, repetitive listing of names, everyone's name, but over and over again, Kline's name. The boy's shaking grew worse, and blood appeared on his lips as he bit through the soft skin on the inside of his mouth.

Francoise tried to calm him, forcing his shoulders down, urging him to be restful. Karen wiped the bursting sweat from his face, and Francoise felt, rather than saw, the silent tears she cried, perhaps feeling something of the sisterly love she had always found it difficult to discover for Adrian.

And then Adrian struck.

It was sudden, and horrifying; the shaking stopped and the empty, terrified features hardened into a mask of pure malice. Instantly Francoise recoiled, but then she was sprawled out on the boy, wrestling with his hands as they dug deeper, more killingly into Karen's throat. The girl gagged, her eyes wide and popping, her face bloated and red.

Adrian's fingers were white, the tension and pressure of his enormous strength squeezing and twisting as Francoise frantically tore at the tiny limbs.

She finally hit him in the face, knocking him on the jaw, then on the cheek, then hitting him blow after blow on the head until the mask of anger and hatred became confused; he relaxed his grip on Karen and fell backwards, choking up vomit and blood that pooled about him and might have drowned him if Francoise hadn't upturned the bed and toppled him out of it.

He lay face down on the floor, absolutely still, and his breathing became hoarse and pained. But Francoise's attention was on Karen, who was silent and terrified, touching the hideous blue and red marks on her throat and trying to ease her breath through her windpipe without pain, for the cartilage had been compressed and hard breathing would have been unbearable.

And downstairs the front door bell rang, and Kline's voice drifted up to her, loud and anxious: 'Who's been playing silly buggers?'

'Lock the door.'

By her tone Francoise let Edward Hunter know she was absolutely insistent. 'Lock him in. You let him out at your peril.'

'My *peril*?' Edward sneered and grinned, but in his face there was something that told of his cynicism not being sincere.

'You saw what he did to your daughter.'

'That was a fit. He often gets them. He can't control his muscles, and I agree, he gets dangerous. I *shall* lock the door. And the windows are locked too, but he could still break them to get out.'

'Someone must always be outside, watching to make sure he doesn't do just that.'

'Then Madame Jeury, I suggest –' Biting back the anger, Edward nodded and changed tack, almost wearily. 'I suppose you're right. Very well, we'll arrange that.'

He turned to the door to Adrian's room and opened it slightly, staring at the sleeping boy. Then he closed and locked it and showed Francoise the key before placing it above the door frame. 'He's heavily sedated, now. I don't think he'll be going anywhere.'

'You'd better pray not. Whatever you say, whatever Lee says, that was not a fit brought on by the shock of an explosion. The demon wants Karen dead, and it wants other people dead as well; but most especially it wants Karen dead and I don't understand why. So watch your daughter all the time, m'sieu. Lee can look after himself. But Karen may be in a lot more danger than we suspect.'

'From the demon . . .' said Edward in amusement.

'From ignorance,' said Francoise coldly.

The police had been and gone, investigating the shot (which had been reported by a neighbour), and Francoise was amazed that they had not sensed something wrong. Young policemen, inexperienced, were more interested in the rapidly recovering Karen, and her flashing brown eyes, than in the sad man, with his sad son, and the sad – how frighteningly close they had come to being tragic – events that had required the presence of the law.

Francoise, quite shaken and yet unbothered by her superficial cuts, remained seated and watching all, and slowly a sort of clarity was assumed by what, for a while, had been a most confused and misty scenario. Simon Belsaint was resting upstairs; the rest of them were here, in the lounge. The curtains no longer had holes in them; June had changed them that quickly. The French-woman had watched June running around, tidying, cleaning, talking in small, incessant ways, as if the mere emission of breath – no matter how meaningless – were a welcome catharsis of the effects of shock.

Edward, mournful and pale, drank and drank and drank. God, how much whisky went into him. And yet he never staggered, never winced, or slurred a word as he talked in a booming, monotonous voice . . .

Kline rattled around, chirpy, angry, excited . . . he was still going on about the stone, and scripts, and the name of the beast. His face was boyish, eyes, mouth, wrinkled cheeks, grinning as if nothing tragic were important, and it was just, by Christ! the sun actually *touched* the font at a certain time every day, and the symbol – what symbol? – therefore had touched it, and the museum was full of Latin, a delightful curator, photographs of the church . . . How important! How to the point! And the demon was there, he believed her, he believed her . . .

And he was so sorry he hadn't believed at all, great danger, great danger, and the sun strikes the font every day through the symbol of the face of Christ. Christ! What the hell, what's he saying?

Edward drinks, drinks, drinks, and Don is comforting Karen, and talking about his father: Wouldn't have done it if I'd had some sway with him, but he's never listened to me. Tim was his favourite.

Violins. Karen chokes. I'm going to kill Adrian.

But you mustn't say that dear!

Sweeping of glass, the voice, from June, as glassy and as tinkly as the glass she swept. And Kline went on, and on: the font must be pulled out, like a tooth, gotta see the base, gotta see if the fragment fits . . .

The symbol, the symbol . . .

Drinking.

I'm going to kill Adrian, before he kills us all. Don't say that Karen. Adrian's your brother. Not my brother. Karen your father's right, you must understand him. The bastard, the bastard, he's possessed, Francoise knows it, why don't you listen, listen, we're all going to die unless we listen, the bastard is possessed; listen, listen, listen –

'SHUT UP! ALL OF YOU! STOP . . . STOP TALKING, STOP EVERYTHING!'

And a sudden, shattering and resonating explosion, and blood, and blood!

And silence.

Francoise had collapsed in the corner and Kline, in two minds as to what to do, ran to her first. He had noticed how pale she was, how quiet she had been; she had stayed in the corner, watching them, while he had explained about the museum. Her face had seemed taut, tense, and he had known she was ill; but that sudden, hysterical outburst had shocked him, and prepared him, emotionally, for the second explosion of the shot-gun, and the awful spray of blood and wood splinters from the hallway.

As Edward ran to the body of Simon Belsaint, Kline dragged Francoise's limp body to a chair and sat her down.

Karen was crying, but most noticeable of all was a terrible, wind-like moaning which after a second Kline recognized as Don.

He went to look. Simon Belsaint had been upstairs lying down. Now he had come down to the hall and picked up the shot-gun from where Edward, with Edward's exact thoughtlessness, had placed it in the hatstand, ready to be taken away when Don and his father went home.

With the second barrel – Christ, no-one had thought to unload the second barrel! – he had clumsily and inexpertly attempted suicide, and had discovered what many others had discovered before him: how difficult it is to achieve such an end with such a gun. Nevertheless, the gun had gone off, and a considerable amount of Simon Belsaint had gone off with it – his shoulder, neck and face had taken the brunt of the blast, and he was almost unrecognizable as he lay in the hallway, with his son staring down at him, reaching out but unable to touch his father.

'I just don't believe this,' said June, and instantly fainted. Edward, finished on the phone to the hospital, was sick. Everything became unreal.

Hours had passed, and yet it was only midnight. Kline had stayed with Don in the hospital for as long as Don had wanted to stay. Eventually it was obvious that there would be no word until the morning. The emergency operation would be long, and tedious, and the atmosphere of the waiting room was unbearable and a constant reminder of death.

When they got home they discovered that the police had come and stayed. They were angry, this time, as angry as was Kline, as angry as Edward, and they just didn't believe, now, that there wasn't something going on.

A plainclothes policeman, whose name Kline thought might have been Underwood, sat solemn and tired in an armchair and talked and talked: he questioned and probed, and of course Karen wasn't going to keep quiet about Adrian, and Edward and June argued between each other, and Kline tried tactfully to let the man know that this was something best left to the experts, which in this case the police were not, and suspicions were aroused.

There was no question of it not being an attempted suicide. But somehow that explanation did not satisfy. Midnight came and passed, and Underwood remained. He was angry and he did not believe Edward Hunter when the doctor kept saying, 'It's grief.

Really, just grief. Please leave us alone. There is nothing you can do, or find out, that you don't already know.'

'I hate that sort of patronizing shit,' said Underwood, and silenced Edward instantly. The policeman scratched the dark stubble on his chin and looked from one to the other of them. He was a young man, aggressive, and there were years of experience in the arrogant, searching way he kept the others on their toes, watching him, never comfortable with him. Suddenly he straightened in his chair and reached down to the floor for his empty cup. 'I'd like another cup of coffee, somebody. Please. You are not getting rid of me, and I'll tell you why. There is something in this town that dislikes you Belsaints . . .' As he spoke he glanced at Don, who was sitting pale and drawn, somewhere between numbed and hysterical silence. By now everyone knew how distant had been his relationship with his father.

As June took Underwood's cup and vanished to the kitchen, the policeman watched the youth, almost frowning. Don was magnificent to still be conscious, to still be calm, without the effects of pills or medications to assist the inner spirit. He watched and listened, and only occasionally did Kline notice a tear or two drop from his eyes to be lost, unwiped, unhidden, against the paleness of his skin.

Underwood said, 'In the past five years there have been over twenty attacks on people whose name is Belsaint. You're all related, I expect – distant cousins, and so on. I expect you know this. Perhaps no-one else knows but there are many Belsaints in the area, not just in Higham. It's a very old family, one of several such, and its roots go back centuries. The man who died in St Mary's church a few days ago – perhaps you read about it – his name was Belsaint. People with that name have complained of being attacked by night, by someone in the town. We've never pinned him down. It's as if there were someone with a grudge against you all. It's as if . . .' he hesitated, staring at the pale-featured boy, then lowered his gaze. 'It must be said. It's as if someone is trying to kill you all, or drive you to suicide.'

Don did nothing, said nothing, staring at the detective with empty eyes, a blank expression.

Meanwhile Edward was righteously furious. 'What a tactless thing to say!'

And even Kline said, 'Surely this can wait. It's hardly a good time to start talking about murder.'

'Please, Mister Kline,' said Underwood with restrained impatience, 'I know what I'm doing.'

Angrily, Kline said, 'You do *shit*! That guy's father just got blown . . . excuse me . . . just had a near fatal accident. You sit here talking like it happened a year ago. You're cold, but nobody else in the room is.' He turned to Don. 'Let me drive you home.'

But Don shook his head. 'I'm alright, thanks. I want to know about this. I'm feeling okay, quite calm. I want to know . . .'

Surprisingly Underwood frowned. 'You want to know . . . what?'

'About my family. I want to know what's on your mind. Have you an idea about this grudge?'

Edward stood and rested a hand on Don's shoulder. Perhaps Hunter himself was more distressed than the boy, and found the conversation difficult to listen to. 'Don, don't talk about it now. You'll distress yourself. Go home.'

'What to? To that house? No thanks.'

'Well, go to bed. Karen will show you which room. If you must talk then talk in the morning.'

But Don shook him off, his face reddening with anger; in his eyes was that intense look of urgency, of desperation. 'I want to know now, I've got to know. I've *got* to. God almighty, I'm nearly all that's left. And . . . and something . . .' he trailed off, staring at Kline. The American instantly felt uneasy, frowning as he leaned forward.

'What is it, Don?'

Don shook his head, but that terrified look didn't fade from his eyes. 'It's this sort of whispering . . . like a voice. It's so compulsive. It terrifies me . . .' As he spoke so Karen and Edward exchanged pointedly worried looks; the girl was thinking of her own 'compulsion' nightmare, Kline guessed. 'I keep waking up to it,' Don went on, 'like from a nightmare. I keep hearing voices, which don't say anything, and I keep . . . I keep . . .'

'Come on Don, keep what? Tell us. Get it out your system.'

He stared at Kline. 'I keep wanting to kill myself. I don't of course, I stop it, I fight it . . . but, oh Jesus! My father said just this, a year ago. It's a terrible compulsion to kill . . . to end the agony . . . I feel it now . . . how easy to strike and drain away, to put it past me, to no longer be a part of the grief . . .'

'You *must* fight it,' said Francoise after the long silence that followed Don's almost inarticulate emotion. Francoise had come alive for the first moment in hours, and she leaned forward, meeting the boy's gaze.

Don said, 'But why do I feel it's so right? Why do I feel that to do it would be to destroy some evil in me?'

'The demon makes you do this,' said Francoise. 'Don't give in.'

'What demon? What the hell are you talking about?' said Underwood, but when he looked from Francoise to Kline he found himself looking at a man who was not only surprised, but astonished.

Kline was staring at Don as if he had just seen the secrets of the Universe written in his face.

Underwood, shaking his head, said, 'You have something to tell us, Mister Kline?' He glanced away as June Hunter returned with his coffee.

Kline grew solemn. 'No,' he said. 'But Don has.' He looked at the boy, then at Francoise. 'For once, my gorgeous, you are wrong. Not the demon.'

Underwood repeated, 'Mister Kline, you have something to tell us?'

'I repeat, Don has something to tell us, not me. He doesn't know it . . .'

'No,' said Don, shaking his head in confusion. 'I don't.'

'But he has a whole lot to tell us. The only problem is, how to get the information out of him.'

And that was all he would say. Underwood finally gave up, finished his coffee, and walked from the house, making vague threats that he would return. He was unhappy and dissatisfied with what he had heard and what he had learned, but he seemed to grasp that he would find things growing no clearer even if he stayed until dawn.

Before he drove away, however, Kline set in motion his scheme to raise the font from its deep embedding in the ground below the church. 'If you really want to learn something,' he said, as Underwood regarded him with some suspicion from his car, 'You'll have to yank that font out of its hole and have a look underneath.'

'And what do you imagine that we'd find there? And what would it relate to?'

'To everything. To what's happened here tonight. To the man who died there a few days back. To mysterious attacks in the street. To suicides. To an exorcism of that font by a crazy, heroic priest. To a man who used horses to pull the font from its setting and hacked at it with a sledgehammer until something killed him, but he had still done what he was supposed to do.'

Underwood shook his head, yawned. 'This is all nonsense. What are you, some sort of joker?' There was restrained anger in the man's voice, and in his eyes. Kline reached out and grabbed the shoulder of his coat.

'Nonsense is one thing it isn't; there's one thing you'd better get clear, and fast, and that is that something big, something wild is going down here, and there are certain things that have to be done, and certain things that have to be confirmed. I want that font out of the ground, dangling at the end of a crane. How the hell do I do it? That's what I'm asking you. I can't just walk up to the Mayor's office. I figure you and your bloodhounds are my best bet. That font is the key to a whole lot of things, and you really ought to be looking underneath it.'

Kline touched the side of his nose and winked elaborately. Underwood's laugh was cynical. 'That font hasn't been moved for a century. Someone had bashed about at the surrounding tiles . . . I suppose that was you?'

'Indeed it was. Maybe I saw someone bury something down there . . . a weapon . . . pushed down deep into that clammy stuff down below the tiles and the concrete. Did you look?'

'We could look again. But the font goes deep. It hasn't been moved . . .'

'It was moved a hundred years ago, and it now sits lower than it did then: I spotted that by comparing pictures. It took a while, but I got it. Someone has hacked the base off. I want to know if I've got a bit of that base in my office. I'll bet I have.'

'And if you have?'

'Then . . .' conspiratorially, seductively, Kline went for the kill. 'It's ritual killing, Inspector Underwood. Ritual killing, and you've got something on your hands that you've known about and ignored for centuries.'

Now Underwood looked interested. He stared at Kline, then looked through the windscreen of his car and chewed absently at his lip.

'What are we going to find beneath that stone, Kline?'

'I told you, I don't know. Not for sure.'

Underwood smiled, but the smile was on his lips, not in his eyes. 'A body?'

'Maybe.'

'If there is, Kline, you realize that I'd have to arrest you on suspicion of knowing more than was good for you.'

Kline stared at him. 'I shouldn't like that at all.'

Underwood laughed sourly. 'Let me explain it simply then,

Mister Kline. If you want to lift that font you most certainly can – on applying to the Home Office with your reasons.'

'But that would take weeks.'

'Months, more like.'

Exasperated, Kline said, 'But I need it out of the ground *now*. How do I do that?'

'By convincing me that there's evidence beneath it relating to a serious criminal matter.'

'And then I'm under suspicion for having known about it, right?'

There was a twinkle in Underwood's eyes as he said, 'Not if your belief is based on having seen suspicious movements in the church, which you have now dutifully reported to the local police.'

For a second Kline didn't get the drift. Then he smiled broadly.

'Why, Inspector Underwood – damned if you're not trying to help me.'

Underwood shrugged solemnly. He stared at Kline. 'There'd better be something worth seeing underneath it, Mister Kline.'

'There *will* be,' said Kline, knowing that for Underwood there would be *nothing* of interest, but caring only to get the font lifted.

Underwood wound up the window. As he did so Kline heard him say, 'Whether there is or isn't, there will be in my damned report.'

'When does it get lifted?' called Kline. Underwood answered, 'Tomorrow.' Then, thinking of something else, he wound down the window again. 'Listen, Kline. I'm doing you a favour, right? But whatever you do or don't see below that stone, I want to know about it in detail. However stupid, however way out, and however threatening to the integrity of this family, I want to know about it. Clear?'

'Absolutely clear,' said Kline. He backed off as the Jaguar raced off down the drive into the early morning darkness. He waved after it.

Turning back to the house his eyes lifted and he glanced at the room where Francoise was staying; for a second he thought he saw someone standing in the darkness, between the slightly parted curtains, watching him. His first thought was that the figure was Adrian, but Adrian was sedated . . . perhaps it had been Francoise, or Karen.

It would have been so easy to have just passed it off, but Kline, now, was in grim and determined mood. He raced into the house and stood below the stairs, looking up at the landing. He could hear low voices from the lounge, and counted: Francoise, Edward . . . June . . . Don . . .

Only Karen's voice was missing, and at that moment she appeared from the kitchen, holding a tray of mugs. Kline smelled chocolate. Karen said, 'There's one for you, if you fancy some.' The words were warm, but the look she gave him was pure ice.

Kline said nothing. He walked upstairs and unlocked the door to Adrian's room. Adrian was asleep. Sound asleep. As he stood there regarding the boy he felt cold, like a sudden cold breeze, and turning he thought he saw someone darting downstairs. By the time he had reached the banister and peered over, there was nothing to be seen.

He locked Adrian in again, and joined the others. Don was crying, Karen sitting with her arm around him, looking as miserable herself. Edward was regarding his mug of chocolate, turning the pottery around and around in his hands, saying nothing. Everyone was very pale. The air still smelled of shot, and of blood, and it made Kline feel queasy.

He went to the drinks cabinet and poured himself a large scotch.

He was thinking of that figure. Twice, now . . . twice. Once he had seen it vanishing into the garden, and now it had been watching from the spare room. A dark figure, tall, man-like.

And he knew that Karen saw it, for she had told him. It terrified her, and yet she felt drawn towards it, as if it were able to influence her will, causing her to compulsively follow. And if she had followed, where would it lead her?

Almost certainly to her death.

CHAPTER SIXTEEN

By two in the morning June and Edward Hunter were in bed, and Don had also retired, with his thoughts and sadness; he was using Karen's room, and Karen had spread out her sleeping bag on the floor of the spare room, where Francoise had been quartered.

But Francoise and Kline stayed up, tired and shaky, but enjoying the sight of the lowering level of scotch in Edward's drinks-cabinet, and pleasantly basking in the warmth it was affording them.

They kept the fire on; even with new curtains, heavy and dark, the coldness of the November night could reach through the empty window and chill them. Anywhere in the room but close to the fire it was freezing.

'I think, then, that you have decided I am right,' said Francoise. She sat, huddled in an armchair, legs drawn up beneath her. 'No more of this poltergeist madness. You *do* believe there is something evil in the stone.'

'Not poltergeists,' said Kline, raising his glass. He watched her steadily, watched every flicker of expression on her face, and the way her skin grew darker as she flushed slightly beneath her tan. 'You are right that something is there. I believe what you saw. You call it a demon. I'll call it a "dark force".'

'A dark force . . .' repeated Francoise. 'I see what you mean . . . it is much more realistic than "demon".' She was being light-hearted and Kline made a face at her. She said, 'Anyway, I call it a demon–God.'

'A demon–God? Like Odin? Yes, I like that. A jumped-up demon, a low spirit with stolen powers, who has raised himself to Godhead. Is that what we've got in the stone? The Norse god of war . . . Odin? Wutaan?'

Francoise shrugged, sipping her scotch. 'Maybe. Maybe something similar to something that became the God of the Northmen. Maybe similar things have become all the Gods. Maybe even the Christian God.'

Kline disagreed. 'The Christian God is different. He embodies many things that are ancient, but they are secondary additions to his mythos. The Christian God was a man incarnate, and was full of goodness, and a strong concern for the elements, not of fire and air and water, but of society, and man. He is a different thing to this . . . whatever it is.'

'Cruachos.'

Kline shivered as she spoke the name. 'Yes. Cruachos. He, it . . . whatever it is, is part of the earth, like all ancient gods, all ancient demons. Their elements *are* the fires and winds of the world, and the clammy mud, and solid rock that we stand on. They are deeper, more primal than Christ. I think they are more a part of man than Christ was, or is. The Christian God replaced the old demons, pushed them into the shadows, but they still lurk there, they still exist. Shadows. Echoes.'

'And imprisoned in their own elements, still alive, still vital and angry, and angrily waiting for release.' Francoise spoke quietly, staring beyond Kline, into a depthless area beyond her focus. She spoke suddenly in French, a long moment, a gabble of words, her eyes half shut.

Kline said nothing as she fell silent, and she smiled, staring at him. 'I'm so tired speaking in English. I wish you spoke good French, I could relax a while. My head is spinning, trying to think of the right words always. It is very hard, Lee . . .'

'Then let's sleep. You'll feel more alert tomorrow.'

But Francoise shook her head. 'No. There are things that must be said now, while we are alone. Lee, we must be so careful. This thing is so powerful, and even the shadows it projects are powerful. I don't believe that Simon Belsaint was trying to commit suicide . . .'

'I don't either.'

'Don't interrupt me. Let me say it. This thing, this Cruachos, is feeding off us. What exists in us all, such things as psychic powers, strange and not so strange, they are all left from the time of man's closeness to the mud and the clay he came from. They are very strong elements within us, and this being is feeding on them, strengthening itself from them. From me especially. I think I did much damage when I came close to it, and I must not go near the stone again, or I shall perhaps help it to pull itself from its prison completely.'

Kline agreed, nodding soberly and thoughtfully as he watched the glowing bars of the electric fire. He said, 'Tomorrow I shall search the base of the font, and see what I can see. But I'll tell you something . . . whatever I find I don't think will matter that much of a damn. There is something more important to be found in Don.'

Francoise leaned forward, interested and awake. 'I know. You said this earlier. I have tried to read Don, through the signet ring he wears, but I have got only normal memories . . . nothing strange. But what is it makes you know this? Is it instinct? The great Lee Kline intuition?'

'I guess so.'

Francoise smiled. 'I trust that intuition, Lee. So tell me. What do you think Don can tell us?'

Kline laughed. 'I don't know. Perhaps . . . perhaps a key. I'm searching for a key and I keep thinking I've found it. But now . . . I really think I have it. I think Don is the key, and not just him, but all his family, all the Belsaints.'

'I don't understand.'

'Perhaps that will be all our fates,' said Kline. 'But tomorrow I'm going to ask for someone's help, someone I saw once, an old man . . . a hypnotist. He knew Arnall Bloxham, and I think he probably learned from Bloxham. This man gave a talk at our Institute about some of the things he had learned about the past . . . he's very like you, in a way. Only with a different technique.'

Light began to dawn in Francoise's face. She was at once puzzled and excited; she smiled, eyes bright, and pointed at Lee. 'Bloxham . . . the man who can hypnotize people back to their previous lives . . . and you're asking him to do this to Don?'

Not Bloxham himself. A man of similar talents. Bloxham once took a woman back to York, in Norman times, and that woman recounted her previous death. He did that with several people, and if someone remembers their death in a previous life, well, you really have to talk in terms of reincarnation. But this man, he's different. He gets both reincarnation and something else . . . he gets memory surfacing, inherited memory.'

Francoise looked blank. 'I didn't think that was possible.'

'Apparently it is, though many biologists still disagree. Memory is some sort of chemical store in certain cells of the brain, and new memory results in new chemicals being formed. But this man – his name is Wegenheim, Doctor Brian Wegenheim – points out that the memory chemical, RNA or something, is part of a complex system that includes DNA, a self replicating chemical, and there is something called reverse transcription by which that DNA can be modified, and RNA can do the modification. He thinks it's possible that crucial, important, or emotionally strong memories can become recorded in the DNA, which is inheried from generation to generation, and he thinks that any such changes in one cell somehow get sent to all the cells of the body, including the germ cells –'

'Excuse me?'

'The sex cells.'

'Oh. Them.'

'Yes, them. In this way you carry memory forward through the generations. He thinks you forget the memories consciously, but they are still there – they are never lost. If he's right, and if he can get through to Don, then I think Don's inherited memory – if he has any – should tell us some very interesting things.'

Francoise laughed. 'And you used to call *me* crazy!'

'I used to call you crazy, but you're not crazy. I'd have thought some dark force living two thousand years in a stone was crazy, but it isn't crazy because it's happening. You told June Hunter that there is truth and there is belief . . . you're right, and that's what was working on me all today. You can believe in God, but that doesn't make God a truth, except that it doesn't matter, does it? Provided you act in accordance with the beliefs as if it *were* truth; and it goes the other way. Demons in stones is a belief, a crazy belief, and I've not been able to accept the belief as truth; but for Christ's sake, I was always regarding this thing *as* a belief, as something you believed in, and June believed in, and I somehow was always associating it with "God as belief" – unprovable, therefore not a truth in the strict sense of the word. But this thing isn't unprovable. It isn't a *belief* that you have, it's certain knowledge. I'm confused, and confusing you –'

'Yes!'

'– but let me just say that it was the way I approached the problem that was wrong. I do believe in your dark power. The demon aspect is still a belief, but the truth of its presence . . . yes . . . not poltergeists, not Adrian. Adrian is the pawn. Somehow it uses Adrian as a focus. It visits this house through his mind . . . we see it as a shadowy figure, usually running from the house. It can exert some will through Adrian, it can call, beckon, encourage to follow, and with Karen that seems to work, but its will is weak. It is securely trapped in the stone, and can project an image of Adrian. It plays games like that –'

'I *know*! I told *you* that . . .'

'But the most important game –'

'The watching game.'

Kline slapped his knees. 'Right! Watching us, attracting us, and one by one, it hopes, destroying us. It called me here somehow, through the fragment that had come into the Institute. Once here it had to keep me here, and it set up events, played games, to keep me interested. Perhaps it was watching me, trying to see if I was the best man for the job of releasing it, but I wasn't. When I fetched you, you were. Now it has to get rid of me because my interference could be destructive, and perhaps . . . perhaps I know too much. Francoise, it has even worked through *you* . . . remember? You told me to go, that I was useless . . .'

'Yes,' she said, frowning. 'I felt bad about that. I don't know why I said it, but I didn't mean it.'

'Cruachos meant it. It meant it very desperately, when it spoke through you, and when it spoke through Karen.'

He sat back, staring at the woman, feeling his pounding heart slowing, calming. Francoise sipped her drink, deep in thought.

She said, when she finally spoke. 'Despair. It is such a strong emotion. When I touched the stone I felt it, overwhelming, almost stifling: there was Adrian, and much much more. Yes, the beast is trapped, and it is losing patience. Perhaps being so close to its release has made it impatient, and that impatience makes it more violent than it should be, and also . . . it makes more mistakes. Time has eroded the hold upon it, and it surely senses the end of its confinement.' She closed her eyes. '*Mon Dieu*, Lee. This is so frightening, so crazy. This sort of thing doesn't happen in our modern world, does it?'

Kline said nothing. There was, deep within him, a terrible fear, an awesome anxiety. He was tense, could feel that tension in his muscles, and his stomach. There was pain in his body brought on by apprehension. He had known it during examinations, or before a date when he had been very young; and this was much worse. He found it difficult to even think straight; Francoise was going through the same thing. This was an age of supersonic flight, and a strange jargon associated with Space Technology, and fairy stories as children's tales, and religion as a source of intellectual patronizing. Two people sitting in a room, terror-stricken at the thought of an earth-demon being released, was somehow . . . not sensible.

It was what made Kline so difficult, for he knew, now, that he had a fault – he could not adapt to the bizarre, and it was thirty-two years of living in an otherwise normal world that made him so slow to adapt.

The principle of evolution was adapt or die; not so simple, of course, and it was not the individual that mattered, but the family group, and thus the species. But Kline was a species unto himself, and he had come close to dying due to his non-adaptation. Now, however, he had made the change. Francoise was right when she said there was something evil about to get loose and wreak whatever havoc it required to fit itself into a world that, to the men who had called it here, could not even have been conceived, let alone imagined.

'They must have come a long way,' said Kline quietly.

Francoise frowned. 'Who?'

'The men who captured this Cruachos.'

'The priests,' she nodded. 'I'm sure they did. They felt like they were outsiders, regarding the world of gold and marble with great envy. They really wanted power, and they knew that the power of armour and weaponry opposed to them was very great – too great. They worked so hard to get a weapon on their side that was invincible – a demon God, something from the Other-world that was immune to fire and spear. Their desperation was almost tangible, the fear, the horror, the realization that they had unleashed a whirlwind of anger.' She stared at Kline for a moment, puzzled by something. 'But how did you know they'd come from the West? I sense it now, in retrospect, but I didn't say that at the time.'

'They brought their coded writing with them – Ogam, a peculiar script. They left a prayer in that script near the stone, presumably after they had successfully contained Cruachos.'

Francoise spent a long time considering that, then quite suddenly she sat up, bright, intense: 'You said a prayer? Are you sure?'

'What else. A few Latin words, *for ever and ever*, that sort of bullshit . . . just fragments, very hard to read. Yes, I'd have said a prayer . . . what would you say?'

Francoise said nothing, just stared at him waiting for the coin to drop in his head. And suddenly, as if the thought had been there all the time, Kline saw what she was thinking!

He frowned and could not help himself smiling almost cynically. 'You surely don't mean some sort of *spell*! Do you? A witch's spell?'

'Of course a spell!' she said, almost angrily. 'What else?' She had swung her legs off the chair and leaned forward now, as Kline sat before her, heart pounding, thinking hard, thinking very hard.

Nothing was said. They stared at each other, and the word flapped between them like some dark thing that neither wished to catch for a moment.

A spell! The magic words, the verbal symbols of fictional magicians and witches that could – at a distance, and at the whim of a good or evil mind – cause something to change. A spell! Why not?

'They wrote it down,' she said. 'The magic prayer that confined the beast, they wrote it down. They buried it by the prison itself, so that throughout time it could be used to keep the beast trapped.'

'It's too simple,' said Kline.

'By whose standards?' said Francoise sharply. 'Oh come on, Lee. Think of who we are dealing with. It makes sense. Those words are the spell we need . . .'

Now Kline sat back on his heels and shook his head. 'There's only a fragment of it. Not enough to be of use. Most of the words are obliterated, and quite obviously the slabs of stone were once far larger. Much of it was lost, years ago. But listen . . .' he leaned forward. 'That spell would have been used on the stone in the church. It might be there, locked there, recorded. Perhaps you could sense it all. There is enough in the museum for you to get an idea of where to focus. Perhaps you could read the whole spell!'

She shook her head, brushing locks of brown hair away from her face, and tenderly touching the white plasters on her scalp. A momentary worried look fled across her fine-boned features. 'No, Lee. I mustn't. To touch it again, oh no . . . Lee, for my sake and everyone else's sake, I must be kept away from the stone. It will use me to get out. It truly will. And it might kill me too, once it no longer needed me, and I have some interest in not letting that happen.'

'But we may find that we *need* to know the words those ancient priests used. We know the symbol, but without the words . . .'

'The symbol you saw in blood?'

'Right!'

'What do you think it was?' Thoughtfully. 'Not something that Cruachos would have approved of?'

Kline shook his head. 'No way. That symbol helped keep it there. A hundred years ago it influenced someone and made him hack that symbol from the stone . . . I'm sure of it. I'll be even surer tomorrow.'

'But why was the symbol in blood? Why did Cruachos allow that man to paint it? Ah, games again . . .'

'That's all I can think of. To keep me interested, having sensed my interest in such symbols. Blood washes away, so it was not much of a hardship to let the symbol be drawn there for a while.'

Francoise laughed. 'This is the best time of the day, Lee – here we are, warm, relaxed, full of whisky, and jumping to conclusion after conclusion.'

He shared her moment of humour, but said, 'Less of the jumping, Francoise. There really seems to be some sort of awareness of Cruachos in this community. A subconscious awareness. I wonder if it all ties together – the large number of people called Belsaint, as if something were keeping them here. The stone having its symbol obliterated. A church with that same symbol in its window placed so that the sun would cast a shaft of light, taking that symbol, from top to bottom of the font every day – until something made the priest break the glass – getting rid of the pagan abstract, perhaps? Or rationalizing the destruction of the most potent guardian force under the influence of a pagan God? And this compulsion to suicide, the need to kill . . .' he sat back and narrowed his eyes. 'It makes a sort of sense, but not a total sense. Lifting the font will help. But I want to know what lies inside Don Belsaint's mind. I want to know if his family goes back to the time of this visit from the West by the men with the power to work "magic", such power that could rend a Universe to get what they wanted . . . and if they could do that, what else could they do?'

Francoise said, 'I don't know. And I'm too tired to think. Tomorrow will be a very hard day, Lee. Let's sleep.'

'I shall sleep here, in this chair. How about you?'

Francoise grinned and curled up into a tight ball in the armchair. 'Me too,' she said. 'I like to sleep like a cat.'

The new day began at sun-up for Kline. Don was in the room, pacing restlessly, and the moment he sensed Kline was awake he came over, stripped back the curtains and allowed the diffuse but bright light of dawn through the empty window and into the room.

Kline shivered and put the fire on immediately. 'What are you doing up so early?'

Then he saw Don's face. The youth was terrified. It was in his eyes, his face, the way he stalked about the room, glancing at Kline, and at Francoise, and occasionally stopping to shiver, to hold his own body in his arms, thinking, thinking . . .

'I know it's going to be bad,' he said, 'but I don't want it to be bad, not yet, not until I've got my own strength of will back.'

'I understand, Don,' said Kline, and led the boy to the kitchen. 'But your father will pull through.'

Don was shaking his head. 'He won't. I know he won't. It's always been this way . . . there is no will to live in our family; serious illness was always fatal; an accident was always fatal. None of us have the inner strength to pull through. Oh Jesus, I'm so bloody scared.' He walked to the kitchen window and stared into the grey dawn.

Kline made coffee, strong, sweet, almost undrinkable, and after a while Francoise woke and came and joined them. She was sleepy, crusty about the eyes and she said that her mouth felt like an old flannel. They watched seven a.m. come, staring at their hands, or the table, or the garden, and soon afterwards Don became ill, going into the toilet below the stairs and retching. When he came out he looked white in the cheeks, and dark around the eyes, and soon he was cradling his head in his hands and giving way to the awful tide of grief that had for so long threatened to engulf him.

June Hunter rose, brisk, noisy, and then Edward arrived. 'I

have to go to London. I'll be back shortly; I think I'm needed here more than I am in town, but I must just get my office in order.'

'Of course,' said Francoise coldly.

Edward glanced at her sourly as he shrugged on his coat. 'I shan't be long. Adrian is sleeping quietly. So is Karen. I suggest you try and keep it that way; let them sleep as long as possible. Don, keep your chin up, lad. Your father will pull through. And you know you can stay here, with us. There'll always be someone around. Anything you want, lad. Anything at all.'

Don nodded, wordless, miserable.

Edward departed.

Soon after Kline went into the lounge and closed the door; his voice, monotonous and controlled on the telephone, seemed to speak forever as he began to track down the hypnotist, Brian Wegenheim. He had no idea where to begin, and by the sounds of it starting with the obvious had not worked.

It was an hour before Francoise, now alone in the kitchen, heard Kline obviously speaking to someone more interesting. She heard him cajoling, pleading, explaining. She heard him swear, then control himself and apologize. She heard him say, 'A boy's life is at stake, this really is most important.'

June was in the garden, using up energy, time and thoughts by digging over the overgrown vegetable patch. She was well wrapped up and Francoise could hear her singing to herself. Karen had come down, spooned down a quick breakfast of cereal and then taken Don out for a long walk. Adrian slept on.

When Kline appeared from the lounge he was angry. 'Damn the bastard's mercenary nature!' he said bitterly, sweeping past Francoise and into the garden. 'June? I've got the man, and he seems prepared to help. But he wants money. I haven't got any goddammed money, so what can you afford?'

June wiped a dirty hand across her face; her breath frosted in the cold air and she thought for a second. Francoise wondered whether she was thinking of cash, or of her responsibility to pay for something that scarcely seemed to involve her. She was sceptical about this whole idea of Kline's, perhaps because she was resentful of its focus not being Adrian.

'How much does he want?'

'I haven't asked. I can find some. Can we find a hundred between us do you think?'

'I expect we can. I think I can afford fifty. Won't he help us for nothing?'

'I'm afraid not. He says his is a rare skill, and if he gets known as someone who'll help out in times of crisis then his main business ability will go. He has a point, screw him. One hundred, then.'

He turned and went back to the phone. Francoise heard him say, 'We can offer you a hundred pounds. We've had three deaths, a fire, an explosion, and an enormous hospitalization fee for the old grandmother of ninety seven. A hundred pounds.' There was a pause. 'You're right. There is no grandmother. It's still a hundred pounds.' There was another pause. 'Dammit, don't haggle with me. One hundred, not a damn penny more. Come on, Doctor Wegenheim, we're not setting a precedent; the least you can do is take a cut in fee for something this important. Right . . . right . . . that's absolutely right. A hundred pounds. AND expenses, yes. And all the whisky you can drink and keep coherent. When can you come? Tomorrow . . . fine . . . I'll tell you how to get here, Doctor, and don't you go and let us down. A lot of people need your skills more than you realize.'

CHAPTER SEVENTEEN

It was mid-afternoon before progress began to be made towards lifting the font from its foundations. Kline and June Hunter went first to the police station, and were told to go on to the church, and to stand clear. By the time they were entering the ruins, forcing their way through a dense crowd of puzzled and interested spectators, the crane was in position.

No-one, as far as Kline could discover, seemed to know what was going on, and within the ruins he found a small circle of people standing, watching the two men who were securing ropes about the stone font. There were three policemen there, and two men in dark-grey suits, both middle aged and rather tetchily talking to the officers and casting irritated glances at the crowd.

June shivered inside her car-coat and looked about her. People watched them, but only with that curious nosiness that meant Kline's arrival was something to distract from what was going on. Kline went up to one group and asked why they were standing there. He smiled pleasantly, but made his hostility felt.

'There's nothing to see. It really isn't that much fun, so why hang around?'

People shrugged and some went; others stayed. More arrived, watched for a few minutes, then left.

Kline went through the crowd and spoke to the police. Once they knew who he was they seemed to relax. 'What are we going to find?' one of them asked, and Kline opened his brief case and drew out the Higham fragment.

'Where that came from, hopefully,' he said; the men shrugged and walked away.

The crane was ready. Its long arm was angled above the walls from outside and it came close to the top of the ruin. The font would be pulled up vertically with as little damage to its setting as possible.

Underwood arrived on the scene, acknowledged Kline testily, then spent a few minutes talking quietly, away from the American, with his uniformed men.

In the crowd, watching, Kline saw June Hunter looking almost apprehensive. He could understand why – they were about to tamper with her only source of contact with her son, and no doubt inside she was resentful of that fact. She had insisted on coming with him to witness the lifting: perhaps her prayers the night before had been for some miracle, or some revelation that would bring Adrian closer to her.

Suddenly worried for her, noticing how pale, how tense she was, he walked over to her. 'You look worried.'

'Yes,' she said quietly, staring at him. 'I can't help thinking that maybe . . . well, maybe we'll damage part of Adrian doing this. How do we know what might happen?'

'Maybe we'll release him.'

June looked angry, but softened. 'Don't play games. My God, wouldn't it be wonderful if that *did* happen?'

'As you say,' said Kline, 'who can know what will happen, or what we'll eventually have to use to get him out.'

Conversation was made difficult by the sudden roar of an engine, and the lifting was underway. As Kline turned back to the font he caught sight of a tall, angular man in a dark suit. He was watching from the side of the church, and his eyes were filled with anger, and confusion. He stared at Kline, and after a moment acknowledged the American with the slightest hint of a smile. When his glance shifted to June Hunter he went solemn, and when June looked over her shoulder she looked away sharply. 'Oh hell, it's that awful priest.'

'Father Alexander. Here to watch and pray.'

'He's an awful man. He shouts abuse at me in the street. I hope he goes away, he frightens me . . .'

Kline reassured her. 'He'll not come close to you today. I don't think he wants to come in spitting range of you.'

'Good. Lee, they're beckoning to you.'

Underwood had called out to him and now Kline went back to the font and waited for the final lift. They had tested strain, or something, and were ready to go.

Standing back, watching, Kline felt a great thrill pass through him. He held the Higham fragment, and watched as the rope of the crane took the strain, and the font became subject to a greater pressure than it had ever known.

For the last time Kline looked round to make sure June was alright. This time she smiled at him, waved at him, and he nodded. He noticed to his relief that Alexander had vanished.

Even before the slack had been taken up, and the pressure commenced, Kline began to feel the power of the beast trapped within that dull and uninteresting looking piece of rock. He felt the heat on his skin, the stifling sensation of being trapped in an enclosed room with the sun heating up the walls and no way to breathe fresh air. His skin tingled, and he felt it pinched, and there was the flapping of that bird, and a sense of wind, and desertion. The bird circled, and the crowd who watched the operation seemed to drift away, beyond some screen, or veil . . . they became unreal . . . Kline glanced round, looked for June and saw her as if from a great distance. He saw her smiling, but she might have been part of a dream.

There was a loud sound in his ears, like the beating of a heart, but faster, more sonorous. His skin began to hurt, and he resisted, and with resistance he felt that tentative irritation go away.

The font cracked and creaked, and the rope shook with the strain; it slowly came from the ground, wrenched from plaster and tiles, and there was a sound from the crowd, a sort of applause, a cheer . . . the great moment coming close.

Instantly Kline felt a huge wave of shock pass through him, and intense fear, a loud scream of anger. He felt his wrists gripped and he dropped the fragment of stone. He fought against the pressure that was trying to throw him to the ground, and he knew his smile was broad, his teeth clenched, a look of determination that in no way belied the effort and determination he actually felt. He resisted the beast, and the beast grew angry. He felt the scorching heat of it, and the angry hatred of it; it tried to throw him down; it tried to affect everyone, driving them back, pinching them, perhaps trying to use this concentration of blank minds to make a further step towards its escape.

But Kline resisted, grinned at it, shouted at it. For just a second as the font rose inches from its bed he sensed Cruachos as perhaps Françoise had sensed it, a cruelly malevolent man-shaped beast, tall, broad, its face somehow not a face, yet watching, watching . . .

He felt a fleeting fear; he felt Cruachos sense that fear and try again, and again he resisted, fighting to ignore the pain and the discomfort, and suddenly the beast had withdrawn, was gone from him.

His skin tingled and hurt, and it was red in places, but now the pressure to control him had faded.

The time taken to lift the font had been a matter of seconds, seconds that had been drawn out against his internal time scale in the same way as he had lost hours before when exploring these ruins for the first time. The stone font dangled four feet above the level of the church floor, and where mud was being washed away Kline could see how much more ragged and unsculpted was the lower part. The font was all of ten feet high, and looked very like a tooth, with its smart, fashioned upper half, and its root-like lower half.

Underwood was crouched by the hole, peering into it. Two policemen held the stone still as best they could and searched the dark, dirty surface for anything of interest.

'Mister Kline?'

Underwood's voice was challenging. Then, surprisingly, the policeman's tone changed as he repeated. 'Mister Kline. Could you come here a moment?'

Kline walked towards him. Underwood was touching part of the stone, right near the base. 'There's some sort of pattern . . .'

'Of course,' said Kline. 'The man who tried to destroy it only half destroyed it; that was probably sufficient for the purpose . . .'

He walked up beside the detective and stared, excited yet calm, triumphant yet complacent. The fragment of symbol was similar to that fragment on the rock he held. Slowly he reached out the Higham fragment and placed it against the jagged gash in the side of the font. He moved it about for a few seconds before quite suddenly it seemed to fit. It wasn't a perfect fit, but then the man in the last century had been possessed of enormous strength and had made a reasonable job of the demolition. But as Kline held that small piece of rock in place, and saw how the symbol was more complete, and noticed how the rock surfaces *did* knit together along a few inches, there was no doubt in his mind, no doubt at all, that fragment and font belonged together, and that somehow the symbol was a cause of fear and concern to the forces of the past that lay within the stone.

'You can put it back now,' he said.

'Just like that?'

'Why not?' said Kline. 'You'll not find anything else.'

And as Underwood looked irked and confused, he walked away from him. June stared at him blankly as he came up to her, and she said, 'It was happening to you again, wasn't it. I could see.'

'Not very powerfully,' said Kline. 'I don't think it wanted trouble. I don't think it really knew what was happening.'

There was a tap on his shoulder and when he turned he found himself facing a slightly angry, but still reasonably tolerant Underwood. 'I'd like that explanation now, if you're ready.'

A mile away, in the now tidied lounge of the Hunter's house, Francoise Jeury finished what she was saying and sat in silence for a few seconds, staring at the carpet. The man who sat opposite her shuffled restlessly, and she glanced up and smiled. 'It all sounds crazy, I suppose,' she said.

'Not at all. It all sounds quite appalling.'

She agreed with that, sensing the hidden fear and anxiety in his voice. He had come from the church where the font was being examined, and he had introduced himself as a friend of Lee Kline's. He had once – he had told her – been the priest of St Mary's, before the fire, before the tragedy. His name was John Alexander. And Francoise had just told him everything she knew, everything there was to know.

'The boy is evil,' said Alexander quietly. 'He shares his evil with his mother; between them they are every bit as threatening as this . . . this dark soul imprisoned in the font.'

'They are pawns,' said Francoise, disturbed by the man's hatred. 'They are used. I was used. What is in the stone threatens us, frightens us, and will destroy us – perhaps by our values it is an evil thing, but our values are not its values. Wouldn't you want to escape such a hideous prison?'

The priest was stiff and restrained. 'You defend this beast?'

'No. I defend nothing. I just hate to hear you talk of evil, when you should be talking of desperation, and a different value of life . . .'

'I would agree with you to a greater extent than perhaps you know. But the boy . . . he is polluted by both the evil of the beast, and the evil of his mother. Is he locked away?'

'Safely, securely. For his protection as much as ours.'

Alexander relaxed slightly, clasped his hands before him and stared at the ceiling, at the gouged plaster. Suddenly he looked sharply at Francoise. 'May I ask for another cup of coffee? I've not had lunch, and I feel quite empty.'

'Of course. I'll go and make it.'

She smiled and left the lounge; the moment she was out of the room Alexander rose from his seat and walked into the hallway after her. He paused by the stairs, looking up them, and after a second he began to mount them.

Above him, in one of the rooms, Adrian cried out again. This was twice in the space of an hour. The first time he had cried out, suddenly and hauntingly, he had caused Francoise a moment's apprehension. But he had been silent after that. Francoise couldn't imagine what had caused that disturbance: she imagined he was dreaming.

Hesitating, as again that unearthly sound came from the boy's room, Alexander felt a cold chill on his skin, but shrugged it off. He wanted to see the boy. He wanted to see the face of the evil that had caused his church to be destroyed. He always carried with him a small bottle of Holy Water; with a pocket bible and crucifix he was thus equipped for any religious emergency, even though he himself did not value Holy Water, finding it to be a tedious acknowledgement to an ancient, archaic tradition.

But now he drew that bottle from his coat pocket and stepped to the closed door of Adrian's room. He turned the handle, found the door locked. A moment later he noticed the key above the door frame. He unlocked the door and stepped into the greyness of the room.

Adrian was awake, laying quiet, regarding him. The boy's breathing was loud, almost pained. There was a sickly smell in the room – quite literally, an odour of vomit. Alexander peered more closely at the boy and saw the signs of sickness on his chin and chest. For a second the more human part of him wanted to call for Francoise, to clean the boy, but he didn't call for help. He closed the door gently and walked to the side of the bed.

He reached down for Adrian's hand, felt the warmth of it, the flaccidity of it. The boy didn't move, remained staring at the opposite wall, breathing loudly through his open mouth.

Unscrewing the bottle of Holy Water, Alexander liberally sprinkled the boy's hand, then head, tensely waiting for the screaming and the twisting. Nothing happened. The boy shivered, shook his head so that sparkling droplets fell from him. Alexander let go of his hand and smiled almost cynically. He stared at the bottle then placed it back in his pocket, tightly done up.

He removed his crucifix from his breast pocket and kissed the naked, silvery figure of Christ. Then he placed it against Adrian's lips. The boy made chewing motions with his mouth, and touched the figure with his tongue.

'I've seen children near tear themselves apart when I've done that,' he whispered to the boy. He straightened, smiling, thinking of those few times he had been in the presence of the Possessed. Possession it may have been, he wouldn't deny that, but it was the psychological belief that the crucifix should destroy them . . . the effect of too much film and TV, and books and comics, and also of too much indoctrination in the way of faith. People could become quite hysterical when they thought there was a demon in them that hated all things Holy. The power of suggestion . . . in so many cases he had known that was all there was to it. The power of suggestion.

He smiled to himself and walked round the bed to get a better view of the boy. He stared at him hard for a moment and after a while the empty gaze altered slightly to meet his own.

'Hello, Adrian,' said the priest, and was answered in that childish, hoarse voice.

'Now I'm angry.'

'Oh, you speak, do you? And coherently too! Who are you angry with, Adrian? Who with?'

'Kline. Kline. Kline.'

'Not with me?'

'You're already dead.'

Alexander felt a wave of discomfort, a fleeting shock. It was the certainty with which the boy spoke, the self assuredness. Alexander began to have an idea of what truly possessed this boy – nothing external, save perhaps the callousness and ignorance of his parents. Across the end of the bed, he was sure, he faced not possession but disease, disease of the mind, untended, uncared for, malignant. But did the boy *himself* believe he was possessed?

'Who am I speaking to? Adrian? Or something else?'

Adrian laughed. 'Is there a difference? Isn't that why you played your religious games with me?'

'If Francoise is right, then there is a difference. A boy's body, the mind of something quite appallingly evil. I'm not frightened of you, whatever you are – Adrian.'

'Oh yes you are. Everyone is frightened. Fear is . . . fear is the key, don't you know that? My father says that all the time. Fear is the key. They key to the soul, the key to intelligence. Fear is alive. Fear is food, my food. I love it. I soak it up. I grow strong on it. You *are* afraid.'

'Your power is impotent. You are trapped. I fear nothing that is trapped. None of us fear you, we fear only what you represent.'

Adrian strained to sit up, the tendons and veins of his neck standing out as he forced himself onto his elbows; he seemed half drugged. His face was distorted into an evil mask of glee. 'It doesn't matter,' he said slowly. 'Fear is fear. And I shall soon be free again. I shall, I shall.'

He laughed and settled back, his eyes narrowing. A blankness came upon his face and Alexander frowned. 'I don't believe there is anything abnormal about you,' he said quietly. 'I've always known that. This is a game, Adrian, a game of living death – your mother must convince everyone that when I let you slip I really damaged you. She must rationalize the terrible thing she did for revenge, don't you see that? She burned my church in fury. Now she had come to believe in your living death because if she doesn't, then there was no reason for the burning. Her evil is so strong, so powerful, that I believe it has genuinely changed you. But you're not possessed, or damaged – you're just overwhelmed by hatred. I pity you . . . I truly do.' He turned away. He realized, as he left the room, that he was cold with sweat, and that his heart was racing. He closed and locked the door behind him. Glancing along the gloomy landing he saw an open door to one of the rooms, and he thought he saw Francoise standing in the darkness beyond it. She seemed to be beckoning to him, and he said, 'Francoise? Is that you?'

When whoever it was had disappeared into the room he frowned. He glanced back at Adrian's room, then unlocked the door and peered inside again. Adrian was still there. Puzzled he walked towards the room at the end, forgetting to lock Adrian's door again.

As he stepped into that end room, cautious, concerned, again calling for Francoise, so Adrian walked from his own room and followed the priest into the darkness. The door closed. There was silence.

The silence might have lasted a few seconds, or a minute. Then there was a scuffling and someone cried out, a man's voice, deep, afraid.

The cry was heard by Francoise who came running up the stairs. As she hesitated, close to the landing, one hand on the bannister, eyes wide and afraid, she saw that Adrian's room was open. Where had the cry come from? A moment later there was more scuffling, and the sound of a chair falling heavily to the floor. It came from the spare room, her room, the room at the end of the landing. She stepped up the final stairs and approached the door, and just as she reached out to the handle, confused and terribly apprehensive, there came a hideous shriek of pain and terror. As she stepped back from the room, Alexander's head was rammed, shockingly and splinteringly, through the thick wood of the door, as if someone inside had thrown him like a javelin and the door had not been strong enough to stop his bloody passage.

Francoise gagged and nearly fell down the stairs, and there was a moment of appalling inaction as she stared at the blood and torn flesh of the priest's head, and the way his mouth moved, and his dulled eyes seemed to stare at her, liquor running like tears in a glistening stream from the angle of his jaw.

Edward's car swept past them as they walked slowly, thought-fully, along the High Street towards the house. June didn't notice it, but Kline did, and pointed to the sleek shape as it overtook a slower, older car and vanished into the distance.

'Not only late, but he didn't even notice us,' said Kline.

'He noticed us,' said June. Kline laughed. She was so sure of the fact that it seemed unimportant to query it.

'He's quite a sonovabitch, your husband.'

'Isn't he just?' said June, and then with a sweet smile. 'But as one to another, I'd have thought you would have approved.'

'Now what does that mean?' said Kline wearily. June shrugged, looking slightly ashamed.

'Nothing.'

As they walked Kline shook his head. 'I'm beginning to lose track of you, June. You seem to be less on my side than you were. I thought you *wanted* my help.'

She looked up at him sharply, frowning. In her face was something of hurt, something of panic. 'I do. What makes you say that?'

'Since I came back with Francoise you've been hostile to me – not directly, but indirectly – sort of distant.'

'It's *your* help I want,' said June sullenly. 'I don't trust Francoise. Anyway, I tried to show you what I felt yesterday. I was shaken, but in the trees, with you on your own, I suddenly felt very secure again.'

Kline, impulsively, put his arm around her shoulders. 'I know.

I appreciate that. But for Christ sake, why don't you trust Françoise?'

'Oh, I don't know. Irrational reasons, I suppose.' She watched the traffic for a moment. 'She's very close to you, isn't she?'

'Why?'

'Just asking.'

Kline drew his arm back and thrust his hands deep into his pockets. 'Does that bother you? Don't you think I could help you if I was having a sex thing with Françoise?'

'*Are* you?' June's face was flushed, her expression one of concern.

'I did in Brittany. But not here, not now – there's not much opportunity is there? It's all very casual, June. Not that it's any of your damn business.'

June said nothing for a moment, walking stiffly, solemnly beside him, her head bent forward just a little so her hair hid her face. Kline said, 'I thought it was just that I made you feel secure.'

'It is, *damn* you!' she said angrily. Her face was brightly flushed, her eyes wild. 'I just don't know if you can mix business with pleasure and still do good business!'

Before Kline could retort they both stopped and turned to watch an ambulance weaving through the slowing traffic, its blue light blinking frantically, its siren loud and harsh. It flashed past them, exhaust fumes black and unpleasant, and the traffic lurched forward again. June walked on, still watching the distant white van. Kline followed it too, and quite suddenly he swore.

It was as if they had known but could not move, could not react until they had seen it turn into what was obviously the Hunter driveway.

'Oh no!' cried June, starting to run. Kline hesitated only a moment before he too felt the power of panic and ran the few hundred yards to the house.

He was there before June, searching the faces of the people who stood beside the front door watching the stretcher being slotted into the ambulance. It was a man who lay on it, his face bandaged, the sheets drawn up to his chin. Kline, seeing that everyone he expected to see was in fact there, walked up to the stretcher and felt quite relieved, then shocked, to see the priest. The man's left eye was bandaged, his right half-closed and dull, but he had the strength, and the sight, to turn and look up at the American. There was no blood in his lips, or face, and with the plasters covering what were obviously extensive scratches and gashes he looked horrendous, corpse-like. But a smile touched his lips, just quickly. The eye regarded Kline with some expression that Kline thought might have been pity.

Then he was gone, safely in the antisceptic womb of the ambulance, on his way to join Simon Belsaint.

As the ambulance circled and left the drive Kline found himself facing a grim detective Inspector Underwood, who stared hard at him, then shook his head. He it was who led the way inside, but Kline remained on the drive, shivering, as Francoise came towards him.

When everyone had gone the woman put her arms around him and hugged him. She was very upset, and Kline could tell she had been crying. 'He said he was your friend. I'm sorry, Lee. So sorry.'

'He wasn't my friend. I just knew him, that's all.' Kline looked after the ambulance. 'He was a crazy padre who I met just once.'

'Not a friend? Why did he say he was? Oh, I see. To get me to talk.' She smiled bitterly. 'And for his lie he . . . oh God, Lee, it was so awful. I think worse than Simon Belsaint last night.' Her bear hug deepened, strengthened. Kline stroked her dry hair, quite absently, but slowly let his lips come down against her head, kissing her. She looked up, looked at his lips, then kissed him quite hard.

'What was that for?' he asked afterwards.

'I needed to.'

Kline drew her back to him, enjoying the close feel of her body, the warmth rising from her. He smiled to himself because he was remembering similar words from June Hunter.

'What happened to the priest? He get thrown out of a window?'

'Through a door,' said Francoise, shivering violently. 'It was awful. He was just – just all covered with blood. It looked worse than it was, but what strength to do such a thing!'

'That's my next question . . .'

Francoise looked up at him and shook her head. 'There was nobody in the room. Or if there was they got out when I fainted. I did that, yes; I fainted. Terrible isn't it? I couldn't stand any more and I just – blackened out.'

'Blacked out.'

'Blacked out, yes. Oh Lee, it was so ugly, so . . . *vicious*.'

Kline saw Underwood standing in the lounge, beyond the empty pane, watching and listening. He had left the church before the American, and presumably had hardly touched down at the police-station before he had been called back. He was grim-faced, but somehow questionless. Kline had explained to him what he

247

believed to be happening, and no doubt the thoughtful policeman was wrapped up in a mixture of emotion and confusion, trying to sort out the probable from the crazy.

Kline whispered, 'I can't face that cop any more.'

'Me neither. I wish he would go away.'

'I don't suppose he will. Let's walk down the drive.' He took Francoise's hand and they strolled slowly, staring at the gravel, Kline trying to ignore the biting chill. 'Why did Alexander come? Just to ask questions?'

Francoise shrugged. 'I suppose so. He said he was your friend, that you'd told him a lot about what was going on, and why didn't I bring him up to date while he waited for you.'

'So he knew about the dark force –'

'The demon!'

'Alright, the demon,' Kline laughed as Francoise kicked him in a half-hearted way. 'And he knew about Adrian, and the stone font . . . he knew about the font? About what is in it?'

'I told him.'

'And what did he say?'

'Nothing. But he went to see Adrian, I suppose, when I went to make coffee. I heard him go upstairs and didn't think there was any harm in it. Adrian was sedated. Although . . .'

She hesitated, and Kline stopped, out of sight of the house now, surrounded by the high earth banks bordering the drive, and the thin wall of trees. Traffic roared and choked past them a few yards away where the main road headed west, but both of them felt alone, isolated for the moment, relaxed.

'Although what?' Kline prompted, and was intrigued by the confusion in Francoise's face.

'He cried out. Twice. The first time was very bad, very loud. It only lasted a second, but it sounded like pain, really pain. I've heard Adrian crying out several times while we've been here, but this was different. He did it again, then fell quiet. I mean, there was nothing I could do. He was still asleep and quite peaceful.'

Kline released Francoise's hand and huddled inside his jacket, staring at the traffic. 'I wonder . . .'

'What do you wonder?'

He looked at her, thoughtful, perplexed. 'Adrian gives an unusual cry in his room. And in the church –'

'An unusual deed!' Francoise had seen the way Kline's mind was working. 'The font is pulled from the ground, the boy cries out. Do you think it in some way . . . hurt him?'

Kline let his gaze drift beyond the trees, and the town, to the church and the crane and the dark thing that lived there. 'The link between them must be very powerful,' he said, 'if it was pain that he felt. A powerful link can be broken powerfully.'

'I agree. If the link is that tangible, we can *shirr* it, we can release him.'

'Shear it,' repeated Kline with a smile, realizing what she had said. Francoise snaked an arm about his waist.

'Let's go to the house, Lee. It's too cold. And the sooner we go up the sooner the policeman will leave. I think he senses something strange, but doesn't know what.'

As they walked back up to the house Kline explained that he had told Underwood everything. Francoise hesitated before stepping through the front door into the warm hallway. 'Lee, I told the priest about Adrian, and he was badly hurt. He might have been killed. Now you've told the detective, and I think we should warn him that . . . well, perhaps he now is also in danger.'

'Perhaps. But he seems very sceptical. I'm wondering if the sceptical might be secure, but those who believe, and cannot be of use, are the real ones in danger.'

'Maybe. But if so, why was Tim killed? And if you doubt that that was an accident, as I do, then you must doubt that Simon Belsaint tried to kill himself. Why him? He knew nothing, he wasn't a threat to this demon.'

Kline was aware that Underwood watched them from the hallway. Nevertheless he ignored the man and said, 'We don't know that. And that is what Don will tell us tomorrow, with any luck. There is something about the Belsaints that is intolerable to this beast. I know it, I just know it.'

'There is something about you that is intolerable too,' said Francoise. 'You are not afraid. Perhaps it tried to kill the priest so it could feed from his fear, like it feeds from confusion. I said this before. But you are not confused, now, and you are not afraid. You are a danger to it. You must always be on your guard, Lee. It attracted you here and kept you here by using your own curiosity –'

'Don't remind me,' said Kline bitterly.

'It doesn't need you. It doesn't need anybody but . . .'

'But who, Madame Jeury?' asked Underwood, startling the woman.

'But me, Inspector. Me. I have what it needs to get out, it knows it, it knows I know it knows . . .' she laughed. 'We know everything, and now we wait.'

'What do we wait for?' asked Underwood. 'Another killing? Another mutilation?'

'We wait for it to make its move. It plays a game with us, a nasty scary game. It knows we cannot destroy it, and it knows it is too powerful, and too far escaped, for us just to go away and leave it. It is watching, all the time. It is sensing everything, and it is waiting for the right moment. And as it waits, it kills, or tries to kill . . . it kills anybody who might conceivably be a threat to it.' She looked back at Kline. 'And that means you, Lee. Most particularly that means you.'

An hour later June was standing in the ruins of St Mary's, hands in the pockets of her car coat, her gaze fixed on the grey stone font. A brisk wind blew her hair into disorder, but she made no effort to retain her groomed appearance. Her face was white, almost pinched with tension. She could hear traffic distantly. She could feel the coldness on her skin. She could smell the stones of the church, the smell that had been her constant companion for so many years. None of these sensory things mattered to her – they had never mattered before, they could not matter now. Only one thing concerned her.

'Adrian . . .'

As she whispered his name she stepped forward and touched the font. Then she dropped to a crouch and pressed her face against the cold stone. 'Adrian,' she said again, and began to cry, eyes tight closed, mouth twisted with grief – her lips were wet with tears and she tasted these and they were a part of the deep despair she felt. She broke her nails on the stone as her fingers tried to claw into the fabric of the font, to rend the grainy stone and tear down to the part of her son that was trapped there.

Then, as so often before, she felt the heartbeat. She stopped crying, sniffing very loudly and wiping the wetness from her cheeks. The whole stone seemed to gently reverberate with the sound of a heart beat, and slowly she replaced her hands on the font and closed her eyes. 'Adrian . . .' she whispered again, and felt the way the beat of the heart speeded slightly. In some part of her mind she knew that it was her own heart that was beating, but she felt close, now, so close to the memory of her son. And yet, even as she sensed him, came close to him in his confining space, she saw the running, then docile, then smiling, then angry shape of the boy that was called Adrian, and who lived in her house. She drew her hands away from the stone and for the first time felt coldness on her cheeks, the cool of her drying tears.

Behind her there was movement and she tensed up, expecting to see the priest, Alexander, but then she remembered . . . there would be no more following her, no more street confrontations, no more loud and obscene abuse. She even found a fragment of pity for him, a moment's regret that he should have been so devastatingly punished for his hatred.

Then she turned, still crouching, and saw Francoise standing in the porchway, looking anxious, but smiling. The French woman beckoned and June rose to her feet, wiped her eyes again and left the church.

Francoise was waiting outside, cold and apprehensive. 'I don't dare go further inside, not yet,' she said, and smiled half-heartedly. 'I wanted to talk to you, June.'

'Alright. Let's get a hot drink.'

They sat in the warmth of a snack bar and sipped what passed as coffee. 'At least it's hot,' said June, and Francoise grimaced.

'I still can't drink it.'

June watched her. How tired she looked, how concerned. She recognized instantly, now that she put her mind to it, just what it was that attracted Kline – the fine features, the full lips that gave the appearance of having just been kissed; and her green eyes, slightly slanted, with their perpetually knowing look, a look of experience and a look of hunger. Francoise communicated so much through her eyes, so much passion, so much concern.

Suddenly aware of June's scrutiny Francoise looked a little uncomfortable. She said: 'Are you very slightly in love with Lee?'

June was shocked at the bluntness of the question. She felt her face grow hot. 'Not even *slightly*!' she replied, stiffly, awkwardly. 'What the hell makes you say that?'

Francoise shrugged. 'Just a feeling.'

'Well thank God you're fallible!' June pushed her cup away from her, staring hard at the other woman. 'In case you hadn't noticed, Francoise, I've got a few things on my mind at the moment. Bad things. What makes you think I've got the slightest interest in Lee as anything but someone who can help?'

Francoise reached out, her eyes shining – with amusement, June wondered? – and touched her fingers to June's fist. June relaxed.

'I'm sorry. It's just that when things *are* as bad as they are for you, well – falling in love is a very good defence.'

Now June laughed. 'Francoise, I lost the need for defence a long time ago.'

'Good. Don't be insulted, June, please. All my life I've had to be frank and honest with people, and perhaps it makes me blunt and perhaps insulting.'

'I'm not insulted – just intrigued to know why you could think I felt that way towards Lee.'

The appalling thing was, June acknowledged secretly, what struck me about Lee in the first place was everything I liked about him – perhaps I *do* have something for him; love out of despair? Has he sensed it, I wonder?

Francoise said, 'When you're with Lee, I've seen you, you're relaxed, even warm. When I'm there too you are distant, cold – I sense tension in you, and resentment. I thought perhaps you resented me because you weren't the centre of his attention any more.'

Keep calm, June urged herself, smiling thinly. She doesn't mean to be offensive . . .

'I was never that, Francoise.'

'Why *are* you resentful, then?'

'I don't know. Silliness I expect. But not frustrated love, I assure you.'

Francoise grinned mischeviously. 'But you'd like to go to bed with him. I can tell that –'

June tried to laugh dismissively and failed miserably. 'I suppose I would, yes. If circumstances were different. I'd not given it much thought, if you must know.'

'I don't think that's true, June. Perhaps now you are confused about your son, perhaps now it's true. But earlier, before I came and saw the stone, before Adrian became so active, then I think you did fall slightly in love with our American.'

June shook her head, meeting Francoise's gaze directly. 'Not true. But yes, I admit I thought of sleeping with him. He's an attractive man, in a dishevelled sort of way. And now perhaps you'd like to tell me what the *hell* that has to do with you?'

Again Francoise took June's hand, this time more firmly. 'June, you must understand me – I know things about people that even people don't realize they know. Most times I can contain that knowledge and yet not be deceitful. But now, I *dare* not contain that knowledge. There is so much tension and conflict in you and in the family that I feel I *must* act to reduce it. I must therefore be honest with you, and I must try to make you accept what it is you are and have become. I must make you aware of your confusion and then it is not eating away at you.'

June said, 'It all sounds very honourable. Are we still talking about Lee?' She felt cold inside, like ice. She sensed that something awful was about to come from Francoise, and yet she knew it was just tension within her that was tightening her up – she hated the sensation of knowing how open she was to this Frenchwoman.

Francoise said, 'Lee is not important, not now. You must face the fact that you are silently jealous of me –'

But I'm not – am I?

'That you know Lee and I are lovers –'

Yes, I know that, you bitch, I know that.

'Please accept this fact, and forget it, and try to remember that Lee and I are both outsiders – you and your family are the important thing, and we are just helpers in a difficult situation. Please relax with us both, and co-operate, and don't feel resentment. We both desperately, urgently, want things right with Adrian.'

June smiled grimly. 'I believe that, Francoise, but I can't help feeling you've made things worse in my head. I'm probably suicidal by now, torn apart inside by my womanly wrath at being wronged.'

'Yes, I can see you are,' said Francoise with a smile. She squeezed June's hand and let go. June laughed and looked around at the rest of the café's customers. She was right, of course – her attachment to Lee had been very tentative, very shallow – a shadow of her dependence upon him, and a dispensable shadow.

'So –' she looked back to Francoise. 'Now that I'm off Lee's back, and his male ego is undented, what else? You suggested that I was confused. What am I confused about?'

Francoise said quietly, 'Why don't you tell me?'

'Okay, I will. My son is in the stone. My son is in the house. Where is my son? Where, Francoise, is the real Adrian? Can you tell me that?'

'He's where you really believe him to be.'

Exasperated with Francoise's calm retort, June said, 'But I don't *know* any more. I'm confused. I'm sure I sense him in the stone font, trapped there, like an animal – but . . .'

'But what?'

June shook her head. 'But how can he be in two places?'

Francoise smiled and sat back in her chair. She stared hard at June for a moment before saying, 'Perhaps it's possible in a way we don't understand. Perhaps it isn't true that he is.'

'I'm not wrong about the stone.'

'June, I'm not implying you are. The stone is not the question at the moment. What is important is the *boy* in your house, and whether you were wrong about *him*.'

'I don't know any more.'

'Oh yes you do. You know very well. And you know why you are still confused.'

June smiled humourlessly. 'Wonderful. Enlighten me.'

'You don't need enlightening.' Francoise was almost angry. 'Think about yourself, your life, the past years – it's so simple it's silly. When you look at the boy now you don't see Adrian, you see Edward. You see his triumph, his sarcasm, you see him saying, "I told you so". You see yourself humiliated by a man with whom you have been pointlessly at war for so long. You see your integrity threatened, your intellect diminished, your life made unbearable. You see all these things and you cannot cope with the thought of them. But you see them because you have lost your understanding of Edward. He's not vindictive – he's desperate. He's not cruel and sarcastic, he's defensive! Next to his son's well being the thing he cares about the most – believe me, June! – is being close to you again.'

They sat in silence for a long while. June's mind was in a turmoil, incoherent thoughts and images, and through it all Francoise's totally determined look, her sense of absolute certainty.

'You think so, do you?' said June, finally.

'I *know* so.'

CHAPTER EIGHTEEN

The greyness of the November day deepened and passed quietly into dusk and evening so that almost without Kline noticing, the house was in darkness.

For the fourth time in less than an hour Kline walked upstairs and stood outside Adrian's room. The boy was running about in there, laughing and kicking things. Kline could hear toys being scattered, and bedclothes being pulled off and dragged about among the debris in his room.

For a normal child there might have been some cause for imagining this to be eccentric, high-energy behaviour, somewhere at the boundaries of, but within the confines of, normal behaviour. But this boy was not normal. And this boy was sedated! He had been given enough of a sleeping draught to knock Kline out for twenty four hours; it surely should have had at least half that effect on Adrian.

Kline unlocked the door and let it swing open. The boy stopped, turned and stared at the intruder. The room looked like a disaster zone, with the paper and plaster torn and gouged from the wall; the curtains had been torn down, the panes of glass cracked. Toys and clothes lay strewn about the floor, and the bed was in ruins. The boy himself, breathing hard, stood naked before Kline, holding a toy crane . . . the arm of the crane had been twisted and it was this that had been used to gouge the walls. Plaster covered him, especially his hair, which lay matted and damp in an appallingly untidy array abou this scalp.

Green eyes sparkled. Boyish mouth grinned.

Then he was off again, racing about the room, hacking at the walls and kicking with his bare feet at anything that came into his range.

Quietly, Kline said, 'Don't worry, Adrian, we'll soon get rid of your passenger.'

Abruptly the boy stopped and leered at the American. In his boyish, husky voice, in an otherwise perfect mimic of Kline's more aggressive manner of speech, he said, 'You'll do *shit*.'

'You've lost,' said Kline. 'You're just a vague effect on this boy, a passing touch. You know that, we know that. Without the boy you're totally ineffectual this far from the church, so you can't afford to lose him. But we're not going to let you use him.'

'You got the place surrounded, eh, Kline?' The words sounded false, unreal from the boy's lips; and behind the sneer, Kline thought he saw panic in Adrian's face. 'Jesus,' said the voice from Adrian's body, 'You are one dumb *asshole*.'

'Very good,' said Kline. 'But don't overdo it.'

Adrian grinned wide and maliciously. 'You think you can keep me prisoner, do you?'

'Better, even, than the stone.'

The boy laughed, shrilly. 'Firstly, I can dash my brains out, right? On anything, bed, window-sill, wall – anything. Then what happens to your cosy *fucking* household?'

The mimickry was frightening. Even Kline recognized his own mannerisms, his own voice . . . almost.

'Secondly, I'm sedated, right? Look at me, Kline, I'm sedated – I'm a prisoner of drugs!' He made an elaborate and sarcastic sound of humour. 'I can get out of here any moment I please, right? Right! But I don't want to do that, Kline. I like being here, and besides, I've got a killing to do.' He laughed again, staring Kline straight in the eye. 'You're afraid, now. I like that! I like smelling your fear shit. I really do. And you really are *full* of it, Kline. All of you are. And it's *tasty*.'

There was a moment of silent scrutiny, boy of man, man of boy, a moment that might have been re-assessment, or challenge, and then Adrian laughed; then he stopped laughing; then he sat, almost instantly jumping to his feet again, and running. He ignored Kline, running round and round the room in that aimless circle of negative energy.

Kline closed the door and locked it, listening to the thump of Adrian's feet as they took him round and round the room, then towards the door. There was a crack, loud and painful to hear, and Adrian's fist had smashed through the wood panelling of the door, and its fingers extended in a cocky wave. The hand, smeared and scraped with blood, withdrew and the running began again. Kline stared, almost in disbelief, at the hole, and thought of the strength that had been needed, and the control of pain . . . and he felt cold, cold, and went downstairs.

He glanced outside the house. Every hour or so a police car drove up to the house, turned and went away again. As surveillance went it was worse than useless as far as Kline was concerned. The family would be taking it in turns to watch the grounds from the kitchen; but if Adrian was to escape he couldn't possibly do so without *some* noise, either the smashing of a window, or the further destruction of his door.

Kline found Edward, June and Francoise seated around the big pinewood kitchen table, facing a spread of cold meats and salad that was inappropriate both to the climate of this time of the year and to Kline's appetite. He sat down, however, and helped himself to liberal portions of the food.

Francoise sat beside him, picking at her vegetables, while both Edward and June ate hungrily and hastily, perhaps making up for abstinence during the preceding hours.

'Karen and Don . . . they at the hospital?'

He spoke officiously and irritably. He'd much rather both of the youngsters were here, where he could keep an eye on them. He didn't like the idea of Don being practically on his own, even though the hospital was some miles from Higham.

'You don't think that's a good idea?' said Edward. 'But it must be safe somewhere . . .'

Kline wanted to say that yes, Don was probably safe from the demon, from Cruachos, but for Christ's sake Doctor it wasn't that demon that bothered him so much as what was in Don himself. However, he said, 'Just so long as he's here when this unlikely sounding man arrives tomorrow.'

'Wegenheim . . .' said Edward thoughtfully. 'I've never heard of him. I looked him up today, when June rang me. But I couldn't find out anything about him.'

'You will, soon enough,' said Kline, forking ham into his mouth and chewing noisily.

Above them, over another part of the house, Adrian's monotonous running, the rhythmic thump of his feet, ceased. All of them glanced upwards, stopping eating as the familiar sound ended. 'What's he done, collapsed with exhaustion?' said Edward. 'Maybe I should go and see.'

As if to prove him wrong, Adrian's running began again. Edward laughed, and all of them relaxed. Kline wondered whether or not he should mention the damage to the boy's door, but he decided not to, not just yet . . . it would only cause tension, and perhaps panic, and everyone, especially June, needed time to gather their reserves, to relax. If the boy had cried when he had struck the door, yes. But he did not seem to have hurt himself, scratches were not important, not now, not yet.

'Active little bugger, isn't he?' said Edward, and laughed as again the sound of running stopped. This time they took no notice.

'Why isn't the sedation working?' asked Kline. Edward shrugged.

'If I knew that, I might know what to use to calm him. I don't dare give him any more. It might not be working, but it might still be damaging in high doses.'

Francoise placed her fork and knife neatly on her plate and pushed it away. 'The sedation isn't working because you can't sedate the energy that's powering him. That's not Adrian, that's the stone demon. Can't you even comprehend that?'

Edward frowned, unhappy with what appeared to be an emerging consensus that this outrageous state of affairs was actually occurring; and yet unable to argue any more, all fight gone from him. He looked tired, heavily shadowed under the eyes, and the expression on his face, reserved for both Kline and Francoise, was undeniably resentment. He said, challengingly, as if struggling to keep his aggressive spirit flowing, 'So what happens now? Do we just live out our lives listening to my son swearing and spitting, running about? What do we do? Why are we so complacent? Shouldn't he be exorcised or something . . .' that cynicism again. 'Or at least, why do you insist he stays here, and not in the hospital where he belongs if what you say about him is true? If the boy is disturbed . . .'

'The boy is carrying a parasite,' said Francoise. 'He's not disturbed, and he's not as posseseed as Cruachos would like. But the influence is there, and we must remove that influence. And we must prevent it ever reaching out to him again.'

Edward leaned forward, staring at her hard. He waved his hand in a come on, 'By doing . . . by doing . . . come on, don't stop there. Finish it, tell me what your plan is, tell me the antibiotic you are going to use?'

'Why don't you shut up?' said Kline. 'We're all quite sick of your voice.'

'I want to know why I'm listening to you!' shouted Edward. 'Don't you see that, Mister Kline? I want you to explain why I'm sitting here doing *bugger all* when my son is in danger of his life. Can you explain that to me?'

Kline said, 'You know we're right, that's why. And you know that we're the only help you've got, no matter how much or how little you care to trust us, or like us.'

'That's right,' said June coldly, reaching out to collect up the plates. 'So why don't we *all* shut up until this hypnotist comes tomorrow.'

As she stood so Kline saw the tension in her face, and in her hands, which shook as she carried the dishes to the sink. She stopped by the sink for a moment, leaning heavily against it, and slowly lifted her eyes to stare at her reflection in the glass, mirrored by darkness and the kitchen light.

Her scream was shrill, brief, startling. Kline threw back his chair as he too saw the face that seemed to watch from her own, wide-eyed, distorted; it was staring in from the night and had startled June, rather than revolted her.

It had been a glimpse, that was all, a brief sighting of that same face, the face of the beast. Kline ran to the back door and flung it open, but in the darkness there was nothing but the skeletal, ghostly shapes of the trees against paler clouds in the sky. Nevertheless, he sensed it was there, watching him.

Francoise's tug on his sleeve was urgent, protective. 'Don't go out there, Lee. Stay in. Remember what I said.'

'Come with me,' said Kline, But Francoise backed away.

'It's out there,' she said, 'I can feel it.'

'So can I. Francoise, come *out* here . . .'

He stood on the paved patio outside the kitchen, drenched in light from the house and watching the darkness beyond that distorted circle of brightness. 'Don't be afraid of it, Francoise,' he called. 'This is just a part of it, a reflection . . . it is hardly powerful at all.'

'Then leave it alone,' called Francoise. 'Don't bother with it.'

Peering into the darkness Kline saw the shape, taller than a man, but man shaped, its wide-jawed head turned towards him, the lips drawn back to expose teeth which gleamed in the faint light that reached down the garden. He could smell it, or perhaps he imagined that. But he felt drawn towards it, drawn compulsively. It seemed to be beckoning him.

'Don't be afraid,' he shouted again. 'The thing feeds on fear, and can be fought by the will. Come on Francoise, come and get a look at it.'

Games.

The word was there, in his mind, almost before his eyes.

Games.

The demon played games with them, trying to outguess them, trying to trick them into moves that might seem right at first, but which were in fact beneficial to its escape.

Games. Beware of them!

Kline hesitated, sensing the trick. The shape of Cruachos moved out of sight, away into darkness. A moment later a white shape flitted through the night, vanished.

It was Adrian. June screamed his name and raced into the garden, but Kline – thinking fast – ran to bring her back. 'It's a trick!' he yelled at her, holding her struggling form. 'Adrian's still in his room!'

'I know!' she screamed, 'Which means *that's* Adrian!' But though she struggled, he would not let her go, and soon Edward came out and tried to calm his wife.

Francoise shouted, 'Come back inside. Please. Come into the light.'

June relaxed, staring to where she had seen the boy. 'That was Adrian,' she said, almost tearful. 'That was him, *my* Adrian . . .'

Edward re-assured her. 'It was an illusion. Isn't that right, Mister Kline?'

'A trick,' said the American, and added almost without thinking, 'to get us out of the house.'

Stunned for a second he found himself staring at Edward in whose eyes was the same instant and shocking comprehension. They both raced into the kitchen, and Kline, being younger and faster, reached the stairs first. He stopped there, staring up. There was, he imagined, little point in going further. The door to

Adrian's room was open, the lock ripped off. The sound would have been loud, but short, and it was perfectly feasible that in the excitement of moments before they had not heard it.

Edward was already at the front door, noticing that it was open though not damaged. He stepped out into the night, Kline following. A small, battered toy car lay on the gravel. Edward picked it up and turned it over in his hand. When he turned to Kline there were tears in his eyes. June came running out of the front door, pushing past her husband; she ignored Edward, had eyes only for Kline. There was something about her, something that made the American stop and anticipate the worst.

She ran up to him and struck him with her fist, on the cheek, then on the jaw, then on the chest. The words she spoke at him were lost in the hysterical, almost manic scream of her voice. Then she was gone, down the driveway and into the night, her voice crying Adrian's name, her body lost into the anonymity of Higham.

'For Christ's sake everybody keep calm, stay together!' yelled Kline, and then saw Francoise watching him. He realized that in his own confusion, and anger, and hurt, he too had been hysterical, running a few paces after the woman, then running to Edward and dragging him towards the house. He calmed himself, gripped Francoise's arm and felt her strength, her steadiness.

'What do we do about her?' he said.

'She doesn't threaten Cruachos,' said the French woman quietly. 'It has no reason to kill her. He only needs to keep Adrian from her. She will be back, Lee. In the meantime, can we please try and keep our heads?'

Edward was shaking very violently. Perhaps it was the number of shocks having built up and finally reached him. His teeth chattered as he huddled inside his baggy sports jacket, his arms folded, his eyes wide as he stared into the night. 'What do we do now? What do we do?'

'Firstly, we try and calm down,' said Kline. 'Then we must all try and find Adrian. He can't have gone far. But we *must* stay together. His strength is unreal in a boy's terms, but there's more than a boy's hands at work, and we've got to keep together.'

But Edward shook his head. 'I'm staying in the house. Adrian may come back, and there should be someone here. Kline – find June, get June back. She'll get knocked down or something in her present state; she doesn't know what she's doing. Get my wife back. The boy will come back soon, I know he will.'

Kline's first instinct was to bundle him into the car, but he felt

Francoise's negative feelings on the matter and glancing at her saw her shaking her head. 'He may well be right, Lee.'

Leaving Edward behind them, they drove away from the house and along the High Street, then up and down the side roads, scanning doorways, alleyways and gardens. They ended up in front of the church, staring at the ruins, and Francoise began to shake. 'Get away from here,' she said quietly. 'I'm not ready yet, not ready to get so close again.'

As Kline drove off he glanced over his shoulder and saw June Hunter emerging from the porchway into the church. She looked around her, obviously still frantic,, and then, breath frosting in the crisp air, began to run along the street in the direction of the museum.

Kline stopped the car and watched the woman carefully in the street waiting until he was sure of the route she was taking, and then he did a tight circle in the road and drove in pursuit. He turned up the road where she had gone and saw her, skirts flying, arms restlessly brushing at her hair, and reaching out to walls and cars to steady herself. He followed fast, pulled up beside her and jumped from the car. She saw him and ran even faster, but he caught her and stopped her, and when she wrestled with him he was rough, dragging her back to the car despite her screams and anger.

'I've got to find him!' she screeched, biting his hand. 'Let me go you bastard, let me go.'

'You'll *never* find him this way,' shouted Kline, and Francoise came out of the car and helped restrain her.

'He must find somewhere warm,' said Francoise. 'He must find a huddling place, or he'll get so cold he'll have to come home.'

They had disturbed the neighbourhood and found themselves with an audience of inquisitive local people.

True to form, and even more vindictive, Kline advised them where to go, and he and Francoise virtually manhandled June into the cramped interior of the Austin. She beat at Kline as he started to drive off, reminding him over and over that it was through his thoughtlessness that Adrian had escaped. Kline kept grimly silent, angry both with her and with himself. Francoise finally calmed the woman down, and there was a brief time of tears.

They continued to tour the streets of the town, but kept returning to St Mary's, slowing as they drove past in case they caught a glimpse of the boy. June said she thought she-had seen him going in there, but it must have been a trick of the light because there had been nothing but darkness and desolation inside. The crane was a stark silhouette against the sky, its narrow arm reaching out above the church, the long chain and great metal hook swinging slightly in the night-winds.

'He could be in there, hiding in the recess,' said Kline. 'I ought to take a look.'

'You'd be a fool if you did,' said Francoise. 'That might be just what Cruachos wants.'

'Why would he need to run away . . . ?' said June, quietly, calmly, and yet with an hysterical, almost grief-stricken note to her voice. 'I don't understand.'

'He panicked,' said Kline, hoping that his insincerity would go unnoticed. 'He just panicked. He'll be home.'

'But will this thing in his mind let him?'

Kline exchanged an uneasy, puzzled look with Francoise, then shrugged almost imperceptably. What *did* this woman believe? Her new concern for the body of the boy had taken Kline by surprise, although he knew she had seen much of Edward's point of view. 'It has no reason not to,' he said. 'It knows we daren't harm the boy, and it has demonstrated quite sufficiently that we are unable to keep it trapped forever. It's use for Adrian will soon pass, and it has no reason to harm him.' But while it needs him, he thought coldly, it's going to keep him hidden.

'We've got to stop the attacks,' said Francoise pensively. 'And to do that we would have to stop putting pressure on Adrian, and therefore on Cruachos. But we *must* find the boy, and we must keep watching him as Cruachos watches us.'

Back at the house they found that Don and Karen had come back from the hospital. Karen seemed revived and full of colour, but Don was still morose, still very upset. His father was 'comfortable', but quite obviously not yet out of danger.

'Are you sure you don't mind being hypnotized?' said Kline as they sprawled out in the lounge. Don shook his head.

'I don't mind, if you really think it will help Adrian. Maybe it'll help this bloody depression, too. Christ I feel bad, really bad.'

Karen sat down on the arm of his chair and playfully wrapped her arms around him. She kissed the top of his head and made some remark that Kline didn't catch. Don smiled narrowly, and reached up to take her hand. He closed his eyes and settled his head back and Karen made a face at Kline, a sort of 'he'll be okay, leave him to me' expression.

June wouldn't remain still, thinking about Adrian, continually reminding everyone that he was out there, alone, in the freezing night. Edward had been in touch with the police again, and they had assured him that they would spread the word around for people to look for the lad. For an hour Edward had phoned the parents of any child he knew had visited Adrian, or attended the same school as Tim. They had all, every one of them, promised to take a look around the area where they lived and ring him back if they saw anything. Every half hour Edward went round the house, looking in the rooms and the cupboards and the garage, and then went out to the garden, with his torch, and searched among the trees. Every time he came back with nothing to report; the phone never rang, and June grew more and more restless, not content with Kline's assurances that many people were looking for the boy, and they themselves could do no better than to relax at home, and get some rest. At midnight she was off again, out into Higham, but this time less frantically, less hysterically; she was wrapped up, and had a torch with her, and Edward let her go without comment. Edward himself, shattered and drained by so much that he could not comprehend, walked quietly to bed and fell into a deep, disturbed sleep.

Adrian did not come back that night, and June appeared at dawn, dishevelled and grimy, tired in body, absolutely exhausted in her mind. She had spent the night walking about inside the ruined church, hoping for some sign of her son. She had touched the font and spoken to Adrian, but she had not felt he was there as strongly. Kline was puzzled by this strange declaration, but after June had gone upstairs to crash out for a couple of hours, Francoise explained what really should have been obvious to the American.

'She has started to acknowledge Adrian, the real Adrian, as her son. It's simple. Because he talks, because he is behaving if not normal or human, at least energetically, she is beginning to accept that he really is the boy she gave birth to. Consequently her obsession with the stone declines; her mind is rationalizing the way she begins to understand how much she was obsessed by letting her feel that the boy is emerging more and more into his own body. But Lee, she must have been in terrible danger last night, being so close. What whim makes this Cruachos kill, or attack, or leave alone I just don't know – the need, occasionally, for fear, perhaps, or to remove a threat to it, or to play a game with us . . . so many different reasons, and I think she was probably very lucky, last night. Very lucky indeed.'

CHAPTER NINETEEN

Brian Wegenheim arrived during the mid-morning. He was a portly man in his early sixties, ruddy of face, and with an easy smile. He was elegantly dressed, and drove a sleek, black car that Kline, without thinking too hard about it, thought might have been a Daimler. A man of obvious affluence, and easy confidence. He wore a shiny; wavy toupee, whose youthful colour and rather too perfect arrangement of hair made it stand out unnaturally, but after a while even Karen, who at first was intensely amused by the wig, forgot about it, and listened to the man.

He bickered with Kline about Kline's attitude on the phone, but the words exchanged were only half-heartedly angry, and Kline was in a giving mood, by design of course. Wegenheim drank a cup of coffee while talking easily to them all about hypnosis, and how he would work with Don. Don listened intently, soon colouring as his mind was taken from his upset to this bizarre state of mind that Wegenheim believed he could achieve, not just in Don, but in anyone.

'I am quite convinced,' he said in a cultured English voice, with just a touch of affectation about it, 'that we carry memory forward. I really don't want to go into the mechanical details of how it might work, partly because I'm not the biochemist who has confirmed that such memory *could* occur, and partly because I think there is far more than a biochemical reason for it. It's all very well, you know,' (Kline sighed as he detected the lecture coming on, and Francoise grinned at him as she sat across the lounge, her fingers entwined, her face registering all the intrigue she was feeling), 'it's all very well knowing that a sort of *reverse inscription* can occur in the chromosomes by the little messenger chemicals,' he emphasized the word, and twiddled his hand as if the gesture somehow spelled the words, 'that get formed when we store memory, but who's to say that complicated chemicals *are* the only type of memory? Nobody, that's who. We get electrical memory, you know . . . well of course you know.'

'Of course,' said Kline.

'Of course,' said Francoise with a smirk.

Edward Hunter, seated irritably by the electric fire, said, 'What's all this got to do with my son?' Shadowy eyes watched Kline, and turned on the puzzled features of Wegenheim. The psychologist stared at Edward for a moment, then looked back at Don. Ignoring the intrusion he went on: 'Electrical memory. So who's to say there isn't a third type, much more easily transmitted? That's what I want to know. Nobody knows, of course, and the only real evidence for it might come from this sort of exploration of inherited memory by hypnotherapy. You see? So it's all very fascinating, and all very challenging, but what it all boils down to is,' he took a deep breath, then smiled. 'The further back we go, the longer it takes. So if you want me to regress you to . . . when? Roman times? It'll take some hours, and maybe even some sessions.'

Kline leaned forward. 'Doctor –'

'I'm not a doctor.'

Surprised: 'You're not a doctor?'

'That's what I said.'

'Then I beg your pardon, I must have misunderstood. *Mister* Wegenheim, we don't have time for several sessions, and we are not interested in anything that lies between Don *now*, and what his mind may have carried through the ages. We want something from, well, as you say, a generation from Roman-occupied England; and we need the information fast.'

Wegenheim considered that for a long moment, staring hard at Kline, then glancing back at the pale-skinned boy. 'What information precisely. Do you know?'

Kline shrugged. 'I wish we did.' And thought, with not a little bitterness, this might all be a bloody waste of time! This could be the day that the famous Kline intuition takes a tumble. Laughed out of court, and out of Higham, and back, stuck with a Frenchwoman who's terrified of using her skills, and a boy very much possessed by something we don't really understand, except in words such as Ancient God, Dark Power, and Supernatural Force.

He said, 'My feelings, a sort of instinct born of a skill as an observer, is that Don is a sort of key, that whatever he tells us will somehow trigger a fuller understanding of a very strange situation.'

'What strange situation?' Intrigued, Wegenheim leaned towards him.

But Kline shook his head. 'I don't want to get into that, Doctor – sorry! *Mister* – Mister Wegenheim. It's complex, and time is short. I'd like you to go ahead and do your thing –'

'Do my thing?' Wegenheim laughed. 'Do my thing. Right. I'll

do that, I'll do that right now. My thing. Yes.' He seemed highly amused.

Kline gave him a wry look. 'Afterwards,' he said more gently, 'I'll paint a picture of possession that will blow that toupee right through the ceiling.'

Wegenheim went upstairs, and with Karen helping, tidied her room and pulled the curtains across so that it was dimly lit, and peaceful. The spare room would have been a more obvious place for the session to occur, but the possibility of using it was never raised. The hole in the door was an ungentle reminder of what had occurred there previously.

Wegenheim was reluctant to allow anyone to watch him at work, but finally agreed that Kline and Francoise Jeury could be there as Don finally relaxed, and broke through the inevitable barrier into his past. While Wegenheim hypnotized the youth, and took him easily back through his childhood to that first quite fundamental, and – as Wegenheim explained – often impenetrable barrier, his own birth, the other two waited outside the room.

Kline listened at the door. Wegenheim's voice was low, relaxing. He spoke rhythmically but actually induced the state of hypnosis by asking Don to repeat a number, while Wegenheim himself spoke the number, over and over again until the repetitiveness of it almost drove Kline to sleep.

'I've never seen that used before,' whispered Kline, but Francoise shrugged.

'I suppose he knows what he is doing,' she said.

There were questions, then, and occasional laughter. Wegenheim asked about Don's earlier years, and every so often Kline heard the firm order, 'You are ten years old, and this is eight winters ago'. Step by step Wegenheim decreased the hypnotic age of his subject.

He was still doing this when mid-day came and passed. He had been alone with Don for an hour and a half. Kline was amazed, but had hardly noticed the time. Nevertheless, he began to grow restless.

Quite suddenly there was a cry, and Don shouted something; it was so sudden, and Kline was so distracted by his own irritation, that he failed to make sense of the words, but the sound brought him to the door, staring at it anxiously, wondering whether to go inside or not. Francoise had been downstairs, and he called to her now. She came running, puzzled by the fact that he was standing staring at the closed door and not going in.

'What is it?'

Feeling slightly foolish, Kline shook his head. 'I thought . . . I don't know . . .'

And at that moment the door opened and Brian Wegenheim glanced, frowning, out of them. 'Come inside. Quietly. I don't understand this.'

In the dimness of the room, illuminated only by a desk lamp turned to face the white wall so its light was scattered very diffusely, Don's sweat-drenched face was gleaming. He lay out on the bed, relaxed in posture, arms by his side, feet splayed. His eyes were closed, and his lips were moving. The water from his pores could be seen to be emerging and dripping onto the pillow, which was saturated.

Wegenheim was disturbed. 'I'm anxious because he is not behaving quite as I would have expected. The moment I encouraged him back beyond his birth he cried out in a strange language, gibberish, and then started to make a frantic gesture, a sign . . . in the air . . . he's stopped now, but . . . well, I'm afraid I'm going to have to terminate this session. It could be dangerous. There is something disturbing in the boy.'

Kline walked forward to look at the strange tension in Don's features, the eyes closed, but rolling behind their lids, the lips smacking together almost childishly. 'Where is he now? What age?'

'Early childhood. I had to bring him back, very fast. When the subject instantly becomes violent, or upset, I have to bring them back and get the session witnessed.'

Francoise said, 'Then you have experienced this before, this violence.'

Wegenheim pushed a hand through his toupee, dislodging it slightly; he took a distracting second to re-adjust it. He smiled nervously, then loosened his tie. He walked round the bed, still staring at Don, and using his own handkerchief to mop at the sweat on the boy's face.

'He was instantly angry, instantly . . .' he sought the right word. 'I suppose afraid. Something frightened him. This language . . . normally you get English, the language that is embedded, you understand? Whether or not they are experiencing something Greek, or French, or whatever, all people working in the field of hypnotherapy have seen the same thing: the language spoken by the subject is the subject's language, though often with a strong inflection. You remember the sailor? One of Bloxham's subjects who remembered a life – and in this case we are probably

267

talking about a spiritual passage, rather than a memory retention – as a sailor, Trafalgar sort of time, and spoke with a strong accent, not his own accent. I've known that, and I've known people with retained memory of a French ancestor speak English.'

'You never have people speak another language?'

'Sometimes, yes . . . a fluent speaker in a language that is the language of an ancestor often uses that language. And once or twice, among the English words, I often hear foreign words, often unrecognizable foreign words . . . Greek, perhaps, as it once was spoken, or Old English. But only occasionally. It makes sense, of course, that an English subject would speak English, because what they are expressing is the meaning, the sense of the word, which is the same for all languages. They simply express the meaning and the sense in their own naturally embedded language.'

'But Don spoke a foreign language, one that you didn't recognize.' Kline stared hard at the boy, feeling the hair on his neck prickle intuitively. 'Take him back again.'

'I daren't,' said Wegenheim, and suddenly all confidence was gone, all self assuredness vanished. He seemed a man humbled by inexperience, a man afraid of his own talent.

'You must,' said Francoise emphatically. 'For his sake, for the sake of someone else.'

'I *daren't*,' repeated Wegenheim. 'I am afraid of what might happen. I've not . . . I've not seen this sort of behaviour before. Instinctively I know there is something wrong.'

'There *is* something wrong,' said Kline. That's why you're here. Goddam it, this isn't some asshole experiment we're asking you to do; it's life and death, life and *death*. That boy is in trouble. Maybe you can find out why. We're asking you to help, to risk a life and help, not conduct some experiment for all our petty titillations.'

Wegenheim's lips were moist, slack, and he stared at Kline through eyes filled with regret that he had even come here in the first place.

'Life and death,' he said. 'Who will take the responsibility?'

'I will,' said Kline. 'Now get him back again, take him back . . .'

Abruptly Wegenheim nodded, pressed his hands together and wiped the palms of them against each other. 'Very well. Very well.'

Kline was relieved; he glanced at Francoise and smiled. He reached out for her hand and she took it briefly, squeezing it. Wegenheim had sat down on a hard chair, close to Don. Again he mopped the boy's face, then he said, 'We are going to try again, Don. We are going to try and take you back beyond your birth. You are such a very young child, warm and secure in your house, with your toys, and your mother and father . . . can you feel that warm security? Now we go back, back by days and weeks, now by months. You are new-born, and now you are not-born. This is a gentle journey back into that snug darkness before your birth. Can you feel the relaxing darkness Don? Curled tight, alive, and relaxed, the journey back to your father is but a moment . . . you are in your father now . . .'

For all this unorthodox suggestion Don had remained still, motionless but for the running of sweat down his face.

Now his fists clenched and his eyes opened. His fists came up to his face and tried to hide his mouth, and there was something, in his eyes, of stark fear. He stared at the ceiling, and slowly his legs began to twitch as if he were shaking with uncontrollable fear.

'Relax, Don. This is relaxing, this is a peaceful journey . . . what can you remember?'

And then the words, meaningless, gutteral. They poured from him like water, his mouth open, the lips stretched, the teeth clacking as if he tried to bite the meaningless syllables back.

And among them: Cruachos! Kline distinctly heard the name, the word, spoken gutterally, with the emphasis different, but that word nevertheless, and other words like it.

It sounded like German, and then Welsh, a bizarre mixture of different consonants, run together tightly, without the softening, rounding effect of vowels.

And over and over again, *Cruachos!*

Don thrashed about on the bed as he spoke these words, his head turning from side to side, his clenched fists hitting the soft counterpane as if to help in the alleviation of some pain.

Wegenheim was quite pale watching this, and again and again he cast anxious glances towards Kline, but the American just shook his head, determined that he should make some sense of Don's nightmare.

'Take him back further,' said Kline. 'Do it again, from his father to his grandfather.'

'Very well,' said Wegenheim, unhappily, and began his insistent whispering of words, of journey instructions.

Slowly Don calmed. He relaxed and as Wegenheim coaxed him back through the new childhood he became quite peaceful. And then the journey back to a previous life, and instantly the same thing, the same thrashing, the same guttural, explosive sounds, and the name *Cruachos*, repeated and repeated.

And his left hand stretched out before him, fingers spread, moving in a circular pattern, then a cross-shape marked in the air upon it, and the air symbol repeated while Don screeched in a high-pitched, almost desperate way, staring at his hands, seeking some release from an agony no-one else could feel.

It was that same symbol he marked out, that same bizarre and unfamiliar pattern from the font.

'Can you get him to speak English?'

Wegenheim hissed angrily at the interruption, but he began to coax the boy to speak his natural language.

Kline said, 'Use the name Cruachos as a prompt. Try it . . .'

'What is Cruachos?' asked Wegenheim, and Don screamed, his hands outstretched, repeating the name then shouting gutturally.

'Speak in English, Don. Tell us in English, what is Cruachos?'

'Trap!' cried Don. 'Bind! Trap! Bind! Bind earth! Bind stone . . . bind it, bind it!'

'Bind what, Don? What do you want to bind?'

Again an explosion of guttural language, followed by Don sitting up, the muscles of his face and neck tense, his eyes bulging, his lips drawn back.

Wegenheim stood and placed a hand on the boy's shoulder. 'Lie back, Don. Relax.'

Don obeyed. Wegenheim said, 'Bind what, Don? Bind Cruachos?'

'Cruachos . . .' repeated Don. 'Cruachos. Bind stone. Bind earth.'

The thrashing of his body grew worse, while no sound emerged from his lips. The three of them watched him, amazed, confused. Wegenheim looked at Kline and said, 'I don't know what to ask him, Mister Kline. I'm at a loss.'

'Ask him who he is.'

'He's his grandfather. These are his grandfather's memories.'

'By the sound of it they were also his father's memories. Maybe they're even his own, but you didn't manage to release them. Maybe they're memories that don't belong to any of them. Old memories, powerful memories, carried forward from a momentous event in one of his ancestor's pasts. Ask him who he is.'

Trying to relax the boy for a moment, Wegenheim bathed his face, and stroked his arms, which after a while ceased to be so tense; the terrified jerking of the boy slowed, the eyes half closed.

Saliva dribbled from his lips and Wegenheim quickly wiped it away.

'Who are you?'

Don's reply was incomprehensible and Wegenheim repeated the instruction to speak in English, and then asked the question again.

'Belos . . .' said Don, 'Belos, belos . . .' he turned his head and moaned, his eyes closed. Then he yelled, 'Bind it! Keep it bound! Drench the stone, drench the stone . . . I've got to drench the stone, I must . . .' He sat up and struggled against Wegenheim's grip to try and get off the bed. The older man forcefully pushed him back, and again succeeded in relaxing him.

'You are called Belos. Is that right? That's your name?'

'Caragok. Caragok . . . warrior of the Blue Shields . . . Caragok . . .'

'Are you Caragok?'

'Proud Caragok whose lodge is built upon the heads of the people of the Bull swords . . . I am Caragok . . .'

'Are you a warrior Chieftain?'

'Gundergodok my Chief . . . great warrior . . . Gundergodok who wears the horns of the Stag, carries the earth-blade of the Blue Shields.'

'And you are a warrior, you are Caragok.'

'I am Caragok, who runs on the right hand of the Stag . . . my lodge bears the Blue Shield of my father, and his father . . . challenge Gundergodok before the Moon of Lug over the Hill.'

'What is your tribe?'

Wegenheim's questioning was relentless, calm, while Kline and Francoise stood with hardly a breath escaping their lips, their eyes wide, their bodies tense with the joy and the shock of what they were hearing.

'What is your tribe?'

'Blue Shields . . . people of the curved blade, people of the Blue Shields, people of the Winter Sun, from the Moonlands of snow, in the far away . . .'

'How long have your people been here?'

'Twelve times my father's death.' Don turned his head, tears running from his eyes. He seemed distressed by something.

'How many moons of Lug over the Hill were in your father's death?'

His father's lifetime, thought Kline, adjusting suddenly to what was obviously an heroic way of marking time. He glanced at

271

Wegenheim, much impressed with the way the hypnotist picked things up.

No answer for the moment, Don's head turning from left to right, faster, faster. Then he said, 'Many . . . many . . . my father sired five sons, died grey, a grey head, a proud grey head. His shield hangs in my lodge, his head across it . . . fine head . . . fine man . . .'

'If your name is Caragok, who is Belos?'

'I am Belos. They have made me the Belos . . . the belos an natic. Fine warrior, now must guard the stone, guard the stone. Trap it, bind it . . . I must drench it . . . I must drench it . . . DRENCH IT!'

The scream brought Wegenheim to his feet, easing the suddenly frantic boy again. He fought against Wegenheim's restrained grip, and Kline came over to assist in keeping the boy on the bed.

'We must stop this,' cried Wegenheim. 'It will hurt him, damage him.'

'No!' said Kline loudly, crying out as one of Don's nails raked his cheek. He forced the boy back and Wegenheim calmed him. 'We've got to stop,' he said desperately, as Don relaxed again. 'We've got to stop . . . please, Mister Kline.'

'For God's sake, can't you understand that this is more important than his *life*? We *must* find out what he is!'

'He's the guardian,' said Francoise, and both men looked at her.

Kline stared hard for a moment, then nodded his agreement. 'He is, isn't he. He's the original guardian of the font, the Belos an natic . . .'

The words made the hard-breathing boy tense, and murmur something, staring at Kline through wide eyes.

'Belos an natic, the Guardian of the Stone . . . it has come down as Belsaint.'

He glanced at Francoise, not smiling, but his eyes sparkling.

'That's certainly pleased you, hasn't it?' she said.

Kline said that it had.

'Well it hasn't pleased me,' said Wegenheim angrily. 'It seems to me, Mister Kline, that you are substantially without feelings for this boy. But I am not. The session is ended. Please get out while I bring him back.'

Don was quiet again, staring at Kline, his hand clenched on Kline's sleeve. Wegenheim fixed him with his angry gaze and then pointed to the door. 'Out.'

Kline said, 'No way. You're not finished yet. If you finish, Mister Wegenheim, then one thing is for sure . . . so is this boy.'

'I have no proof that that's true,' said the hypnotist, vindictively, almost triumphantly. 'You tell me this, you appeal to the deeper emotion in me, but as far as I'm concerned, Mister Kline, you're a bloody liar. You're interested in something this boy has to offer, but you don't really care what he has to go through so that you can get that bloody something. No, the session is ended. Get out and let me bring him back.'

Before Kline could speak, angrily and pointedly, Francoise snapped him into silence. She stepped forward and squeezed his arm, giving him a look that said, 'In the name of God, keep your mouth shut'.

Then she reached down and stroked Don's saturated face, before straightening and addressing Wegenheim. 'Lee is loud and ignorant, and to a greater degree than he believes, you are right in your assessment of him. It is something he will learn, and learn to hate. But I assure you, Mister Wegenheim, that this boy's life is in danger from himself. What we are looking for is a clue to how we may stop a terribly evil thing from ruining his life, as it ruined his father's and his small brother's. Believe me, he is unusual . . . you have seen this . . . what he keeps in his head is like nothing else on earth. He knows secrets that we must have. If we do not have them then something will be released into this world which may well destroy even you.'

Wegenheim frowned. 'Me? Why me? I'm nobody . . . I'm just an outsider.'

Kline watched the panic in his face, was amused and irked by it.

Francoise, with incisive and very French poignancy, calmly told him why. 'Do you ever feel you are being watched, Mister Wegenheim? You should, because you are . . . we all are. There are evil eyes watching you now, and you can be thankful that the hands that go with those eyes are tied. It looks as if Don, and those who came before him, have been instrumental in tying those hands. But the eyes have seen. They have seen you learn of things which must be kept from man, or they threaten the mind *behind* those eyes. You are now in danger of your own life. Your only hope, like me, like Lee here, is to keep going, to keep searching.'

'You maniacs!' cried Wegenheim, in genuine fury. He looked from one to the other of them. 'You tricked me here, you got me here knowing full well that I'd be risking my life. You irresponsible –!'

'Don't cry over spilled milk,' said Francoise, the phrase sounding idiosyncratic with her strong French accent. 'Just get back to Don, and accept what I say. If you want to live, get probing!'

She acknowledged Kline's expression of startled approval.

Wegenheim stared at them. More sweat ran from him than from his subject and after a moment he wiped his already soaking handkerchief across his face. He took a deep breath then closed his eyes. A minutes silence later, less flushed, he nodded abruptly and sat down by the tranquil figure of Don. 'I am very angry about this,' he said quietly. 'And you will be hearing from me again. For the moment, yes, I shall do as you say. But you shan't get away with this . . .'

'Just do the job,' said Kline icily. 'We're wasting time with all this crap.'

Wegenheim composed himself, then said to Don, 'Who are you?'

'Caragok. I am Caragok, the Guardian, the Guardian . . .'

'You guard the stone?'

'The stone on the hill, yes. I must give my life to keep the stone intact, to keep it trapped there. The tribe has appointed me to this. I must die for the tribe . . . I must die . . . I must shed my blood if the earth binding is destroyed, I must drench the stone if the stone binding weakens . . . drench it, I must drench it . . .'

'Caragok . . . listen to me . . . listen to me, Caragok . . . are you listening?'

Don's head moved frantically, side to side, eyes closed. Then: 'Yes.'

'Answer all questions you hear, even if the voice is not mine. Do you understand?'

'Yes.'

Wegenheim looked up at Kline. 'You ask him. I don't know what you want.'

Kline knelt down by the bed. 'Who appointed you the Guardian of the stone? Who made you Belos an natic?'

'The black priests, the ones from far away where the mountains hide them.'

Wales, thought Kline, or possibly further, possibly the desolate western mountains of Ireland. He said, 'These priests, the black priests, from whom do they hide?'

'The Legions, the iron helmeted men of the Legions. There are so many of them. Dark shields, always marching, marching, rattling as they march, and singing, like a single man, but so many men. The Legions. We shall take our land back from them, and the black priests have come to help . . . but . . . trap the darkness, bind it, bind the darkness, bind *Cruachos* . . . I must drench it with my blood, I must say the spell . . .' His cry was shrill, terror stricken, and then his lips moved, but no words came.

Kline said, 'Cruachos is bound, the darkness is bound, tightly, tightly, in the stone. All is well, Caragok, all is well . . .' Slowly Don relaxed, his breathing laboured, but slowly becoming shallower.

Kline prompted, 'The black priests came for conquest, is that right?'

'To conquer the Legions, to win their land. We should have done it, we are the People of the Blue Shield and our valour is great, the strength of our arms like the strength of a storm wind, relentless, ungiving . . . we should have fought alone . . . punished for it, punished . . .'

'And was Cruachos released?'

'It escaped . . . it turned against us . . . it destroyed us . . . I am the Guardian . . . I must drench the stone . . .'

'Was the darkness trapped successfully?'

'Trapped in stone . . . the dark priests managed to find the spell . . . trapped it . . . stone in earth . . . but sacrifice must be made, or binding will weaken . . . must sacrifice all the time . . .'

'How many tribesmen, like you Caragok, how many like you have been made such Guardians?'

'Many . . . some are Guardians, some are prayer givers, some are givers of blood . . .'

'How do you know these men? How are they known? How are the givers of blood known?'

'Givers of blood, the givers of blood . . . harok ga cra . . . the spillers, the sacrificial wolves to the stone . . .'

'And you are the Guardian of the stone, the belos an natic. How was this done? How were you made a Guardian?'

'Spell . . . a prayer to the earth . . . the priests cast the spell, and the deep parts of my body will carry the spell into my sons and their sons, until wind and rain erode the strength of the stone and the strength of Cruachos . . . the dark one is bound to the stone, bound by earth, but feeds from earth, from its ancient earth . . . must keep it tight, keep it locked, but can never weaken it, cannot lift the stone . . . safer to keep it on the rise, can guard it . . . can protect it . . .'

'Caragok . . . Caragok . . . the dark one, *Cruachos*, is nearly escaped . . .'

'NO! Must drench the stone!'

Kline and Wegenheim wrestled the suddenly panic-stricken boy back to the bed. 'Listen to me, Caragok . . . you must tell us what to do . . . what to do . . .'

'Blood! Any blood, drench with blood . . . and the spell . . . say the spell . . . let me go . . . let me go . . .'

'What is the spell? What are the words? Say them. Say them.'

Don screamed. 'For me . . . me alone . . . I am the one, I am the Belos an natic, I am the one . . . let me go . . . let me go . . . let me go . . . too late soon. Too late to stop Cruachos . . .'

'The *words*. I am also a Guardian of the stone. What are the words?'

But the boy suddenly collapsed, exhausted and broken. His eyes were open, his breathing deep, but all tension was gone, all fight left him. Wegenheim stood in the sudden, frightening silence, and stared at his subject. Kline drew back, sweating, breathless, his head spinning with what they had been told, and frustrated to the point of screaming with what they had not.

'So close . . .' he said. 'Something . . . God, I'm out of breath.'

'Why not let the boy himself say the words . . .' Wegenheim stared at Don as he spoke. 'He said "any blood", animal blood would do . . .'

'But he will use his own,' said Francoise. 'I think we must choose to believe that; he is motivated to kill himself, and that we cannot allow.'

Wegenheim rubbed his face thoughtfully. 'He must be brought back,' he said, and this time there was no uncertainty in his voice, no question. Kline watched Don, felt his whole body shaking and trembling, just as Don's was trembling. Francoise took his arm, led him from the room.

Behind them Wegenheim's voice began to speak softly, 'The journey starts, Don, the journey back to your own life, forwards, through the years.'

Kline closed the door, leaned against it, his own eyes closed.

'My God.'

'I knew all this. We have not learned any more . . . except about the Belsaints.'

Francoise was pragmatic and cold. Kline regarded her coolly, then agreed. 'You sensed the spell, yes, you told me. I remember.

276

But now we have twice been in contact with that spell, and twice failed to get it.'

Francoise led the way downstairs. In the kitchen Edward and June were sitting pale, tense, hostile. They said nothing as Kline came in, staring up at the two of them as if they were total strangers.

Then June, her words like ice, said, 'Have you enjoyed your fun and games?'

'Very much,' said Kline, equally coldly, but he relented, acknowledging that such aggressiveness was out of order. June looked absolutely shattered, her face lined and dark, her hair a chaos of curls and tangles. Edward looked not much better; he was strangely quiescent, almost dead as he held June's hand and stared vaguely at Francoise. Kline said, addressing June, 'I'll take a drive around the town in a minute – have a look for Adrian. Will you come?'

June said, 'In case you hadn't noticed I've just *been* out looking for him. I was out all last night – I'm the only one round here who seems to care enough for the boy to search for him!' Her voice had risen to an almost hysterical pitch. She drew her hand away from Edward as she stared angrily, almost challengingly at Kline. Her eyes were shadowed, tired; almost glazed with bitterness. 'The only people out there who seem in the slightest interested are two reporters from the bloody *Chronicle*! They're out there now, Lee – go and see – *they'd* like to find Adrian! A great story! The police aren't doing a stroke; Edward sits here as if he's glued to his chair – and you and the Madame play bloody stupid experiments! Thank God I'm at least looking for the boy. If it were left to you lot he'd freeze to death.'

Edward looked embarrassed, almost apologetic, as he urged June to calm down. 'Shut up, Edward!' she said coldly, and smiled with an equivalent degree of frost at Kline. 'Yes, Lee, thank you very much. I'll help you look for my son. Most kind of you.'

Edward leaned back in his chair and shook his head. 'Adrian will be back. I have a feeling he will. We should just sit quietly and wait for him, and when he comes . . .' empty eyes turned on Kline. 'When he comes back we get him to hospital, to care. We get him the treatment we should have got him a long time ago.'

Karen had been out, wrapped against the cold, buying a few supplies. She came in now, with a small bag of groceries. She saw Kline, saw the sweat on him, and she looked immediately worried. 'Where's Don?'

Francoise reassured her. 'He's fine. The hypnotist is bringing him out of his conditioning right now.'

'Did you learn anything? Did he help at all?'

'Yes indeed,' said Kline bitterly. 'He helped a lot, then stopped at the crucial moment.' He found it hard to keep an unwanted element of anger out of his voice. He was quite convinced that it had been the atmosphere of tension in the room that had prevented Don finally revealing the spell – the *spell*; it was hard to credit that he believed such things existed – which would push Cruachos back into its rocky tomb. If Wegenheim had just been quiet and done his job, Kline was convinced that they would now be sitting here with the answer to all their, and especially Adrian's, problems.

Karen busied herself putting things away. She had seen nothing, and none of the people she had spoken to had seen anything of Adrian either. She had also looked in the church, but had felt so suddenly panic-stricken that she had fled the ruins almost immediately.

Francoise shook her head and said something in her own language that Kline thought might have been, 'stupid girl'.

At length Wegenheim appeared and accepted a double scotch from Edward, who broke with his depression for a moment to find his manners.

The hypnotist sat at the table and stared at his glass. There was absolute silence, which Kline eventually broke.

'Have you ever seen anything like him before?'

Wegenheim shook his head without looking at the American, then drained his glass and winced. As the burning went away he relaxed, and smiled.

'Good stuff. Very good stuff. No, no, that'll do me adequately thank you, Doctor Hunter. Adequately. Have I met anything like Don before? No. Emphatically not. I would have thought that much had been obvious. I have never ever experienced a regression in which a memory was so strong, so dominating. When Don was under hypnosis without regression he was himself. But the moment his living identity was shut away, the moment he became another life, his father, his grandfather, he became not – as I would have expected – a shadow, a fragment of those two ancestors, but a strong manifestation of this Caragok, who I take to have been a Briton living in the Roman Province, and rather bitter about it. I've never known that. I've never known such an ancient memory so dominant through subsequent generations.'

278

'They put a spell on him,' said Francoise quietly, and Wegenheim glanced at her.

'A spell? Do you believe such things existed? Magic?'

'Of course. Don is proving that, I can prove it, there is a church in this town that can prove it. Of course we believe in what you call magic. I might call it the paranormal; you would call part of it a *regression*. Isn't what you've just done magic?'

'Oh my dear woman –'

'Don't be stupid!' shouted Francoise. 'Of course it is. Magic is a word that is used to cover things that cannot be explained by science.'

'No it isn't,' said Kline easily.

'Well, almost! Many things called magic at the time were called that because they appeared to be miraculous, or bizarre. My powers, your powers, these would once have been classified as witchcraft. So yes, I believe in spells, because I believe in the power of the mind, and I believe that the mind of even someone with no manifest powers can be instantaneously channelled or harnessed by, perhaps, a symbol, or a word, or a group of words. You see? Even you agree with me.'

Wegenheim had been nodding thoughtfully, staring at Francoise as she had addressed him in an excited, half angry way. 'I was thinking,' he said quite brightly, quite earnestly. 'That Don showed all the signs of a very ancient hypnotic conditioning. The strength of this memory, and the fact that he met an ultimate block to talking about this memory, is all very suggestive . . . I'd say he had been deeply and thoroughly hypnotized in his ancestral guise, this Caragok. They must have known more than we think,' he went on, frowning at the thought of it. 'Those dark priests – the druids. My goodness, they must have understood the mind better than even I understand it. They knew . . . I can't believe that they wouldn't have known . . . that their particular form of conditioning would be transmitted from generation to generation. Perhaps they did call it a spell, but it was a very rare and very real talent they possessed.'

He glanced at his watch and rose to his feet. 'I really must go.'

Kline walked him to the door, with Francoise close behind. 'You seem more interested in him now than earlier. If we need you again, and we might . . . are you available?'

His answer was Wegenheim's hand extended, palm upwards, in a position ready to have something placed in it.

'Oh yes. Your fee.' Kline drew an envelope from his pocket and opened it, showing a cheque from his own account made out for a hundred pounds. Wegenheim smiled as he inspected it, then he said, 'I would prefer not to come again. Your attitude, and what you, Madame, have told me hits me where I hurt the most, in my basically cowardly interior. But I must say, if you do need to take this young man into a second regression . . . well, perhaps I will come back. Same fee.'

He abruptly left. Kline watched him drive away, then closed the door, standing in the gloom of the hallway and watching Francoise.

Francoise said, 'If Don reaches an hypnotic block against telling us the spell, then what do we do? Without knowing the ritual by which we fix this thing back in its prison . . . why would they block that information? I don't understand.'

Kline shrugged and led the way back into the kitchen. 'So it remains in the family, in the genetic line.'

'But why? The more people who knew it the better, surely.'

She had a point. An answer occurred to Kline instantly. 'Maybe *two* spells! One to trap, one to release. Perhaps it was felt that at some time in the generations to come it would be acceptable to release Cruachos, perhaps they felt they were close to understanding how to control it with more facility. Don's job, then, the job of all the Belsaints was to guard the stone, but when the time was right, to release and use the demon to their own ends.'

They had stopped again, thinking hard, the both of them, running all the events and feelings of the last few days through their minds.

'That man, a hundred years ago,' said Francoise, 'Perhaps the demon tricked him somehow, made him try and release the font's hold . . . perhaps he was the one of the Belsaints, and he started to use the wrong spell, thinking it was the spell for trapping the beast again.'

Kline said, 'He seemed to do nothing but destroy the symbol.'

'The essential first step! Perhaps the symbol was a warning symbol, a design that blocked any use of the releasing spell. When the time was right the symbol would be erased, the releasing spell operable.'

'That's why it made the priest smash the glass window . . . it makes a conclusion-jumping sort of sense. But if it's true, then Cruachos has only to get a Belsaint, or someone, to use the wrong words and it can escape . . . the first step has been taken, and never undone.'

They passed into the kitchen. Edward was walking in the garden, and Karen was busy scraping some potatoes for an evening meal. June regarded Kline steadily, her dark eyes still bright and alive with anger.

'How about Adrian? Are we going to look for him? Are you going to drive me? My bastard husband is so sure he'll be back he won't even let me have the car.'

'Sure, I'll drive you.' He turned to Francoise first, though. 'Cruachos wouldn't let us get near enough to carve the symbol back, or even paint it. Would it?'

'What would be the point? If our thinking is right on this then the symbol itself is unimportant to the spell now. I can't believe it would have let a man paint it in blood just to tease you, otherwise. No, we must find the words, *then* carve the warning symbol.' She laughed, shaking her head. 'Listen to me. Already I'm assuming we are right!'

'Never mind that, for the moment. The thing is, how do we get the words? If Don is conditioned not to give them, then it must be you, Francoise. You have to go peering into the past again, you've got to resurrect those words from the stone, from what *it* has carried forward.'

Francoise folded her arms about her body and turned away from Kline.

'You *must*, Francoise . . . for Adrian's sake, for all our sakes.'

'Do it, you bitch,' said June, not comprehending what the talk was about, but presumably reacting almost instinctively to the sentiment she understood. Francoise laughed at June's words, but said, more solemnly, 'Lee, I can't. I daren't. I know what I feel and I feel that Cruachos could grip hold of my mind and pull itself out. I can't explain . . . if my strength of will is not big enough to hold it back, it can use me to escape *without* the spell.'

'You don't know that for a fact.'

'I *know* it. It is too dangerous. Anyway, there is something we've both overlooked, something that helps . . . it should have been obvious.'

Kline waited, staring hard. 'Well, for Christ sake what?'

'Adrian crying out about the time the font was being lifted from the ground. What did you say happened when the stone came up?'

'Nothing much. Cruachos had been playing its games with me, just a little . . . it gave up, exhausted when the stone came up.' Comprehension like lightning, flashed through his face. 'Christ! You think it withdrew from Adrian at that moment?'

'I don't know. Maybe. Upstairs just now we heard Don say a lot of references to earth binding, and stone binding. And he said, at one point: cannot lift the stone. You remember that? He said, cannot lift the stone so must keep it guarded. Lee . . . I think this thing feeds from earth, is strengthened by its deep contact with the earth. When the stone was lifted it weakened, withdrew. But that would also weaken the stone's hold upon it, eventually. The ancient peoples couldn't hold the stone like that, swinging above the earth for generations. Wood rots, they knew that, and perhaps it was too difficult to build a stone support. It was safer to keep the thing powerful, yet powerfully trapped and constantly guarded. Throughout the generations the appointed guardians would . . . sacrifice themselves to keep the spell strong, drenching the stone . . . they are sensitive to its escape, they can tell it, and then the self destructive urge, the *spell*, took hold of them. Don should be sacrificing himself to the stone; it's his job, his inherited, incredible job, to open his arteries across the stone and drive it back with the words that were known so well two thousand years ago.'

Kline placed his hands on his ears, closed his eyes, shook his head. 'Wait a minute . . . wait a minute . . . there's something . . . Yes, the man who died when I first came to Higham. Why didn't *he* manage to resecure the binding of Cruachos?'

'He was *used*. Cruachos has been flexing his muscles for years, attacking people who come in range of his power. Perhaps the hypnotic spell is not as strong in some Belsaints as in others, but they still feel drawn to the stone . . . and then Cruachos can make them dance a dance of death at its own whim. Two types of suicide, Lee, not one! Some of them inherited self sacrifice, and some caused by Cruachos itself!'

And Kline was thinking that perhaps Cruachos had been flexing its muscles a little more than they had realized – perhaps although Simon Belsaint's finger had been on the trigger of the gun he had turned against himself, perhaps there had been a voice in his head. The same voice that Kline was convinced had been whispering to Karen when she had begged him to leave, to get the hell out of Higham now that he could only interfere with Cruachos's plans, and no longer help.

Not just the ghost of the beast haunted this place, then, but the ghost of its voice, of its influence . . .

He watched Francoise as she sat down, looking drawn and tense, staring back at him as if waiting for him to voice, now, what had become the obvious conclusion from their understanding of the suicides.

Kline said, 'So if we pull the stone up again . . . Adrian is released?' Francoise shrugged. 'And then,' he went on, 'we need words, and . . . we need a sacrifice. Is that it? A sacrifice!' He sat down next to her, staring at June, whose face registered all the bafflement she felt. Karen was leaning against the sink, her face pale and angry, her gaze fixed penetratingly and coldly on Kline. Kline knew what she was thinking: Don. She was thinking that he was suggesting Don should be killed. He shook his head. 'A sacrifice,' he repeated. 'Listen to us. Are we really serious about these things? I can hardly believe I'm saying these things rationally.'

Francoise reached out and pressed his arm. 'Lee, think for a second. A spell to keep it there, using blood . . . but Don said *any* blood, not necessarily death-blood from a human. Perhaps, yes, his conditioning is to kill himself, perhaps that makes the spell stronger –'

'*Jesus!*' screamed Karen. 'You sound like a couple of maniacs! What the hell is all this? Kill Don? Death blood on the stone? You're talking about a human life, a human being . . . you can't just –'

'Shut up!' shouted Francoise. 'And listen.' Karen was instantly quiet, her face red and hot, her eyes wide and angry. 'Listen to what I was saying! We must stop Don getting near to the stone or he *will* kill himself. I'm *sure* of that. But if we can find the words we can use . . . chicken blood, cat blood, anything. That's what he said, I'm sure I heard him right.'

'But those words are elusive, Francoise. They are blocked in Don. And you won't touch the stone and try and sense them. So what do we do?'

Francoise looked at him long and hard, coming steadily to a decision that obviously pained her. Finally she lowered her eyes and nodded acceptance. 'It must be me. But first, let's try and lift the stone again. That might make it easier.' She glanced at June. 'And perhaps . . . just perhaps . . . it will release Adrian, and that is its human host taken from it. Without Adrian it is less influential, but not, I suspect, less powerful.'

CHAPTER TWENTY

The crane had not been moved.

It towered over the church, a yellow, painted-steel monster, its tapered limb extending above the recess where the font lay quiet. Birds perched on that great girdered arm. They watched.

Underwood had wanted the crane left there in case he should decide to pull the stone from the ground again, and this time explore the pit more thoroughly. He was dissatisfied with Kline's reasoning and explanation; he was suspicious. His nose for trouble meant he could not assume that Kline's request to lift the stone had been everything it seemed. He had ordered the crane left in position for another day, and now he hurried after Kline and Francoise as they walked towards it. The man who would operate the machine was half in, half out of his cab, waiting for instructions.

As Kline approached him he shouted, 'Someone's been tampering with the cab! They've bent some of the controls!'

'Didn't you lock the door?' asked Kline, an edge of intolerance in his voice.

'Of course I bloody did. Look!'

He pointed to where the door had been forcibly jemmied open; the metal was bent and gouged.

Underwood inspected the damage, then asked if the crane was operable. The man grunted that it was, that the damage inside was very superficial.

Kline found Francoise staring at him thoughtfully, and he said, 'You think Adrian?'

She shrugged and smiled very thinly. 'Of course.'

Kline touched some of the marks on the crane's chassis. 'I'd have thought a boy who could throw a brick the length of his garden would have made a better job of sabotage than this.'

Francoise laughed. 'He probably thinks he did a good job. Would you know how to sabotage a time machine?'

'The boy?' said Underwood, breaking in on the conversation. 'He's not turned up, then?'

'Not yet. Unless one of your cars has found him.' Underwood shook his head. Kline wondered if the police search had been rather half-hearted.

As the crane-operator flexed the arm of the machine, and let the cable lower into the church, Kline led the way inside the ruins. Francoise tugged at his arm, pulling back, disturbed by the thought of what might happen.

'It's like before, Lee,' she said. 'I can't feel it, but that means it's gathering strength.'

Kline was insistent, determined. He pulled her towards the

font. 'Fight the bastard. It's only trying to scare us, to confuse us as to how powerful it really is.'

'It's powerful,' murmured Françoise, as if Kline needed reminding.

As before, there were light ropes about the stone, and the great metal hook was being looped through a chain-link connection, ready to take the strain for a second time. Within the shade, beneath a grey and overcast sky, it was depressingly cold. Kline felt none of that heat, none of the ghostly echo of a bird, or running. Françoise too, though she shivered and held onto his arm, watched less anxiously, the lack of awareness of the beast perhaps welcome, the ominous fact of that quiescence put from her mind for the while.

One of the men tying up the font called that it was ready; he turned away from the stone as, across the wall, the crane's engines revved up, and the hook lifted, pulling the slack chain taut –

The man had looked at Kline with an exasperated expression, perhaps confused and irritated at the interference that was taking them away from more important work.

The next moment he was bowled over onto his back, screaming. His colleague had been thrown against the wall of the recess and now staggered out, clutching his face with fingers that seeped blood. He was yelling.

A wind was blowing.

It came from the baptismal recess itself, swirling about the ruins, sending up great clouds of fallen leaves and dust. The two men who had been working on the stone were again struck by something unseen, one of them staggering right into Kline who caught him, but not firmly enough to stop him being sent flying further away, his neck badly twisted, his whole body racking as it was turned and broken by the angry wind.

Françoise turned and ran, then stopped, dropping to her knees with her hands clasped to her ears. Kline couldn't be sure in the noisy gale, and above the sudden screeching of the crane, but he thought she might have been screaming.

When he turned back to where the stone lay he could hardly believe his eyes.

The hook was swinging to and fro with increasing violence, the ropes having been sheared clean through so that the stone was no longer bound. As Kline stared in frozen disbelief at that wild swinging motion, so he realized that the crane was in fact trying to pull the hook up to the top of its ride, but that something was preventing it. The crane's motor was roaring and whining as the driver fought with the controls without success; some immense force was keeping that hook extended . . .

And without apparent effort suddenly snapped the heavy piece of metal from its chains, and cast it across the church, directly at Kline.

He jerked his body to the side, twisting his shoulders and ankles to avoid that killing flight. The great hook clanged to a stop by the brick porchway, and Kline – his heart racing, his eyes bulging – just leaned forward, hands on his knees, and stared at it.

He grew conscious of Francoise, gripping his arm, shaking him. When he straightened and extended his hands they were shaking. He laughed, nervous, frightened. 'Christ, that was close.'

The man who had operated the crane had come into the ruins and was now staring in considerable disbelief at the detached hook, where it lay. Underwood was with him, his overcoat slung across his shoulders. He walked over to Kline, shaking his head, frowning.

'How the hell did that happen?'

Kline said nothing. Instead he turned to Francoise and touched her gently on the face. 'I think it realized as much as we did that uprooting it would weaken it. It probably didn't notice a hundred years back, so it made a mistake yesterday. I think it just told us that it's not going to make the same mistake again.'

'You're right,' said the woman, and then abruptly walked towards the font. Kline ran after her, stopped her.

'Are you sure?'

'Am I sure what?'

'Are you sure you have the strength . . .'

'After doing all that, Lee,' she waved a hand at the crane's hook, 'what makes you think our friend here has much strength left? If it can be weakened in one way, then maybe it can be weakened in another. That took a lot of effort. I think now is the time to get near to it again, to peer into the past. OK?'

Kline shrugged and watched her as she walked up to the stone, and immediately, without hesitation, rested her hands upon it. Then she walked around it, stroking it, getting the feel of it, and then again, this time facing Kline across the bowl of the font, she closed her eyes, palms outspread upon the cold rock surface.

It *was* weakened by the earlier exertion – that was the first thing she sensed, before it withdrew from that momentary contact of minds, hiding deeper in the shadows of those images that she could receive with her strange and powerful gift.

The boy was crying, a distant, depressing sound. There was running, the sound of a man running through a tunnel, perhaps, or along the passageway of a stone building. His running was frantic, as if he fled some horror, some unseen, unheard source of evil – she could hear his breathing, laboured, painful – she could hear his murmured words, not prayers, fragments of words that told of his regret, his growing conviction that he would at any moment be struck down . . .

A girl screamed; she tensed as the sound erupted through her mind, flooding into her through the cold touch of her flesh upon the ageless stone. As the scream died, as she sensed death, the sour smell of blood spilled in sacrifice, she saw Karen's face, distorted with pain, wide-eyed with some unfelt agony: then slack, the eyes rolling up, the lips opening as death took her.

It filled Francoise with a terrible sense of apprehension, but as Cruachos manipulated her mind as powerfully as it could, trying to hide the deeper, etched memories of the stone – those memories over which it had no control – so she knew she was being tricked. These faces, the familiar, these sounds, the disturbing, were a show put on just for her, to weaken her resolve, to upset her . . .

The force of her rejection of those images sent them scuttling down into the darkness and Karen's face seemed to fade, to dissolve, though still a girl screamed as she died, her scream drowning, for the moment, the frantic chanting of the men who struck life from her body. Francoise felt shaky, weak in limb, and knew that her whole body must have been racking and shaking with tension. But she was here, now, and there was no breaking off.

She searched the shadows, the dark places of her mind, the howling anguish of the stone, of the lives and deaths that were caught in the stone, and she worked her way steadily towards the time when Cruachos had first been imprisoned here.

Snatches of words caught her attention: *mists of earth and sky* . . . *dark horns of the moon* . . .

They were words that she sensed by meaning, not by sound, and she repeated them in the language she was not familiar with, as she heard them, again and again, struggling to hear more, struggling to sense the full message of that ancient spell, for this was what she heard . . . the words that had been spoken by the dying men who sought to undo the terror they had wrought.

Cruachos emerged from the places where he was hiding. He tried to force her back, and she felt those awful fingers on her skin, the yanking, painful tugging of her hair, the twisting of her flesh so it burned and tried to weaken her.

Blood flooded through her mouth as her teeth closed on the flesh of her lips, but she stood her ground, and wrestled with the weakened force of the earth, denying everything that was placed before her as a source of confusion.

She seemed to see Antoin, running through a stone passage, blood streaming from his mouth and body, his arms reaching out towards her, his lips mouthing her name. He tumbled forward and climbed to his knees, and he clutched with bloody hands the great spill of entrails that had been slashed from his living body . . .

It choked her, panicked her to see this, but with the blood pounding through her head and her heart she fought to stay calm, to ignore the screams of the man she had once loved so much.

She saw Kline, vicious, callous, speaking words to her that thundered into her mind, revolting her, angering her.

And she saw Adrian, begging her to help him escape, his tiny hands spread wide in a desperate gesture for release; his face cried, the sound was the sound of wind.

The wind hit her, two thousand years of storm-wind, and rain, beating at her weakening mind as it had beaten at the stone; snow and frost froze her and cracked her, and baking summer suns made her sweat and squint, the glare of the orb hiding the visions that were recorded here, waiting for her to sense them. Wind and rain swept before her, the darkness of the elements, and the fire-storms of invader after invader, revolting her with their atrocities, and the cruel way they drove the peoples of this land before them.

Such a confusion of images, such a game, played so powerfully, so desperately . . .

Words: *Mist of earth and sky, dark horns of the moon* . . .

Sensed through the swirling images, and the screaming sounds of nature . . . and of something not so natural. Gradually they emerged, the words of the spell, the most ancient exorcism of them all. No bells or books or candles, no Christian words, with images of hell and heaven, but words nonetheless that inspired her with their power, words that hit at the force they attacked, drove it backwards, frightening it, locking it away.

They were words that had been etched in stone; through the eyes of the dying she could see the process, the stooped figure of the cowled man who made the marks on the slabs; they were words that were repeated across the decades, emphasizing the entombment, consolidating it. They were the words that battled the gradual release of Cruachos, frustrating its tenuous, tricky attempts to escape the crystal prison where it was bound.

There were words, then, that were as gentle as lark song compared to that original spell, the first process of binding, the panic-stricken priests making sacrifice to the stone to drench their spell with blood, and make the bonding of demon to rock as strong as the rock itself –

Francoise knew she was smiling, knew she was confusing Kline who watched her with such ill concealed anxiety. She sensed him, his puzzlement, as strongly as she sensed the stone. There was no way she dared communicate with him, to reassure him. The smile helped, that smile that must have seemed so enigmatic, so meaningless to the observer, who could not know that it was merely relief, relief at seeing for certain how unnecessary a sacrifice was when the task at hand was merely the re-securing of Cruachos, and not its total capture.

As the power of Cruachos increased so Francoise concentrated the harder, crying out as the tension in her body began to pain her. Over and over she repeated the snatches of words that she could hear, saying them loudly and searching her mind for the rest of them. So many spells, so many words, so much poetical exhortation of Gods and Earth, the people of this time being greatly skilled and very much inclined to speak in great, over-blown prose as they called for a good harvest or hunt.

But the spells she sought were there, stronger than these others which were mere reflections from the minds of those who manipulated the stone and the evil power they were forcing into it. Again she sensed that duality of purpose, the spell to call it forth, the spell to trap it, the key, in words, that could turn both ways. She narrowed her mind, tried to ignore the screams and storm sounds that were whirling through her mind's ears, tried to acknowledge physically that the rotten smell of decay, of bodies putrefying, was just an image, and not an actuality. She kept her stomach down, her body in a state of tension, but not in a weak and helpless state of physical illness. The words, the words . . . slowly they came to her, so slowly; the powerful words that accompanied a sacrifice – Karen's face again, her head brutally ripped from her body, her viscera draped like linen across the stone, her hands, blood-smeared, gripping the stone in death, powerfully, scratching so shallow that the marks were almost wiped away by the first puffing breeze of spring, but scratching deeper in a way that could not be seen . . . not Karen, of course, just Karen's face, a game, a game, to weaken her resolve . . . the girl who had died, young, so young, unspoiled save by the skin-clad priest who had dragged her there, giving her the pain of a brutal rape to extend the power of the spell, the efficacy of the sacrifice . . .

And slowly, emerging from behind the short, sharp, blunt cries of magic, the flowery, poetic words of the retaining spell, the guardian spell, that which had been left for posterity in the minds of the Belsaints, and those others, those families that had now been practically wiped out, destroyed, by the gradual, insidious workings of the emerging beast.

Mist of earth, grey veil of sky, Lug's shield of cold and white misting the dark horns of the moon, dark shadow of earth . . .

They came, these words, as if suddenly released to her from a locked cabinet . . . as they tumbled through her mind she began to speak them, mimicking with her hands the circular, winding gestures of the men she saw – so darkly – standing by the stone two thousand years before, faces turned to the skies, bodies swathed in dark cloaks, the gleam of bronze and gold amulets decorating their chests . . .

As they said the words, so she said the words . . .

As they made the magic passes, so she made the magic passes . . .

She smiled as she sensed Cruachos withdrawing, unable to work its will upon her and make her say the wrong words; she almost cried out with triumph as she sensed the magic working, the words, like those of an exorcism, working in some inconceivable way to manipulate the raw forces of evil, to strike at them, to drown them . . . to drown them . . . to drown them . . .

Its scream of triumph, its raw cry of pleasure, almost knocked her to her knees in utter despair!

It was so sudden, so unexpected, such a brutal shock, shattering her false moment of glory.

She smashed her head down against the font, feeling the solid, cracking impact drive her senses into whirling chaos, as Cruachos fled from its prison, escaping into a world that could scarcely credit its imaginary existence, let alone its real life . . .

'NO!' was the only word she could scream as she passed into darkness.

How unfair, how brutal this trick, this terrible trick. Games had been played and games had been won; she had lost, Cruachos had won, had won its freedom by so confusing her in her mind that instead of speaking the words to trap it, she had spoken the spell to aid its release. And she had *known* it would try and trick her, she had *known!*

Its laughter was the raucous mockery of a bird, of a thousand vultures descending to feed upon the vibrant carcass of the freshly dead . . .

It was gone, then; gone from the stone, gone from her mind:
Into the church:
Into the recess, facing Kline, who swore and stood, and backed away, his eyes popping, his mouth open in dumbfounded, silently hysterical shock.

He glimpsed it for just a second, towering above the prostrate form of the French woman whose final frenzied contortions had nearly smashed her skull against the font and knocked her cold. It regarded him, and he it, and for a second he was sure he was dead because it would not miss this opportunity to kill him.

Like a man, yet unlike a man, huge in form and frame, its head seemed to flow from the leathery, muscular substance of its chest – eyes, huge and bulbous, watched him from the great head, eyes that seemed impossibly far apart, separated by a ridge of flesh that flared out into a mockery of the human nose; its mouth, impossibly wide, like an impossible smile, split the face across – a thick tongue probed out to taste the air of freedom, and lick across the gleaming teeth which that smile exposed.

In the instant of that contact of eye there was a contact of mind – it swept through Kline like the unnaturally cold wind blowing from the recess, that froze his body and knocked him stiffly backwards. The shape towered over him, flowing into the night, and its voice in Kline's skull was deep, almost broken, almost ecstatic, louder than the wind that shrieked through the ruins.

unbound no pain no trap unbound into wind expansion such power now such power now adapt to earth and sky new place power destruction of opposed energies much energy malicious forces must repress must show strength great strength grubbing things that fight me free like wind home place of birth gone now no way back world of shadows to enjoy now destruction of kline thing destruction of france thing –

And like an iron fist some invisible hand closed around Kline's throat and crushed him until he gagged, then wrenched him round and threw him bodily against the stone wall of the church. He fought it, heard its bird-like shrieking, its laughter, knew he had moments left, seconds only . . .

Then the pressure on his body relaxed and he slumped heavily into a tight ball.

Gone. Fleeing upwards, outwards, into the bitingly cold November afternoon, just the frantic sound of wings, growing more distant, an unearthly, haunting echo of a sound that – as a symbol of the beast's desire for freedom – had haunted this church for more than the time the church had been standing.

Kline screamed, with fear, with hurt, with panic. The sound came from him like blood, like tears, flowing about him and taking the terror from his body, carrying it away on the wind. He became quiet, touched a shaking hand to his throat, felt the way his whole body seemed to vibrate uncontrollably. His hair whipped about his face; dust, even fragments of tile were flying about the ruins in a chaos of disturbed energy. The wind seemed to come from nowhere, and to go nowhere – leaves, caught in its blast, swirled in through the porchway and out through the empty roof – figures, human figures, crouched, tearful, panic-stricken, their clothes and hair tossed and torn in the impossible storm.

It moaned, this wind, deep and baleful, rising and falling in pitch as it rose and fell in strength.

Slowly Kline stood, conscious that it grew dark, that the sky was so filled with dust and smoke and debris that the daylight was being obscured. He saw Francoise's slumped shape by the font, but for the moment, bracing himself against the storm-wind, he edged his way around the wall of the church until he came to the porch –

And stepped out into mayhem.

Uprooted trees, scattered bodies and cars that burned and sprawled about the road as if they had been dropped at random. Thick smoke rose from where a bus was almost invisible behind the licking flames that consumed it and through the flames Kline could see the shapes of passengers on the upper deck, still seated, charred black into gruesome silhouettes of the human form. Men screamed, staggered against the wind that fanned the flames. Children and women ran sobbing, hysterical; all were dishevelled, most were bleeding, their faces twisted masks of incomprehension and fear.

It was as if a bomb had exploded. As he leaned against the church, clinging onto the wall to stop the gale from throwing him backwards, Kline could not see a single window that was not broken, nor a car that was not dented, or buckled, or burning – and for every figure that moved, there was a figure dead. Through the howling wind, the sound of human terror grew and became all the noise in the world.

Kline, the flesh on his body feeling like it was pulled so tight it would split, turned and stumbled back into the ruins. He walked warily towards the font. The air stank of some vile excretion, perhaps an all too familiar gesture by the demon, the lingering odour of decay to symbolize its power, the power it would use to find its place in a world as far removed from the world of the Britons as their world had been removed from that of Cruachos.

The wind dropped, then died away completely. The tension in Kline's body lessened and he felt he could breathe again.

He pulled Francoise to her feet, took her weight as she collapsed against him, then knelt, easing her body to the ground, reaching up to touch the fiercely grazed skin and darkening bruise on her forehead.

'My God, what have we done . . .' he whispered, the words drifting away from him into the stillness. He could hear the sound of sirens, many sirens, soon so loud that they drowned the screams and sobs from the street.

There was something about this place, now, this small grey, recess in the Christian building, that was more peaceful than before. He touched the stone, as he cradled Francoise's unconscious form, and found it lacking in something. Perhaps it was just suggestion. Perhaps his mind painted the pictures of peace on the basis of its certain knowledge that the stone had lost its hold upon Cruachos. Without being told he had guessed what had happened, and he didn't know what to do next, he just didn't know.

'Underwood!' he called, irritable that for all the policeman's insistent lingering on the scene, he was never there when you wanted him. 'Underwood, for Christ sake! Where are you?'

He looked up, glanced towards the far end of the church. Underwood had been near him, watching as Francoise had been in communion with the stone. Now he was sprawled against the end wall, where the altar had once been, curled as if asleep; except that his body was hunched towards the wall, yet his face, staring blindly, was watching Kline, twisted impossibly far about the axis of his neck.

In his arms Francoise stirred, then screamed.

He calmed her, forced her back to lie against his legs. Her hands gripped his arms, her eyes widened, filled with all the fear she had felt. 'Oh God, Lee . . . oh God, oh God . . .'

She was whining, like a child, like a dying woman. Kline comforted her, stroked the hair away from her saturated face.

'What have I done, Lee?' she said, then murmured words in her own language that Kline strained to hear.

'Easy,' he said. 'Take is easy. What's done is . . .' he didn't finish the sentence. No, dammit, what's done is *not* done, not so

293

quickly, not so easily. But for the moment, yes, they had lost. 'What's done can be undone,' he said.

Francoise made a sound like a sob, then buried her face in his arms for a moment, letting brief tears express the release of her tension, the release of her enormous aggravation with herself. She wiped her eyes and sat up, touched the grazed skin on her face with almost theatrical tenderness.

She shook her head. 'What a fool. What a bloody fool, Lee. I should have known . . . I really should have *known* not to trust *anything* I felt. My God . . . I've released it. I've completely released it.' She looked at Kline, her eyes filled with panic. 'What are we going to do?'

'Easy . . .' he said, meaning her, not the task in hand. She relaxed against him, then shook her head angrily. 'I was a fool.'

'We are all to blame,' said Kline.

'No. I knew it would try and trick me, and nevertheless I let it trick me.' She stood up, brushing herself down.

Kline said, 'It has killed a lot of people. It killed Underwood. But for some reason it didn't kill us. Don't question it, just thank God.' Francoise looked towards where the man's body lay, and said something softly, something sad.

'It could have killed us easily,' she said. 'It was on the point of doing so – it held back.' She looked sharply, anxiously at Kline. 'There has to be a reason for it, Lee. Not luck.' She put her hands to her face. 'I need a towel.'

'Use this.' Kline stripped off his leather jacket and passed it to her. She laughed, a sound that pleased him. Wiping her face thoroughly she handed the garment back to him with a grimace. She seemed to become suddenly angry, staring at the dead man, then at the font.

'Okay, Lee, you're the man who's so full of ideas. What do we do now?'

Kline laughed bitterly, glad that she was angry, now, glad that she had shaken off her shock. 'How the hell do I know?'

She mimicked him, scornful: '*How the hell do I know!* You *should* know, Lee. You're a man whose thinking progresses by the destruction of different views. Surely it's obvious!'

Icy fingers, like cold fingers, the fingers of evil, whipped through the ruins, progressed towards them as noisily as the uniformed men, and the intrigued and horrified spectators. Kline said, 'I suppose now you can read the stone without pressure, without fear.'

She reached out to touch the font, and Kline, after a second, reached out to encompass her hands with his. Francoise laughed, quietly, almost ironically. 'Mon Dieu, Lee, that feels good.'

'What? My touch?'

She nodded, stroking the dark hair on his fingers with her free hand. 'You're a bastard, Lee, you always were, you always will be . . . but you are so strong, and your touch makes me feel –' eyes, wide, gleaming, devoid of fear, watched him. A moment only. A closeness.

Men came up beside Kline; they were white-faced and afraid, looking young and awkward in their smart blue uniforms. They were confused, too, and the confusion made them angry. They spoke words that Kline didn't hear. The touch of his hand on hers, hers on his, thrilled him for the moment; in those days in Brittany he had made love to her, kissed and touched her in ways more intimate than many married people knew. That had been sensual. This single touch, like that first touch of an ancient stone monument, filled him with joy. Real joy.

'Adrian is not there.'

The words, technical, to the point, broke through his momentary lapse of concentration, dragged him back to stark reality.

'What do you mean, not there?'

Their touch had ended. Francoise, still shaking, was leaning on the font, her eyes half closed, her fingers splayed, feeling, touching each sensual contour of the carved rock. 'No. There is no sense of him, nor of Karen. Oh Lee, it's so obvious. They were games, cruel games, and we must tell June that.'

Kline stared at her, but saw June Hunter, her face, her hopes, a single image already corroded by her gradual acceptance of the boy who lived in her house as her son . . . now that image was shattered. Her obsession had been just that . . . an empty obsession that had kept her alive, whilst all the time the son she so desperately sought was in her house, in her flesh, harbouring a parasite that kept him empty, almost blind. Cruachos had played with her emotions, played a game with her, the game of belief . . . because of the way it played it induced conflict in the house where his eyes were living, watching . . . and on that conflict it fed, and through that family it grew aware of the world beyond its stone prison.

A cruel game, an empty obsession, and yet without it, perhaps Adrian would have stood even less a chance of release than he now had.

Release.

The word jarred at Kline, made him frown. He stared at the policemen, at their youthful faces.

'Was there an explosion here too?'

Kline looked blank for a moment. 'Explosion? Yes – sort of. No, more of a blast.'

One of the men glanced back at Underwood. 'He's dead,' he said unnecessarily. 'Did you see what happened?'

'A blast – it didn't seem to come from anywhere. It knocked him over – it knocked us all over. That's all we saw. We were studying the font . . .'

'Trying to lift it. I know.' The man pushed his cap back and stared at the crane. 'Blast twisted that too, by the look of it.'

Kline looked up, but said nothing. They would find out the truth soon enough; for the moment Kline was content to let them speculate on the nature of that blast.

As the police surveyed the church, shaking their heads and talking quietly and anxiously among themselves and with the ambulance men who were now on the scene, Kline thought about Cruachos, and why it hadn't destroyed him or Francoise? Why just an innocent man, who might have known more than was good for him, but who surely was not the sort of man who would have used that information?

Francoise was saying, 'It's here, Lee, much clearer, much easier to read. Horrible . . . horrible . . .'

'What is? Adrian?'

Angrily she snapped at him, 'Adrian's not here, Lee. I told you. That was a game, a vicious, nasty game to keep . . . I don't know . . . to keep us distracted, perhaps. No, I mean the spells are here, the words. Easier to see.'

Kline reached for a pen and fumbled in his pockets for paper. He had none. 'I'll write them down,' he said. 'Just a second.'

He turned to one of the uniformed men, who were still standing there as if frozen, and begged a notebook. Francoise said angrily, 'Words aren't necessary Lee.' As she spoke she drew back from the stone, staring at it, then at him. 'The spell I used has set Cruachos free, but not totally free.'

'What do you mean? Where?'

She said, 'It's somewhere, in one of us, in someone . . . in Adrian, completely in Adrian. For a second it was free, but the spell has bound it to a human body. It *must* be Adrian . . . he was here, outside the ruins for a while . . . now, instead of releasing him, it looks like we've totally possessed him. But that's why we're alive, Lee; it only had a second, a moment to attack before it was bound more permanently in the body of its messenger. It knew we could resist it, because we've already resisted it, so it struck down what it saw as the weakest easiest of the opposition; it eliminated the one man it knew it could eliminate. A potential hazard out of the way, it now has only two to conquer. Me and you, Lee. And it will do everything it can to destroy us, because we have the one thing it fears – the key to re-entomb it. It will destroy us unless we can destroy . . .'

When she said nothing more, he prompted, 'Unless we can destroy Adrian? Is that what you're saying? After all this, after everything we've done to help June, we must now destroy what she has taken years to find?' He shook his head. 'No way. I can't go along with that, Francoise . . . I just can't . . .'

'Don't be a fool!' she said. He frowned, upset by the sudden contempt. 'If he has to die he has to *die*. That's all there is to it. Don't you know that? Can't you see that? We're not talking about one life any more, we're talking about many lives, yours and mine included, and the Hunters, and the Belsaints, and maybe everyone in this town, and beyond. We're not talking about one boy, we're talking about something that can do . . . My God, I just don't know *what* it can do! So keep your sentimentality to yourself, you fool. There is no *place* for it, not now, not any more.'

She was right, of course, and it made him feel sick to realize the fact, and sicker to think of June, and how they would tell her, and what she would do . . . and Edward, who was right all the while, and who now would have to share in the tragedy, and it would break him, Kline knew that instinctively . . . it would break him.

'Dammit!'

'Why do you say that?' Francoise, softer, now, reached out and took his hand. She was smiling, and he returned the gesture.

'It makes me feel bad, that's all.'

'So now we see the real Lee Kline,' she said, smiling almost ironically. 'Not the bastard, not the cold fish with no feelings, just a man with a heart, but without the courage to live his life without a mask.'

'Bullshit,' said Kline easily, glancing at her. 'It just . . . it just makes me feel bad, that's all.'

She let go of his hand. 'Well don't feel bad. Because I don't think it's necessary. Adrian must be here, near the stone, but to trap Cruachos back in the stone . . .'

'A straightforward spell? A few words, a few gestures? Come on Francoise . . . what is it? Tell me.'

'A blood sacrifice. It's necessary. In the way it was originally done, just a blood sacrifice, not necessarily Adrian . . . but a *human* blood sacrifice, Lee, committed across the stone, the blood to be daubed across the mortal body of the host.'

She was white as a sheet as she spoke these impossible words. Kline listened, feeling distant, unreal. Sacrifices, human sacrifices, across stones, in rituals as long dead as the Gods they had been made to . . . perhaps it was all nonsense, perhaps the old ways were just that, old ways that could be improved on. Perhaps there were drugs, or electrical treatments, or psychiatric exorcisms that could do the job just as well, but who could know what they were? And who had the time to find out?

A sacrifice. A *human* sacrifice . . . with the words, and the gestures, and the crisis would be past . . . and someone would be dead, and who would pay the debt for that?

'Are you sure?' he said quietly, staring at Francoise who shrugged.

'How can I ever be sure? I know only what my senses tell me. It worked before, Lee . . . I can sense it working. One must say the words and one must die . . . Adrian would be the obvious choice, but it doesn't have to be Adrian. It could be anyone, anyone who is strong in life, so that they can be strong in death.'

And as he turned away from her, to walk across to Underwood's body, Kline could find nothing in himself to express what he felt other than raw and humourless laughter.

It took an hour before the police allowed them to leave. Their statements had been taken, and Underwood's body removed along with those from the street, Kline, again using every ounce of his persuasive skill, failed to convince the sombre faced men that it would be pointless closing off the ruins.

But how did they all die, they kept saying. How could Underwood in particular have been so twisted if no-one touched him?

Kline managed to keep himself from heavy handed sarcasm. He played it innocent, shrugging and shaking his head. Amazing, isn't it? And I just don't know.

And since there were enough people who had seen his body lifted by unseen hands – that sudden, staggeringly powerful wind – and flung against the stone wall of the church, at length the police let them go.

'We've got to find Adrian,' said Francoise as they ran from the church. Kline reached out and took her hand, slowed her down.

'Somehow I already knew that. And this is a big town.'

'And Adrian is very strong now,' said Francoise as they walked to Kline's car. She stopped, tugged him round. 'Lee, we must be so careful.'

'I already knew that too. But what choice have we got? We've obviously got to get Adrian back to the stone, but this thing is obviously not going to risk letting us do that, is it, so we may assume that Adrian will fight us. And I've seen the way he fights . . . the strength of ten? By now he must have the strength of a hundred.'

They jumped into the Austin and roared in a tight circle in the road before weaving through the traffic back towards the house. November dusk was touching the sky, and everywhere lights were going on inside houses. It would be dark soon.

Francoise had been thoughtful for all the journey back to the house. Now she said, as they stood on each side of the car in the Hunter's driveway, 'A hundred? No . . . no, Lee. That's not possible. There's always the possibility of far more strength than you are aware you have. Adrian can do horrifyingly strong things but that means he must push himself to the limit. The limit his body can take is the same, Lee. It's high. It's potentially lethal, but surely he can't have increased his strength ten-fold again. His muscles and bones wouldn't take it.'

Kline shrugged. He was thinking of a priest, thrown bodily through a wooden door; of a brick hurled over a hundred yards down a garden. He said, 'I hope you're right. Come on.'

They went back into the house.

At first glance the house was empty. It was in greyness, and in the lounge, with the curtains pulled, it was pitch black. Apprehensively Kline switched on the light, but the place was deserted.

'They must all be looking for Adrian,' he said, and Francoise agreed.

But she went to the stairs and shouted, 'Anybody here?'

She was answered by an hysterical scream of *yes*.

'Karen . . .' she said as Kline came running. They raced upstairs, Francoise tripping on the top step and swearing loudly. They went to Karen's room and found the girl standing by the door, her face wet with tears, her body shaking.

On the bed Don lay full length, twisting and thrashing, but making no sound. 'He's been like this for ages,' said Karen, tears running freely again as she stared pathetically at Kline. 'Ever since . . .' she broke off, bit her lip and looked at Don.

'Ever since what?'

'We were at the hospital – his father –' She could hardly bring herself to say what Kline knew must have happened.

Simon Belsaint was dead.

She said, finally, 'We were with him when he died. He never woke up, just stopped living – it was so sad, he just . . . sighed.'

'When *was* that Karen?'

'An hour or so ago. We came back here. Don was really crying, but then he went like this. It's so frightening. What's the matter with him? He looks so ill, so white . . . that's not what should happen, is it?' Again she gave way to fear and emotion.

Kline went over and tried to calm the agitated boy, but Don screamed out and knocked Kline's hands away. Francoise helped restrain him, and Don stared up at them, eyes bulging, lips drawn back and white with tension. His breathing almost hissed between his teeth, like a snake, an animal.

'He has sensed the escape,' said Francoise softly, hoping that Karen wouldn't hear. 'Perhaps when his father died some intangible responsibility was awakened in him. He instantly knew of Cruachos being free. Now he needs to get it back. Everything in him has only a single direction, now. He must trap Cruachos back in the stone, and to do that he must also sacrifice himself. His body, his mind, his instinct for survival, all are resisting the programmed instructions, but those instructions are slowly overwhelming him.'

'What are you saying?' said Karen loudly, agnrily. 'What are you whispering?'

Francoise led the girl from the room, reassuring her with soft spoken words. But Kline heard Karen tear herself away from the older woman angrily. 'What's the matter with Don? Is this something to do with him being hypnotized?'

'It would have happened anyway,' said Francoise, and then Kline heard her swear.

A moment later Don struck out and hit him on the cheek, sending him staggering. The boy began to scream, shouting what sounded like a name: *Morawyn, Morawyn!*

Instantly Karen had come back into the room, and a moment later, having hesitated and stared at the boy, she was reaching for him.

'Caragok!' she cried, and seemed – to Kline's astonished eyes – to be trying to run to him, but her feet remained frozen to the ground. Her hands clenched, then reached again, her face twisted in agony, tears flowed from eyes squeezed tight shut, as if she fought against something.

300

Don jumped from the bed, tried to run to her, but he too seemed caught, frozen to the place where he stood, and for a long time Kline and Francoise watched the bizarre sight in stunned silence, the two youngsters each screaming a name at each other, each trying to reach the other.

Suddenly Karen collapsed, curling into a heap as she fell to the floor, her body racking with sobs. Don became quiet, his voice fading away with shock, his eyes staring. Still his hands reached towards Karen: slowly he began to whine, and slowly his hands came up to mask his face, to hide the grief there.

'Morawyn . . . Morawyn . . .' he said, and sat down heavily on the bed. Francoise helped Karen to stand and the girl welcomed the protective arms that encompassed her. 'What happened?' she said. 'I had that dream . . . so intense . . . that awful dream . . .'

'Tell me about it,' said Francoise, and this time, as she led the girl from the room, there was no fighting.

Kline sat down by Don, stared at the boy's ashen face, wondered what to say, what to do. 'Were you dreaming, Don?' he said.

'I don't know,' said Don. 'Horrible . . .'

'What was it? What were you seeing?'

'Karen . . . Morawyn . . .' he frowned. 'A girl . . . a girl . . .' he seemed overwhelmed by his own recollections. 'Oh my God, how horrible. I remember, now . . . I've had this dream before . . . as a child. I used to wake up, reaching for the girl, but she was being dragged away and . . . and killed so horribly. A knife, splitting her open, and I would always see it in my dreams. Poor Karen . . .' he looked at Kline. 'I don't understand. What the hell is going on?' At once he started to shiver, to shake quite involuntarily. He hugged his arms about his body and rocked backwards and forwards again, and Kline heard his breath come fast and hard again. He could hear Don almost breathing words, unfamiliar words.

'Fight it, Don,' he said, and thought: fight *yourself*, Don, fight that which has been in you for two thousand years.

It was almost impossible, of course. Don had no idea of what was happening to him, but again he started to cry out, to yell words, a mixture of the unknown, and English, and Kline heard him saying, 'Drench it . . . soak the stone . . . I must . . . I must . . .'

He dragged Don back to the bed as the boy made a sudden rush for the door. Don fought him, and Kline used all his strength to twist his arms behind his back and then drag him back inside.

He ran from the room and locked the door behind him. Don started to kick and punch at the heavy wood panelling and Kline was glad to see that the youth could not make any progress with its destruction.

'They're out looking for Adrian.'

Kline turned as Francoise spoke from behind him. 'Edward and June. They must find him . . . oh Lee, if they don't . . . if they don't.'

Explain what's going on,' said Kline, above the screaming and ranting of Don Belsaint. 'What's Karen got to do with all this?'

'Nothing,' said Francoise. 'I'm sure of it. All I can think is that she's a little bit psychic like me, like lots of people. Being close to Don, and to Adrian, she has sensed something tragic and it has haunted her.'

'The girl in the river . . . the dream she talked about . . .'

Francoise shuddered as Don's voice began to get hysterically angry. She nodded. 'I think that Caragok, this ancestor of Don's, was forced to watch his girl, his wife, perhaps, being taken from the river and sacrificed. The memory, deeply hidden in Don, was somehow seen by Karen who became identified with it. Cruachos saw this and played on it, but I think for its own ends.'

When Kline said nothing, just frowned and shook his head, she said, 'I think it saw her as a potentially powerful sacrifice, just like the original sacrifice, this Morawyn. I think it must have believed she threatened it because of this, because if she was used in sacrifice it would be very strong. It might explain why Adrian was so aggressive towards Karen . . . when she came home this time Cruachos knew she was a sort of threat; in previous years it has not been so important. This time it panicked, made Adrian say those horrible things, and enforced them by making him bite through his finger.'

Kline was confused, his mind reeling. 'But surely Timmy was more of a threat . . . he was a Belsaint, why didn't he respond instinctively to the presence of Cruachos in Adrian?'

Francoise reached out and squeezed his cheek, smiling thinly. 'I don't understand the rules any better than you do,' she said. 'Perhaps . . . perhaps it only watched and spoke through Adrian . . . perhaps he was never *physically* possessed, even a little. Perhaps there was nothing for Tim to respond to. I know, it's hard to believe any of these things, to understand these things, but we've got to start thinking differently if we're to save Adrian.'

'And unless we can get him back to the font, everything is pointless. Let's go look for him.'

CHAPTER TWENTY-ONE

Karen watched them go. Inside her there was only coldness, fear, the sort of emotion that leaves you drained and unresponsive, even irresponsible. She could hear Don sobbing and almost without thought she walked along the landing and reached for the key of the door. After a second she turned it and stepped into the room.

Don immediately stopped his noise and stood. He walked to her and reached out to take her shoulders in his hands, pulling her close. For a second she tensed, wondering if he was going to be brutal with her, but he relaxed and kissed her face.

'Adrian . . .' he said.

'I know,' she said, and for a moment just concentrated on hugging him. 'I'm going to kill the little bastard. He's done all this, and caused all this. I'm going to kill him.'

'In the church,' said Don. 'It must be in the church, by the stone font.'

She looked up at him and then smiled, stretched out to kiss his cold lips. 'Whatever you say.'

Don released her and ran down the stairs, as fleet, as silent as that dark figure that had so often haunted her nights. She heard the front door slam, and when she had remained alone in the darkness for a few minutes, listening to the heavy silence, she found her coat and left the house as well.

She ran lightly, and easily, the half mile to the Belsaint's house. The place was in darkness, but she knew where the key to the back door was kept because she had often used it while waiting for Don to come home from work. She unlocked the door and slipped inside, not turning on the lights, because she knew the police, in their confusion and misunderstanding, were regularly checking the place out.

Upstairs.

She found Don's room and pushed the door open. She went swiftly to the desk and switched on the small, anglepoise lamp. The room was at the back of the house, and the heavy curtains were pulled.

For a second she glanced around the room, at the chaos of clothes, and the unmade bed. Books and models lay scattered everywhere, and about the room was the dull smell of metal. The walls were covered with Don's replica guns and swords, and armoury quite magnificent in its versatility. Not all of the weapons were working models, but she knew one that was.

It was a blunderbuss he had made for a school project, four years ago. Double-barrelled, heavy, no-one at the school had realized it would *work*; no-one had thought to ask, and Don hadn't thought to tell them. She reached for the gun, now, and hefted it, feeling the weight, the balance. She worked the double flintlock mechanism and sprang the trigger, and she felt the power of the brilliantly made replica, and smiled as she thought of what it would do to Adrian.

The coldness in her grew more intense, the thought of Adrian made her mouth taste sour, her blood race. If, somewhere in her head, the voice of reason spoke to her, told her that she was not being rational, she ignored it. Adrian was the cause of all this horror, all this hatred, all this grief – Adrian was *it*. Adrian had made Don go mad, had threatened his life – Adrian had made Don's father try to take his own life, Adrian! Adrian! Adrian and his hateful, mean games – Adrian!

She *had* to kill him. She *had* to make things good again.

She found Don's tin of gunpowder and in the poor light of the desk-lamp she measured large charges of powder into each barrel and tamped them down as she had seen Don doing so often. She found his small tobacco tin of lead shot, emptied from his father's twelve-bore cartridges, and loaded each barrel with what she imagined was an over-adequate amount of the lethal material. This she rammed home, and shook the gun as she had seen Don do; nothing rattled. What was next? She had to think for a moment, but she completed the charging of the barrels as best she could and felt pleased with the job. She primed the priming-pan, using the finer black powder that Don had always told her was important. She covered the pan with the ice-cold frizzen, and stroked the whole complex, beautiful firing mechanism.

She was grinning as she left the house, the snub-barrelled gun wrapped in the oil-cloth that Don used to carry the replicas whenever they went out into the pine-woods to shoot.

She returned to her own house. Since she didn't know where to even start looking she thought only that the house was the safest, most obvious place to wait for the boy, who must – she sensed – eventually come looking for her.

A confusion of images and senses, a feeling of being lost, hopelessly lost. He walked unsteadily, his body cold, his mind alive with growing panic. Familiar images, familiar smells, glimpsed fleetingly, then lost against the dark faces of this unknown place. This was freedom and yet it overwhelmed him, he could not cope with the strange darkness of it. He moved through that darkness, instinctively walking towards the west, following a route towards the one place he sensed was home, his haven . . . the place he knew so well. There were other places, glimpsed darkly through half closed eyes during the time of eternity before the now, and there was one place, a darker place than all, where for a moment he stopped and wondered, staring from the security of the shadows at the dark eyes of the building, and the lifelessness of its walls. But then he moved on, walking past this place of his nightmares, until trees and gardens hid him, and he progressed more confidently, more sure of himself in this time of his greatest trouble, and yet his greatest triumph.

'Stop a minute! Over there . . . isn't that Edward?'

Francoise had spotted the figure of the doctor, standing hunched and cold in the security of a darkened shop doorway. He was watching the activities in the High Street, his face was lit by the bright lights of a television crew. As Francoise saw him, he slipped from the doorway and walked away from the reporters.

Kline pulled into the kerb, two hundred yards away along a narrow side street, and said, 'Wait here.'

Francoise laughed, as if to say *I'm going nowhere on my own*.

There was a new chaos in Higham, now, a chaos of water gushing into the street, of smouldering fires, of fire-engines and ambulances, and the silent, but obtrusive flashing of blue and yellow lights. There seemed to be police everywhere, walking alone or standing in groups, discussing each and every detail of that sudden explosive gale that had ripped through Higham town centre and exploded every lamp, and shattered every window.

Quite clearly they thought there had been an enormous sequence of explosions and the television news services had confirmed that much. Bomb disposal units, army men in large numbers, were poking through the fire-gutted wreckage of the bus, and several cars that had burned along with it.

The artificial yellow light that bathed the place was unnerving, at once brilliant and discomforting. Kline avoided anyone who looked like a reporter and scanned the crowd for Edward. He saw him, distantly, staring at the church of St Mary's. Kline walked briskly towards him. Before he got there Edward had moved away from the High Street and Kline, with an anxious glance at the chain cordons round the church and the police cars parked on the grass banks, darted after the doctor.

There was no reason why anyone should have associated the failed effort to lift the font with the sudden explosive gale that had wrecked the street. Only Kline and Francoise had been aware of the escape of Cruachos; only Kline had glimpsed the shape of the beast. Underwood alone had had an inkling of the dark forces at work in his town, and it was quite apparent that he had told no-one of what he was learning. The church was cordoned because a policeman had died there, because there appeared to have been a blast there too.

But how long, Kline wondered, before the police found a few scribbled notes on Underwood's desk, perhaps, or remembered how the crane had been buckled when it had tried to lift the font, and thought to connect the crane and the explosion, and then came back to Kline with a little more determination than earlier?

He put the thought from his mind, hating to think of the consequences of police interference now. He caught up with Edward in a quiet street. Distantly a police siren wailed and both men glanced in the direction of the town centre.

'Any sign of him?' asked Kline.

Edward shivered and shook his head. He looked tired, dishevelled. There was a haggard look about his face, a tension there that was twisting his features horribly. 'You?'

'Nothing.'

'It's so bloody cold,' said Edward. 'He can't survive this weather long.' He looked sharply at Kline. 'You been back at the house?'

Kline nodded. 'I left Karen and Don there. Don's ill – his father finally died.'

Edward considered that and shook his head. 'I'll go home too, I think. I'm getting too cold, too cold inside.'

'Good idea,' said Kline. 'Where's June? Have you seen her?'

Edward glanced back towards the High Street. 'A few minutes ago, she was down there, near the church. She keeps looking there. She's quite hysterical.' He looked hard at Kline, confusion, anxiety apparent in his every feature. 'This explosion . . . do you think . . . . ?'

'Do I think what?'

Edward shrugged. 'Could it have been Adrian? Or June?'

Kline stared at Edward for a second, torn by a decision he found difficult to make; Edward did not yet know of the escape, but worse, he didn't know of Kline's belief that Adrian was now totally taken by Cruachos, totally possessed . . .

The moment to tell him came and went, and Kline bit his lip angrily. He couldn't help thinking that it would kill Edward to know the truth. 'I don't think so,' he said.

'It makes things so much harder . . . so much harder . . .'

Edward walked away, cutting through the back streets towards his house. Kline stood below a bright lamp and watched the distant confusion; darkly, above the houses in this street, he could see part of the church, its walls eerily lit by the flickering blue light of a police car.

A gentle wind blew his hair, rustled leaves in the street.

He didn't notice it for a moment, started to walk back towards the main street.

A window shattered loudly. Someone screamed. Kline stopped.

He looked into the distance, at the dark houses, and the bright windows, turned back along the street and became aware of that insistent breeze . . .

'Oh Christ!'

It hit him like a fist, sending him staggering backwards – fingers of wind tugged at his clothes, wrenched at his skin. He grabbed the lamp-post and winced as it was silently plucked out, and the glass from it scattered on the gale. Windows and lights were going out all round, the explosive sounds muffled in the howling storm. Gates and concrete garden figures flew like leaves, and above the shrieking of the wind – the awful cry of human fear.

It was here, nearby. Was it looking for him?

Back along the road he saw something hazy, a confusion of leaves and wood, a whirling of wind and light, an area of obscurity that moved swiftly across the town. A body was flung from it, an old man, broken and crumpled as he sprawled on the pavement. Kline lurched after the holocaust, fighting against the haunting wind. An unearthly scream stopped him – he watched horrified as two bodies, both naked, were tossed through the air like rag dolls, splitting open as they struck and were impaled upon the metal railings outside a school.

As if suddenly aware of him the whirlwind turned, came towards him.

Kline glimpsed nothing but confusion and a hazy human shape in the middle of that centre of destruction. He thought he heard his name called, and laughter, deep unhuman laughter. A door was ripped from its hinges and hurled towards him. It glanced from his shoulder, agonizing, almost fatal. A child came running through the empty socket in the house and was flung on the wind straight into Kline's arms, then whipped away, as Kline hung on for his life to the lamp-post, and dashed, screeching and finally silent, against the school wall.

And hands reached for Kline, and tore at his eyes.

He turned and fled.

Words:

strong strong kline thing useless now termination of energy regret strength necessary possession necessary strength of kline thing destruction

Kline screamed as he felt the life squeezed from him, his heart clasped in icy fingers, the blood in his body frozen, the air sucked from him . . .

He burst into the artificial light of the High Street, stumbling on the pavement, gasping for breath.

Abruptly the grip upon him was gone and he stumbled, released from the invisible fingers that were trying to haul him back, away from the centre of the town.

The holocaust was gone, vanished into darkness. Kline watched for it for a while, massaging his chest where his heart was in considerable pain. Then, still breathless and in agony, he walked quickly back through the confusion of people and vehicles and almost fell into the car, where Francoise was waiting.

'My God,' she said, reaching out to touch the sweat that poured from him. Instantly she had gathered what had occurred. 'You saw him!'

'It was defensive. I couldn't get near. It's strong, Francoise . . . really strong.'

'The strength is limited, Lee. I just know it. Cruachos is gathering strength ready to transfer to an even stronger host. It's the only way it can do it.'

'Is that why it weakens so suddenly? It could have easily killed me . . . Christ, it killed four people while I watched.'

'It's confused, Lee. It doesn't know the rules, it can't control the energy it uses, it needs.'

Kline recovered his wits, used his shirt to mop his face and then nodded vigorously. 'It wanted me . . . now I understand. It thought I was acceptable as a new host, and tried to take me; it tried to knock me senseless, but when I fought it weakened, decided that it would have to kill me, to destroy me.'

Francoise laughed abruptly, humourlessly. 'Now I understand. That's why it didn't kill us yet. I suppose we *must* explain our luck that way.'

Kline looked at her. 'It thinks – thought – we are ideal for its purpose. But why? Because we know so much that *it* needs to know?'

Francoise shrugged. 'Perhaps. It is unsure of itself, uncertain. It is triumphant, yet confused. It hesitates when it should be destructive, destroys unnecessarily out of a sort of frustration, a release of frustration.' She looked at Kline. 'When it escaped, I felt it very strongly . . .'

Kline was thoughtful. 'I felt something too – its triumph, its destructiveness . . . something else.'

'Homesickness?'

He smiled. 'Yes, but something else. It regards us as interfering and insignificant – like grubs, yes, like *grubbing* things. But it has nothing on which to base any judgement. Our minds touched, but there was no *meeting* of minds, no common ground – it understands us no more than we understand it. It's totally alien to us, and we to it. This destructiveness is a defence; I don't think it has any real understanding of the way it hurts us. And I don't think it is concerned to find out.'

'But it must still be destroyed,' said Francoise. 'We could never communicate with it. It belongs to a different world, and this is a shadow world to it, and a shadow world in which it must now stay forever – as you say, it is so different to us that it will never allow itself to relate to us. It *must* be destroyed, trapped again.'

'And in the meantime . . .'

'And in the meantime, as it adjusts to its new freedom, it will seek us out. It has to, Lee. It has to possess us or kill us, and I think it now knows that possession will be too difficult. Since we know the way to trap it, it must eliminate that knowledge from us. So it must take the chance and stay in the area, playing a game of war with us, instead of hiding so that it can consolidate its strength.'

Kline laughed, grim, almost sour. 'That's great, then . . . So we get the boy to the font . . .' he trailed off, staring through the side-window, away from Francoise. Something was working at him, and he was conscious that Francoise had seen this.

She said, 'What are you thinking?' Her voice was soft, soothing.

Kline looked back towards her, but couldn't meet her gaze. 'I was thinking of a dead man.'

'Which dead man is that? Many men died today. Underwood? Do you mean him?'

Kline shook his head. 'The man who has to die if Adrian is

to be saved. What are we doing sitting here, thinking about how to get the boy to the font, when we still . . .'

'We still what?'

He met her gaze. He hoped she couldn't see what he was thinking, desperately hoped she couldn't read him, like that open book with pictures. There were things that had to be kept hidden from her, for a while at least, until it was too late for her to interfere.

Not waiting for him to answer her question, she answered it for him. 'When we still need a sacrifice, you mean. We still need a volunteer.' She shrugged, smiled. 'Don't worry yourself about it, Lee. We have a volunteer . . . don't look so shocked! Of course it's me. Who else?'

'You're not serious!'

'Deadly serious, Lee. Someone has to die, and if we discount the possibility of killing Adrian himself – and Edward and June both will try and stop us doing that, and so would you . . . you know you would. Well then, who is left? Just me.'

'I don't understand.'

'Why not? It seems very straightforward to me. To make the magic work what is needed is a sacrifice, made during the speaking of certain simple symbolic words – important words, mind you. Very important. You *have* memorized those words, haven't you?'

'I have memorized them,' said Kline irritably, unable to tear his gaze away from this matter-of-fact woman who was so calmly telling him of her plans for self-destruction. 'Trust me, will you?'

'So! Yes, I trust you. I have to trust you. And when you say the words I shall quietly open my veins. Lee, it seems bizarre, perhaps it seems melodramatic, almost noble . . . but what other alternative is there? It was me who let herself be tricked by Cruachos, who ultimately let it loose. I was responsible . . . just me. It should be my life that pays for the mistake. It seems to me a simple question of honour, and economics. A life is needed, my life should be offered.'

'Just like that.'

She shrugged. 'I have contemplated suicide so many times, Lee, you cannot imagine how many times. This is nothing new to me, nothing extraordinarily frightening. I have contemplated death many times, and each time have decided that death was as pointless as life. This time, for the first time, there is a point to death. I am not afraid, Lee. There is something I very much regret, something that makes me bitter, and bitterly sad . . .

something . . . but even that cannot change the *rightness* of this action.'

'You're too bloody cool,' said Kline, half angry, half distressed. They sat in silence, for a while, staring through the dirty windscreen of the car, their hands touching affectionately, but their spirits far apart. For a long while there was just their breathing, the groaning of equipment in the High Street, the frightened sounds of people hurrying home, perhaps scared of a second 'explosion'.

'It's funny,' said Kline. 'But I never figured you would think like that.'

'You don't know me very well.'

'I thought I did. But I didn't guess you for a martyr.'

She looked sharply at him, frowning, cold. 'Are you being cruel? That sounds cruel to me, unnecessarily so.'

Kline squeezed her hand, then turned to her and put his arm round her shoulders. 'It wasn't meant to be. Really. It's just . . .'

'Just what? Just that you don't want me to die because of some selfish reason in you?'

Kline repressed the surge of irritation he felt. He closed his eyes and kissed her hair. His heart was thundering, almost painful as he reached a moment when he would put into words something he had hitherto only thought about. 'Don't mock me, Francoise. I know what I am, I know what people think of me.'

Her hand touched his knee. 'I think a lot of you.'

'Maybe you do. Most people don't. I don't give a damn, you know that. It's just that we've both been chasing Adrian for the same reason. Only you didn't know that I intend to die, to be the sacrifice.'

His heart was working so fast he thought it would burst; he was overwhelmingly hot, baking in the small car; the sounds of the town had slipped away, unreal murmurs in the background; the muscles of his neck were tense, painful. He had said it! He had said what he had felt was right for the past two hours, the sacrifice of his own life for a cause far greater than any one man's survival. It had to be him, it *had* to be, and yet if he thought too hard about it . . .

And suddenly he realized that Francoise had laughed at him.

'Now, Lee, that *is* melodramatic.'

The heat, the tension in his body, evaporated in an instant. He felt cold, as cold and rigid as stone.

She was saying, 'Damn you, why should you want to die? Why should you *need* to? You have everything to live for, and you know it. I don't believe you are a man who would knowingly sacrifice himself.'

'Then you don't know *me* very well.'

'Oh yes I do. I know you very well indeed. You are doing something to try to frustrate me, to stop me. I know it, you must admit it. You are not the self-sacrificing type, and don't try pretending you are.'

Kline withdrew his warm hold upon her and sat stiffly upright. He was very angry as he turned to her. 'Listen, Francoise, and listen good. You have something that must not be lost . . . a talent . . . a sensitivity. You are far too valuable to sacrifice yourself in this way, and you must not do it. Besides, I am stronger than you, stronger in body, which may be needed, and stronger in will.'

Francoise smiled cynically. 'You are, eh? Well, that's good if it's true, but I don't think it's true. You're too self centred, narrow minded. And that's the truth, Lee, that's all the truth there is.'

'And I agree,' said Kline softly. 'Which is why I say I'm stronger. This thing can feed off confusion, can play on it; it played on your emotions, mixed you up and tricked you, and you'd better believe it can do it again. But me? No way. I'm too *narrow*. You can't bend the sort of aggressive self-centredness that I've got. Think about it. It's true, right? If anyone has a chance of fighting the boy, it's me. You just make sure you've got your words ready. Okay?'

There was an icy silence, an embarrassed, awkward quietness.

Francoise's face was a torrent of confusion and anxiety, deep thought and difficulty. Finally she reached out for Kline's hand and lifted it to her lips. The kiss was long and sincere, and Kline saw how her eyes were closed as she touched his skin with her tongue. The kiss ended but still she held his hand as if she held something precious, stroking the hairs on his knuckles, tracing the boney contours of his joints; she stared at her own fingers, painting abstract pictures of some deeper emotion on the dark skin of his wrist. She said, 'Lee, it wouldn't work. It just wouldn't work.'

'Why not?'

'Because . . . oh my God, what do I say? It's so difficult. It sounds so insulting.'

'Say it anyway.'

Still stroking his hand, growing closer to him with that intimate touch, she said, 'I know why you are doing this; I know what is going through your head. I respect you very much for it, but I can see how it will not work perhaps more clearly than anybody. Lee, I know you've come to understand yourself a little better, perhaps a lot better. I've seen this, I've sensed it. You are a man who builds hopes and shatters hopes, as easily as a child might build a sandcastle and then kick it down. You don't mean to be destructive, but you *are* destructive, and this destructiveness comes from your terrible pragmatism. Everything must be proven, must be seen to be true; everything has only one practical solution, and nothing, not sentiment, nor economics, must get in the way of that practical solution. There is much in what Edward fears about you, much about you that has threatened the family, more so even than this dark spirit from the stone. Now perhaps you understand this, and I know that you feel it your duty to atone; perhaps you don't think of it like that, but you must admit that you are rationalizing some deep feeling of guilt when you say your weakness is in fact a strength that can be used to fight this thing. You are being noble, in both a nice sense and a feeble sense. I think you genuinely believe you must be the sacrifice to the stone, and I love you for that . . . but then you know that already, don't you? You know I love you, that's something that you're well trained to detect –' she broke off, hot, awkward; she kissed his hand again and Kline felt the tingle of sweat on his skin; he touched her hair, frowning, wanting to say something to her but unable to summon the correct words.

She laughed quietly, still not looking at him. 'This is what makes it so difficult. So very, very difficult. Lee, deep down, deep inside you, there is this same very pragmatic man that we see on the surface; it's a man with a basic instinct for self-survival at any cost. Right now you firmly believe in the rightness of taking your life to save . . . God knows how many lives. But when it comes to the moment to do it, you would *not* do it. Your instinct would take over . . . oh Lee, look how much of your life is founded on instinct, on intuition! You would cynically say, what the hell am I doing here? I must be mad! You would, you know. You'd say it, and you'd let the moment pass, and the chance for release would be gone as well. So it must be me, Lee. I am the only one who can do it.'

After a frozen few minutes Kline said, 'What makes you think you don't have those same instincts? Why wouldn't you back off at the last moment?'

Francoise laughed. 'Because my determination is honest, whereas yours is not. Don't be angry. Truth is all that matters, not convenience.'

'We'll see,' said Kline. He started the car and drove angrily away from the shambles of the town's centre.

He drew up before the house and climbed stiffly, still angry, from the car. Francoise walked round to him and stopped him as he was about to step up to the house; her hand on his arm felt good and after a second he closed his own hand about hers. 'Don't be angry with me,' she said.

'I'm not. You're right, I just hate admitting it.' He smiled at her.

'I'm glad you said that,' she murmured, and stretched up to kiss him. 'Lee . . .'

'Yes, I know. Francoise, do you think that if I really loved you as well, do you think I could let you go through with the sacrifice?'

'I don't think – if you loved me – that you would let me, no.'

Kline touched her cold nose with his finger. 'And I'm not going to let you,' he said, 'so there.'

And at that moment there was a girl's scream, and a deafening explosion of sound from the garden.

'That was a shotgun!' cried Kline. 'Christ almighty, someone's shooting at Adrian . . .'

They raced through the dark passageway between front and back doors, and found themselves in brilliant light – kitchen light – watching as Edward wrestled with his daughter, who screamed angrily, almost hysterically, at him. She was holding the gun – it looked to Kline like a blunderbuss! – which was still billowing white smoke. Kline, his eyes sharp and watching for the slightest detail, noticed that it was a two-barrel gun, and only one barrel had been fired. For a terrifying moment Edward found himself standing, both his hands on the barrels of the gun, but standing in front of them, watching Karen as her finger curled around the trigger.

Then the girl started to cry, her grip leaving the gun so that Edward drew it from her with ease. Once he had the blunderbuss free of her he reached up a fist and smashed it hard against Karen's head, causing her to scream louder, and stagger back against the wall.

Kline, not expecting such violence, ran forward and stopped Edward from hitting his daughter again. 'Are you mad?'

'She tried to kill Adrian!' cried the doctor. 'I saw her, aiming. He was in the garden, walking towards her, and she would have blown his head off if I hadn't got to her first. She's a killer! She would have killed him!'

314

'You might have killed *her* with a blow like that,' said Kline, quite calmly, and Edward stared at him, breathing hard. He looked at Karen, at the graze on her cheek and the sullen expression on her face, and then his own face twisted with anger and grief.

'What am I doing?' he said. 'What am I doing?'

'Fighting for your son,' said Kline. 'As we all are.'

'You should have let me kill him, daddy,' snapped Karen, full of hatred, not just for her brother, but for all the adults who stood about her. 'What do any of you know? What do any of you care? You keep talking about helping the bastard. But he's a killer, he's evil. You should have let me kill him.'

Francoise led the girl into the kitchen, comforting her. Kline stared at the gun, shaking his head. 'What a bloody lethal thing.'

'There would have been nothing left of the boy,' said Edward quietly, watching the gun as Kline examined it. 'My God . . . Adrian! He ran off again . . .'

He turned and went towards the darkness, staring across neighbouring gardens for a sign of the boy, shouting at the lighted windows and the silhouettes that watched him.

He walked slowly back to the house, grim, angry. 'He won't come back now.'

'He will,' said Kline. 'But not for a while. For the moment we have to find June, get everyone together, in one place. Where's Don?'

'I don't know. He's not upstairs. I saw Adrian from upstairs.'

Kline was instantly angry, then instantly calm again. 'Damn! Well, we'll just have to find him too. I locked him in the room . . .' He realized, then, that Karen would have let him out. 'We have to get everybody together, to stop any more stupid games like this occurring. Adrian came here once, perhaps because the house represents security, and he's still confused. Now he's run off elsewhere, but you can be sure he'll be watching us. He doesn't dare let us out of his sight for too long.'

'You talk like he's possessed,' said Edward, and instantly realized what must have happened. Kline, at the same moment, remembered that he had not told either Edward or June about what had occurred.

Edward said, 'Oh Christ – not *that*! It's not got him completely . . . !'

Kline said, 'He came back to try to kill us. Not Adrian, of course, but the thing that has possession of him. Francoise and I

315

are probably on the top of its list . . . you and June also, I would think. That's why I say we must all keep together.'

'Right . . . right . . .' Edward, ashen faced, almost unbelieving, led the way into the house, vanished into the lounge. Francoise and Karen stood sullenly in the hallway, watching Kline. 'Where to now?' said the girl bitterly.

'Nowhere,' said Kline. 'We stay right here. Francoise, take her into the lounge. You don't move from the lounge unless I tell you. Is that clear? Here, take this.' He passed the gun to Francoise. Karen walked into the lounge on her own, sat down opposite her father who stared at her almost uncomprehending.

'Empty this without triggering it if you can. It's too dangerous to have lying around loaded.'

Francoise weighed the gun, and held it gingerly. 'Alright.'

Kline hesitated, staring at her. She met his gaze, frowned. He said, 'He'll go back to the church.'

'I know.'

He spoke softly, so his words would be inaudible in the next room. 'We can't leave these two alone, not yet. Where the hell are June and Don? They'll start screwing things up!'

'Relax. You told Edward? About the escape?'

'He guessed.'

'Then I think that soon the shock will pass, and he will find his daughter again. A few minutes, a few hours . . . and then . . .'

Again Kline froze, but said, 'And then we *both* go to the church. Francoise, I insist. We *both* go. I say the words, while you . . . oh God, I can't bear to think about it.'

'Compassion yet!' She smiled in the darkness of the hallway, touched his cheek. 'You're crying, Lee. That's not good.'

'It's very good. You should try it sometime.'

He smeared the tears from his eyes, and glanced into the lounge. 'I'll lock the windows and doors. In case Adrian *does* come back we must arrange a rota of watching from a front and rear window. Go and unload that gun.'

As she went into the warm room and sat down, Kline walked to the back door, closed it and locked it. He slammed the windows closed, locked them, then went through the upstairs rooms, locking the windows there too.

His final call was at the front door. He checked his pocket and found the folded knife there that he had picked up from Edward's tool chest, below the stairs. With a last glance at the lounge, where Francoise talked loudly and light-heartedly, trying to keep spirits high, he made noises with the door bolts, then stepped outside onto the drive, closing the door quietly.

He let off the hand-brake of the car and pushed it in a tight circle, only just managing to turn it round to face the drive in a single motion. He let it roll quietly to the road, then started up and drove swiftly, excitedly, to the church.

There were still people about in the streets, but the crowds had mostly dispersed and the police were nowhere to be seen. A few carefully placed lights were all that was left of the earlier brilliance. Through the semi-darkness Kline could see that the porch of the ruined church was guarded by just a single chain slung across its width. The wreck of the bus had been dragged away in the last half hour, and apart from the unnatural darkness of the streets, it was hard to tell that something akin to an explosion had occurred here earlier in the day.

A police car was parked a hundred yards from the church of St Mary's, its occupants awake, but regarding the far end of the town. Kline felt caution was in order.

He stood in darkness, against the rear wall of the church, and smelled the lingering odour of burning, watched his breath frosting in the bitter night air.

There was so little time. Francoise would be following him already, he knew that. Even now he could imagine she was running down the driveway of the house. She would be in the High Street in minutes. He had to find Adrian, and . . . release him . . . all in the space of a few moments, and now it occurred to him that this gambit was probably the most pointless thing he had ever done.

He was gambling on Adrian being inside the church, hiding there now that the confusion and chaos was gone, now that attention was removed. It was the obvious place for the boy to run to having been driven away from his own home by a shot-gun blast. Perhaps Cruachos was weakened, had come to its host's home to hide; in its confusion perhaps it sought the sanctuaries of the boy. Now it would surely have sought the sanctuary of its tomb, the place it knew so well.

Kline fumbled in his pocket and drew out the knife. His heart thundered as he thought that this was the moment of his own supreme sacrifice, the self sacrifice that would save so much, and so many.

I must be mad . . . I have so much to live for . . .

He saw, in his mind's eye, a broken child – a strange, strangely red doll, sprawled on the pavement. He felt sick. He saw two people, their flesh still warm from coupling, impaled viciously on the railings of a school . . .

And Cruachos was still *weak*.

The sacrifice was not too great. He tried not to think about it, to linger on the fact of there being no more of tomorrow, of anything, an end to him, a termination . . . he felt his eyes sting, remembered moments from his boyhood, places and friends . . .

He shook them away!

A child, broken in the streets – the first, just the first. This thing from the shadows, this force of violence – not evil, just alien, alien in the way it regarded this world of 'grubbing things' – this Cruachos *had* to be destroyed, or it would destroy everything that had been built upon the seed of those same men, those same foolish priests who had brought the violence upon themselves, two long millennia ago.

It was not too great a price: his blood, his life, for freedom.

He ran quickly round the church, doubled, hugging shadows, his eyes on the police car, his ears keen for the sound of running, a voice, the sound of movement, anything . . .

He stepped across the chain and slipped into the darkness of the church. He stumbled . . .

A body lay sprawled there. He caught his breath, thinking that it had to be June; but when he stooped and touched the face he felt the sharp edge of stubble. As his eyes grew accustomed to the darkness he recognized, dimly, the unconscious features of Don Belsaint. The boy was frozen, almost as cold as death, but not quite; he was breathing; blood had congealed on his skull, and on his hands, and there was grey discolouration on his cheeks; he had known Cruachos's particularly unpleasant wrath, but he had not been killed. This puzzled Kline, confused him . . . why hadn't Don been fatally attacked? What had Cruachos to gain by leaving him alive?

There was movement in the church, down where the baptismal font stood.

Instantly Kline was alert, his hand still resting on Don's face . . .

Confusion . . . puzzlement . . .

He smiled as he realized that this was intended to take his mind from the deed at hand. Don had been spared simply so Kline might do just what he had done – find himself thrown by the incongruity of it.

Cruachos would not get the edge by doing that! Kline pushed all thoughts of Don away from him, rose to his feet and stared into the gloom, his mind alert, his determination strong. He knew Cruachos was here, could feel it, could almost sense it.

Gradually his eyes adapted and he saw the stone, a vague outline in the black. And by the stone, standing there, watching him . . . Adrian.

For a while they stood there, quietly, watching each other, and Kline relaxed his body, fought to reduce his apprehension, knowing that this would be food and drink to Cruachos, and a good weapon against him in the battle to come. Then he walked towards the boy, his hand in his pocket touching the knife, eyes fixed on Adrian's. He said nothing, though he was inclined to be insulting, taunting. He wanted to be strong, but for the moment there was nothing to be strong against. He did not feel threatened; he felt none of the alarming imaginary symptoms of closeness to the entity that he had often felt before. He felt just cold, quiet, increasingly perturbed.

This too he fought down. But the boy was so passive, so . . . scared looking.

Adrian's face was open, innocent. His mouth was slightly agape, his eyes wide; he watched the man walking towards him, then suddenly took a step backwards.

Kline stopped.

'There's no way out,' he said. 'You're going to have to kill or be killed.' He smiled, grimly, triumphantly, feeling an enormous surge of confidence, but aware – and wary – of the likelihood of a trick.

Suddenly, perhaps overly confident, perhaps acting more instinctively than anything, he ran at the boy and grabbed him by the collar of his pyjama shirt, pulling him back to the font and bending him backwards across the stone. He opened the knife and screamed with emotion, feeling the blood surge through his head and heart, as he held the cold blade against his own wrist.

The words of the spell ran through his mind and he began to speak them, but the passiveness of the boy, the quietness, the inactivity . . .

'Fight!' he cried suddenly, the magic words lost, for the moment. Adrian's face wrinkled up in fear, and tears filled his eyes. Kline watched amazed as the boy whined and cried, for all the world like a new-born baby; then he guessed the trick and went back to the task at hand.

'You can trick Francoise, but not me.' He pressed the razor sharp edge of the blade against his wrist and pushed, but he hesitated, watching the dull, silvery gleam of the blade, feeling the pain.

Beneath him Adrian squirmed, trying to get free – it was not the enormously powerful strength of the creature from the supernatural world of the past, but the almost pathetically inept efforts of a boy of seven.

Adrian was crying quite loudly. Kline heard the sound through the dull thunder in his own head, watched him through spinning, dizzying images, almost unable to focus on the child.

'Oh CHRIST!' he said aloud, and quite suddenly he was panicking.

He couldn't do it! He couldn't do it!

'CHRIST!' he screamed, and angry, furious with himself, he raised the knife and slashed it down at his wrists, cutting the skin, drawing blood, but missing just about everything vital there was.

Adrian shrieked in panic as he reacted to the American's fury. Kline knew that he must have seemed as wild and crazy as a beast of prey, but awareness of this seemed unimportant . . .

He *had* to say the words, he *had* to drain his life . . .

He *had* to win!

And then behind him there was movement.

Behind him there was laughter. Agonizing pain in his neck! A blade thrusting deep into the muscle, grating against the bones of his spine.

He twisted as the blade was withdrawn. His own knife fell free to the ground, and he stared at the triumphant, grinning face of Cruachos . . .

June.

It had gone into June, finding her confused and conflicted persona as easy a target as the mindless void of the child. June, then, and not Adrian at all, whom everybody had suspected, and no-one had thought . . .

June! *June!*

She screeched again, like a bird, the shrill cry of a bird, and the knife flashed down a second time and drove into his belly, splitting him open with a ripping sound that was part his clothing, part his flesh. The warmth of his body spilled across his fingers, bubbling up from his lungs. Again the knife struck him, in the shoulder, deeply down into his body, draining life from him, like blood, like the power of his mind, fleeing the useless corpse . . .

There was thunder. Warmth and stickiness erupted over him, drenching the stone against which he lay, dying. He heard words,

Francoise's voice; strange words interspersed with hysterical sobs, and he recognized those words; he was aware of the heavy, broken corpse of a woman lying across him, faceless, almost headless, the knife still held in one of the hands, its point touching his cooling flesh, unable to make a fifth incision in him.

There was a whirling sound, like wind, like panic, like the storm sound of heartfelt terror, and briefly as he slipped down the stone, born down by the dead woman's weight, he saw the tall shape of a man rising above him, twisting and fighting some invisible foe; it finally seemed to drain into the cold air, dissipating completely, and beneath his body the stone font seemed to shake, to tremble, to grow warm, then cold again. He thought he heard an unearthly scream.

Then there was a woman crying, reaching out to touch his face, whilse acrid smoke billowed from the gun she held, choking him, choking him . . .

CODA

From too much love of living
    From hope and fear set free
We thank with brief thanksgiving
    Whatever gods may be
That no life lives for ever;
That dead men rise up never;
That even the weariest river
    Winds somewhere safe to sea.

The Garden of Proserpine
Algernon Charles Swinburne

CHAPTER TWENTY-TWO

On a crisp, clear Sunday in late February, Francoise Jeury walked quietly up the gravel drive at the front of Edward Hunter's house. She was frozen, hunched up inside her beige raincoat, her hair tied back in a heavy, woollen scarf. She was pale, looked very tired, very drawn, and the slowness of her walk was because she was apprehensive.

Somehow time had ceased to have any meaning since she had killed June Hunter. The memory of that appalling moment, when her finger had jerked the trigger of Don's home-made gun and June had scattered her life across the stone, lived with her, a vivid image of darkness, of white billowing smoke, of Kline screaming her name and clawing desperately at her coat, as if by clinging to the fabric he could cling to the life he was losing.

And a memory, too, of that stone font. Even Don had sworn what she had sworn, over and over again at the interminable inquest, that the stone font had glowed red at the instant of June Hunter's death, the redness of some inexplicable and immense heat; it had burned part of the dead woman's corpse, and had even burned Don himself as he had helped drag Kline away from that haunted rock.

Poor Don, she thought again, remembering the boy's face as clear as if it had been this morning that she had been watching the agony in him as he had described his father's death. Now that it was all over he had vanished, fleeing from Higham, fleeing the place that had held him there all his life, and his family over the centuries. Now he was looking for a life so far away, so different, that not even Karen could be a part of it, and that, Francoise, knew, had almost broken Karen's heart.

She walked to the front door, stood there for a moment before reaching out to the bell. But she hesitated before ringing. Instead she walked around the side of the house, to stand by the gate that led into the long, rear garden.

She had heard a child's laughter, and recognized Adrian's voice.

Adrian was running about the far green. He was swathed in thick coats and scarves, and being chased by Karen, herself wrapped up tightly and bulkily against the cold. Edward Hunter stood close by, his hands thrust deep into his pockets, his face a mask of pleasure as he watched Adrian's antics.

Francoise watched the boy too, smiling as Adrian laughed hysterically on being caught by Karen. He was too big for her to swing up into the air, so she merely tried to tickle him through his clothes, and Adrian erupted into giggles, twisting away from her and running off again.

For a child of his age it was peculiarly infantile play, and yet for this boy it was wonderful play. When Karen stopped, breathless with the chasing, her breath frosting in the cold air, Adrian ran back to her and tugged her sleeve. Francoise heard his voice, begging her to play some more.

Karen said she was worn out.

Quite suddenly the boy saw Francoise standing there, down by the gate. For a second he stared at her blankly, then he said loudly, 'Who's that lady?'

Edward turned and Francoise heard him swear quietly. He said something to Karen who began to chase Adrian again, and the boy soon forgot the stranger. Karen, though she laughed, continually glanced angrily down towards the gate.

Edward walked across the garden and came up to Francoise. He didn't smile, or acknowledge her, but just said, 'Please go away.'

Francoise nodded sadly. 'I shan't stay. I only came . . . well, to see how Adrian is.'

'He's fine. As you can see, he's a very lovely, very active, very *ordinary* little boy. He's his age in every way except education, and he's learning very fast. He's a bright boy.'

'I'm glad about that.'

'Thank you for asking. But please, Madame Jeury . . . I don't want you here. Please go away.'

There was something almost pleading in his voice; he was not angry, nor offensive, just desperate that the new peace should not be disturbed.

Francoise felt her eyes sting, glanced beyond Edward at the running, laughing child, freed at last of the presence in his mind that had kept him from developing properly. 'I had to do it,' she said, the words almost choking her. She met Edward's gaze. 'It had taken her . . . there was nothing I could do. You *do* understand that?'

For a moment she thought Edward would explode angrily; his face had flushed, his eyes narrowed in a deep, concerned frown. He watched her, his eyes almost dull; the smile that touched his lips finally was a desperate attempt to control the emotion that had surged through him at that moment. 'Understanding it doesn't help accept it,' he said quietly, bitterly. 'But yes, I know you had to do it. Justifiable homicide, as the court so eloquently put it.'

'Please believe that it was,' said Francoise, searching Edward for some moment of softening, some sign that he would help raise the awful burden of guilt that she felt. She couldn't bring herself to look at Adrian. 'I never wanted it to come to such a tragic end,' she said. 'I wanted to help . . . both of us wanted to help.'

Edward said nothing for a moment, and Francoise saw that he was shaking. He was having difficulty, now, in meeting her gaze. 'I don't bear you a grudge. I know that there was something evil in my son, something repressive. I said so all along, but June wouldn't listen. I also know that that evil went *into* June. For God's sake, I can't explain why that stone glowed red like that. I can't explain anything. I still don't know if I was right or if June was right about Adrian . . .'

'Does it matter?'

Edward frowned. 'Does it matter?' he repeated, and now, in his eyes, was that haunted expression that so frightened Francoise when she saw it; the man truly looked his age and was shaking as some turbulent emotion welled up within him. 'Does it matter? Does it *matter*?' He laughed cynically, sharing some obscure moment of disbelief with himself. 'It's *all* that matters, now that Adrian is well again. It's *all* that matters.'

Francoise, wanting to say more, now found herself lost for words. 'Goodbye, Doctor Hunter,' she said.

Edward said nothing. But as she turned to go he called after her and she stopped, turning back to him. He said, 'I'm . . . I'm sorry about Kline. I thought the man was a bastard, but I'm deeply sorry. I know you were very good friends.'

'Yes. Thank you.' She watched him for a second, her face quite expressionless, her eyes searching. 'Thank you.'

She turned away again and this time walked uninterrupted down the drive.

Kline's battered old Austin was parked across the road and she ran to it and climbed into the driver's seat, shivering in the chill and slamming the door after her. For a minute or so she sat in silence, staring through the windscreen, trying to fight back the tears of anger and frustration that she desperately wanted to shed. Distantly she could just see the green in front of the ruined church. The font was no longer there. It had been taken a long way away, and suspended in chains in the air, weakening that which lived there again, making it harder for it to escape. That much, at least, the Home Office had been prepared to do, and it was enough. The story had broken, of course, and for a few days the newspapers had gone wild; but when answers had not been forthcoming – either at the Inquest on June Hunter, or privately – their interest had waned, as newspaper interest always does. Now the clamour had died down, and the Higham Incident was just one more supernatural story that would periodically be resurrected in order to make 'good copy'.

Calming down a little, feeling the tension in her stomach drain away, Francoise said, 'He's sorry about you, Mister Kline. He thought you were a bastard, but he's deeply sorry.'

'So he still thinks June killed me?'

She turned to look at Kline and smiled. He was still very pale, and he had difficulty turning his body because of his stomach wound. His left arm was in a sling. 'Somewhere, deep inside, he knows you're alive. But he wants to think of you as dead, and as far as he's concerned that's the way you are.' She smiled thinly. 'It's part of his own process of re-adjustment. Don't begrudge it him.'

Kline shrugged and winced as shooting pain reminded him not to be too violent. 'I don't begrudge that man anything. I just think he's cracked.'

Francoise pressed a finger to his lips, silencing him. Her look was earnest, imploring. 'Don't say that, Lee. Please. Don't say that.'

Taking her finger away she leaned forward and kissed him. Then she laughed. 'You bastard,' she said.

'Why? What did I do now, Madame Jeury?'

'Nothing. You're a bastard that's all.' She was smiling, no trace of the shadow of a moment before. 'I'm glad you're a bastard, Lee. Only one such as you would still be alive after that attack.'

'Well, I agree with that. It never occurred to me that I might have been dying. I can think of death, of my death, but it's a sort of fantasy. The idea of it seems unreal.'

'Of course – you're the survival type,' she said cynically.

'Most people are,' he said. 'It's the animal in us.'

'And don't I know all about the animal in you.' Francoise slapped the steering wheel, cutting off any further comment from Kline. She glanced back at the house and made impatient noises. 'Where to, Mister Kline? Where can I chauffeur you today?'

'How about going to Church? It *is* Sunday.'

'Bad joke,' she said grimly. 'I know. Let's drive out to Stonehenge!'

Kline groaned. 'Christ, no! Not that. I couldn't stand it . . . all those standing stones, all those lintels.' He looked at her. 'It might turn out to be the Bronze Age equivalent of Alcatraz.'

She met his gaze, momentarily startled, and after a while they stared silently through the windscreen, watching the traffic as it rumbled past them.

All Futura Books are available at your bookshop or
newsagent, or can be ordered from the following address:
Futura Books, Cash Sales Department,
P.O. Box 11, Falmouth, Cornwall TR10 9EN.

Please send cheque or postal order (no currency), and
allow 60p for postage and packing for the first book
plus 25p for the second book and 15p for each additional
book ordered up to a maximum charge of £1.90 in U.K.

B.F.P.O. customers please allow 60p for
the first book, 25p for the second book plus 15p per
copy for the next 7 books, thereafter 9p per book

Overseas customers, including Eire, please allow £1.25
for postage and packing for the first book, 75p for the
second book and 28p for each subsequent title ordered.